PATH ⚙ OF THE
TITANS

BOOK 1: SYSTEM ACTIVATION

TIMOTHY McGOWEN

PATH OF THE TITANS - SYSTEM ACTIVATION

A LITRPG EPIC FANTASY

PATH OF THE TITANS
BOOK 1

TIMOTHY MCGOWEN

ILLUSTRATED BY
CHRISTINA P. MYRVOLD

EDITED BY
CANDACE MORRIS

RISING TOWER BOOKS

Fantasy /LitRPG/Gamelit

OTHER BOOKS BY THE AUTHOR

Haven Chronicles

Haven Chronicles: Eldritch Knight

Short Stories/Novellas

Dead Man's Bounty

Exiled Jahk

Last Born of Ki'darth

Reincarnation: A Litrpg/Gamelit Trilogy

Rebellion: A Litrpg/Gamelit Trilogy

Retribution: A Litrpg/Gamelit Trilogy

Order & Chaos

Arcane Knight Book 1: An Epic LITRPG Fantasy

Arcane Knight Book 2: An Epic LITRPG Fantasy

Arcane Knight Book 3: An Epic LITRPG Fantasy

Arcane Knight Book 4: An Epic LITRPG Fantasy

Arcane Knight Book 5: An Epic LITRPG Fantasy

The Elemental Realms

Nexus Guardian Book 1: A Fantasy LitRPG Adventure

Nexus Guardian Book 2: A Fantasy LitRPG Adventure

REVIEWS ARE IMPORTANT

Every review matters, get your voice heard. Follow me on Amazon to get informed when my next book is released!

https://www.amazon.com/stores/Timothy-McGowen/author/B087QTTRJK

Join my Patreon for early Chapters!

https://www.patreon.com/TimothyMcGowen

Join my Facebook group and discuss the books

https://www.facebook.com/groups/234653175151521/

SPECIAL THANKS

I wanted to give a special thanks to those that helped bring this book to its current state.

Candace Morris - Editor and Super Hero.

Dantas Neto, Sean Hall, Hugo Morais. (Elandar) - Proofer

I dedicate this book to my fans. Without your loyalty and dedication I'd never be able to craft so many wonderful stories.

CONTENTS

CHAPTER 1
ADVENTURE

Knox felt his sense drift. Something was close by, but he couldn't tell what it was just yet. Instead of revealing his awareness of its presence, he continued his work of cutting away at the tree before him.

Thwack. Thwack.

The sweet release of exertion filled him as his axe bit deep into the wood under the practiced blows of an experienced woodsman. He fingered the shaft of his axe with each swing, shifting his grip to avoid blisters.

He had decided long ago that even though he was a natural woodsman, he wouldn't stay one for the rest of his life. What would his father think if he knew what he was planning? It didn't matter, and he wasn't going to let him dictate his life any longer. His father couldn't stop him, no one could.

Under Common Law of Laurdenar, any citizen born of any station or house had the right to challenge his destiny within a Dungeon. He would become an Adventurer.

The winds shifted and he caught the scent of a predator behind a forty-year-old pine marked for cutting. A Dire Wolf by the feel of it.

Knox's dark brown hair blew with the wind and his vibrant blue eyes scanned the horizon. His sense was his best tool against threats, and he reached out with it.

He shifted his weight to his other foot and swung downward —his axe flying from his hands and landing with a loud crunch. He caught sight of a moon-grey swish of a tail as it turned and fled from its hiding place.

Dire Wolves could be dangerous, they had above average intelligence and were unwilling to let themselves die needlessly. Being just dangerous enough that you *might* kill or maim your opponent went a long way when you lived at the edge of civilization. One of the less monumental reasons why Knox decided he wouldn't live and die as a woodcutter. He had to be an Adventurer. He recovered his axe and went back to work.

Thwack. Thwack. Growl.

Knox's sense shot out like a web of fine silk, and he prepared for the attack.

At the last possible moment, he rolled to the side, having a good idea of the Dire Wolf's presence now. Without looking, he raised his axe and swung behind himself, turning to face his attacker. His quick blow did the job of keeping it at bay.

The Dire Wolf was different than he expected. His keen sense only gave him a general feel and location for the beast. The strong thick fur was marred by traces of dark blue, almost black, gashes. One of the wounds that traced the Dire Wolf's frame crossed directly over its left eye. A bright blue glow emanated from one cunning eye, where the other looked normal, if not a little bloodshot.

Regardless of its odd deformities, Knox had no plans to kill the wolf if he could avoid it. Trouble was, he knew he couldn't avoid it. The odd infection that drove the Dire Wolf to attack when it would normally flee, couldn't be ignored.

The wolf pounced again.

Knox easily avoided the swift attack and delivered one himself. Like a hot knife through butter, his axe head slid through the wolf's abdominal wall and into the unprotected internal organs. The axe's arc finished, and blood dripped from its sharp edge. The Dire Wolf stumbled another few steps before collapsing from the devastating attack.

Knox observed his fallen foe and reached out with his special sense but was unable to detect the warm glow that he'd always attributed to the signs of life. He had downed the creature in one blow, whatever had driven this Dire Wolf to forgo its natural instincts had also weakened it significantly.

A bird cawed in the distance and Knox approached his kill. Cleaning this carcass and trying to salvage its hide would be useless. Whatever the infection was, it had eaten through the Dire Wolf and ruined it thoroughly.

He would report the attack and the dead wolf to the foreman after his shift, not wanting to waste any more time that could be spent felling trees. The more trees you dropped, the more money you were paid.

Wolves were common in the forest of Feralease. The King's guard was—in theory—supposed to provide safety to all the workers of his realm. Feralease was on the Easternmost edge of

King Wilham's domain and only tax collectors, Adventurers, or people looking to be forgotten, ever traveled this far out.

An older Adventurer, Dernal Dorntooth, had arrived in town this very week. You could set your calendar by Dernal. Each year after the last snowfall, he arrived like clockwork.

Dernal was a short—by Keenlen's Vale standards at least—and sturdy man with amber-colored eyes that spoke of knowledge untold, and black hair that was long enough that he kept it in a tight bun atop his head. He had a shrewd and sensible way of talking that was more growl than speech half the time. It was like he only wanted to speak a few words at a time and any time Knox's questions drew more out of him, it looked like it pained him.

Despite Dernal's frequent visits to the town, most townsfolk kept clear of him. Adventurers didn't have the best of reputations this far out. Too easy for one in power to act without fear of consequences.

It wasn't as if there wasn't an authority in the area. There was a Guild-controlled Dungeon a few days' journey from the town, and a Guild Charterhouse bordering the Shadowfall Swamp.

Tavern gossip suggested that the charterhouse was only there to hunt the powerful creatures that lurked in the swamps, giving strong Adventurers a chance to advance further down the path of power. It was a day's journey from the Mires Gloom Dungeon, which put it just a few days' travel from their town. Its exact location wasn't common knowledge. Even the most up to date maps of the area didn't show the location of the Dungeon or the Guild Charterhouse. The Dungeon made sense, as it was bad luck to put a Dungeon marker on a map, but why they hid the location of a Guild Charterhouse was anyone's guess.

Thwack. Thwack.

The wind blew through the trees cooling Knox's sweat-covered arms. He took it in with a deep breath, appreciating the smells of the forest as he continued to work. He loved being a woodsman on most days. Although, he had seen too many lives wasted in mediocrity not to take measures to change his fate to avoid a life as stagnant as the Shadowfall Swamp.

That is where Dernal Dorntooth came into the picture. Knox wasn't like most townsfolk, and he took every opportunity he could to speak with Dernal. Just this week he was finally going to do something he had wanted to do for the last three years, ever since Dernal agreed to the bargain.

He was going to buy a weather-worn set of enchanted armor. That would put him just above the bare minimum—according to Dernal—that it took to get into a Dungeon group and survive.

The bellow of a low horn cried out in the distance. It was quitting time. Knox let his sense span through the forest like a spider sensing vibration in its web, as he turned himself toward the town. He located his friend Terrim not far off from where he had been working and changed his direction to intercept him.

He was a tall man, much taller than anyone had any right to be, with a decently muscled body born from countless hours of cutting down trees. His eyes were a keen emerald and his hair the same color as Knox, a darker brown. He had a perpetual grin on his face that was at odds with how grim his face looked. He appeared most days to be angry smiling at people, but Knox knew that was just his resting grim face and not a true expression of the joker beneath.

"Today's the day," Knox shouted up to Terrim as he finally caught up to his freakishly tall friend.

"What's that?" Terrim asked, turning his attention toward Knox. "Oh, you mean you are going to finally let Beth have her way with you?"

Terrim's words were followed by a burst of booming laughter that could easily be mistaken for the echoing crash of a fallen tree somewhere in the forest. Knox joked daily that Terrim should take a job with the town watch, one yell from him and the entire town would hear it.

Terrim in turn liked to take a too-close look into Knox's love life, or the lack thereof. It wasn't that Knox didn't like the

5

company of the opposite sex; he was just busy. Between his job as a woodcutter, repair work with Mr. Tome, and taking care of his drunken father, he didn't have much time for a social life.

"Har har, Ter," Knox laughed sarcastically, swinging the handle of his axe to rest on his shoulder. "You know I only have eyes for Danielle."

This caught Terrim's attention and Knox had to dodge a lumbering punch. Terrim tried a few more halfhearted swings as Knox expertly nudged himself out of the way at the last moment. Terrim wasn't trying to do him harm, Knox knew, but if he didn't pay attention, a blow from him—playful or not—was likely to land him on his ass.

"Stay still you shit-fly!" Terrim boomed, his attacks abating. "You know I'm planning on asking Danielle to the summer feast."

"It was a joke, Ter," Knox said through a series of chuckles. "Besides, today is the day I tell my father that I'm going to be an Adventurer!"

"Hah." Was Terrim's only reply.

"I'm serious this time, Ter. I've finally saved up enough money and I've spoken with Dernal, he has the armor."

"Dernal?" Terrim asked in surprise. "The old bastard that cheats at cards in the tavern. *He's* the Adventurer you've been talking with?"

"Sure is," Knox said proudly.

"Well good luck, I say," Terrim sneered, his nose pointed down toward Knox as he spoke. "I don't need to tell you, but your father is a bastard, and you know he won't be happy to hear you want to leave."

"To hell with my father," Knox snapped, the words leaving his lips before he could stop himself. He tried his best not to talk down about his father, but it was hard. He really was a bastard. Nearly eight years back he'd been injured in a woodcutting accident and had stayed mostly drunk since. He got a small amount of coin each week, but he wasted it on booze without fail. How he'd earned a weekly stipend from the crown Knox didn't know, but it was one of the few mysteries about the sad old man. Knox's mother had died during childbirth, or so he was told, and that left just him to care for his father.

The edge of the village came into view, a vast assortment of mismatched buildings.

"Good luck talking to your father," Terrim said, moving away toward the tavern. "I'm going to grab a cold drink and a hot meal, come meet me afterward if you can find the time."

Knox smiled after his friend, but the smile didn't last. He had to talk to his father, and telling him anything, even good news, ended in an argument. Finding the foreman, Knox reported the incident with the wolf and gave directions for its recovery, before heading toward town.

Nearly two thousand townsfolk called this area home, only half of them lived within the main walls of the town. To the East lay the Forest of Feralease, and further out the Shadowfall Swamp —a place where no one in their right mind would live. To the North and West lay the Spike Peak Mountains that pierced the clouds. They ran from the Endless Sea's edge to the capital city of Sedriseal. And finally, to the South lay the Valley of the Dead, where most of the crops were planted and animal stock grazed.

Of course, most townsfolk just called it 'The Valley' and avoided the official name given by the original settlers.

For a village so far out of the way, Keenlen's Vale was a prosperous place. A river ran off Valespring's Lake with a strong current that made trading with the capital city a lucrative endeavor. Getting trade to run back to the town was an issue. The water's current and elevation of the river made traveling back nearly impossible.

So, the town's goods moved downriver in wooden barges that would be taken apart and sold upon arriving. Every month they'd receive a trader or two that would bring an assortment of exotic items into the town. These same traders would bring down tokens of wealth, mostly coin and exotic spices, rewarded from the supplies the village provided.

Truth be told, Keenlen's Vale was almost entirely self-sufficient and only truly considered themselves citizens of the realm when they required some type of royal support or trading was involved. The kingdom rewarded inner-realm trading over foreign trade by a reduced tax. But, considering how far out Keenlen's Vale was outside of anything regarded as civilization, inner-realm trade was really the town's only option.

Passing beneath the shadow of several steep structures, the town's administration buildings, Knox made his way to the western most side of the town. He encountered a few hellos and hey there's but didn't come across anyone he was overly acquainted with and therefore avoided getting pulled into a longer conversation. The nicely painted white buildings at the center of the town soon faded away. He found himself surrounded by dilapidated structures seemingly placed at random on the edge of the west side of the town; a place where the town-planner had failed to impose rule of law.

Knox was home.

He stood without speaking outside his childhood residence and examined the runes that no one else seemed to be able to see. They looked as if they were scratched directly into the wood, but upon closer examination, he had been surprised to see that the wood was left untouched.

He had reached puberty when he had first noticed them, thinking they were a trick of the light at first, he'd ignored them. But after finding his mother's diary, he had learned the truth. His father refused to speak of runes or Knox's mother. More than once his father had tried to dispose of her diary, but Knox was clever—or at least more so than a perpetually drunk father—and had been able to keep her words safe.

She was the biggest reason he wanted to be an Adventurer. He wanted to be like her, a powerful magic-user. He assumed that is what she had been, why else would she write about nail-biting dungeon adventures and sketch magical runes?

Turning his attention past the runes and onto the house,

Knox mused at its construction. It stood two stories high—the only home in this area to be so—but that was the only thing that made it stand out. The exterior walls were flaked with old white paint, more wood than paint showing. The window shutters were recently fixed, but Knox hadn't spent any money on newer wood, just added new nails, and fixed the failing hinges.

The door was his pride and joy. He had made it with the help of Mr. Tome's tools. It stood out against the house, being well sanded and stained dark. It stood strong on its hinges and made their home the only one in this part of town with a door that could lock, securing his precious few belongings.

Knox stood at the threshold of the door—his hand lightly touching the doorknob. Previously rehearsed conversations ran through his head as he took several deep breaths before pulling the door open. His father never bothered to lock it, he doubted that he even knew that the door *could* lock.

"I'm home, Father," Knox called out as he entered the dimly lit entryway. "I've got work to do for Mr. Tome later tonight, did you want me to pick up food from the tavern?"

"You little shit." Came his father's voice from the back room. His father was in a foul mood. Knox guessed by the slur in his voice, that he had consumed the entire week's ration of alcohol and would expect him to get more.

"What did I do now, Father?" Knox responded, moving through the house and into his own room, another luxury that most on the west side of town didn't enjoy. The room was modest with a bed, a rundown dresser, and a single window, no glass but with strong shutters. He began to swiftly undress in preparation for a bath. Mr. Tome complained that he stunk up his workshop when he came straight from the forest after a day of cutting down trees.

"You'd spen' all our money on fancy food to impressh the whoresh in the town?"

Knox smiled at the ridiculousness of the sentence his father just said. Did he really think buying food from the tavern would impress women or was he just that drunk?

"Are *you*," Knox asked, emphasizing the first part and projecting his voice louder as he moved into the small washroom, "planning on cooking dinner then?"

It didn't take him long to draw a cold bath. He could hear his father try to stand and subsequently fall back down with a loud crash in reaction to his words, Knox ignored the racket.

"How dare you shpeak to me like that." Came the eventual muffled response. "I'm your father! You'll show me some reshpect!"

Knox could hear his father's voice get closer as he spoke and made it a point to bathe quicker. Just as he finished scrubbing his sweaty hair, the threshold darkened, and his father hobbled into the room.

Knox shot to his feet, ready to defend himself if his father was drunk enough to attack him. Water dripped down Knox's muscled form as he pretended to be unconcerned by his father's presence. His hair, dark and wet from the bath, dripped down his back as he reached for a towel to dry himself off.

His father huffed and puffed but did nothing. Knox studied the form of the once strong frame of a broken man. His father's gut had overtaken his waistline by a factor of several inches and his too-tight shirt that had fit him perfectly before the injury struggled to hold it in. He had black hair atop his head, different from the brown of his son's, and an unkempt beard. His left arm was a stump just below the elbow and he leaned heavily to one side.

"How many treesh did you get today?" His father's voice was far less threatening when faced with the obvious strength difference between them. Knox slipped into his trousers, careful to check for trouser snakes first, and regarded his father carefully before speaking.

"Nearly two dozen, I didn't have time to finish the last tree because a wolf tried to take a bite out of me," Knox said, unable to hide the smugness as he spoke. Twenty-three was an impressive number of trees, considering the work that had to be done after felling them—stripping the branches and such.

"Tshh, I could do three dozen on a bad day," his father said, turning to leave the washroom. "You're too careful, if you'd trust your instinctsh you could shtop putting my name to shame. If I hadn't been injured in that freak accident, I'd be running that operation by now!"

Knox listened to his father's ridiculous ravings but said nothing to disparage him further. He still had to tell him about his plans to leave and be an Adventurer, and that would do plenty to set him off.

The thing about his father that really irked Knox was he'd lost an arm but was still in good enough shape to do something, be it marking trees or working with the foreman as an assistant. But tell that to his prideful ass and you'd hear an earful about how he was worth so much more and no one really wanted him to work anymore. That he was 'better off' staying at home and keeping the house in order. Of course, he did nothing to keep the house together, wasting away all his money and time with the drink.

Several minutes later, Knox was dressed into a fresh set of clothing and made quick work picking up after his father. After making sure everything he needed to do in the house was finished he approached his father in the sitting room. The room had a large table and two chairs in fair condition. His father, Askar Trelling, the former woodcutter, sat in the better chair facing a low burning fire.

He held a half-filled mug of some Felish Ale that Knox had purchased from an exotic vendor last month. Apparently, he hadn't hidden that cask as well as he thought he had. The unique purple-red color of the ale stained his father's lips giving him an asphyxiated appearance as he sat staring into the fire.

"I'm going to be an Adventurer," Knox said.

His father didn't move or say a word. Knox considered checking if he had died, but finally the old man shifted in his seat.

He was still alive it seemed.

After continuing to stare into the fire for another minute, he spoke.

"No, you're not." His voice was solemn and lacked the fire from only minutes ago, even his drunken slur had dissipated.

"Yes, I am," Knox shot back, confused by his father's monotone response. "I've arranged for Terrim to check in on you while I'm gone, and if the dungeon run goes well, I can move us both out of the west side and into one of the nicer homes by the Townhall."

Knox did his best to regurgitate the prepared lines he had been rehearsing for weeks.

"And with all the magical items I could get, I might even be able to find a way to heal you!" Knox's words trailed off as he spoke. His father had shifted his gaze to him, and his dark brown eyes were filled with a quiet rage beyond anything he could recall seeing there before.

His words were barely a whisper. All the slurring and drunken speech fled as he spoke. "I should have burned that damned diary. Leaving me, just like she did. Get out."

He stood ready to respond to any number of angry retorts his father would throw at him, but this? This quiet rage and request for him to leave caught him completely off guard.

Knox turned and left.

CHAPTER 2
DANGER

KNOX APPROACHED THE NICER, eastern edge of town where the tavern sat. It was overrun and reminded him of a mungle trap, filled to the brim with bugs. He halted mid-step as he examined the building—the sun was just cresting over the northern mountains. Even in the dimness of the cool evening, Knox could tell something wasn't right.

The building was one of the biggest in town, a series of three tavern owners had come together to build it and technically, they remained three separate taverns. By the look of the outside, you wouldn't be able to tell, the wooden construction with the clean white paint and large signs out front of the three main entrances being the only hint to it being separate establishments. Once you took a step inside though, it was clear that the three worked together. The entire space was open and each of the back walls were lined with bars to tend to the decently sized population of the town.

Only during festivals or disasters did this many people crowd the taverns at once, and the festival was still a week away. Deciding that he wasn't going to find anything out by standing outside, Knox made his way into the taverns. Most just called the building the Three Ladies, but each specific tavern was named after the wife of the owner: Patti's, Brea's, and Sheena's. Knox preferred to just think of them as the three ladies.

The atmosphere inside was tense and, despite how crowded it was, Knox weaseled his way deeper into the crowd.

"Something has to be done." A loud grizzly voice spoke above the rest of the crowd's chatter. "And it *must* be done tonight!"

The crowd inside profusely agreed with cheers and loud shouting. Terrim was among them, and Knox made his way to stand next to the beanstalk standing among the short grass of people. He was tall enough that they made eye contact before Knox made it halfway.

"You know the Gigorf family that keeps the farm that runs up against the Forest?" Terrim leaned down and asked Knox.

"Yeah, that's Frederick's family, right?" Knox asked, scrunching his brows as he waited for the inevitable bad news.

"Yeah, he was out visiting his family, which is why he didn't show up for work today. Well, turns out something got them," Terrim said, his voice quiet as he spoke. "They are saying it might have been a monster from that dungeon, maybe even a creature from Shadowfall Swamp."

"Impossible!" Knox said. His thoughts turned to the Dire Wolf that had attacked him earlier and he began to speculate. His mind raced as he began putting facts together. "Dungeon creatures can't live outside a dungeon for long! It is a well-documented fact." In truth, he'd heard as much from Dernal so it might as well be taken as fact. "It could be a creature from Shadowfall Swamp, but it seems unlikely that it would come this far west, what would be the point?"

"The boy's right," another voice said from directly behind the pair. "The dungeon is young—one, maybe two hundred years old."

"Dernal!" Knox said, slapping the burly Adventurer on the back. "I was hoping I'd run into you, but it can wait. What do *you* think got the Gigorf family?"

Dernal Dorntooth peered up at Knox through a steady stream of smoke from his pipe. He wore light padded armor, a large dagger at his waist, and a sour expression on his face.

"Damned if I know."

"Could it be some kind of sickness that got a bear or Dire Wolf to be overly aggressive?" Knox asked, growing excited as he considered whether such a sickness would be magic related. "I ran into a Dire Wolf and was forced to bring it down while working today. It had veins that ripped up through its skin and totally ruined the pelt, maybe it had something to do with that?"

"Could be," Dernal said, letting another long puff of smoke spill from his lips.

"You're a great help," Terrim cut in, bending slightly to see the short, stout Adventurer.

"Dernal, have I told you recently how much I love the eloquence you speak with?" Another voice, this one was young and vibrant, Murdoch Adam, the mayor's son.

"Hhmm," Dernal said, nodding his head to the newcomer.

"Knox, are you saying you've encountered some type of diseased animal?" Murdoch asked, turning his attentive gaze to Knox.

"Yep. I let foreman Bill know. I killed it, so we could still take a look if it's important."

"Hmm, we may just have to do that. Fabulous, yes indeed. But first, I need to quiet this room, or they'll burn down the forest looking for something that likely isn't even there."

Knox watched as Murdoch took command of the room by just walking next to the tall burly ringleader who continued to shout about taking action and how they needed to avenge the blood of their fallen.

Murdoch was tall, muscled, and kept an impossibly straight posture as he walked like someone stuck a really long pole up his backend. He kept his appearance and dark hair neat and tidy, as rigidly in place as his back. His stiffness aside, he had all the commanding presence his father used to have and more—his father had been stricken by a sickness as of late and his form continued to wither despite the attention of skilled healers. The room quieted under his gaze and waited for him to break the new silence.

Murdoch let his intense purple eyes wash over the room but said nothing.

After an awkward amount of time, he finally spoke.

"My fair and beloved townsfolk, you are right to demand retribution."

Another awkward pause, followed by squirming in the audience, while Murdoch eyed the crowd.

"You are right to expect action. I would have you know that I have put together a team of talented hunters and justice will be served in memory of the fallen."

Knox covered his face to muffle his laughter. Not many people knew Murdoch Adam as he did, and he knew Murdoch was loving having all eyes on him. He was very self-important but also an irreverent bastard when he thought no one important was listening.

The crowd appeared pacified by his quick and awkward speech and began to disperse. A few questions were called out, but none were acknowledged. Knox watched Murdoch make his way back to the three of them, still standing to the side by the walls.

Terrim gave Murdoch an awkward head tilt as he approached and flashed him a shit-eating grin. Murdoch, Knox, and Terrim all exchanged a quick chuckle hidden by a series of coughs.

Knox was going to miss these two if he decided to go elsewhere when not Adventuring. But that wouldn't be for a while. By all accounts that Dernal had given him, the local dungeon was fairly weak and would be well-suited for a new Adventurer's first five to ten years, depending on their skill.

"Team of talented hunters, hmm?" Dernal asked, blowing a stream of smoke into Murdoch's face. Murdoch was visibly irked by the sweet-smelling smoke and swiftly dispersed the cloud.

"Why yes," Murdoch said. "First thing in the morning my skilled team will go and deal with the wild animal or whatever it might be. You three are free tomorrow, right?"

The trio echoed a collective, "Shit."

"You do know there are actually hunters or guardsmen that can handle this?" Knox asked. The crowd had thinned, leaving the four of them to sit at a table to sip their beers while contemplating what the morning would hold.

"Yes, yes, my dear Knox. I know very well that we have those employed by the town for this very work, but..." Murdoch's smile widened to ridiculous proportions as he spoke, "we have Dernal! And with his help, we could come back looking like heroes!"

All eyes snapped to Dernal who had just taken a long swig of his drink. By the time he was done, the mug had been emptied and his face had taken on its usual look of boredom. But he didn't answer right away. He pulled out his pipe and packed in some more green herbs, preparing to light it.

"Core's mine," Dernal said, his voice low and scratchy as he lit up his pipe and took a long pull. Smoky tendrils snaked up and around his face and when the cloud of smoke cleared, Dernal wore a small smile of his own.

Knox nodded knowing what he meant. After a quick look at the remaining companions at the table, he knew he was the only one that understood.

"Dernal thinks that there must be a good chance that the creature has developed a Monster Core, they are used in enchantments and are basically a currency for Adventurers," Knox said, straightening his back as he spoke. He loved knowing what others didn't. Not counting the Adventurers that passed through the town, Knox thought he knew the most about dungeons, magic, and complex runic systems.

He wasn't sure if that was really anything to be proud of, considering how small-minded most townsfolk tended to be. If it didn't have to do with their crops, prices of the grain for the day, or the state of the weather, then it was usually deemed silly nonsense that didn't deserve a second thought.

Knox was different and yearned to know more. He wanted answers and he was willing to put himself at risk to get them.

"Mmhhmm," Dernal said through another puff of smoke.

"Okay, Murdoch," Terrim cut in, his booming voice grabbing everyone's attention. "Why should we go? You think I want to die like the Gigorf family?"

"Well, you see," Murdoch leaned in as if speaking a secret, "only Frederick's younger brother and parents were found mangled and dead." Murdoch took a long swig of his drink. "So, Frederick could still be alive. I'd think you'd want to help out a friend in need?"

"Well, shit," Terrim shot back and took a long swig of his own drink.

It was true. Frederick had been a good friend to them, and it didn't feel right leaving a fellow woodcutter to the whims of a monster.

"We leave tonight," Dernal said, standing and adjusting the dagger at his waist. "Knox, come with me."

"What's that now?" Murdoch said, his voice losing all its former bravado.

Despite only asking for Knox, the entire group followed Dernal up to his room on the second floor of the tavern, ascending the creaky wooden staircase.

"Armor," Dernal said, when Knox caught his eye and gave him a confused look.

Knox put his hand to his coin purse and pulled out the remaining coins, Dernal took them without as much as a glance in their direction.

"Do we all get armor?" Murdoch asked, a measure of his confidence returning.

"You haven't heard," Terrim said, chuckling. "Our boy Knox has decided to buy some magic armor and become an Adventurer."

"You *are* a mad lad!" Murdoch said as Terrim finished. "You know I want to have fame and fortune as much as the next guy, but Adventuring? Like into actual dungeons? You are as mad as a Titan."

"Much of the lore surrounding the Titans doesn't withstand rigorous scrutiny. If these beings truly existed, I'm skeptical that the tales we've been told are even true," Knox said, doing his best to sound confident in a subject that was mostly mythos and legends.

"Titans are just myth and fable," Terrim said, joining into the discussion.

"Get inside and put the armor on," Dernal said, moving to a chest at the foot of his small room and opening it. Inside sat a tarnished grey chestplate with several straps. He moved closer and looked inside after Dernal removed the chestplate. An assortment of smaller armor pieces, none of which he knew the names of, were spread out across the bottom of the chest.

Knox initially paid little attention to the armor until he focused on the pieces, and they began to illuminate under his gaze. Runes of all sorts began to glow on each piece, woven together in a familiar fashion like the runic formations bordering his home's doorframe. The flowing script linked at two distinct points to the adjacent rune. The runes were tightly compacted, and several were ones he'd never had a chance to study, as they weren't a part of his mother's diary. He silently cursed himself for not bringing his notebook but remembered with a chuckle that this was his armor now, so he could examine them anytime he wished.

Dernal provided him with a tight-fitting gambeson that sat just above his knees, before helping him into each piece of the armor. In all, it included coverings from head to toe: helmet, chestplate, leggings, bracers, gloves, boots, and even leather pauldrons.

Turning to admire himself in the small mirror that hung on the far wall, Knox gasped. He looked amazing. He really didn't look much different than a fully garbed guard, but this was the first time he'd worn any kind of armor and he felt majestic.

The armor was a mix of brown leather straps and grey tarnished metals, but to Knox's eyes, he was glowing under the power of the runes. To him, he looked like he could be a Titan of Legend.

They had made it to the edge of town before the first hiccup in their plan happened. Murdoch had put on a very fancy suit of leather armor that Knox was sure wouldn't stop many teeth. He also wore a thin saber at his waist, the kind that was said to be used for gentlemen duels in the capital city, not a weapon for hunting.

Terrim brought up the back of the group, his long cloak making him look like a tall, pitched tent as he walked with his axe at his side.

Knox hung his axe from his waist, using a loop likely designed for a sword as the perfect fit.

"You three look ridiculous." Came a distinctly feminine voice —Beth.

"Shit Beth, you scared me," Terrim said.

As Beth came into the light of Dernal's torch, Knox smiled. She was stunningly beautiful with fiery red hair, pale skin, and emerald-green eyes, none of which was easy to see because she was fully covered by her guardsman armor and held a bow at the ready. Beth was a guard, not born in the area but she had lived here long enough that most accepted her as one of the townsfolk.

"You inspire confidence, Terrim," Beth said as she walked up to Knox and slapped him in the ass. Knox grunted from the casual attack against his backside but said nothing. "But I can't trust you to keep my Knoxy-woxy alive. How ever will I bed him if he is dead?"

"Oh, hells Beth," Murdoch laughed. "You are truly an example of fine guardsmanship, are you drunk on duty again?"

"Do I get a say whether I want to be *bedded*?" Knox asked, reaching down to remove Beth's hand from his ass as it returned for another squeeze. It wasn't that he didn't find her incredibly attractive, but damn, that girl was so sexually aggressive that he wasn't sure if he'd be able to keep up.

"Coming?" Dernal asked Beth.

"Sure am."

Dernal grunted and kept walking. The group followed him, now one more person strong.

They left the town on the east side and stuck to the road. Knox listened with his special sense as he walked and felt several predators out hunting in the light of the moon, but nothing approached them on the road. It took nearly an hour to walk to Gigorf's farm and what little conversation they had ceased as they approached.

Three bodies had been stacked on the porch, awaiting burial. But the blood. The blood was everywhere. Even under the light of the moon, it was easy to tell that Mr. Gigorf hadn't gone down easily.

At the edge of the wheat field was a bloody scythe that must have cut into whatever had attacked poor Mr. Gigorf.

"Spread out and look for tracks," Beth ordered. Without question, everyone began to study the ground for tracks. Everyone but Knox.

Knox was studying the blood pool next to the scythe. A strand of some kind of black cord had caught his eye. It was darker, but it looked strikingly similar to the veins that had covered that wolf.

"Dernal!"

"Hmm," Dernal said as he approached. "What?"

"See that black cord? That is what I saw on the Dire Wolf earlier. It made it overly aggressive, and it attacked when it would have normally run."

Dernal leaned over the pool of blood and with a gloved hand picked up the black cord, it twitched under his touch.

"Magical infection," Dernal said, holding it closer to his face and then showing it to Knox. "You see?"

Knox focused and was surprised to find that he could. There was a very faint blue glow surrounding the blackened cord. It looked like the faint glow you'd get on your hands after crushing a glow bug on your arm.

Dernal moved his torch down to touch the black cord and it went up in a puff of smoke.

"Volatile," Dernal said, scratching his beard.

"What does this mean? Do you know what we are up against?"

"No."

Knox just nodded and let his sense push outward, looking for any sign of life. To his surprise, he found something. Not the usual squirrel, wolf, or cow, but a human. Closing his eyes, he pushed his sense harder and narrowed down on a location.

"Someone is under the house!" Knox called as he turned and ran toward the human he had sensed.

His party fell in behind him as he approached the house. It

was a simple farmhouse, three, maybe four rooms large, and built up off the ground several feet. A wooden lattice ran along the bottom of the home to prevent wildlife nesting beneath the raised space. Next to the backdoor, the lattice had been broken and a bloodied smear led beneath.

Now that they were close enough to see underneath the home, they could also hear the whimpering.

Frederick was alive.

CHAPTER 3
BATTLE

"ARE YOU ALRIGHT?" Knox shouted beneath the house at the bloodied mass that could partially be identified as Frederick.

A new startling burst of whimpering sounded from beneath the house. Knox decided that getting Fred from under the house was going to be messy, and he didn't feel like ruining his new armor.

"Terrim, since you have the longest arms, why don't you reach out and pull him out?" Knox asked with a raised eyebrow.

"He could be injured," Terrim said. "Do you think it is a good idea to move him at all?"

"Hmm," Dernal said, brushing past him. "Surprised at you." Dernal shook his head at Knox and a sense of shame washed over him at the same moment.

Knox blushed in embarrassment. He should have been down there and trying to help. He had spoken in jest but knew that if Terrim had followed his orders he wouldn't have stopped him.

Murdoch stood behind the group with Beth. Neither seemed keen on getting too close to the blood, but by the look of them, it was for two separate reasons. Murdoch looked like he might throw up, and Beth just looked haunted.

Dernal handed his torch to Terrim and crawled through the blood-covered dirt until he reached Frederick, seemingly uncaring about his own cleanliness.

"He's weak," Dernal called out from beneath the house.

"What do we do?" Knox asked while trying to remember which roots help slow bleeding. He had tried to learn alchemy and study the different types of plants, but that had been a short-lived experiment as he didn't seem to have the knack for it.

"I'll heal him," Dernal said, his voice rising just above a whisper, but Knox heard, and from the perplexed look on Terrim's face, so had he.

"Did he just say?" Terrim asked.

"Yeah," Knox answered.

"He can do that?" Terrim asked.

"Yeah."

"Did you know?"

"Yeah."

The quick back and forth ended as a small flicker of blue light came up from under the house. Knox knelt and paid attention to what Dernal was doing. He remembered when Dernal mentioned that he specialized in Life energies, a Healer.

Dernal held a hand over Frederick and Knox thought he could faintly hear the whispered words. *Fael Thunkar Foal Resoria*. He recognized a few of the runes but it was hard to tell, as he'd only read runes, and on one other occasion he had actually heard a few spoken.

Fael and *Foal* were both related to heat in some way, but he hadn't a clue about *Thunkar* and *Resoria*. The blood around Frederick began to move, being pulled back into him. After half a minute of moving blood and repeated chanting of *Fael Thunkar Foal Resoria*, Dernal stopped.

"Done all I can," Dernal said, sweat trickling down his brow. Frederick must have been close to death for a small healing like that to take it out of Dernal. Of course, Knox didn't know what it took to heal, surely just saying the words wouldn't be enough. For all he knew, even healing small wounds took a great deal of effort.

Knox watched Dernal slowly edge out of the crawl space with Frederick being pulled along with him. He wore a mangled shirt, pants, and boots. It was odd, though; nowhere Knox looked could he find any blood or wounds. It would appear even the blood from his clothing was sponged away during the healing. As his body was brought under the full light of the torch, Knox saw the signs of the attack. Instead of gaping wounds, there was faintly reddened skin. The healing had worked even better than Knox could have imagined.

Fred lay where Dernal deposited him, breathing even, steady gasps of air. After only a few minutes, Fred began to stir and wake up. Knox moved to his side and helped him sit up.

"How do you feel?" Knox asked, supporting Frederick.

Frederick didn't answer, he just stared forward while whimpering.

"Back," Dernal said, moving to take Knox's spot on the ground next to Fred. He pulled out some kind of green herb, maybe the same stuff he'd been smoking, and put it into Fred's mouth.

Frederick didn't resist and chewed on the leafy herb mechanically.

"What was that?" Knox asked.

"Numb his mind a touch," Dernal answered. "He's in shock."

They waited for the herb to do its work while Beth and Murdoch kept watch.

After several long minutes, Fred just blinked and seemed to snap out of it. He looked around the group from Dernal to Knox, Terrim, Murdoch, and then finally rested on Beth.

"The-They are de-dead, m-my family..."

Knox watched Fred begin to weep and cry out in pain, not physical pain, but the deep emotional pain of losing a loved one.

Stepping forward, Knox placed his hand on the shoulder of his friend.

"We are here to avenge your family and kill whatever creature did this," Knox said, keeping his voice firm and steady as his friend wailed in pain beside him. "Please, I know it won't be easy, but we need you to tell us what happened and what did it."

Fred's jaw pulled in tight, and he began taking in long sharp breaths, eventually settling into a passable calmness.

"It wasn't right," Frederick said, his voice still shaky. "That owlbear wouldn't die. Father put a scythe straight through its head after it took down Johnny, but it just kept slicing with its blackened dead body."

"All black or black veins?" Dernal asked.

"Wha-what, black veins? No, the entire thing was just a dead, leathery-looking black color."

"Is there anything else you can tell us? Did you see which way it went?" Knox asked while rubbing his grieving friend's back.

"Toward the mountains," Fred said, motioning to the high peaks in the distance. "And I'm not sure but I could have sworn there was someone else with it, but I only heard her and wasn't able to see where the voice had come from."

"Her?" Knox asked.

"Yeah, it sounded like a young girl," Fred said. "She was

singing a nursery rhyme but the words she used were different than I'd ever heard, if it weren't for the tune that she was singing it to, I wouldn't have known. It sounds crazy, but she was singing *Victory over the Deep* but the words she used... It was all turned around and backward. *Victory to the Deep,* she said. It was unsettling."

Knox looked to Dernal to get a sense of his thoughts, but he had pulled his pipe out and his face was lost in a cloud of smoke that seemed to linger around his head.

"Well let's kee-," Knox began to say, but Dernal cut him off with his own words.

"Anyone not in Tier 1 Enchanted Armor leaves now."

"Now wait a sec-," Murdoch and Beth said at the same time, but Dernal cut them off as well, speaking more words in a single sentence than Knox had heard from him since meeting the man.

"This is a magical issue and the chance that unenchanted armor would last more than a moment against it is minimal. All of you but Knox, take Fred, bury his family, and return him to the safety of the village, now."

Murdoch and Beth stared daggers at Dernal while Terrim helped Frederick to his feet and walked him toward the front of his home.

"You think just because you have a dag-," Beth began to say.

"Hhmm. My dagger has nothing to do with this, you are a fair warrior—I'm sure—but this won't come to a matter of weapon blows."

Dernal raised a hand to stop Murdoch from speaking.

"He will make it to the town with the healing I've done. Take credit for this kill, my lordling, then wait here until we return with proof of its demise. Damned kids."

This seemed to pacify Murdoch, but Beth just looked even more annoyed. Both turned and walked to the front of the house without further argument.

"You really think the two of us will be enough?" Knox asked after everyone else had left.

"More than enough," Dernal said through a thick haze of smoke.

Knox had found tracks that matched the description Fred gave and signaled Dernal over.

"It looks like an owlbear for sure," he said as he grasped his smooth axe shaft.

"Hmm. Small Core of an owlbear explains the disease spreading further, magical beasts are more resistant. Be on your guard."

"Owlbears are magical, right?" Knox asked, scratching his head. "Are you sure?"

Dernal said nothing, but gave Knox a look that said, 'Am I sure? I'm fucking Dernal Dorntooth. Yes, I am sure.'

Dernal took the lead and Knox followed closely behind. He did his best to remain silent and stealthy like Dernal but failed spectacularly. With each step he broke a twig or ruffled leaves that announced his presence to any predator listening. Normally a very skilled 'soft foot', he was utterly aware of his faults when measured against Dernal.

The woods around them quieted as they stalked the steps of the owlbear—a single pair of tracks so far. Lumbering pines swayed under the weight of an unfelt wind and a single cry pierced the silence.

Hhhuuooo-garlll

It was the hooting roar of an owlbear!

In the distance came a steady *flip-flop... flip-flop.*

"It has caught our scent!" Dernal said, turning toward the sound.

"Do we have a plan or?" Knox asked.

"Kill it, but don't damage the Core."

"Good plan." Knox said, rolling his eyes.

The shadows were thick between the trees and Dernal's torch did little to illuminate the source of the distant *flip-flop... flip-flop.*

A thicker shape of blackness, like a silhouette made of pure darkness, waddled through the trees on its rear legs and into sight.

The owlbear stood at least seven feet tall and waddled awkwardly from side to side. The thick cords of black leathery veins bulged out of its already sizable girth, making the monstrosity nearly spherical. The arms with their wide palms and hooked claws flailed about on either side. As it walked, its arm slashed into a nearby tree, splintering it and throwing bark out toward the two of them.

"Avoid the claws and beak and we should be fine," Dernal said, moving to flank the owlbear on the left as Knox went to flank the right side.

The owlbear threw back its head in anger and cried out as they approached.

Hhhuuhhuuooo-garlrllrrll

Knox mused that this might be easier than he had expected as he focused on the owlbear with his special sense. He could barely make out the owlbear's touch, it seemed weak-probably close to death.

He raised his axe, ready to strike as soon as Dernal made his move. However, instead of attacking, Dernal motioned Knox forward. Knox charged, swinging his axe high, hoping to take the owlbear in the neck. His excitement and eagerness to prove himself to Dernal overtook him and he let his special sense drop.

Knox's axe stopped several inches short of reaching the owlbear. Strands of the leathery black cords had unraveled from the owlbear and held Knox fast. They didn't cut into him, but he was unable to move his weapon, arms, or torso.

Panic overtook him and he felt his sense shoot outward all around him. The owlbear no longer felt weak. It gave off waves of anger like the torrents of rain that accompanied a powerful storm. Using his sense as a shield, he pushed back against the overwhelming fury radiating from the monster, for it had truly become a monster now.

The swish of a blade caught Knox's attention and he tilted his head just in time to see Dernal go in for an attack. The owlbear was slow to react, but the tendrils of black had no problem keeping up and quickly entangled Dernal as well.

All around Dernal, a soft blue light grew and pulsed into white burning light. A new sound filled the forest clearing.

Scccrrrrrrrrrrrr

It wasn't the scream of an owlbear, but rather the sound of its flesh searing away.

With a wicked laugh, Dernal unclenched his fist, light shot from his palms striking the blackened fleshy appendages. It had taken only moments, but Dernal and Knox rolled free from the wounded, corrupted owlbear.

"On your feet!" Dernal called and Knox rolled to the side and onto his feet.

The owlbear could be seen beneath the black tendrils as they withered and moved over the top and into its flesh. It looked like a bucket of earthworms trying to consume a squirrel from the inside out.

Knox looked at Dernal and they exchanged a quick head nod before he rushed in to attack the exposed owlbear with his axe. The wind tore against him as he rushed forward, axe raised. The smell of sweat mingled with a faint acrid aroma as he closed in on the owlbear.

His strike slammed into the exposed flesh and cut deep. The pain to the host spurred the blackened cords to a new purpose. They took hold of Knox and began entangling him again. He could feel the cords working against his flesh, trying to find a way inside of him. The struggle to keep his mouth closed and body moving reached a fever pitch when he heard additional battle cries.

A new burst of light from Dernal loosened the blackened cords and Knox rolled to the ground and away.

To his left and right stood his friends, weapons raised to fight off the monster.

Beth wasted no time unleashing her bow against the owlbear. Several loud screams echoed into the moonlit night as each of her arrows found purchase.

Terrim swung his massive axe down on a tendril that tried to snake closer to the small group, severing it completely and spraying black liquid from its ruined end.

Murdoch moved with surprising speed, cutting, and poking at the owlbear while avoiding the tendrils by a hair's thickness. It was as if he could predict their movements before they even made a decision. He cut away at the monster like a wraith in the moonlight.

And then there was Frederick. He stood, staring down the owlbear with hate, shame, regret, and fear mirrored in his eyes. He held tight to his father's scythe and began to slowly walk toward the monster.

Knox readied his own axe and wiped the sweat from his forehead. A swell of pride built in his chest seeing his friends standing by his side, ready to fight with him.

"Keep up the pressure!" Knox called, getting himself ready for another attack. "Terrim, Fred, come in with me, and let's end this blight."

Dernal's beam of light cut out and Knox studied him for signs of fatigue. Sweat dripped freely from his face, but he gave Knox a reassuring nod.

Murdoch kept moving and striking the owlbear's tentacles whenever he could, but the corruption was moving quicker now that Dernal's attack had ended, he would have to retreat soon or be overcome.

Fred fell behind as he continued his slow steady walk, and Knox and Terrim ran ahead, axes at the ready.

Several medium-sized tendrils shot toward Knox, but just before they connected, Terrim was there and cut them aside. Knox pushed through the opening that had been made and brought his axe down hard. Red blood, not the black stuff of corruption, spewed forth in a spray. He had hit a vital artery and with his special sense surging, he felt the owlbear's power wane.

"Keep up the attack!" Knox screamed, as arrows flew within inches of his head striking the open gash he had made.

A thin blade nearly nicked his ear as it slid past and into the open wound. Knox rolled to the side just in time to see Terrim plunge his own axe into the owlbear.

One of the owlbear's arms swung down and caught Terrim in the chest before he was able to throw himself out of its path.

"Arrrhhhggg!" Terrim screamed and fell backward, a swath of red following him.

"Bring it down now!" Dernal's voice rose over the din of battle and snapped Knox out of his shock. White light smashed into the owlbear, and several new areas opened for a possible attack.

Knox caught sight of the claws coming down and missing Murdoch by a hair and decided what he needed to do was disable the owlbear's natural weapon.

Ripping away stray tendrils, Knox went to work. Back and forth he wove through the fight, cutting and gouging open wounds. Finally, he was in a position to take one of the claws and he twisted around to ready his axe. The blade caught just above its claws, biting deeply.

Instead of taking off the claw as he'd hoped, it stuck fast, and Knox found himself without a weapon. A light flashed in his eyes, separate from the attack, and his head began to ring from pain.

Blinking through the daze, he pieced together what happened. After his axe had been ripped from his hands, the owlbear must have swung to strike at him and the stiff smooth solid wooden handle knocked him upside the head.

In his position on the ground, he saw Fred walk past him. Black tendrils cut at his flesh, but he pushed forward. Knox struggled to his feet, weaponless but protected by his armor.

Fred wasn't protected and the attacks began taking their toll.

Several of the smaller tendrils entered and lifted Fred, pulling him toward the injured owlbear.

"Fred!" Knox cried out and charged the owlbear weaponless.

Fred didn't cry out as the black tendrils entered him through every single cut he had. He barely flinched as he was brought closer to the owlbear, the scythe still clutched firmly in his hands.

As soon as Fred was moved into the ideal range of the owlbear he screamed, pulling his other hand free and taking a two-handed grip on his weapon.

"DIE!" Fred cried as he brought the scythe down into the owlbear's head.

Whether it was his raised-up position or the rage he held inside from the loss of his family, or just dumb luck, Fred had done it.

A loud crunch filled the area and the owlbear went still. The tendrils still squirmed and moved, but no longer tried to attack. Knox reached Fred, catching his bloody form as he fell from the tendrils' grasp.

"Finally!" Beth cried from behind them.

"Move aside," Dernal said calmly, though his voice carried a certain relief in it. Knox shifted his weight to allow Dernal access to Fred, but Dernal walked past them.

Knox watched with a mix of horror and wonder, as Dernal plunged his dagger into the owlbear's head.

"It best be intact," he said as he worked.

Fred groaned in pain and Knox put pressure on Fred's biggest wound, trying to stem the blood.

Knox watched as Dernal pulled free a gem the size of a walnut, with a dim blue light shining forth.

"Hhm," Dernal said, before pocketing the gem and turning back to Knox and Fred.

CHAPTER 4
CLEAN UP

KNOX SURVEYED THE BATTLEFIELD. Fred lay in his lap, breathing shallow and raspy. The owlbear was dead. The black leathery infection that had clung so tightly to it had disappeared into the woods. Just to his left under the light of the full moon, he could see Terrim sitting up, blood still pouring out of his chest in a steady stream.

"Dernal, they need your healing! Quick!" Knox shouted.

Dernal turned and seemed to notice the injured for the first time.

"Right, who first?" Dernal asked, looking expectantly at Knox.

"Heal Fred, this is only a flesh wound," Terrim said, his voice weak.

Dernal looked at Knox seemingly awaiting an answer.

"Heal Fred," Knox said.

Sloshing through the mud and blood of the owlbear, Dernal moved to kneel next to Knox.

This time he had a perfect view of how Dernal healed.

Moving his hand in odd gestures, something Knox hadn't read about before, Dernal began his chant.

Fael Thunkar Foal Resoria, Fael Thunkar Foal Resoria, Fael Thunkar Foal Resoria!

His chants grew to a fever pitch and blue light shone from his hands as they swiftly moved between four unique patterns.

Fred's breathing returned to normal, the raspy shallowness to it gone. His eyes closed and his body relaxed.

"Is he...?" Beth asked from somewhere behind them, her usually jovial tone had gone dark.

"Well, what is it?" Murdoch asked, he moved closer to get a look, "Is he healed yet?"

"He'll live," Dernal said, rising and moving to Terrim.

The once rosy complexion of the green-eyed giant had turned a sickly white. He was barely holding himself up in a sitting position when Dernal got to him.

Not wasting any time, Dernal began his chant.

Fael Thunkar Foal Resoria, Fael Thunkar Foal Resoria, Fael Thunkar Foal Resoria, Fael Thunkar Foal Resoria.

It didn't take long to see it begin to work. Blood that had bathed Terrim only moments before moved up and back into his body. As the blood returned so did his rosy complexion.

Knox let loose a breath he hadn't realized he was holding.

"You feel alright?" Knox asked Terrim, delicately moving Fred off of him, being careful not to wake him.

"I'm fine, just need some rest," Terrim answered, laying back into the muck and mud.

Knox was used to seeing dead bodies. Even their small village had its fair share of accidents or wild animal attacks. You didn't live on the edge of civilization without seeing some measure of death. But Fred's still body reminded him too much of a dead corpse and he caught Dernal's attention.

"Are you sure he'll be fine?" Knox asked, Fred's face was still very pale. "Recover well, friend, and may the Titans not impede your travel to the next world if it is your path."

It was an old saying, one that Knox had read in his mother's notes, but it felt right to say. His own people had no special death rites. Although each and every member of the village would be quick to tell you that if you aren't burning the body then you had better bury it deep or risk it coming back to visit you. Old superstitions of times long forgotten.

"He'll live," Dernal said, putting a comforting hand on Knox's shoulder.

Knox felt a wave of grief taken over by hopeful resolve and he welcomed the new emotions.

He scanned the tree line with his eyes and his special sense. Nothing, not even the usual wildlife he expected. Then, suddenly, he felt the barest prickle of life.

Turning his gaze to that area of trees, Knox saw something. Between two great pines was a small, almost insignificant silhouette. His eyes had traveled over that spot at least three times before his sense had directed him to it. As best he could tell it was a little girl, as Fred had mentioned, but she held a small farmer's sickle out to the side.

That is when the words reached his ears.

Victory, Victory, to the deep ones went the victory. Gone for now, we come again, victory, victory.

A cold shiver ran up Knox's spine as he listened to the haunted words.

"What was that noise," Beth asked. Knox turned away from the silhouette for only a moment to glance at Beth before returning his gaze to the tree line.

The girl was gone. But the tune repeated in his mind several times before he could shake himself free of it.

"Nothing," Knox finally answered Beth. "Let's see if we can collect anything useful from the owlbear and get back to town. These woods are giving me the creeps for once."

"These woods have always given me the creeps," Beth said, turning to follow Knox back toward the owlbear.

Knox led the group back to the farm and they tended to the burials of all the family members. Meanwhile, Dernal began to search through the house.

"Do you think it's right to just go through the things of the recently dead?" Knox asked, calling through the open window toward the noise within.

"Evidence," Dernal shouted back. "You do the same. Check the perimeter before we set off."

The rest of the group worked to get the bodies buried, while Beth tended to Fred. Knox took it upon himself to check the perimeter like Dernal suggested.

His eyes twitched back and forth along the edge of the thick forest. At any moment he imagined something would come out and scare him, but nothing came. His axe was still at the ready. He wasn't scared, he told himself, but the image of the small silhouette, the sickle, and then that eerie tune had him on edge.

He was so intent on scanning the tree line, his eyes darting back and forth, that when his foot hit something heavy, he tripped and fell into the mud. The ground was cold, and he felt the wet dirt seep past the gaps in his armor and into his pants.

"Well, shit. I've had the armor for all of one night and I'll probably set it to rust before the week's out," Knox mumbled to himself.

Looking around the area he found the object that had tripped him. It was a book.

The book glowed with the vibrant blue of magical runes. He didn't recognize any of the runes, only noticing they gave off a consistent blue glow across the cover and along the edge of the pages. Focusing his mind, he tried to dampen his sense and sure enough the glow dissipated.

It was an old book, made of cracked leather and gold embossing on the cover. The words weren't runes, but they also weren't any language that Knox was familiar with either. In the center cover of the brown cracked leather book, was a triangular blue gem, cut with many facets.

The moon shone brightly above him, and the facets caught the light in the most beautiful ways, shimmering like magical dust trapped just below the surface.

He reached out and touched it.

It pulsed and he was shocked. Dropping the book back into the mud, Knox recoiled in surprise. Not only was the book not covered in mud, but it also floated several inches above the ground. The words on the cover had changed and made sense to him now.

It read, "Personal Journal of Ramses VanClark of the Highest Seat of the Fourteenth Reign of Stars, Destroyer of Mangulous the Dull, and speaker of the Ancient Tongue."

Knox's head hurt as he read the words. Reaching out, he tried to grab the book again. He was able to pluck it from the air without the tome shocking him. Putting the book under his arm, he went back to meet up with the group.

The sun was just beginning to peek above the trees as they approached the town gates.

"Who goes there!" A voice called down to them.

"How are you just seeing us now, Jeremy, you half-wit? If you've been sleeping at your post again…" Beth let her sentence trail off, giving Jeremy the chance to fill in the threat with his own imagination.

"Is that you Beth? What are you doing outside the walls?"

"Open the gate, Jeremy," Beth answered back with a deadpan voice.

"Oh, right," Jeremy answered back, his overly curly dark hair could be seen peeking out the side of his helmet even from this distance.

There was a click and the sounds of grunting that Knox could only assume were Jeremy pulling the wheel that allowed the heavy wood portcullis to be raised. Knox tried to remember who Jeremy was, but most of the current guard members were older than Knox and he hadn't had the chance to get to know many beyond learning their names and their faces.

Officially, the town guards were employed by King Wilham, but unofficially appointed by the mayor's office. As such, it wasn't a job that had much turnover. It was easy, boring, but stable.

"Don't worry everyone!" Murdoch proclaimed, raising his arms in the air as if he were about to make an important announcement. "I will take care of reporting the events to the people. I will be sure to spare no detail and I think I might even be able to arrange a donation, to which all of you will get a portion!" Then, seemingly only noticing the half-dead Fred standing beside him—he'd woken up and insisted on walking halfway back to town—he jerked in surprise. "And of course, I will tend to our injured friend as well. A warm bed and a hearty breakfast will be your reward, you brave soul."

Murdoch seemed the least affected by the night's adventures, short of Dernal who always looked slightly bored while he puffed on his pipe endlessly. Knox, on the other hand, felt like he had just lived the longest day in his life.

"Hey Ter," Knox said, moving in close so only he could hear.

"Do you think I can crash at your place? I don't really think I will get any sleep at mine. That's if my dad even lets me inside the house."

"Oh," Terrim said, he shifted uneasily before finally saying. "Well Knox, I mean, you know we only have the one bed at my place and well, I guess I could put a blanket down for you on the ground if you don't mind..."

Knox read the hesitation for what it was and sighed. "Nah, I'll find someplace else to sleep for a few hours." He could tell something was bothering Terrim and didn't want to pressure his friend after what they'd all just been through.

"I've got a place for you," Beth said as she caught up with the pair. She put her arm around Knox's shoulder, pretending like the larger pauldrons didn't make the move awkward.

"Look Beth," Knox began to say, then thought better of it and decided to see where the conversation would take him. "Actually... yeah sure, where do you have a place for me Beth?"

Beth's grin went wide, and her eyes seemed to smile as well.

"My bed of course," she answered. "I've been renting one of McNailey's rooms, I have my own entrance and everything. The bed isn't that big, but we can both squeeze in if we try."

"Is there room on the floor for me to sleep?" Knox asked. "I'm not looking for a tumble right now, what I need is sleep."

Beth just laughed and led him away from the group toward her home. "If you say so," she said, but her grin expressed that she wasn't done trying to pull him into her bed.

Knox had seen the pair of small one room homes before, but he hadn't known they were rented rooms until Beth told him. They walked through the nice part of town and there was a fair bit of foot traffic, but no one had bothered them and soon they arrived at her front door.

The door was something Knox could appreciate. Mr. Tome most likely had built it, if not the entire building. He noted the craftsmanship of the wood and the framing as they entered.

The room was simple. It had a bed with a trunk at the foot of it. As well as a small nightstand and a single dresser with a water pot and bowl for washing.

"It isn't much," Beth said, seeing Knox look about the room. "But it's home."

"It's perfect Beth, thank you for giving me someplace to sleep in peace," Knox said, emphasizing the last bit. He began to try and remove his armor, but Beth hurried over and without asking, helped him strip it off. It truly was not a one-person job, removing armor.

He would have to see about renting one of these rooms himself and apologize to Mr. Tome for missing last night's work. He also hoped that the foreman wasn't upset at him for missing work this morning. But those worries were for another time, right now, he needed rest.

Beth ran a hand down his chest, earning a warning glance from Knox. She feigned ignorance, focusing on unfastening his bracer. Clearly more skilled at disassembling armor, she had him down to his underclothes in just a few minutes.

"Take those off as well," Beth said, her brown eyes running the length of Knox's body. "You are covered in mud, I can grab you a change of clothes, but you aren't going to sleep like that."

Knox gave her a long hard look before responding.

"I need a moment to clean off my armor, if you could run and get me a long shirt from someplace, that would give me enough time to clean the armor and myself," Knox said. His armor really did need to be wiped clean at the very least, but he wasn't keen on stripping naked and cleaning himself in front of Beth.

Beth smiled, turned to the dresser, and pulled out an oversized long shirt.

Damn, Knox thought, *well it is what it is.*

"Help me out of my armor first and we can help bathe each other," Beth said, her voice sounding all business.

"I'll help with your armor, but I'm not bathing you," Knox said, his resolve holding firm despite the beautiful woman in front of him wanting him to take her clothes off.

He took his time to help Beth remove her armor until she stood in her very worn and very see-through underclothes. He averted his eyes as best he could, but he'd seen more than enough, and she wasn't trying to hide it.

"Look, Beth," he said, but she stood up, almost pressing herself against him. "Not tonight. Why don't we catch a meal together sometime and we can see where it goes?"

They knew each other well enough, but he'd never gone on any dates with her. Most of the interactions were during group activities and she'd slowly decided that Knox would be the main target of her flirtations.

Beth let out a sigh and Knox had to avert his eyes again, a sizable hole in her shirt giving him a view he hadn't asked for. "Fine. But I'm not going to wait forever. You are handsome and all, but a girl has needs. Here, take this blanket and try not to snore too loud."

With that, she threw Knox a blanket that he caught deftly midair. She then pulled out another from the chest at the foot of her bed and curled up under her blanket while making noises that stirred things inside of him.

Damnit, this woman was being impossible, he thought as he tried to make himself comfortable.

Knox awoke to the sound of the door shutting. It seemed Beth had left for guard duty and Knox was finally given some privacy to get his things together. He had thoroughly enjoyed the sights of staying in Beth's room, but he would need to secure his own place to live. He decided he would not be going back to live with his father. Let him be someone else's burden for once.

His clothing and armor had been cleaned, but not by him, and were neatly placed atop the chest. The plans to clean them before slipping off to bed had vanished the moment he'd laid his head on the pillow.

It seemed like odd behavior for Beth, she rarely kept within the bounds of what most folks considered proper womanly behavior. Knox wasn't one of those who dared to think Beth was anything remotely resembling weak. Not that he thought the other women were weak either, it was just rare to encounter a woman like Beth, one that was as ready to put on a dress and dance as she was to suit up in armor and fight off an owlbear. He had to admit there was a certain attraction there and he began to wonder if he'd made a mistake in not taking up her offer the night before.

Knox had to stop himself. He couldn't remember the last time he'd spent so much time thinking about a woman. Beth had really left an impression on him. Peeking out the window to check the time of day, he realized several things at once.

He'd missed a day's worth of woodcutting and now he was about to be late helping Mr. Tome. On top of that, he was very hungry.

Deciding to address his hunger first, before he was needed at Mr. Tome's workshop, Knox dressed himself and put his armor inside Beth's trunk. He trusted her enough not to mess with it, enchanted armor or not.

He was just about to leave the room when a glint of light caught his eye. It was the book he had found last night and had somehow nearly forgotten about it. It was as if the very thought of the book after picking it up, had fled his mind. Now that he thought about it, no one, not even Dernal, had asked him about the book, which seemed odd. Knox stared at it and his mind wandered.

Sometime last night, it had been pushed beneath the space under the dresser. Moving to retrieve it, Knox grabbed the heavy tome and sat down. The pages were thick and yellowed. The book itself glowed in the same all-consuming light as before, no visible runes to decipher. Concentrating to turn off his sense, Knox opened the book to a random page and began to read.

Journal Entry # 1 – 1065-11 Fallen Titan Standard Time

It has been decided by a vote of the council that I, Ramses VanClark of the Highest Seat of the Fourteenth Reign of Stars, Destroyer of Mangulous the Dull, and speaker of the Ancient Tongue, would be sent to investigate the convergence of ley lines in the Gorr'ahm Sea. Creatures of unspeakable power and destructive potential have been sighted and confirmed by the council's own eyes.

Something had to be done. We voted. I lost. So here I am, having booked passage of the finest pleasure ship that the kingdom had in port, and sitting in an overly decorated room writing my experience down for later review by the council members.

-The same day, long into the night.-

The captain says we won't arrive for an entire week. I should have tried to connect a portal to one of the Serifian isles, but no, I will follow the advice of my esteemed council members who suggested that the magical crossing of lines in the area could affect the spell. They are of course correct, but a week on this swaying hell-driven boat might just be my death. I will not return to this report until something of actual value presents itself.

Knox blinked and flipped to the first page. It was the same passage. It was as if the book would only allow itself to be read in a specific order. He read the passage again. He didn't recognize a single place named. Once more he read the passage, this time aloud. When finished, he turned the page and a new entry revealed itself.

Journal Entry # 2 – 1065-25 Fallen Titan Standard Time

So much has transpired since my last recording, I hope to communicate the full series of events.

The trip took just under a month, the winds favored our journey, until we arrived at the aforementioned area. With my channels open, I followed the ley lines to a chain of previously unrecorded islands. That is where the first of several setbacks occurred.

We were met by a creature of indescribable horror, and it assailed our boat. It appeared to be several sea-life predators smashed into a mishmash of teeth, fins, and claws. Whatever its previous life had been, it was a thing of nightmares now, and it would have shattered us from the very sea that we rode upon if I had not been here.

Using my mastery of the water and my deep understanding of gravitational forces of the planet and sea, I was able to slay the wretched beast.

But that caused another, unfortunate mishap. The blood of this nightmare beast caused the metal bands that held several important parts of the ship together to melt away. My best guess concluded it was a type of acid released into the water. Had we been any further away, it could have been diluted enough to do us no harm. So, you see, it was the command of the captain to bring us closer so that I may slay the beast and not my own actions that caused this incident.

I digress. We were able to make landfall on the smaller boats they carried aboard, and our luck be damned, they also fell apart, but not before we reached the surface of one of the larger islands.

Within a week we'd lost half of the crew, the captain included. Our foodstuff had been lost to the sea, but several edible plants had been found. It wasn't until my own private food store also ran out, that I realized what they had done.

My first bite into the so called-edible plant sent me abuzz with power. Those not attuned to the ways of the world would have no way of knowing that for the last few days they'd been poisoning themselves with the power of creation. Without proper cycling techniques, I too would have fallen prey to such essence-rich plants.

Those that didn't die began to change. Just this night I was forced to flee. Those remaining had lost what little sense of self they had and have become slaves to the powers of this island. I kept several separate notes on their condition and possible remedies, none of which amounted to much.

I fear I will be forced to open a portal back to the Academy and the awaiting council.

Tomorrow, I plan to go deeper into the island and trace the source of the converging ley lines. I find myself hungering for the magically enriched plants, but I know that even as a master of the arts I could be overrun by the power, yet still, I crave it...

A cold chill ran up Knox's spine. He had read the words aloud and could almost see the things in his mind's eye. The sea creature of nightmare, and men changing into inhuman monsters. He shut the book and put it into the trunk along with his armor.

He would keep reading, but not right now. Although he felt slightly less hungry after reading, he knew he needed to eat, so he stepped out into the evening light and made his way to the tavern.

CHAPTER 5
GIFTS

THE THREE LADIES Tavern was abuzz with energy and livelihood. Knox was greeted with cheers from several of the patrons at the bar, the news had obviously gotten around that they'd dealt with the owlbear responsible for killing the Gigorf family. Knox wondered what tale Murdoch had spun and how closely it resembled the truth. They would have to talk later so that he could be on the same level with whatever extra details had been sprinkled into the tale.

Scanning the brightly lit room, Knox found Dernal sitting alone at a table and made his way through the crowd to join him. The room was filled with the bustle of hard-working men and women who had spent their day laboring. A part of Knox felt bad that he had missed out on his day's labor, but there was no helping it. He had done a great service for the village by slaying the owlbear, and only but himself seemed to care that some work had been missed in the doing of it.

"Good evening Dernal!" Knox said happily. He slid into a sturdy oak chair opposite Dernal. The stout man stared up at him with brilliant, amber-colored eyes. He wore his normal light padded armor, tan leather hide with golden edges made of a ragged looking thread. His black hair fell loose around his face, where normally he had it in a tight bun. Smoke rose out of his mouth and curled around his bushy black beard.

"Where's your armor?" Dernal asked, more smoke puffing from his mouth as he spoke.

"It's safe," Knox assured him. "I'm grabbing a quick bite to eat then I have some work to do for Mr. Tome. No reason to wear armor while working with wood."

"Hhmm, we are leaving the morning after the Sun Harvest Festival," Dernal said, looking up as another man approached. It was Ferlin Goship, the local blacksmith.

"Aye I hear you's two were the ones that brought down that owlbear. I'd like to buy you's a round of drinks!" Ferlin had a way of talking that Knox could only describe as smushing all his words together in a vain attempt to make everything sound like a single long word.

"I could use a drink, but it'll have to be a quick one, I don't want to keep Mr. Tome waiting," Knox said, smiling up at the dark-haired Ferlin. He looked about what you'd expect a black-smith to look like, big brown beard, bushy eyebrows, dark brown eyes set against sun-darkened skin, and muscles enough to lift several anvils at once, if the size of them meant anything.

"Right, two ales over here," Ferlin boomed over the low roar of the tavern. "There is one other thing. I hears you stripped that owlbear clean and was wondering if you'd found a buyer for the claws yet? I've experience working with owlbear claws and for a price I could fashion several daggers, or even a gauntlet of sorts if yous be interested."

For whatever reason this seemed to pique Dernal's interest, and he looked up at the man for the first time.

"You've worked with essence infused materials?" Dernal asked.

"I've got a smattering of experience, mostly owlbear, mind you, so I think I could make a good go at it," Ferlin said.

"Hhrm. I'll swing by later," Dernal shot back, shooing the man away afterward with his hand like someone would an annoying dog.

"Right sir, of course, look forward to it." And with that Ferlin made his way out of the tavern.

"You think he will be able to make something with the owlbear parts?" Knox asked, noticing a grin on Dernal's face as he took another hard pull on his pipe.

"Maybe," Dernal growled, keeping most of his thoughts to himself as per usual.

The drinks arrived and Knox took this opportunity to order some food to-go before the serving girl, Lisa, went on her way.

"Before I head off," Knox said, grabbing Dernal's attention from the drinks that had arrived. "Have you heard of ley lines or the Gorr'ahm Sea?"

Dernal stopped mid-gulp and placed his mug of ale aside. He eyed Knox as if he were reading his mind. Knox watched as the bearded man lifted his long, bent pipe to his lips and took a quick puff.

"Hmm," Dernal answered before another long pause began.

"Hmm?" Knox shot back, his foot beginning to tap beneath the table.

Taking a deep breath and looking like he was preparing to exert himself, he spoke. "I'm as knowledgeable as any Adventurer my stage so, yes, I've heard of ley lines, but only in a general sense. As for the Gorr'ahm Sea, I think perhaps you mean the Gorhm Sea? It is half the world away from our little corner of existence. Where'd you hear these names?" Dernal asked, his eyes still locked on Knox.

"Here and there," Knox answered back. Dernal had asked him on several occasions where he had learned the meaning of several runes and other bits of magic he was able to uncover, but Knox hadn't given up his source yet and Dernal always backed-off eventually.

"Hhrm. Right, here and there," Dernal said, mimicking Knox's voice. "One of these days you will tell me, and you'll be better for it."

Knox just smiled at Dernal. Happy to keep a measure of secrets from the old Adventurer who always seemed to know more than he should.

"Beth tells me she gave you quite the ride last night," Dernal said, just as Knox tilted back his mug for a swig of ale. The contents of which sputtered forth, wetting the front of his shirt and a measure of the table.

"The hells she did," Knox said back, more embarrassed than mad. Beth was not shy about her sexuality or her sexual desire at all, but Knox knew she hadn't gone about announcing that they'd finally had sex throughout the entire town, especially when they'd done nothing of the sort. She wouldn't... would she? He asked himself before deciding that no, she would not.

"Hah." Dernal shot back. "Be careful young lad, the adventuring life is full of that kind of fulfilment if it's what you wish, but young wives and kids don't mix well with our life."

Knox wasn't sure how to answer that, so he didn't. There was a special feeling that he had when he realized that Dernal saw

Knox as his type of person, but Knox didn't want it to go to his head, so he thought of other things.

Like how he had found a journal, seemingly belonging to some kind of powerful Adventurer from halfway across the world, out in the dense forest surrounding the town. It didn't make much sense for a magical object, book or otherwise, to be left for anyone to find. Magical objects were valuable, so much so that it had taken Knox countless days of work to save for a hand-me-down set of magical armor for himself. On top of that, Knox was sure that Dernal had given him a better deal than he would have received elsewhere.

"Here you are," Lisa said, dropping off his food wrapped in red and white checkered linens. "Mr. Goship picked up your bill, have a swell day Knox. Be careful out there cutting wood, Bill came in here earlier saying they spotted a pair of bandits. Had to chase them off and everything."

"Thanks for the heads-up, Lisa," Knox said, giving the young girl a smile before downing the last of his drink and bidding Dernal farewell.

Mr. Tome's workshop was a thing of wonder. In a village where space inside the walls came at a premium, his workshop was like a large complex of its own. It even had a six-foot-tall wooden fence that ran around the perimeter, with a main gate access point and a smaller door hidden behind a grove of trees.

Knox approached the smaller entrance like he always did when starting his evening's work for Mr. Tome. There were always a few people who grumbled that the secretive Mr. Tome ought to not have his own large space, but they were always quickly quieted by the mass of villagers who benefited from his inexpensive but high-quality work.

From doors to a village-wide drainage system, Mr. Tome could do it all. For his part, Knox felt like his artistic woodwork is where his true beauty lay, but he had the distinct feeling that that part of the work was what Mr. Tome valued the least, as he had over the past several seasons given most of the repair and new woodworking tasks to Knox.

The door held fast when Knox went to push it open. This was unusual, as Mr. Tome was very good at remembering to unlock it when Knox was meant to come to work for him in the evenings. Looking about, he realized he was running a little late, perhaps Mr. Tome had locked it thinking that he would miss yet another day of work.

"You're late." Mr. Tome's voice sounded from a metallic device above the gate. It looked like he'd attached a funnel to the end of something and hung it just over the six-foot-high wall.

"Yeah, sorry about that," Knox called back. "I was resting up from last night's attack. I'm coming straight from the tavern; I haven't even sat down to eat yet." Knox lifted his package of food up to the funnel as if Mr. Tome could see it, which he clearly could not.

"What attack?" Came the voice again, followed by the clank of several chains and bolts being thrown open. Mr. Tome appeared in the open doorway.

Mr. Tome was a short man; some would say ridiculously so. He stood barely four feet tall by Knox's own guess, but none of that height translated into less of a man. He wore his work clothes, a thick white shirt stained with various greases and sawdust, goggles on his head just below the large bald spot that reflected the weak torch lights to either side of the entrance. They hadn't been burning a moment ago, Knox realized, and made a note to ask about how he'd gotten them to light automatically.

The small man curled his fingers at the edge of his mustache and inspected Knox.

"You seem fine," Mr. Tome said finally. "I've had to finish

Miss Rose's wooden chair myself. Get in here and out of the cold."

He led Knox inside the large workshop, where he had indeed finished Miss Rose's chair and it was a much finer piece than Knox had planned it to be. It seemed that Mr. Tome was unable to work on something and not create a masterpiece work of art.

"Tell me about this attack," Mr. Tome said, picking up a small iron box filled with small gears. He didn't look up as he continued his work, but his fingers seemed to move slower and more carefully than Knox was used to seeing.

"An owlbear killed the Gigorf family, only Fred made it out alive and only barely," Knox said. Inspecting the finished chair and finding nothing he could add to it, he pulled out a ledger and found what project was next on his schedule.

A wooden chest with a hidden bottom for Murdoch Adam.

Grabbing a few lengths of wood, he began to measure out the dimensions he had been given from the work order.

"That's a shame. I made them a fine bed frame some ten years ago, nice family, tipped well," Mr. Tome said. He did that a lot, setting someone's worth in his mind based on how well they paid or how hard they worked.

They were fine measurements to use, but Knox knew that people were more complex than that. Sometimes an awfully lazy man, like Murdoch, could be the best of friends and a fierce protector of those he felt were less fortunate. People were complex, so Knox saved his judgments for when he really got to know someone.

"Yeah, they were good people," Knox finally answered back. "We barely saved Frederick, their oldest son, he got himself injured badly while dealing the killing blow to that owlbear."

"Wasteful," Mr. Tome said, shaking his head.

Knox was about to ask how it had been wasteful, feeling a bit angry at the callous nature in which Mr. Tome spoke, but taking a deep breath realized that he was right, if not in the way he meant. It was wasteful for the owlbear to be allowed to kill unchecked. If

Knox had more training, and better armor, he could have ended the threat before it had a chance to harm Fred more.

Even more than that, perhaps if he became an Adventurer, he could ensure that all the strongest monsters that threatened the village could be dealt with. The village guards were good at keeping the peace and sounding the alarm when monsters approached but they had limited ways of dealing with such attacks short of hiding behind the walls and hoping whatever it was lost interest.

Knox was working himself into a mood and he made a mistake with the piece of wood he was cutting. It was several notches too short.

"Measure twice, cut once," Mr. Tome said from his place at the worktable to Knox's left.

The wood pile of scraps in the corner was relatively empty— what little wood had been thrown there was from Knox's own mistakes. Mr. Tome seemed immune to making mistakes, or at least ones that resulted in wasted wood.

As he returned to the silent work of building out the chest for Murdoch, Knox considered what Lisa had told him as he left.

Bandits in the forest of Feralease. If he became an Adventurer, he could deal with bandits too. The idea of killing a living person gave him pause, but living out as far as Keenlen's Vale taught you a thing or two about people like those. They'd have no issue killing you or doing worse. Hard to have compassion for someone like that.

"You are going through with it then?" Mr. Tome asked, actually looking up from his work for once. Knox did the same, setting aside his tools to look Mr. Tome in the eyes.

"Yeah, afraid so," Knox said. He did feel bad about leaving Mr. Tome without an apprentice, but Adventuring was his true calling, just like it had been for his mother.

"When will you be leaving?" he asked, his hand rubbed the edge of his chin as he waited.

"The day after the festival," Knox said. "But I won't be gone forever. The dungeon is only a few days' journey and from what Dernal told me, you have to wait a few weeks between entering. That, and I doubt I'll be ready by the time Dernal leaves, so I will be back all winter."

"That is, *if* you survive those death traps," Mr. Tome said. "You know, back in my day I went into a dungeon nearly a dozen times. It wasn't for me though. I've got a gift for you; it might help you out when all that fancy magical gear fails you."

Mr. Tome stepped down from his stool and went into his back office, just beyond the scrap pile. Knox could hear the sound of things falling and bells going off, but eventually it quieted, and Mr. Tome came out of the back with a small box, about the size of the short man's head.

"This is a dangerous tool and should only be used if you think you have no other option. And Knox, you must promise me you, and only you, will use it and only on monsters. You must not lose this."

"I promise," the words were out of Knox's mouth before he even had a chance to think about it. What could it be? An object so dangerous that Mr. Tome would want him to swear to keep it out of the hands of others and to never lose it.

Before Knox had much more time to speculate, the box was opened. Inside, sitting on a cushion of red velvet, was a finely decorated metal pipe that curved at the end into an ornate wooden handle. Knox didn't know what to say, or what it could be.

"This is a boomstick," Mr. Tome said. "It is a weapon of deadly consequence and something I regret making. However, you might find use of it. Beneath the velvet lining you will find several small bags of powder, keep them dry and keep them away from fire. Otherwise, they'll burn up so quick that the box might explode. Follow me below so I can teach you how to use it."

Wordlessly, Knox followed, still perplexed at the item Mr. Tome was giving him.

He was led to a hatch in the floor that Knox hadn't known

was there and followed Mr. Tome down into a basement. It went from dark to light in a moment and several torches were lit along a passageway that ran the entire length of the shop above. At one end was an odd assortment of crates and burlap bags. The other end, where Mr. Tome was now leading him, had several burlap and straw scarecrows lined up at several different distances.

Each of them had fist-sized holes in them, some patched and others not. Knox was getting excited to see what this boomstick could do.

"Stand over here," Mr. Tome said, motioning behind him. "You get one chance with this weapon, then there is a lengthy reloading process that I will show you."

And then without fanfare or any additional comments, Mr. Tome took out the large pipe-looking boomstick and held it in front of him. Then, a sound like lightning cracked the air in front of him and a large piece of a scarecrow was missing.

"What in the mother's mercy was that?" Knox said, speaking louder than he ought to. His ears still rang from the loud cracking that issued forth from the boomstick.

"Let me explain it to you. I discovered that a certain mixture of minerals could result in a flashfire. And when you confine that fire into a space where it can't go anywhere, you get a violent reaction."

Mr. Tome pulled out a small round metal ball.

"This is the shot, the object that gets expelled from the tube faster than any arrow could hope to. Now watch while I load it."

Mr. Tome pulled up the velvet lining and pulled out a small pouch full of black powder. He put the entire contents of the pouch down one end and used a bronze metal rod to shove it downward. Then he placed the ball inside, plunging it down as well.

"This here," he pointed to a small metal piece sticking out from the bottom, protected by a loop beneath it, "is the trigger. Pull back this first," he motioned to the top where he pulled back something that looked similar to the before mentioned trigger until it clicked. "Like so, and then squeeze the trigger while pointing in the direction you want the shot to be fired."

He set the boomstick down on a small stack of crates and moved aside, motioning for Knox to pick it up.

Knox held it as if it might come apart in his hands. As carefully as he could manage, he held the handle, aimed the barrel, and squeezed the trigger. Again, sound cracked the air, and a powerful force pushed the boomstick completely from Knox's hand.

"Oh right," Mr. Tome said, waddling over to pick up the boomstick. "Also, hold the handle firmly. Try once more, you do the reloading."

Knox did as he was told, and this time was able to hold on to the boomstick as it fired. His aim wasn't nearly as good as Mr. Tome's, but he did manage to hit one of the scarecrows.

The rest of the night went by quickly, Knox's ears ringing throughout. After he finished his work, Mr. Tome gave him the box and reiterated the importance that no one else be allowed to get their hands on his invention.

CHAPTER 6
HUNTING

SEVERAL DAYS HAD PASSED and Knox found a new apartment where he could finally live in peace. He had just finished a day's work and was heading toward his new home on the eastern side of town when he ran into Danielle, rosy cheeked and humming a song while her black curls bounced along as she walked. She nearly walked into Knox, but between his special sense and the fact he'd spotted her a ways away, he easily stepped out of her path.

He held out a hand to steady her as she stumbled backward in alarm. Danielle was always daydreaming and bumping into things. Knox had grown up with her and she was nothing if not sweet and likeable.

So, it was a surprise when she took one look at Knox and turned as if to run away.

"What's wrong?" Knox asked and Danielle stopped in her tracks, twirling to face him.

She was blushing fiercely, and her breath quickened. "I... uhh..." She cleared her throat and straightened her back. "I want to know if you have a date to the Sun Harvest Festival." The words came out all mushed together and faster than Knox thought someone could physically speak.

Knox studied Danielle and a knot formed in his stomach. Her light blue, almost grey eyes, wouldn't meet his and Knox was at a loss for words to say. He had dated Danielle before, they'd even kissed during their younger years, but the decision to remain friends had been a mutual one.

"What about Terrim?" Knox asked, finally coming to his senses.

Danielle looked confused. "What about him?"

Well, that was a blow to his gut. His friend's love interest didn't seem to even consider him as a potential date. This wasn't too surprising, as Terrim was notoriously bad at expressing anything close to resembling romantic feelings toward another. It was one of his great failings, but Knox had a plan that might help his friend along. If he hadn't asked her yet, perhaps he could get her to ask him.

"Well, he told me he was going to ask you, but I think." Knox tried to think of how to phrase this without throwing his friend into the mud. "You know Terrim," he finally said in a huff, and she nodded—she did know Terrim.

"You don't want to go with me?" Danielle asked. She took a

chance to meet his gaze and immediately averted her eyes, her nerves always getting the better of her.

Knox let out a sigh and pulled Danielle into a hug, she didn't resist, instead melting into him and letting out a sigh of her own. "Look," he said, searching for the right words. "Ask Terrim and he will say yes. We're better as friends, me and you." Then, squeezing her tightly one last time, Knox released her.

"Don't tell him I asked you first, okay?" Danielle said, and she needn't have told Knox as much, because he wished to spare his friend the shame of such knowledge.

"Deal," Knox said, smiling.

With that, Danielle left, heading in the direction of the Three Ladies Tavern now. It was well known that you could place a bet on where to find Terrim after work, and it was always the Three Ladies Tavern on the far-right side at the same table he'd taken for years. One of the chairs at that table had been built especially for the few larger folks of the town, of which Terrim was the tallest.

Before Knox could take much more than a dozen steps closer to the eastern end of town, he felt a presence approaching him, and fast. Turning, he caught sight of Dernal running toward him and a surprised look was on the stout man's face.

"Hhrm. That special sense of yours?" Dernal asked, shaking his head slightly.

Knox nodded and studied his friend and ticket out of this town. His bun was disheveled, and a strand of hair had been knocked loose. His armor, all leather but glowing with runic magic, looked fine, but some of his exposed skin had scratches and even a spot of blood. He'd obviously been in the middle of something, but why had he sought out Knox?

"Care to help me clean up?" Dernal asked, a hungry gleam in his eye.

Knox looked at him suspiciously. "What do you mean?" he asked.

What followed was more words than Dernal liked to speak, but each one was necessary. "I wiped out the bandit problem, but they had several captured monsters that got loose. I need your help to track them all down. Get your armor and sharpen your axe."

"Let me get my armor and I'll ready," Knox said, going into a jog now to get to his residence faster.

That made Knox smile. He rarely needed to sharpen his axe, though he mostly did it out of habit. The axe his father had given him, the only decent thing he'd ever given him, was the sturdiest axe he'd ever used. The few times he'd tried to use another axe, it seemed like the steel dulled much faster and one time he'd even broken the shaft after only a few days' work.

But not his axe, not Scarlet—he'd named it after his mother hoping to lessen the feelings that came with it being a gift from his father. He told only a few people that he'd named his tool, slightly embarrassed by the action as everyone knew tools didn't last forever. But his axe had held up for years now and if it lasted only a few more days, it would have survived his entire career as a woodsman.

Knox reached his apartment and Dernal followed him close behind. With his help, he was armored and armed within minutes. It felt good to wear the armor of an Adventurer, the stiffness of it was pleasant to the touch.

It was only when he had his armor on and they were walking to the edge of the town, where the forest opened up, that he began to wonder what help he could possibly be. Was Dernal perhaps testing his willingness to dive into danger? If that were the case, Knox wouldn't say a word against such an activity. He knew that being an Adventurer meant being in danger, but he couldn't help but wonder if it was for some other reason.

He knew little about the strength of Dernal, but he had seen that he focused on healing and flashes of light as his offensive weapons. Perhaps he wasn't fit to fight so many monsters at once and he needed someone strong like Knox to help? That idea turned in his head for only a moment before he expelled it as being ridiculous. Then he had to fight the urge to ask Dernal if perhaps they should get a few of the town guards involved, or at least his friends who'd proven themselves in battle before.

In the end, he decided against all actions other than following Dernal and keeping his mouth shut. He knew that Dernal wasn't one for idle conversation and if he wanted more help he'd have asked. But no, he'd asked Knox and Knox was going to be enough, he told himself.

Now if he could only get the feeling of butterflies out of his stomach, he'd be all set to dive into battle.

The forest around them was familiar, much of this area had been marked by the foreman for cutting. But after only half an hour they reached an area without any such marks and in the distance a howl went out. More Dire Wolves perhaps? Would they be infected like the previous one he'd faced or was the infection an isolated event? That was a question worth asking, Knox decided.

"Do you know if any of the monsters are infected?"

"No," Dernal said, not even turning his head.

"No, they aren't infected, or you don't know?" Knox asked, realizing he didn't know which Dernal meant.

"Yeah," Dernal said, and Knox let out a defeated sigh.

The sun was close to setting already and he realized he was going to be missing one of the last days he had left to work for Mr. Tome. That stung, but Dernal was his future, and he couldn't risk upsetting him right now. Not that Knox thought Dernal was that kind of petty person, but if he asked for Knox's help, he must truly need it.

Knox let his special sense wash over his surroundings, pushing as hard as he could at the boundaries of it to get a feel for what was out there. Dernal turned to the left and a moment later Knox felt it and turned his attention that way as well.

From this distance it was hard to tell what it was, but whatever it was, it moved with scary speed. Dernal stepped in the path of the incoming monster and said two words over his shoulder that made Knox's blood run cold.

"Giant spider."

It wasn't that Knox was particularly afraid of spiders, he just really did not like them. Of course, he encountered his fair share of normal-sized spiders while felling trees daily, but even those gave him the creeps. No, it was the idea of a giant spider that really shook him. If it had the speed and grace of a normal spider while being as big as he was sensing, then this would not be an easy or quick fight.

He raised his axe and prepared to meet the attacker, when his senses tingled, and he caught the approach of two more beings of equal size and power. Dernal cracked his neck to the side and regarded Knox. He tried not to wilt under the powerful Adventurer's gaze, but it was difficult. Was he measuring him up for his combat potential? Or wondering if it was a mistake to bring him after all?

Whatever it was he was looking for, he must have found it because he grunted and pulled free his own weapons.

The first spider appeared and if it had not been for his sense ability, he'd have found it hard to see. Dernal side-stepped it as it jumped for him, but that left it on a path right for Knox's face, which was fine with him since he was ready. His axe came down and he finally got a decent look at his foe as it slammed into the ground with a wide gash on its lower body.

It was a spider, but the size of a dog or a small wolf, with legs about eight paces wide. It was black and grey, with hairy legs twitching as it tried to right itself. The body leaked blue, oozing blood, and small organs threatened to fall loose from the slashed carapace.

Before Knox had the better sense to finish off his foe, it made it to its feet, and the fight was back on. It lasted all of one second, ending on the heel of Dernal's boot with a mighty crash.

"Get ready," Dernal said, his eyes flicking back to the horizon.

Two more spiders were on their way—or at least, that was his best guess at what was approaching. But it could be anything. His senses faltered as powerful and ancient words overtook him.

Victory, Victory, to the deep ones went the victory. Gone for now, we come again, victory, victory.

Knox's attention immediately diverted from the incoming foes and looked back over his shoulder. He saw Dernal shift uncomfortably as well, but Knox tried to keep his eyes forward. Though, only a dozen feet behind them, he saw that same small shape. Despite the shadows hiding all of her features, he got the impression that it was a young girl once more. She held a sickle and, this time, raised her arm into the air and slashed downward with it.

Tendrils of dark power surged forth, sweeping past both Knox and Dernal, enveloping the two emerging monsters as they revealed themselves. Knox's gaze was frozen on the shadowy figure, unwilling to turn away and lose sight of her again. Advancing toward her direction with his weapon at the ready, he took a step, only for her to dissipate as if she had never been there.

He turned back to Dernal to ask if he'd felt or seen that as well, but the two spiders were upon them, and questions would have to wait. Lunging forward, Knox was caught by a spray of black webbing from one spider, but his axe slashed down and cut most of it away. Scarlet did a good job of not getting stuck, and Knox's grip was like iron on the wood of the shaft.

Pulling with all his might, he managed to get it free, just as more webbing covered him from toe to nose. A flash of white light hit him, and he felt a burning sensation as the webbing burned away. Dernal was there with his palms outstretched.

"Fight!" Dernal yelled, turning Knox's attention back to his opponent, the biggest of the three spiders.

Pulling himself free from the remaining black spider goo, Knox slashed out with his axe just as his opponent leapt toward him. It didn't go down as easy as the first, though, curling up its legs midair and taking the strike on one of the hard carapaces of its spider legs. He dealt a glancing blow and the spider launched past him to land on a tree, legs outstretched.

More black webbing flung itself toward him, but he went into a roll, painful as it was when he hit a rock mid-way, but the move enabled him to avoid the sticky situation.

Forgetting his fear of spiders in the rush of adrenaline that came with battle, Knox yelled in defiance of such a small foe getting the better of him and threw his axe. He hadn't even stood yet, but he put enough force into the attack to split the spider in two. It just so happened that it missed the midpoint he'd been aiming at and instead stuck right into its head, killing it instantly.

"Yeah!" Knox said, pumping his fist.

Dernal was there, watching, as he'd already taken care of his spider. He moved over to Knox and offered him a hand up, Knox took it gladly, brushing himself off after he stood.

"Good job," Dernal said, a look of skepticism on his face, but for what reason Knox couldn't tell.

"Thanks," Knox said, smiling wide as he went over to retrieve his axe. "I think I'm getting the hang of being an Adventurer."

Dernal snorted but said nothing.

"What?" Knox questioned him, his eyes narrowing.

"That was just the warmup," Dernal said, stretching his arms. "Though that black goo made them a bit more of a challenge than I'd expected."

"Did you see the girl this time or hear the voice?" Knox asked, taking an eager step forward.

"Hhmm. Hearing voices isn't a good sign, but I saw the black goo appear, same as you, just not where it came from."

Damn, Knox would really need to get his attention next time so that he wasn't the only one seeing strange visions. He almost wanted to tell him about the journal he'd found, although surely Dernal had seen it when he first retrieved it. But something inside told him he ought to keep it a secret.

A trickle of worry crept in—Dernal might want to take it from him, or perhaps the book had value beyond the information he was learning. Either scenario meant he wouldn't get to keep it, and with so few precious belongings he could truly call his own, it held him in place.

"What did you mean, this was only the warmup?" Knox asked, suddenly aware of what Dernal had said only moments ago.

"Exactly that," Dernal said, then he stabbed into the spiders, checking for Cores. None of them had any, but with beasts so big and strong, they must have been close to forming one.

It was hard to say when a creature of nature became a monster that would have a Core, at least for Knox. He praised all the bits of knowledge he'd been able to gather, but he'd be the first to admit that he knew nothing compared to any real Adventurer. But when you lived in a den of ignorance, even the barest sliver of knowledge made you king.

He didn't like thinking of his town like that, but so many were eager to live lives of mediocrity that it made him feel sick when he thought about it too hard. His father was the worst offender in his mind and the pinnacle of everything he didn't want to become. Sure, he'd had hardship and lost an arm. It wouldn't be easy to come back from that, Knox knew, but to give up entirely and turn to the drink for comfort when he still had a son to care for just wasn't the path to follow.

Knox had only been twelve years old when he had needed to step up and care for his father full-time. Cleaning, making him meals, providing him with his vice, and taking up the axe as a woodsman's apprentice. It wasn't uncommon for someone his age to go out and work at twelve, some did it even earlier, and at the time he'd been all too eager to help.

But when he discovered his mother's journals, which were hidden in the floorboards of the second story room that remained empty, he began to yearn for a life beyond woodcutting. His father never spoke of his mother, even when deep into the drink. He'd gotten whooped severely when his father found out what he'd done—he'd overheard Terrim and him speak about how he'd named his axe after his mother, Scarlet.

It was a dead giveaway that he'd found the journals, as his father had never uttered her name to him before. He remembered the first time he'd read the name at the beginning of one of the journals and a personal passage about how she'd fallen in love with a strong woodsman named Askar Trelling, but there was never any mention of Knox's birth or pregnancy that must have followed them getting together.

Instead, the rest of the journals spoke of her research into runes and unique combinations of the six primary patterns. She suggested that it was possible to mix the primary patterns but had yet to figure out how. Most of what his mother wrote was nonsense to him, even today, but he hoped he'd learn more as he dived deep into dungeons and became an Adventurer.

The rest of Dernal and Knox's hunting trip was eventful and exciting. Although they didn't come across any more black goo, they did take down two owlbears. Dernal claimed the single intact Core that survived the battle, while Knox was given the 'dust' of the broken one.

"It's important for enchanting," Dernal had told him, putting the broken pieces into a small leather pouch, and handing it over. Knox felt that he was getting the short end of the stick but didn't complain. Dernal insisted that one more monster lay waiting for them someplace, but after the Fire moon crossed the highest point in the sky, marking it true night, he insisted Knox return home.

"You know the name of the world, don't you?" Dernal asked, breaking the silence of their trip back to town.

It was an odd question and one that Knox didn't know the answer to. He just thought of the world as the world. Old legends gave odd names to the moons, but he just called them by the elements that legend said they represented.

There was Darkness, the dark moon that was nearly invisible in the night sky; Light, the white moon that shone the brightest in the latest hours of the night; Water, named after the cool blue color and swirls on the surface of it as it glowed overhead. Then there was Fire, the red moon that rose highest at the darkest parts of the night, and Death, the purple moon that was said to only appear when great death or famine were to occur, but Knox knew better as it appeared every five years by his counting and not always heralding death or famine. Lastly, there was the green moon of Life, or some called it Nature. It was always present, even during the day, a green speck in the sky.

None of that answered Dernal's question and Knox looked at him with a confused expression on his face as he tried to recall what a song he'd heard years before had called the world. *It started with a P... was it premiere or prepare or something.*

Finally, he shook his head to show he didn't know and Dernal clapped him on the arm before speaking again. "You will learn much once we leave this place. The world, or so the old legends say at least, is named Premar. If you believe in the Titans or the Great Titan, then we are the first planet in all of creation. Do you believe that?"

He thought about what Dernal was saying and, though his curiosity was boundless, he couldn't help but wonder what any of this had to do with being an Adventurer. He also wondered what had made Dernal so talkative lately, but decided neither would be the proper continuation of the conversation. Instead, he truly thought about what he believed and what he didn't.

He was fond of the idea of Titans, powerful beings that created worlds in the vast emptiness of space. Then there was the Great Titan, the name of which has been lost to the passage of time, who was said to have created the world. Of course, he'd heard some of the myths and legends that Dernal spoke of, but he'd also heard that the Titans were no more. Gods old and new struck them down, but he wasn't sure about the new or old gods either.

Religions of all kinds popped up here and there, but out here in the wilds, everyone remained too busy to worry too much about the powers so great as to lay out their destiny. His father would call it all hogwash, but Titans were also said to be the creators or organizers of magic and that piqued Knox's attention more than anything else. Magic was the one thing he had that connected him to his mother, that and her journals, but he'd read them page to page hundreds of times and still only understood a handful of her runic theories.

"I don't know," Knox finally answered, his mind getting pulled into tangles as he thought about this and that. Then an idea sparked within him, prompting him to ask Dernal the same question. "Do you?"

"I do," he said simply and then the conversation drifted back to silence. The trip back to town was quick after that and he made his own way to his bed once they'd gotten past Jeremy and his incessant questions about how they got outside the wall without him noticing.

Knox crashed into his bed, armor and all, finding sleep within moments.

His dreams were filled with visions of powerful beings with metallic skin, wielding immense power as they forced the chaos of the void between worlds into planets. And with their mighty power, they planted the seed of life on each planet they formed. Some thrived while others withered, but then his dream shifted, and he saw a titanic figure, skin as radiant as polished gold.

Without being told, somehow Knox knew this being to be named Gowlen—or at least that is what the name sounded like in his mind, for he also knew that the language that could speak such a name was far beyond his comprehension. This new figure, a Titan for sure, ripped apart time and space to create a pocket of life far from the others doing their glorious work.

Then a voice from a distant corner of the void spoke into Knox's dream and he shuddered at feeling the endless power that it held.

"I am Mah'kus, hear my words. I am sending someone to help when the time of great need is upon you. Be at peace and have a donut."

Suddenly, Knox awoke and sat up in his small bed. On his lap was a pastry he'd not encountered before; it was a round thing with a hole in the middle. Atop it was a pink substance with tiny sprinkles of every color. His dream replayed in his mind and sweat dripped down his face. He felt a compulsion to consume this, 'donut', and it increased the longer he ignored it. So, doing something his mind knew to be completely ridiculous, he ate the pastry and enjoyed every bite.

It was sweet and light, each bite setting off new and wondrous feelings inside him. By the time he finished, he felt amazing and the gloom of the darkness and the worlds of the shadows that had weighed him down fled.

Knox awoke the next morning from a long night's sleep refreshed but with no new donuts or intense dreams. His back ached from the lumpy bed, but he couldn't remember feeling so great in the past few years.

CHAPTER 7
FAREWELL

SEVERAL DAYS WENT by without much else new and exciting happening. He had a place of his own, sort of, his life as an Adventurer would begin soon, and he was taking Beth to the festival.

She had been upset when he told her that he had found his own place to stay, but Knox knew it was for the best. He had even managed to keep where he was staying a secret from her, worried that she might show up unannounced—which she most definitely would have. Beth knew what she wanted and didn't let things like propriety stand in her way.

He admired her for the force with which she applied herself in all things she did. As a guard, she was diligent and had risen to guard captain within months of taking the job. As a potential lover, she was persistent. He took Dernal's warnings to heart, but he also told himself that he shouldn't refuse her advances completely, as he didn't know when he'd be back or if she'd still be interested. It wasn't like she didn't understand Knox's situation or the fact that he was leaving soon.

Knox shook himself out of his musings and remembered he had a task to get to before he could start his day. He meant to look over the ancient book once more and he'd even gotten a new notebook of his own, bound in leather and with several dozen pages of paper—it hadn't been cheap, but without having to care for his father he'd had the extra money. Besides that, he'd always had more money than he knew what to do with, doing extra tasks and saving for the expensive armor Dernal provided. But with that paid off, coin was filling up his pockets by the day.

He felt a sudden pang of guilt when thinking about his father. Was he doing the right thing, leaving him without his care any longer? It was always going to happen eventually and Askar owned the house outright, so it wasn't like someone could push him out. Although, how would he earn money to feed himself or satisfy his urge to drink everything in sight?

He didn't know and he wasn't sure he cared. But the moment after having such a thought, he was overtaken with the urge to go check on his father. The ancient journal could wait another hour, he'd already told the foreman that he wouldn't be working his last three days, so it wasn't like he had much to do other than work with Mr. Tome and enjoy time with his friends.

Trying not to think about what he planned on doing, but

worried about his father and what he might do if he grew too desperate, he headed out into the early morning.

The green ever-present moon, Life, hung next to the powerful bright aura of the yellow sun and Knox let himself bask in the warmth of the morning, a cool breeze coming down from Spike Peak Mountains. Its peaks were still capped with snow, and with how high they were, it was likely the snow never left. Though winter had only recently concluded, the pass leading to Feralease had reopened, welcoming traders, tax collectors, and Adventurers once more.

Dernal once described his time in Feralease as a vacation from more difficult dungeons and challenges. Despite what he said, when pressed about Shadowfall Swamp, he admitted that the place was beyond him in strength and was an anomaly safe-guarded by the Guild to protect locals. He'd had much to drink that night and he went on to explain that most areas had a ranking of sorts that told you how safe or unsafe they'd be for Adventurers and all of Feralease, excluding Shadowfall Swamp, was considered a beginner area.

That was when Dernal had promised Knox that he would take him from Keenlen's Vale before winter came again and Knox grew excited that perhaps he'd get the armor after all. Of course, he hadn't gotten enough money at that time, but now he'd finally sealed the deal.

All of this ran through his mind, distracting him from what he was truly dreading to think about or do as he neared the west side of the village.

Dilapidated and randomly placed buildings were the norm here, but he navigated them with practiced ease and approached his childhood home with fear in his heart. He shouldn't be afraid, he knew, long gone were the days when his father could get away with beating on him, but in his mind, he was comfortable to admit that a part of that small frail boy still existed within him.

He'd never let that part of him show or give his father even an inch of ground, but it was there all the same. Recognizing it, he believed, marked him with wisdom.

When he finally reached the road where his home lay, he noticed the door was ajar and instantly he was on guard. Moving as swiftly as he could without running, he reached the door and gently swung it open the rest of the way.

What he found inside didn't surprise him but a part of him wished his father had been capable of change. Snoring like a boar, Askar Trelling lay passed out on the floor, his breaths coming in big raspy gasps. Knox was more worried that he'd drown in his own bodily fluids than anything, so he gently turned him to his side. His breathing eased considerably.

Thinking this might be the last time he set his eyes on his father for a long time, he sat and wondered what he ought to do. First, he tidied up around the house as he always had, his father was a bit of a slob. Next, he slipped out and made his way to the market to grab a few food items, simple stuff like grain and vegetables. One last grocery trip wouldn't hurt. Considering that he'd found little to no food left, it seemed sensible and necessary.

By the time he got back to the house, his father had woken up and sat in his favorite chair, a new drink in his hand. He looked up in surprise when Knox entered, but he said nothing. Taking a deep breath and feeling his eyes on him, Knox put away the groceries while trying to think of a better way to leave things with his father.

Unfortunately, no words came, and he feared that any comment would just set the man off again. Instead, he looked at his father, their gazes meeting, and he gave him a single nod before pulling the door closed behind him as he left, making sure it closed tightly.

"Goodbye, father," he said to the street before him, and with that he was gone, heading back to the eastern section of town.

He arrived back in his apartment and locked the door behind him. It was time for more prudent matters to be handled. Opening the single chest in his room, he looked inside.

The ancient book sat atop his pile of armor and other meager belongings. His five most-prized possessions all lying about as if they were last night's laundry. His mother's journals, the armor he'd received from Dernal, the broken Monster Core, the boomstick, and the mysterious tome he'd found out by the Gigorf farm.

Murdoch had filled him in on his version of the story that he had been spreading among the townsfolk a few nights before over a pint.

"I told them the truth," he had insisted. "Maybe I inflated my role a bit, but I made sure they knew it was old Freddy boy who put that foul creature in the ground. Seemed only right."

Knox smiled at the memory. Murdoch was genuinely good-hearted, but he did have the tendency to inflate his part in things. He cared too much about what others thought and too little about the truth.

The heavy tome opened easily, as it had each time. The thick pages and the deep black ink on the pages seemed such an ordinary thing. That was, to everyone who couldn't see deeper. Knox had been making it a habit to keep his sense lowered, and so, with a moment's focus, he switched it back on.

The book lit up in his sight, all blue and glowing. He had spent many nights staring at the book with his sense turned on, hoping to glean some new information from it, but not willing to keep reading its pages yet. To his relief, something did happen the longer he stared at it.

What he first took for a consistent glow, was actually threads of power woven tightly around and through the book. Instead of the runic symbols that his mother had written so fondly about, this magic appeared to work like a woven blanket. The complexity of how the threads were tied together and how they were able to give off the same type of strange light as runes, was completely lost on him, but he was pleased with his discovery, nonetheless.

Today he was finally going to read deeper into the tome. What secrets would he learn from Ramses and his adventure to explore the ley lines? He imagined everything from his rescue to his journey so far, and several instances in between. His curiosity could only be held back so long before he just couldn't stand it.

Opening the book once more, he began to read.

Journal Entry # 3 – 106?-?? Fallen Titan Standard Time

How long has it been since I last wrote? The passage of time and my ability to do more than drool on the ground half-dead have all merged to nothingness in my mind. I will do my best to dictate my journeys here, but I do not claim to remember everything in perfect detail.

I remember that I traveled for several days before reaching the ruins that nearly claimed me as my tomb. The ley lines converged in what appeared to be a small pool of water, but when I reached the water's edge, I fell through it and into a great city of gold.

The fall and its suddenness left me unprepared to protect myself and I was mortally wounded. But mine was to be a slow death. I remember a dim light shining in the distance. It took me an undetermined amount of time to crawl, roll, and push my broken frame the entire way, but I did it.

What I got for my trouble was a golden armored skeleton. Close to death and unsure what to do next, I reached out to examine the treasure. What happened next will change the course of history.

But I grow tired, still not fully recovered from my sleep. I will return to these pages when I have rested.

The writing in the recent passage was far messier than the previous. As if the writer penned it in haste, fearing perhaps he wouldn't be able to continue to tell his tale.

What could it mean that he fell into water to his death or that he'd found a golden city? Surely, he must have injured his head and his ramblings are nothing more than the dreams of a dying man. But that didn't help explain how the book had been sent to the farm or why. Too many persistent questions lingered in his mind, and he had to keep reading and find answers.

The reading of the book seemed to drain Knox. He couldn't pinpoint the exact cause, but he grew tired from even the shortest attempts at reading it. Taking a deep breath, he prepared himself for another passage.

Journal Entry # 4 – 0001-01 Risen Titan Standard Time

My Body, Mind, and Soul are invigorated. I've slept another decade at least, but time has lost most of its meaning in my new form. I am so deeply enthralled by my research and the continued discovery of the Titan System that recalling the events that led me here is becoming difficult, so I have told myself I will not stop until I've recorded my path so far.

I will pick up where I left off previously. I reached forward to the odd skeleton, seemingly covered in gold, and had my first encounter with the Titan System.

My vision was filled with some form of visual overlay that prompted me to choose life or death. I chose to bind myself to the object and become Titan Born. What that means, I am still discovering. What I can tell you is that as soon as I accepted the so-called Ascension to Titan Born, my body was ripped away and a new body formed around my spiritual and mental self. And then sleep came.

I am leaving out the mental, emotional, and spiritual battles I struggled with while I slept and my inability to move off the floor for at least a century, but I have deemed them not necessary.

To think those old codgers on the council thought to punish me by sending me here. Now I will have lived longer than even they could hope to achieve. You might ask yourself, why do I still record these events if no one will ever be able to enjoy them? A part of me still hopes I will be able to return and reveal my findings to the scholarly world at large. Only time will tell.

The Titan System is something that was created in the same moment the great Titans formed the fabric of reality itself—or at least that is what my current hypothesis is—truly I have no way of knowing for certain, but this place I find myself in is one of knowledge and hidden mysteries.

The place I once assumed a convergence of ley lines, is a spring in which the power courses outward. Many of my scholars theorized that this could be possible, I was not among them. So, you can imagine my surprise finding signs of such an outpouring of power.

It would appear that the object I touched was the former master of this city. He also would have been Titan Born, how he died remains a mystery. Further study of the skeletal remains shows no signs of injury, but I don't claim to be an expert at determining death in any form. I can only speculate, based on what I know about my new body, that it was not time that killed him. I appear to need extraordinarily little, if any, nourishment in the traditional sense.

My form draws power directly from the ley lines at a suitable rate. As long as I don't push myself too hard, I should be able to avoid any further unwanted long slumbers. It would appear that the resources of the city and the armor were depleted beyond reckoning. This, I have determined, is the cause of my sleep. Perhaps if there had been enough latent power, I might have transferred to my new body without fear of a long sleep, but that is mere speculation.

The power is prompting me to go out from my new home and gather certain items. From what little I can make of structures in the vast underground city, there is some type of large marvel of mechanical and magical means that connects all the buildings. I can only surmise that the promptings I'm being given are to restore this Titan Engine, as it calls itself.

However, I am unable to venture out in my current form and find the things it asks of me. Endless miles of ocean lay between me and any creature of sufficient strength to provide a Monster Core. Had I any way to brave the depths of the sea I would do so, but alas, I do not.

I will do all that I can do, short of fulfilling the request of the prompt, in hopes that I will be able to engineer a way to find a monster of suitable magical strength. Until a time comes that I am able to do so, I once more end my recordings of the events thus far.

Knox couldn't help himself. The power of the book appeared to be draining him of his energy, but he needed to know more. He turned the page and waited for more words to come.

The page remained blank.

He turned to another page and focused as hard as he could, trying to get the words to appear.

Nothing happened.

Finally giving up, he laid back down on his bed. He knew he had things to get done today, but the passages he had read took more out of him than he cared to admit. It was as if the very energy that enabled him to move about was siphoned from him. This book was as much a parasite as it was a gift. Knox tossed the book to the floor, careful not to damage it, and it hit with a satisfying thud.

His body screamed at him that he needed sleep, but he wasn't ready to drift back just yet. He had provided for his father but skipped any breakfast for himself. He decided that he would eat, then maybe take a nap before he had to go to work with Mr. Tome.

Unfortunately for him, his body had other ideas. He determined that his hunger could wait just as he rested his eyes for a moment or two, then sleep came powerful and overtaking.

His dreams were back on the metallic-skinned creatures he now thought of as Titans, but it was the same dream as before. It started with creation, then the special Titan and ending right before the message about the donut had appeared. He woke in a cold sweat, hungrier than he could ever remember being, and stumbled his way out the door to find food.

CHAPTER 8
SUN HARVEST FESTIVAL

THE SOUND of laughter outside his small closet of a room brought Knox back to consciousness. The smell of the festival wafted into his nose, and he knew he had slept later than he ought to. Moving with the haste that only being late can muster, he quickly bathed himself from a pitcher of water, and changed into the nicest set of clothing he had.

The shirt was white and cleaner than any others he owned. The pants were a deep purple and hung loose below his knees. Slipping on his boots, newly polished black, he tied the strings at the end of the pants tight. His brown hair fell loose around his head, and he quickly remedied that with a leather tie. He was ready.

The early evening air was filled with the smell of sweet wine and savory meats. All around him people walked toward the town center, where large tables had been set up in preparation for the Sun Harvest Festival. Knox was glad to see he wasn't the only one dressed in the new purple-colored attire that old trader Joe had brought into town.

He had worried at first that the color was too feminine, but Joe had assured him that the color was all the rage in cities like Sedriseal and Dalindraw. The majority of his worries were put to rest when he caught sight of the burly Ferlin Goship wearing an entire shirt colored the same as Knox's pants.

"Wondrous color, eh Knox," Ferlin said, noticing Knox's stare. "Oh, if you see Dernal tell him I was able to finish the rush order he put in. Not an easy thing, making a shield the way he wanted. All's I need is the Core he wanted to set into it."

"Shield?" Knox parroted back to the burly man. "So, *that's* what Dernal had you put together for him. I asked and he wouldn't tell me, only saying it was a surprise."

"Oh," Ferlin said, his face attempting to match shades with the reddish purple of his shirt.

"Don't worry," Knox said, chuckling as he patted the large man's back. "I will keep it a secret."

"Thank yous." Was all the blacksmith said before disappearing into the throng of people.

It didn't take long after getting to the town square to find Beth. She stood out against the crowd, not only because she wore a dark green dress, while everyone else wore mostly lighter colors, but also because her beauty was striking. Her lips drew Knox's attention with their deep red color, her eyelids had been painted a green that matched her dress perfectly. Her face, normally a tanned brown from all her time in the sun, had been covered in some kind of skin-lightening powder. He was confident that the only other time he'd seen such a face covering was from a few of the visiting highborn ladies who came to the village a season ago, for what reason he never did find out.

"Is it too much?" Beth asked, looking worried for the first time that Knox could remember.

"You look amazing," Knox said, leaning down to give her a hug. She held him there longer than he would have, but he didn't mind. Not today, not tonight. He planned on enjoying himself.

"You know," Knox said. "You didn't have to get all dressed up for me. I think you look just as pretty covered in mud as you are with all that stuff on your face."

"Well, thanks, Knox," Beth said; she punched him in the arm, and he was reminded that she was no ordinary woman. Dress or no dress, she was probably the better fighter and her punch actually hurt. Making a note to dodge any further playful punches, Knox took Beth's hand and led her to a table.

"Nice pants," Beth said, smacking his ass just as he was about to sit down.

"Beth," Knox said in a low whisper and a grin on his lips.

"Yes?" She answered innocently.

"Save that for later," Knox teased, then put his hand on the lower end of her back to guide her toward Murdoch and the others.

They were set up at the end of the third table and from the looks on their faces, having a grand ole time.

The air was warm thanks to several large bonfires set into the center of the festival area. More food, free of charge, had been set out than Knox remembered seeing the year before. As they made their way across the open area filled with people, they ran straight into a familiar face, Knox's father.

"Excuse me," Knox said, trying and failing to keep the venom out of his voice.

Of course his father would be here, there was free food to be had. His father looked better than he remembered, even managing to wear a clean set of clothes and, if his eyes were any indication, he wasn't drunk... yet.

Knox had made his peace with his father in his own way and seeing him again so soon didn't help with that. He pushed forward with Beth, but his father put up a hand as if to say he wanted to speak. Knox stopped and waited to hear his father's words.

"You better not get that whore pregnant, we have enough-" Whatever else he was going to say was cut short as Knox punched his father in the face, laying him out flat.

"If you hadn't done that, I was going to," Beth said, stepping around the fallen man purposefully and Knox followed.

"I'm sorry," Knox began to say, but Beth stopped him and pulled him into a kiss. It was like lightning danced between their lips for a second and Knox found himself filled with a warmth that made forgetting his idiot father all the easier.

"I'm not," Beth said, putting her hand playfully on Knox's back side. Knox smiled and slyly returned the gesture.

Beth's eyes lit up and a hunger could be seen reflected behind her eyes. She grabbed hold of Knox and started to turn him back toward her apartment. He held firm and nodded slowly.

"Let's enjoy my last night with all our friends, not just each other."

She winked and said, "As long as the night ends with us, I'll weather our friends."

With that, they made their way to the end of the table and found spots between Murdoch and Danielle. Terrim looked absolutely thrilled to be sitting beside Danielle and when she wasn't looking, he shot Knox two thumbs up along with a cheesy grin. Knox knew they'd be here together; Danielle was more than willing to ask Terrim to the Sun Harvest Festival when his own courage fell short.

Terrim often talked about how he wanted nothing more out

of life than a beautiful wife and a dozen little kids to bounce on his knee. Knox, of course, had bigger and grander aspirations, so it was hard for him to relate to the simple dreams of a wife and kids. Life held so much more adventure and mystery; he couldn't let himself be stuck here. But, for tonight, he would enjoy the company he had with the friends that loved him.

"Well, look who we have here," Murdoch said, turning his attention to Knox. Beside Murdoch sat Lisa, all curls and smiles. She had auburn hair, not quite red or brown, and it fell over her shoulders in tight ringlets. She must have gotten a good bit of the purple fabric from trader Joe because she'd fashioned out an entire dress, even making a cute headband that held some of her hair back.

Under the glow of the Fire moon, her hair looked positively radiant. Murdoch was known for going through the women of the village with a speed that even an owlbear's strike couldn't match. But Knox didn't judge either of them, knowing that, fling or not, they'd have a good time tonight.

"It is I, Knox Trelling," Knox announced to the table as if he were pretending to announce himself to some noble's court. It got a laugh from all present, save for Fred who had a thousand-mile stare directed right into the fire.

"How's Fred been?" Knox asked Murdoch, leaning toward him and lowering his voice.

"Just yesterday he moved back out to his farm, said someone needed to get the crops tended to. I sent half a dozen farm hands out to help him; the ones they normally employ have all refused to return to the place. It is a shame really, I tried to tell him he ought to just sell the place and live the bachelor life with me, but you can imagine how that conversation went," Murdoch said, then gave an overly exaggerated impression of Fred staring off into space.

Knox hit him with his elbow, and he stopped the act before Fred could notice. He wasn't ready to let his friend sink off into whatever hell he was reliving in his mind, so he decided to try and talk to him. Getting up, he switched places with a man named Joel that occasionally joined them for drinks.

Sitting beside Fred now, he cleared his throat and Fred's thousand-mile stare broke long enough for him to nod to Knox before he returned his gaze to the fire.

"I hear you went back home to work on the crops?" Knox asked, trying to think of the best way to get his friend talking.

Sun Harvest Festival was all about harvesting the winter crops, those sturdy enough to last out the snow, things like peas, leeks, spinach and the like. They were harvested around the time of the year called First Sun, hence the name Sun Harvest Festival. However, it also signaled an uptick in hunting, so there were plenty of boar and even a few Dire Wolves, roasting over spits in the fire.

Dire Wolf meat was rich and flavorful, unlike normal wolf meat that tended to be gamey and stringy. What made the biggest difference, according to a conversation with Dernal, was the beginnings of a Core forming. Not enough for a full Core to form, but if Dire Wolves lived long enough, they'd form a full Core and even in rare cases gain a certain level of sapience. Knox had time to think over all these topics, as Fred hadn't answered him. Time for a new tactic.

"I'm leaving tomorrow morning," Knox said. This caught Fred's attention and he looked at him with a puzzled expression.

"Really? Where are you going?" Fred asked, suddenly snapped out of his trance.

This was odd, Knox was sure someone must have told him. But with all that had been happening, he hadn't had a chance to inform him personally.

"You know Dernal, the one that healed you, the Adventurer," Knox kept adding bits until recognition filled Fred's eyes and he nodded solemnly.

"Well, he sold me some armor and agreed to take me on a dungeon run. Just one time through and I'll probably have enough treasure to set myself up like a king," Knox said, though he wasn't sure that was true. That was more from rumors spread by ordinary townsfolk and drunkards than anything he'd heard from Dernal or any other roaming Adventurers.

"Sounds dangerous," Fred said, and for a moment Knox thought he might try to convince him not to go. Suddenly the direction of the conversation didn't seem like a good idea after all. Fred had been through so much that it was cruel of him to even mention this stuff. "You have room for one more? If I sold the farm, I bet I'd get enough money to buy some armor as well."

This shocked Knox into silence, he'd been ready to apologize for bringing up the subject of violence, but now he was just plain confused.

"Group's full," said a voice from behind, and both men turned to see Dernal approaching with a mug of ale the size of his face and a huge leg of meat in his other hand.

"But perhaps next year," Knox offered, shooting a glance at Dernal, hoping he'd catch on and play along. Unfortunately, the hint went unnoticed.

"Hmm. Not likely," Dernal said, before taking a huge bite and forcing open a spot next to Knox and Fred.

"I'll figure out a way, maybe even try to buy an extra suit of enchanted armor and you can pay me back. I think it would be great for another Keenlen's Vale man to get out and become an Adventurer," Knox said, trying to salvage the conversation.

"Easier and cheaper ways to die," Dernal said, and Knox flinched at his words, but Fred didn't.

"I'm not afraid of death," Fred said simply. "Not anymore."

Then it dawned on Knox why Fred would suddenly want to be an Adventurer. Something Dernal had picked up on the moment he arrived. Fred was looking to die, or at the very least, to live dangerously. There were many different reactions people had to death out here in the wilds of Feralease.

Some would experience death when a hunting party was overtaken by something that was beyond their capability, be it an owlbear or a powerful Dire Wolf. Those who survived would become nothing more than a shell of their former selves, always on edge, seeing threats in every shadow.

Then there was another kind of reaction that was fairly common. The kind that Fred was having now. Those who experienced death or extreme danger would start to crave it as a way to experience anything but the emptiness and sorrow that filled them. Often, they'd be dead by the end of the season, because out here in the wilds it was all too easy to die when you went looking for it.

That wasn't a fate Knox wanted for one of his friends, but he knew of no way to snap him out of it. Instead, he would do what he knew how to do, just be a friend.

"You've got a long life ahead of you," Knox finally said while lifting his mug and kept it up until Fred did the same. "To a long life."

"To a long life," Fred repeated, and they both drank deeply.

After a few more mugs, Fred lost his thousand-mile stare and began interacting with those around him. The drink wasn't the perfect answer to sorrow, but in this instance, Knox saw its benefit.

Beth pulled Knox away from Fred after a time and they moved over to where dancing was just starting. People gathered and then the men and women separated. It was a simple dance, one that he'd learned early on in his life, although he didn't consider himself any good.

But he would do the dance anyway; it made Beth happy and once it got started, he found himself enjoying the exertion. In and out, through the arms of two girls, and then swirling around and kick and kick. It was fun, he had to admit it, but it also added a dull ache in his stomach as he realized he'd be leaving this all behind.

It would be worth it, he knew, but change was never easy. A part of him allowed himself to follow a train of thought that he rarely, if ever, allowed. He saw himself continuing his life as a woodcutter, perhaps eventually taking over the role of foreman and getting paid more.

He'd settle down with Beth and they'd start a family together. She'd work as much as she was able, he knew he couldn't ever ask her to stop her work completely, that just wasn't something she'd consider. And they'd live a long and happy life together, raising another generation to live out their lives on the edge of civilization.

Or perhaps he'd take Beth with him and move to a bigger city? Anything could happen, he knew, but the idea of taking that path in life left him feeling... incomplete. As if he were allowing some grand treasure to go undiscovered or an adventure waiting to be had. In the end, he knew the one reason he couldn't stay and wouldn't stay: his father.

His mind wandered as he danced, and a frown filled his face. He saw himself losing an arm or maybe a leg and becoming as bitter and hateful as his father. His entire mood soured as he imagined himself being the one thing that drove him to be different. He would never allow himself to become that!

Then there was his mother and the legacy she'd left him. How would he ever feel close to her if he didn't try and follow the footsteps she herself had taken? Nowhere in her journals did it say that she was an Adventurer, but who else would study and know so much about runes and their formations?

Then there was his sense. He could feel and touch things with just his mind, unlike anyone else he'd heard of. He liked to think of it like a gift from his mother, but honestly, he had no idea where such an ability came from, only that he hoped to learn more as he progressed.

The dancing became slightly more complex, and he let himself fall into a rhythm, letting his feet lead him until finally it ended with Beth back in his arms.

The night went by too quickly, and before too long, it was over. He spent time saying his goodbyes to those he cared about, and to those he cared less for, he avoided. To his surprise, especially after their earlier encounter, he noticed that his father hadn't left yet and even tried approaching them again. However, Beth skillfully steered them clear of enduring another interaction with him. Free food and drink would be about the only thing that brought the wretched old man out of hiding, but Knox knew that he'd crawl back into his cave eventually.

It was a perfect night, one filled with friends, drink, and laughter. It ended with Beth sneaking him away to her apartment and for the first time that he could recall, he wondered if becoming an Adventurer was worth it. After moving from his father's home and finally accepting Beth's advances, he was happy. But he knew that he wasn't just becoming an Adventurer to be happy. He wanted power and to see the world. So, when the morning was still early, he slipped free of Beth's embrace, kissed her on the head, and left.

CHAPTER 9
NEW WORLD

BEFORE THE SUN rose above the horizon, Knox took care to pack his belongings. He put his armor on, one piece at a time. Though the task was difficult without any assistance, he managed by himself, even if the fit wasn't as snug as it should be.

The small box that contained Mr. Tome's gift lay discarded next to his bed. He'd fashioned a leather sheath affixed to his hip and placed the extra shots in a small compartment at the end. The boomstick fit snugly within, its handle pointing upward, and an added strap ensured that the powerful weapon wouldn't come loose as he walked. While he took pride in his new contraption, it paled in comparison to the pride he felt for his axe.

A newly purchased thick emerald cloak hung about his shoulders, the ends of which rustled from a subtle draft in his room. He looked down at his most prized possession.

His axe, Scarlet.

It wasn't magical and wouldn't be very effective against magical creatures, but he was a woodsman, and he couldn't imagine wielding any weapon other than Scarlet. Bending down, he gripped the smooth polished shaft. After so many years as a woodcutter, his axe felt like an extension of himself. It had been a gift from his father when he first began work as a woodsman. It was special, and although he knew it wouldn't last forever, he had been lucky and taken good care of it.

Knox, the woodsman of Keenlen's Vale, put his axe on his belt, ready to become an Adventurer.

With darkness barely giving way to the first bit of daylight and a heavy pack weighing on his back, he'd only made it ten paces from his new apartment when he saw Dernal approaching.

"Ready?" he asked. A pack, twice the size of Knox's, rose above Dernal's shoulders, yet there were no signs of him struggling under its weight.

"As I'll ever be," Knox said without a second thought. His path was laid out before him, and he knew it was the right decision. Last night's festivities had momentarily shaken his resolve, but now, as he embarked on his journey, there wasn't a single thread of doubt. Maybe a faint whisper of uncertainty still lingered, but he pushed it down hard and focused on what lay ahead.

"We'll meet with the dungeon group a few hours out of town, they prefer another small town over Keenlen's Vale, so they've already left," Dernal said, his usual gruff and limited words had been set aside for a no-nonsense tone that Knox had never heard from him before.

With that, they moved out toward the gate where Jeremy was stationed, seemingly waiting for them as he leaned hard on his spear.

"Excuse me, but I was told not to let you go yet," he said, looking to either side as if he expected someone else to appear. Knox reached out with his sense and sure enough, there were four figures headed their way.

Dernal grunted as he put a hand on his dagger. Jeremy paled visibly, an impressive feat considering his already fair complexion.

Knox recognized the feel of each of them and put a hand on Dernal's arm. "It's just my friends, Beth probably paid off Jeremy to make sure we couldn't sneak out without them coming to see us off."

Jeremy tried to look anywhere but at Dernal and nodded profusely, agreeing with the explanation Knox had provided.

"Why, there he is! Trying to escape as if last night's meager goodbye was enough to satiate his friends' desires to see him off!" Murdoch was entirely too loud this early in the morning, but Knox just smiled as Fred, Terrim, Beth, and Murdoch approached.

"Good to see you too, Murdoch," Knox said, pulling the man into a side hug as he reached him first.

The towering form of Terrim came next and he smiled at the sight of him. "Don't get yourself killed, alright?" he said, then, instead of pulling him into a hug, he threw a slow lumbering punch, which Knox dodged and ducked beneath, grabbing him as if he were going to wrestle him to the ground. They hugged and released a moment later.

Next came a quiet Fred, his eyes fixated on the ground. "Thank you," he said, holding out a hand to shake. Knox took it and met Fred's eyes. He had a long way to go before he recovered from the death of his family and the trauma of injury, but if Knox knew anything about his old friend Frederick, it was his resilience. He'd survive.

Last came Beth. She didn't say a word at first, just coming up and giving Knox the biggest kiss of his life in front of everyone.

He blushed, she didn't.

With a squeeze to one of his ass-cheeks, she released him and set her eyes to stare into his. "You come back to me, alright?" she said, then with a sly smile on her face she added. "I won't be waiting around for you, but I still want you to come back and see me from time to time."

"Wouldn't have it any other way," Knox shot back, matching her grin. "I'll do my best to stay alive, you all do the same."

A round of nods followed and Jeremy finally stepped aside. "Goodbye, for now," Knox said, raising a fist into the air and turning to follow Dernal into his uncertain future as an Adventurer.

"Leo Patel, John Keller, and Caleb Pool," Dernal said pointing to each man in turn, "regulars in my dungeon group." Then pointing to Knox, he said, "Meet Knox."

"How do you do?" Leo asked, giving an odd bow.

It was clear that Leo was not from around these parts. His hood was up, but it failed to hide his pointed ears or light blue skin. He was of average height and wore a mix of grey and black beneath his oversized brown cloak. With striking yellow eyes and blond hair to match, he was the strangest man Knox had ever laid eyes on. Of course, he'd heard of other races like the elves from the Northern continents and several tribal races like goblins, gnolls, and orcs, but none had ever come through Keenlen's Vale.

"Nice to meet you, Leo," Knox said, mimicking his bow.

"My name's John, John Keller," John said, he seemed eager or overly excited as he spoke, reaching out and taking Knox's hand in his own, then shaking it furiously.

He was an average sized man with short blond hair, a keen look in his eyes, and a grin that could match Murdoch's. He wore leather armor and had daggers at his waist, along with several small pockets that contained who knows what. His skin was pale like someone who rarely got out in the sun and his eyes were brown.

"Dernal told him your name, you nitwit," the one named Caleb said, reaching out and moving his hand upside John's head, however, before the blow could connect, John dodged it deftly.

"Hmm," Dernal said, shaking his head, but the two looked to Dernal as if they'd both been told off and Caleb's follow up attack stopped mid strike. They'd both moved with amazing speed and Knox wondered if he'd ever learn to move that fast.

"Well met," Caleb said, holding a hand outward.

Knox reached out and shook it. Caleb pulled him in and whispered in his ear, forcing his wrist into an awkward angle.

"You better pull your weight, no one but Dernal wanted you along. We don't need extra shares of the essence going to waste."

Knox squeezed his hand back until Caleb released him and stared right into his dark gray eyes. His arm ached from the maneuver, but he wasn't going to let himself be manhandled like that. He looked at Caleb and took him in, he was not impressed.

The man was muscled for sure, but he lacked the height of even Knox, being at least a hand span shorter. Not that he had an issue with shorter folks, but on Caleb he was fine using it as a fault. He wore armor, a mix of leathers and plate, similar to Knox's own, but it blazed with the light of at least a dozen more enchantments. On his back, he had a large round shield with a backpack affixed over it, and at his waist he had a sword. His face was covered in deep scars, one of which ran all the way up to his bald head.

"I'll pull my weight. I've killed an owlbear before. I'm sure I can handle whatever the dungeon has to offer," Knox said, he wanted to show the other Adventurers that he was meant to be here, but he wasn't sure that did it. All three of the newcomers laughed, Dernal just grinned.

"You want any heals this next run, Caleb? Then keep your shit to yourself. Knox is going to be twice the Adventurer you are once he finds his feet," Dernal said, his usual bored demeanor had changed to one of pride and Knox noticed that he didn't even have his pipe out, something he hadn't seen Dernal without since meeting the grizzled old Adventurer.

"Hhrm. One last thing, come here Knox," Dernal said, walking him to the side. "I had this made for you. It suits the protector type more than any others, but a shield for any type of Adventurer is just smart for your first few dives."

Dernal pulled out a round shield from seemingly nowhere, the edges lined with the owlbear claws, and the center emboss-ment had a faint glow to it. It was a magical shield.

"Dernal," Knox began to say but he was interrupted.

"Don't mention it. I used the Monster Core to give it a bit of a kick, but I'm not much of a crafter and neither was that black-smith. It should—again I haven't been able to test it—but it should apply a bleed effect to any creature with blood you hit it up against. You will be running the front line alongside Caleb, our main tank. Which reminds me."

Dernal pointed toward Leo, "He is our main damage dealer, he is a fairly powerful D Ranked Sorcerer."

"He isn't human, is he?" Knox asked, lowering his voice in hopes that he didn't offend the strange humanoid.

"Not exactly, no, he is a half-breed from what he tells me, half human and half something I've never heard of before." Dernal didn't try to hide his response and Knox noticed that Leo tilted his head just a touch in their direction.

Pointing toward John, Dernal said, "John is our sneak, he is an E Ranked Adventurer, but he's on the cusp of making it to D. His essence control isn't what it should be, so he is slow to gather power, but if he stays diligent, he could make it to C Rank before he dies of old age."

"And that man," Dernal pointed to Caleb, "is our tank; as I said before, you will be up with him most of the fight. He is hard to get along with, but he knows his place and he is on the cusp of moving into C Rank, so he can't afford to not be invited to this season's dungeon runs."

"Uh, Dernal," Knox said, trying his best not to sound like a complete newbie. "What are E, D, and C Ranks? Also, what Rank are you?"

"Oh, right, I keep forgetting you don't know any of this," Dernal said with a chuckle. "You are still such an oddity. Your source must be open, and you clearly have some sort of sight ability. How someone managed to open their source and gain a sight ability without help still baffles my mind. Up until a season ago, I really thought you were some runaway Adventurer that got tired of it all and wanted to live his life out here in the sticks. But I'm getting off topic, I'm a C Ranked Adventurer. The leader of this group. I benefit less from such a lower-Ranked dungeon, but I like to think of this as my vacation from a year of hard work."

Knox nodded along, growing more confused than when the conversation had started.

"The rankings are something of a mystery. They are assigned by the Guild based on the aura of the individual. Since you have a sight ability, I can show you how we gauge it. Can you activate your sight? Go ahead and take a look at each of us."

Knox did so, activating his sense and gazing at each of them in turn. Normally when looking at Dernal, even with his sense activated, he saw nothing but Dernal. This time, however, he was greeted by a green glowing hue, with traces of a lighter yellow in it. Taking turns looking at each of the other three, he noted they each glowed a different color.

John was a dark indigo, almost blue. Whereas Caleb had some blue in his aura, but most of it looked greener than anything. Then there was Leo, who had no aura at all.

"Leo is special, he developed his aura mask before C Rank. Unmask yourself Leo," Dernal commanded, and before Knox's eyes his aura became apparent.

It was a deep blue, much deeper than Caleb's, but it lacked any of the green mixed in that Caleb's showed.

"F Ranked Adventurers have a Violet Aura, E Ranked Adventurers have Indigo, D Ranked are Blue, C Ranked-if they let you see their aura-are Green. None of the higher Ranks would ever give you a good look at their aura, so their colors aren't important, but I'll tell you anyway. B Ranks are Yellow, A Ranks are Orange, and S are Red. But you won't see any red auras, as those Ranks might as well be myths. No one in a thousand years has reached beyond B Rank. You, Knox, will start as an F Ranked Adventurer like all of us did, though I sense your Core is on the cusp of E without any training whatsoever. I expect great things from you, whatever path you decide to take."

"It's like there is a whole world just outside of what I knew, and I never truly understood," Knox said, doing his best to come to terms with everything he'd heard so far.

"There is more I need to tell you, but let's get moving. I don't want to spend more nights on the road than I have to," Dernal said, then turning to the rest of the group he ordered them to get ready. Each carried a bag twice as big as Knox's and not a single one of them seemed bothered by the weight.

After several hours of walking, Knox had gone further from his home than ever before. "Finally," was all he said as he took the next step into the unknown.

They stopped for the night, making camp just off the road in a small grove of trees. It was well past true dark, even the Fire moon had passed its apex. Knox felt exhaustion unlike any he could recall, struggling to keep up with the brisk pace set by the four. He even had an inkling that they were holding back for him. It wasn't something he'd like to admit to, so he made sure he kept up, his body screaming at him until they finally stopped walking. He had no way of telling how many hours they'd walked, but it must have been at least fifteen or so.

They were headed for a dungeon said to be about a three day's walk away, and he doubted that the distance would be a match for one more day of walking at this pace. Unless, when the Adventurers told him the distance, they'd meant their pace and not a normal person's. He was learning the hard way already that an F Ranked body was no match for even an E Ranked one.

He'd struggled to do much talking, breathing as heavily as he was, but John had filled him in on several facts about this new world as they walked. John was friendly and the pace didn't bother the rogue at all.

So, he'd learned a great deal of things, including the advantages of ascending in Rank, each level offering special benefits upon breakthrough. While he didn't go into much detail about any of them besides reaching E, which he had personal experience with, Knox marveled over the new information.

Apparently, at E Rank you got a new body, or at least your body was strengthened, purified, and altered in a way that allowed you to survive on less sleep, less food, and less water. On top of all that, you could begin to naturally push out impurities through special nodes inside your body. He even said he'd learned to use his impurities as a kind of poison, saving it in a special place inside of himself that he could then call upon in battle to poison his enemy.

Knox made a note to himself that he ought not make John his enemy, because being poisoned by impurities didn't sound pleasant at all. Besides that, John spoke at length about his role in the dungeon being more tactical and defensive than anything. He said he'd be disarming traps, detecting hidden rooms, and if he had time, fighting monsters. Dernal had grunted at that but said nothing.

Knox was beginning to work out a pattern in the types of grunts that Dernal made. There was the low and guttural sound of disapproval, the longer and drawn out one signaling agreement, and then there was the fast and sharp one that he hadn't quite figured out yet. Deciphering Dernal's unique method of expression proved to be an amusing distraction for Knox.

Dernal then pulled him aside to explain something.

"To truly get your start as an Adventurer you need to go through a purification ritual," Dernal said, pulling out a stone the size of a walnut.

"What does that entail?" Knox asked nervously, eying the walnut warily. John had briefly touched on this but had been silenced by one of the sharp and quick grunts from Dernal.

"You have to swallow it and it will purify your Core; do you think you can do that?" Dernal asked, a serious look on his face.

"It has runes on it that will attract and rid you of corruption that builds up from passive essence consumption, the kind you get from eating, drinking, and breathing," Leo added.

His clarifications didn't help Knox feel any easier about the process of eating a walnut-sized rock covered in runes, a few of which he recognized but what they did he could not say.

"I have to swallow that?" Knox asked, the runic rock seeming to grow in size the longer he looked at it. "I'm not sure I can."

"We've all done it before, it takes a bit of work to get it down, but I haven't heard of anyone choking on one in ages," John said merrily.

"Eventually it will start consuming the good essence, so we will need to get it out of you as soon as possible," Dernal said. Then he tied a string to the walnut rock and Knox felt even more uncomfortable. It looked like they'd be literally pulling it back out of him when it had done its job.

"Normally," Dernal said, "we used the water and punch you

in the gut method, but it wasn't foolproof and didn't always work. I prefer not to take any chances."

"Drink this, it helps," John offered, giving him a wineskin filled with ale. Knox sat down and began to drink a good share of the ale John offered.

"I'm ready," Knox announced, standing.

"Right after the cleansing, I'm going to give you a well of knowledge along with a pill. It should push you over the top to E Rank. You'll want to strip, otherwise you will never get the smell off your armor," Dernal instructed.

Knox took Dernal's advice and stripped out of his armor, wearing only his underclothes. If he understood correctly, he'd be ruining them very soon, but he had more in his pack. The group had built a large fire and was cooking several rabbits that John had caught along the road. His ability to see wildlife and unleash his daggers in killing blows was shockingly effective.

Dernal approached with the rock and another large cup of ale.

"Hmm. Drink, then swallow," Dernal said with a look of grim determination on his face.

Knox drank the ale and held some in his mouth before accepting the rock from Dernal. Taking a deep gulp, he attempted to swallow it. It felt like someone punched him in the throat, but somehow he got it down.

Then the pulling began. His sense had been activated, but it abruptly flickered off. It felt like his stomach was being ripped from the inside outward. He groaned in pain and fell over screaming. It hurt so bad that he was no longer able to think clearly.

There was a swirling vortex inside of him and he could feel it consuming him. He wanted to rebel against it and try to keep hold, but he didn't resist it. Instead, he sat and focused on steadying his breathing while pain continued to rip at his insides.

"Not yet... not yet," John was saying somewhere distant. "NOW!"

A sudden yanking feeling and his world rocked back into normality. The pain snapped away, replaced by a deep exhaustion.

He coughed blood and chunks of something while straining his ability to sit up. He managed to look up just in time to see a black mass twice the size as before, in Dernal's hands. He chucked the ball into the fire, and it exploded in a spray of sparks and flames.

Dernal approached him, giving him a reassuring smile before reaching out with his hand.

"Here, take this," he said, pressing a small glowing stone against Knox's forehead and the world faded away.

He was sitting atop a hill, meditating on the meaning of essence and the feelings inside him, but he wasn't himself. It was as if he were watching a memory of someone else from their own eyes.

The terrain was unfamiliar, but down below, a battle raged between man and beast. This person, whoever they were, was looking for a way to improve their chances in a world hellbent against them surviving. Then something clicked into place and the contents of their Core began to swirl.

Suddenly the world went white, and a new memory formed. It was in the depths of a dungeon, though how he knew this he wasn't sure. He meditated on the type of cycling technique that would be most efficient for fast growth, then like a fog lifting, it clicked, and a new cycling technique was born: The Raging Water's Cycling Technique.

The world flashed again and again, but it went faster now, and Knox had a hard time truly seeing it. However, he was left with impression after impression that helped him refine and decide on his own which cycling path would be best for him. He knew that he'd been given a lifetime's worth of knowledge and study, though how it was given he was unsure.

The world blazed back into place, and he began cycling the Raging Water's Technique without hesitation. However, he knew something was off the moment he started. Instead of pulling in the flood of essence the technique was capable of, it cycled only the smallest, almost imperceptible stream.

"Take this pill and cycle it into your Core," Dernal's voice echoed again, but Knox didn't break off his cycling. Instead, he opened his hand and just as he had—or as the memories had—many times before, he cycled an Essence Pill. The memories were already fading into near nothingness, but the instincts that came with it remained. Intuitively, he knew how to cycle and extract the essence materials from the pill and absorb it into his Core.

He pictured his Core, although small and weak, filled nearly to the brim with essence. The new flood that came from the new pill was too much, and for a split-second Knox panicked not knowing what to do, but he relaxed and let the memories guide him.

Filling his Core to bursting, he cycled essence from the pill and into the small container. Then with his mind, body, and soul, he reached out and grabbed hold of the Core. Pressing with all the excess essence, like a blanket wrapping around a ball, he pushed and condensed. One tiny bit by tiny bit he pushed down his Core until it was half the size it was before, then he pushed some more.

Finally, he felt it happen. His aura shifted, and pain exploded from his body as new channels inside of him opened up. Vaguely, he knew these were natural channels meant to strengthen the body, but it scared him, and he nearly lost his concentration.

But he endured, focusing on why he needed to be different, why he had to be better.

The process of taking a Core from F to E was all about getting a good cycle going around the now smaller Core. So, he began to weave strands of essence like lines of power around his Core in a pattern he'd been taught by the visions he'd had moments ago.

Pain continued, but he didn't stop working until the essence from the pill was consumed and his Core had a vortex of power slowly pulling essence into it while purifying any outside essence within the vortex. What he was meant to do with the expelled essence, he wasn't sure, as the memories hadn't touched on that.

He opened his eyes and the first thing to hit him was the stench. His arms, face, legs, everything he touched had a thick greasy layer of something on his skin. And no matter how much he tried to brush it off, it clung to every inch of him.

"Here," John said, and suddenly a wave of water crashed over him. He'd upturned a huge bucket's worth of water on Knox, but there was something in it that stung. He was then handed a flat and smooth wooden utensil. "Scrape that crap off and try to keep it in one place so we can burn it. The water I threw on you had a low-grade acid in it, it should help loosen it up."

Going to work, he spent the next hour or two—though time lost all meaning while doing such nasty work—cleaning himself free of the grime. When he finally finished, he stripped out of his clothes. The smell was so bad that he no longer cared if they saw his nakedness, and he got another bucket of the acidic water for a final cleanse.

The smell unfortunately didn't seem to wash out of his hair very well, and he eventually took a knife to cut it short upon John's suggestion. What little hair was left atop his head cleaned off easier, and he let out a sigh of contentment.

Knox threw his clothes into the fire along with the gunk left on the ground. He then joined the others by the fire and laid down.

"How's it feel to be truly alive?" a nearby voice asked. His hearing adjusted to the closeness of the voice, and he recognized it as Dernal's. Knox turned to face him.

"Everything feels..." Knox struggled to find a word that fit into how he was feeling. "Enhanced?"

"You've joined the E Ranks; you will find that your senses will be greatly improved. I need to fill you in on a good bit of information, so sit tight and ask questions," Dernal said, sitting atop a fallen log next to where Knox lay.

"Alright," Knox answered, getting himself comfortable where he lay. Someone had put a blanket over him and a pillow under his head.

"I'll start by explaining what just happened to you after we purified your Core. You probably don't realize it yet, but you've learned a great deal about essence cycling," Dernal paused and watched Knox for signs of recognition.

"Yes," Knox said, his mind filled with knowledge he hadn't known before his purification. He looked inward and saw that the essence that filled him, filled all living beings, had begun to move and churn like the beginnings of a hurricane, following the vortex he'd created.

"You will notice that your Core moves and should have a decent understanding of how to get it to continue to move. In its natural and pure state, it will stay in motion like that, but once you begin to eat and breathe the air around us, additional toxins will mix into your Core and eventually it will begin to slow as it struggles to process the toxins. I've used something on you, one you'll have to pay me back for, to teach you how to keep the impurities from taking hold. No one's Core is perfect, and you will gain impurities eventually, but this is the great secret of Adventurers. The cleaner you can keep your Core and the longer you can keep it from stopping, the longer your natural life will be and the further you can advance."

"You see, we are all just creatures of essence and aging is just a reflection of inner impurities," Leo added, from across the campfire.

"What are you saying, Dernal?" Knox began. "Are you saying that I can live forever? Let me guess, you are going to tell me you are really old now?"

"Well..." Dernal said, shrugging. "I am nearly a hundred years old, but I am more an exception than the rule. You see, it is common for Adventurers—if they don't die—to stay in fit, fighting shape until around a hundred years old, but I specialize in Life essence, so I reap additional benefits that you don't see in Ranks E to A. S Ranked Adventurers are the true immortals, though; they are able to completely shut off any additional need to gather essence, thus they do not gain additional corruption."

"Wait, there are actual immortals? Like the Titans?" Knox asked.

"Titans?" Dernal asked, "No they're just a myth. Stories of ancient powerful essence users who tried to control the world. Silly campfire stories." Dernal was opening up and talking more than ever before and Knox wanted to take every advantage of his openness as he could.

"If you say so," Knox said, thinking about the journal he had found and the mentions of Titans.

"Back to my explanation," Dernal said, regaining Knox's attention. "E Ranked users have just as much opportunity to keep their Core as pure as A Rankers, so get serious about maintaining a proper cycle inside. I will teach you more when we get to the dungeon, but until then, spend a good bit of time each night meditating inward to get familiar with your Core. Before I let you get some sleep, I want to explain one last thing."

"What's that?" Knox asked.

"I told you before we purified your Core that you were at F Rank already."

"Yeah."

"Well, you are E Rank now and it is because I gave you a very rare pill that contains purified essence and knowledge contained within a hollow Monster Core. There are methods to impart certain memories and actions into Cores. That particular technique is a family secret that I only share with my pupils. Your newly purified Core ate up that essence and it tipped you over the edge into E Rank."

"I didn't realize there would be this much to learn about being an Adventurer," Knox said, sighing. "I'm not complaining, but I figured it would be more, swinging my axe and learning magical runes. So far, it's been all essence talk, swallowing stones and being told that if I work hard, I can become immortal."

"You don't need to learn everything now," Dernal reassured him. "But it is important that you learn the basics of essence cycling if you want to stand a chance in hell of making it to B Rank before you die."

"Right, before I die in the next hundred years or so," Knox

said, the advice that Dernal had given him before he left about not getting too attached to a lover now made a load more sense. It wasn't that he would be busy running around from one dungeon to another. He would literally outlive Beth three times longer if he didn't die a gruesome and horrible death in a dungeon.

Sleep didn't come easy that night, and when it did come, Knox struggled to keep memories of the magical journal's stories of sea monsters and mad crewmen out of his mind.

CHAPTER 10
TECHNIQUES

"HE GAVE YOU THE TALK?" Leo asked, striking up conversation after their short break for lunch. The blue-skinned man was extremely friendly.

"Yeah, I'm going to be immortal if I work really hard and eat all my berries," Knox said, laughing as he considered the ridiculousness of it all.

He'd gotten used to Leo's strange features and pointy ears. It turned out that Leo and John were both very friendly. He spent most of the morning talking casually with both.

"You are young enough that a push to B Rank might be possible still," Leo said; he grinned but didn't seem to see the humor that Knox saw in the idea of immortality.

"What about you?" Knox asked, "You aren't going to try and live forever?"

"I'm old enough," Leo said; the thinly built sorcerer pulled back the hood of his cloak revealing aged blue skin and deep yellow eyes. "You learn that sometimes a deep basin is as useful as a wide one. My power runs only as deep as a D Rank, but I don't have the resilience to hit B Rank, that's a game for younger players."

"I look forward to venturing into a dungeon with you," Knox said, seeing Leo with new eyes. He must command some awesome power if only his age was keeping him from B Rank.

"My bones ache for the essence-rich environment of a dungeon," Leo said, sighing.

"Oh," Knox said. "So, I've been meaning to ask you and Dernal didn't say, so perhaps it's rude to ask, but what is your other half—if not human?"

"Aw, Dernal has a memory like a sinking ship," Leo said. "Sturdy but filled with holes."

Knox laughed at that and caught a glare from Dernal for his trouble.

"I am born of a human and a Sea Folk, they call themselves Atlari, but most people consider them just a myth, like the Titans of old," Leo said, winking at Knox.

"You don't think the Titans are just a myth?" Knox asked, excited to talk to someone who might actually believe in them.

"I know they aren't," Leo answered. "I've spent countless years exploring the dungeons that only the Sea Folk can gain access to, being underwater and all. The evidence that rests beneath the sea doesn't lie. The Titans are as real as me or you."

"They are or were?" Knox asked.

"I know of no living Titans," Leo said. "But that doesn't mean they aren't around."

"Have you heard of something called the Titan System?" Knox asked, remembering what the wizard from the journal, Ramses, had called it.

"I have not, but I do not claim to be an expert on all things Titan."

This new revelation ignited a glimmer of hope inside of Knox. His drive to learn more, to know more, to understand, burned within him. His first steps had been taken and now the world was open to him.

He gave Leo a friendly head nod before standing and going to the edge of the woods. For a moment, he caught himself fearing what he might find. Would the creepy girl be out there waiting for him with her sickle held at the ready?

These were strange woods compared to the ones he knew so intimately. Perhaps he ought to exercise more caution, but he didn't, and no shadow of a girl appeared to harass him while he let his mind wander.

He'd stood there for several minutes before Caleb walked up next to him. His thoughts of runes and their formations shattered under the pressure of the burly man's presence and his foul mood.

"You'll just get in the way and get me hurt," Caleb said, elbowing Knox hard and if he hadn't moved to the side with the blow, it might have cracked a rib. Hell, if his body wasn't as sturdy as it now became, he surely would have.

"What's your deal?" Knox asked, getting fed up with the man's rudeness. "I'm new, but not completely incompetent."

"I'll bet half your share of gold that you nearly die at least twice during the first dungeon run," Caleb said, his tone turning coy with a touch of sharpness in it.

"You're on," Knox said without a moment's hesitation. Between the shield, his new body, and his boomstick, what were the chances he'd come *that* close to death in a dungeon?

With that, Caleb left him to his thoughts and Knox started to think about his new body, his new senses, and how even his special sense seemed to be strengthened.

He felt at least twice as strong as he had been before, but it was hard to gauge himself without a physical activity outside of jogging—they had been jogging down the road instead of walking ever since Knox received his new body at E Rank, yet it still seemed like they were holding back for him. Deciding to test just how strong he now was, he reached out to a nearby tree branch.

He gripped a branch about the thickness of his wrist, big enough that he'd not been able to rip it free of the tree before his transformation. Pulling with all his might, the branch creaked and groaned under his strength, then suddenly it cracked and broke free. It wasn't a clean break, the tree was healthy and filled with life, but he'd snapped it nearly free with his effort.

Taking his axe out, he finished the cut with one swift practiced strike. Even that had felt different, like the force he could put behind a strike had been multiplied severalfold.

"Looking to learn a strike technique?" John asked, he'd come up right behind him. His special sense took concentration to maintain, so Knox hadn't noticed him at all.

"Strike technique? What's that mean?" Knox asked, putting his axe back and turning his full attention to John.

"Well, there are a variety of techniques you can learn now. Strike techniques are built into strikes, like me with my daggers or Caleb with his sword," John said. "Then there are enforcement techniques that enforce the body, things like healing and buffing allies or yourself. And then you've got the technique that Leo likes the most, expelling. It involves expelling essence out in specific patterns to create spell forms or effects that strike from a distance. Those are the basics at least."

"Striking, Expelling, and Enforcing," Knox repeated. "Got it. And you can teach me a strike technique?" Suddenly he was very excited by the direction of the conversation.

"No, he can't," Dernal said, pushing his way into the conversation. "I'm your mentor and I'll decide when and what you learn."

Knox turned his attention away from a chastised looking John to Dernal. He had his pipe out again—he'd begun smoking during the breaks, but the smell of it was much different than Knox remembered, most likely due to his increased physical abilities.

"Will you teach me then?" Knox asked, he was so close to having learned something cool that he found his tone to sound more frustrated than he'd meant it to be. However, he didn't apologize, instead standing his ground to await an answer.

"You will learn fast inside the dungeon," Dernal said, "but I can teach you a basic enforcement technique that every Adventurer worth their salt uses. It's called Haste and learning it now will help us get to the dungeon within the normal three-day window, instead of four or five days."

"I'm ready," Knox said without hesitating.

"I don't have any Memory Cores for this technique, so you'll have to learn it the hard way. Best to get used to learning things the hard way, though, as Memory Cores are pricey and sometimes not worth the knowledge they attempt to impart."

Dernal continued after leading them back to the fire. "Every living being has an affinity toward a certain type of essence and it is best to focus on that type when using techniques as it will strengthen them considerably. However, I'll first teach you the basics of the technique then apply your affinity once identified."

"What essence type do you use?" Knox asked, unable to restrain his excitement at learning even more. He'd have to add this to his personal study journal. Then, thinking twice about it, he went to his pack and pulled it out along with a pen and inkwell. He wrote down first what John had taught him earlier, then what Dernal said about affinities and essence. When he'd finished, he looked up eagerly at Dernal.

"I use Life essence and it makes me a powerful healer or enforcer, depending on the terminology you prefer," Dernal said, eyeing the notebook. Knox wrote down Dernal's then looked at the others, they each shook their head no, except for Caleb who looked downright angry at the prospect of giving up his essence type. "Don't worry, you'll learn theirs when they start using techniques, whether they want you to or not." Dernal added when he saw the group's reaction.

This made Knox smile and he continued to make a few more notes before turning his attention back to Dernal.

"How do I figure out my affinity?" he asked, unsure of the next steps to take.

"You'll be able to tell by the amount of essence you can pull from the respective auras. For instance, the fire here has enough Fire essence that you should be able to fuel a simple technique, so first, I'll show you how to do the technique and then you can try to fuel it several different ways. The easiest but the more harmful way to fuel a technique is with Pure essence, like the kind that fills your Core."

"Why?" Knox asked, interrupting Dernal as he tried to finish his explanation.

"Simple, really. Your Core needs all the Pure essence it can get to advance, and you can only get Pure essence by filtering out the elements from the essence around you. When separated, the elemental portions of the essence become waste and must be expelled. When you are stronger, this waste can be harnessed into techniques, but first I'll teach you just to simply expel it into the air. So, let's teach you Haste, then figure out your affinity and teach you how to expel the waste. Should be easy enough."

It didn't sound easy enough and suddenly, Knox was worried he might not be up for the task, but he reinforced his will by reminding himself that he was doing what he should, and he was where he needed to be. If ever he was going to be like his mother and understand the things she did, then he had to walk this path.

"Feel the power around your Core and the vortex that is

feeding it Pure essence. Reach out with your mind and grab hold of one of the strings of power that feed your Core and let me know when you've done that," Dernal commanded, he had Knox sit by the fire and close his eyes in concentration.

It was easy to hear or say the words but doing what he asked proved to be a nearly impossible task. Time and time again he tried and failed to grab hold of the energy. It was like trying to catch the wind. Only after focusing himself into a cycling position and clearing his mind did something occur to him. Instead of imagining himself grabbing hold of the power and moving it around like a hand would a stray noodle, he envisioned what he wanted.

He wanted the power to stop feeding his Core and obey his command. Then, just as easy as that, he felt something tugging at the most central vein of power.

"I think I've got it," Knox said, keeping his mind clear as his intentions focused on the noodle of power.

"Now to do this we will have to force open a node inside of you that has to do with physical enhancement, but don't be alarmed. I want to nudge the power down into your groin, and you will find a node there that will accept the power, then I need you to trace the power back to your Core. Try to do that and let me know when you've succeeded," Dernal said, speaking loud and clear.

Knox nodded and began to envision what he wanted. Slowly, but steadily his power pulled away from the vortex surrounding his Core and followed little veins or pathways that he hadn't noticed before. Slowly but surely, he pushed the power down toward his groin, each inch it traveled made his body shudder with power in a way that felt almost addicting. Like a flush of adrenaline and the touch of a chill breeze smashed together and drowned by a cool ale.

When he finally reached his groin, he found something he could only describe in his mind's eye as a lump or another Core of some kind. He pushed against it, imagining the power flowing into it and back out again, but it resisted. He tried again, nearly losing the strand again, but finally on the third try he felt something shift inside of him and power flooded the muscles all over his body.

If he'd felt strong before, he felt invincible now. Careful not to lose focus, he pulled the power back up and connected it with his Core. When he was finished, he opened his eyes and realized his breathing was ragged and coming in sharp gasps.

"Give yourself a minute to adjust," Dernal said, smiling wide. "You've just unlocked your Root Node, the one that strengthens the body more than anything else. Most experience at least a twenty to thirty percent increase in strength from it."

"However, it isn't normally the first node one unlocks," Leo added, looking to Dernal with something akin to suspicion.

"He has the sight, or a version of it already, so I'm taking him down the path of the Iron Body. He'll thank me for it later," Dernal said, directing his words to Leo.

Suddenly, a feeling built up in Knox and he hurled out all of his lunch and much of the water he'd drunk that day. His muscles rippled and strained against his own movements, but just as quickly as the feelings came, they receded.

"What was that?" Knox asked when he'd finally finished clearing out the bad taste in his mouth.

"Your body needed to purge out more toxins and it seems like it chose to do so through your stomach. Good thing too, as it might have resulted in another pair of messed up clothing," Dernal said with a chuckle. "Why don't we start you on that technique now."

Knox groaned, his stomach hurt, and his head was abuzz now, but he straightened himself and nodded his head at Dernal to continue.

"Now that you've unlocked your Root Node, this is going to be extremely easy for you. Take the power that is flowing nicely through your Core channels. You need to forge a new path that intersects with your lungs, only don't push against the node there, and down into your legs. Imagine you're drawing a line or path that branches from the steady flow of essence you've created. This pathway will only temporarily be filled with essence, and it should allow you to infuse them with essence of any type down the line."

Knox nodded and went to work. He used the same mental pressure he'd used before, imagining what the end goal was instead of trying to force it step by step and was encouraged by early success. It wasn't until he tried to spread the pathway around his lungs that he hit a snag. The pathway he was making wanted to push into the node, he could feel it.

But he'd been told explicitly not to allow that, so he focused harder on what he wanted to see happen and imparted his will against the task. After a while, it moved slower but did as he wanted, the task was finally complete. When he stopped, the essence, pure and white in his mind's eye, receded back to the main path between his Core and his Root Node.

"I did it," Knox said, letting out a slow and steady breath. It had been difficult but not impossible.

"Now flush those pathways with essence while also running or moving and see the results of your hard work," Dernal said, clapping him on the back.

Knox wasn't sure he'd be able to do that, but he would try. It took an immense amount of concentration to flush his pathways and the idea of running or moving at all while doing it seemed impossible. For one, he'd only been able to do it before with his eyes closed and his mind focused on the imaginary layout of his internal body.

The first dozen attempts ended in sporadic success. "Even if I get the power moving, I can only hold it for a second," Knox complained, looking to Dernal for some tip or trick to make it easier.

"Perfection of a technique comes with many attempts, you cannot expect to run before you can walk," Dernal responded, but Knox could tell the man was growing frustrated with his failures.

The failures continued for another hour and finally Dernal called it off, saying, "You will practice while we jog and during meal breaks. Do not stop trying."

And so they were back on the road, while Knox attempted and failed to do the technique known as Haste.

CHAPTER 11
HASTE

IT WAS on the third day that Knox finally figured out how to keep the essence flowing while moving. The results were amazing, if not short-lived. He suddenly sprinted ahead of the group, unable to continue going at the slow pace he'd been moving only moments before. Dernal gave an appreciative grunt and John hooted congratulations at him.

He managed to keep it going for a solid five seconds, in which all the others let loose a bit and caught up with him with ease. When his Haste technique suddenly unraveled and he stumbled and fell, Dernal was there, extending a hand to help lift him up.

"Let's take a break and work on your essence affinities," he said, lifting Knox to his feet.

Within minutes they had a fire going, and for the first time since starting the trip, Knox got to see some magic at work. Leo waved a hand and whispered several words under his breath that not even Knox's newly enhanced body could hear. Then, suddenly, a ball of flame fell onto the wood and a fire roared to life.

"He has a high Fire affinity," Dernal said, seeing Knox's eyes widen in amazement. "It's like I said, it's hard to hide your affinity once you start using your techniques."

Leo shot Dernal a look but said nothing in his defense.

"There are six basic essence types and dozens of combined essence types, but those are much more advanced and not something you need to know right now," Dernal said, finding a fallen log and kicking the massive thing in place as if it weren't at least a hundred pounds.

The pair of them sat and Dernal continued.

"Darkness, Light, Water, Fire, Death, and Life are considered the prime essence types, and we will test your affinity for each of them, starting with Fire."

Knox nodded along and looked into the blazing fire, trying to imagine that he could see the essence.

"You have a sight ability, though I don't think it is a full third eye, it should be sufficient to detect the Fire essence if you focus. It will appear as a haze of red, like a second glow around the fire. You will need to cycle while focusing on pulling in just the Fire essence. You will know it is working when that red haze swirls around you and enters your vortex. When you get that far, let me know."

Knox activated his sense, what Dernal called his sight ability, and stared at the fire. It looked much like the fires he'd seen through his sense many times before. Focusing on seeing the red haze, he thought he noticed something around the fire. However, he'd always seen that, sometimes even without his sense focused. It took concentration but he turned off his sense and looked at it with just his eyes. Sure enough, the red haze that burned around the outer edge of the fire, swirling and dancing with the flames, disappeared.

Smiling to himself, he focused, and his sense flared back to life. He went into a meditative sitting position and began to cycle, focusing on not pulling everything, but just the specific red haze around the fire. It was easier than he imagined, and soon it began to swirl in the vortex surrounding his Core, slowly being purified to feed it.

"I've done it," Knox said only minutes later.

"That was fast," Dernal remarked, before continuing his explanation. "Now that you have access to Fire essence, I want you to pull it free from your center and do as you had done when you successfully used Haste. Pay attention to the feelings you get and special attention to how close it feels to using Pure essence. This is what will give us an idea of how high your Fire affinity is or isn't. The closer to the feeling of using Pure essence, the higher the affinity."

Knox stood and readied himself to activate his only technique, Haste. He took a few steps before grabbing hold of the Fire essence and flushing it through as he had done the few times previously when he'd correctly activated Haste. It felt warmer—perhaps that was the right word for it—but other than that, it came just as fast and easy as the Pure essence. His steps blurred as he rushed forward, cutting off the technique, and used the remaining Fire essence to empower himself for another Haste to get back.

The technique ran out halfway back, so he jogged the rest of the way at a decent, but normal, speed. Dernal looked at him expectantly, but Knox just shrugged. "Honestly, it felt no different," he said finally, to which Dernal smiled.

"A powerful Fire essence user. Perhaps I'll let Leo teach you a thing or two after all, but first, let's test the rest of the essence types."

They spent the entire day and night testing the remaining ones. Life essence was easy enough, as they all inherently overflowed with it. Next came the Death essence, as it emanated from a dead rabbit that John had killed for lunch. Following that, they drew Water from water, and Light from the very sun and ambient light around them. As their travels for the day came to an end at sunset, they tested the final essence: Darkness.

Through it all, something strange happened and Dernal no longer looked excited, but rather concerned.

"There is no way that you have high affinities in all of the prime essence types, it just isn't possible," he said, shaking his head after Knox informed him that Darkness essence worked the same as the others. What he hadn't told him, because he feared it meant he was some kind of freak, was that when using Light essence, it came easier than even Pure essence had.

Knox had tried to broach the subject with Leo, asking if it were possible that an essence type could be more effective than Pure essence, but he'd assured him immediately that it was not. Pure was Pure, and essence didn't work that way, he assured him.

Knox wondered if it was a joke, because when he channeled Light essence, he felt almost as if he could fly. Deciding to test how long he could maintain it in the sunlight, Knox began hiding his usage of Haste. He'd managed a twenty second sprint before shutting it off due to strain on his channels.

It was odd getting used to this whole new system that existed within his body, but he was learning the limitations of it day after day. He discovered that he could only maintain Haste for a limited time as it strained the very channels it moved through to an extent that made him fear they may burst if pushed too hard. Leo had informed him that the more he used techniques, the more powerful his pathways would become, and eventually, he'd have a wide network to choose from when activating different techniques.

Dernal struggled to accept that it was even remotely possible that Knox could have high affinities in all essence types. Yet, Knox simply brushed off Dernal's skepticism with a shrug.

"It is how I feel, I don't know what to tell you," Knox said. Worried he'd anger his new mentor, he added, "Sorry."

Dernal grunted. "Hhmm. Don't be. It is a difficult task to identify your own affinities, I just hoped that with your skill with the sight that you'd be more attuned. When we get to the dungeon camp, we will have you read by a practiced sage, someone who has experience reading auras and affinities."

"What of expelling toxins?" Knox asked. He'd noticed a lump of something gathering outside his Core due to his filtering, but he didn't know what to do with it or how to handle it yet.

"Right," Dernal said, grumbling something to himself that Knox didn't catch. "I'll teach you the most basic expelling technique. Do what you did for Haste, but this time, I want you to connect pathways to your palms and not a loop, mind you. You'll find small nodes in each hand but pick a hand and focus on unlocking that one first. It isn't a primary node, so don't expect anything special from opening it."

He was so vague that, at first, Knox wasn't sure what he meant, but he wanted to give it a try anyway and see what he could do. Pushing as he had when he made the connections to his Root Node, he picked his left palm as his target. Using Pure essence from his Core, he pushed and wormed a path until finally he felt what Dernal meant. There was a node there, but it was much smaller than the Root Node and didn't have the same pull.

Doing as he had with the Root Node, he made the connection and instead of looping it back to his Core, he just left it there.

"I think I've done it," Knox said excitedly.

Dernal examined him and nodded. "Looks good to me," he said, and suddenly Knox realized that with his sense activated, Dernal had a glow to his eyes for just a second. Perhaps signs of him using a sight ability of his own? "Now grab hold, this will be more difficult because you really have to grab it and yank those nasty toxins into your channels with just a touch of Pure essence, it'll help reinforce your pathways and prevent damage. Then when it gets to the node, point your hands away and watch it work."

"I think I understand," Knox said, picturing himself pushing essence through his pathways but also allowing the taint of the filtering process to accompany it.

He wasn't as prepared as he thought. The first ten attempts ended in failure. Each time he'd gotten the Pure essence from his Core easily enough, but when it came to moving the lump of hard impurities, they just didn't want to move at all. He imagined, he prodded, and finally he did what he'd first tried to do to the essence. He grabbed hold of it mentally and tugged. A thin noodle-like section came off and followed his directions, if barely.

Thrilled by the success, he realized he had to learn to split his mind a bit, as moving the essence required focus while forcing the impurities demanded sheer willpower. Strangely, he felt that he'd grabbed filtered Flame essence, and when combined with the Pure essence, it almost resembled the color of Fire essence. Pushing, pulling, and forcing it through the channel he'd made in his arm was difficult and time-consuming at first.

By the time he was able to channel it to his open palm, he felt like he was getting the hang of it. He directed his hand away from everyone and it began to come forth in a sudden rush. The moment it hit his palm he felt a pressure build and heard Dernal yell from behind him, "Release it!" Knox focused on the node and mentally uttered the word *release* and a stream of raw and burning flames shot out of his palm.

He felt the blisters form on his hand from the heat the

moment the flames shot out. It lasted only three seconds, but it had shot far enough out that a nearby tree was beginning to burn. Leo walked up to the tree, spoke a single command, and the fire went out.

"That was impressive," Leo said, turning to Knox and regarding him with a curious expression, his brows raised in surprise. "How did you manage to pull only Fire essence from your impurities without training? Typically, a straight expulsion technique like that, without any words of power to guide them or runic hand gestures, would result in a cloud of mixed essence types that wouldn't even be a solid form. You've got a knack for it."

Dernal grunted and put himself in front of Leo. Pointing a meaty finger at Knox he poked him in the chest. "Be straight with me boy, have you been taught any of this before? No one is this good without any training."

Knox sensed an abrupt surge of danger emanating from Dernal. He saw Dernal's aura flare as he raised his hands, palms facing out, and a light began to radiate from them.

"Dernal," Knox said, taking a step back. "What are you doing?"

Light smashed into Knox, bringing with it a soothing cool sensation. Familiar words of power rolled off Dernal's tongue.

Fael Thunkar Foal Resoria!

"I half expected him to raise a barrier spell or activate mage armor," John said, chuckling at Knox as he stood from where he'd fallen to the ground. The burns running up his hands and arms had been healed, leaving only a faint itchy discomfort.

"So did I," Dernal said, walking over to Knox and eying him critically. "You've got some talent, boy, but be careful who knows it. This life isn't all rainbows and sunshine."

Knox spared a glance at Caleb, who appeared oblivious, engrossed in devouring a piece of meat. Pondering Dernal's words, Knox prepared to expel some more impurities. However, Dernal put a hand on him, prompting him to stop.

"I was just going to," he began to say, but Dernal interrupted him.

"Save what little impurities you have for now. If you can pull them out like that again, they'll make a decent enough weapon if you find yourself in a tight spot. Just be careful to project a bit more force into it next time so that the attack doesn't materialize so close to your flesh. In theory, you should be able to hit anything within twenty paces if you can leverage enough mental force against it."

"When do I learn words of power?" Knox used the same terminology that Leo had, though he thought of the words as nothing more than the names of the Runes he'd learned. "Surely I can add some more utility to these attacks, and I'd be more useful."

"When we get inside the dungeon, I will teach you a few spells and striker techniques, but until then, you need to learn to pace yourself. You have talent. Don't let it get wasted because you tried to run before you could walk," Dernal said, each word a growling rumble of finality.

Their break ended swiftly. Several times, Knox mentally practiced doing the fire technique without truly executing it. He imagined facing off against monsters and summoning fire upon their heads, smiling all the while. He could be a powerful axe and shield-wielding caster, or perhaps he could learn to shroud himself in flame and attack full on like a demon of legend.

Though, now that he thought about it, very few demons were said to be fire-breathing monsters. From the tales he had been told growing up, that was more the characteristic of dragons and their kind. But it was said that the last dragons had been slain or driven from human lands over a hundred years ago.

He thought about his ancestors, being so strong that they could possibly control and conquer dragons, perhaps even ride them. There were, of course, stories and legends of ancient dragon riders. But they were more far-fetched than the mythos surrounding the ancient Titans. He recalled a tale he'd heard from a trader, that there was a race of people who shared blood with the dragons, appearing like humanoid lizards, tail and all.

While he let his mind wander, the group began their steady jog again, approaching their destination. Soon Knox would learn to the full extent of what it meant to be an Adventurer.

CHAPTER 12
CAMP

DERNAL HAD REFERRED to the area around the dungeon a few times, as had the others, and each time it had been called a 'camp', so Knox expected as much. When the road curved ahead and he came face to face with stone walls rising at least twenty paces up and guard towers every hundred paces, he thought perhaps they'd taken a wrong turn somewhere.

Wooden gates banded with iron were closed fast, but upon their approach they swung open without a sound. Within was a maze of tents and stone structures, most of which looked to be formed directly from the stony ground. Despite the massive walls and appearance of several stone buildings, it truly looked like a camp inside. Tents and buildings seemed placed haphazardly, similar to the west side of Keenlen's Vale.

If there was any kind of central planner involved with deciding where these buildings were placed, Knox assumed that they must've taken the day off while these structures grew straight out of the ground like weeds. Knox eyed several of these stone buildings, particularly noting a two-story structure with multiple windows they were approaching. Dernal swung the door open, revealing an interior stone-flooring covered in wet mud. Thankfully, Knox's newly enhanced body aided in maintaining his balance as they entered the slick-floored building.

Four days of running had given him increased control, when at first, he'd been very awkward in his new E Ranked body. When thinking of the ranking system, Knox decided to use his sense on the nearby Adventurers, immediately revealing to him a sea of colors.

From violet to indigo to blue, and even a few unveiled green auras, all blazed brightly around him. A particular green aura emanating from one man caused Knox to cringe, as the pressure exerting from him felt as if it would take Knox's breath away.

"Foolish man," Dernal said, shaking his head and grunting in the man's direction. "Keeping his aura out just to push around weaker Adventurers."

"His aura was so..." Knox was at a loss for how to describe it. Oppressive maybe? Strong, definitely.

"Obnoxious," Leo offered, winking at Knox from under his hood.

"Sure, that fits," Knox said smiling, glad that he wasn't the only one affected by it.

The multitude of colors strained his sense, prompting him to quickly turn it off before another green aura approached too closely. There was a roughness about this place that reminded Knox of the Wistful Maiden, a tavern that operated on the west side of Keenlen's Vale. Despite its name, there was nothing wistful about it. Terrim had once dragged him there for a night of drinking, and they both left sporting black eyes.

"We need to get you to the registrar establishment, only they've moved the damned building, so let me ask around," Dernal said, separating from the group and disappearing into the crowd.

"I'm not here to babysit," Caleb said. "I'll see you all later." With that, Caleb left, much to the relief of everyone present.

"He is such a stick in the mud," John complained, elbowing Knox in a friendly gesture.

"He'll be insufferable when he hits C Rank," Leo added, shaking his head as their teammate walked away.

"He must be really good," Knox said, looking at the two.

"Why do you say that?" John asked, not denying it.

"Because you all put up with him instead of kicking him out," Knox said, chuckling.

"True enough," Leo said; then turning his head he added, "Looks like Dernal found the registrar, let's go."

Sure enough, only moments later, Dernal appeared once more and led them through the sea of Adventurers.

Knox felt overwhelmed by the sheer volume of Adventurers, especially given their diversity of equipment. One man had armor resembling a skeleton and wielded a club as large as Knox's midsection, yet he handled it as if it was as light as a feather. To Knox's surprise, his sense revealed that the man had only a Blue aura, meaning he was merely a D Rank.

Two hundred paces away, there was a smaller stone wall with a gate made of dull grey metal directly in the center of the small dungeon town. The entire length of the town looked like it could be crossed in only five, maybe six hundred paces.

"What is that?" Knox asked, pointing to the smaller tower-like construction. It had multiple smaller doors built with people filing in and out from different entrances.

"That's the dungeon. We should be in by tomorrow morning," Dernal said, noticing where Knox's gaze was directed.

"Why would they put another gate around the entrance, are they worried about monsters getting out?" Knox asked, noticing there were several very official looking guards standing by the walled-off section.

"Hmm. Rarely happens," Dernal said with a chuckle. "Adventurer's Guild is worried people might get in without paying."

"You have to pay to get in?" Knox asked. "I thought anyone was allowed to go inside."

"That's true," Dernal said, taking a deep puff of his pipe. "But that doesn't stop the Guild from charging. For the less fortunate, there's a death or completion contract. Poor rates on those. Better to have a sponsor."

"So, you're my sponsor?" Knox asked, understanding what a gift he was getting from Dernal, though he'd never had it outlined for him.

"Mmhhmm," Dernal said in response.

They approached a tent that appeared marginally more official than the other random assortment populating the gated dungeon town. There was a large carpet laid out beneath the tent, which looked only big enough to hold three people comfortably. The light tan-colored tent stood out in its cleanliness, especially considering that every other tent he'd seen were all in various stages of mud-covered deterioration.

A large crest was embroidered on the side of the tent, depicting a grey gauntleted fist set against a white triangular shield in the background.

In front of the tent, there was a small table set out with a burly man sitting in a comfortable looking chair. He wore white armor with a wax-like texture, something Knox had never seen before, and he wondered what material it might be made of. At the center of the guard's chest was the same emblem on the tent, marking him as a Guild Adventurer Administrator.

"What can I do for you Dernal?" the man asked with a surprisingly cheery tone. Knox had expected the man to have a dour mood to match the expression that he carried on his face.

"Well met, Chad, I see they put you on desk duty? Did you get tired of having to clean up Adventurer parts outside the dungeon?"

"Hah, you don't know the half of it. We've had an influx of weak and untrained F and E Ranked groups getting their hands on enough cash and gear, thinking to call themselves Adventurers. I'd say near enough to zero knew shat about essence techniques."

"Speaking of untrained Adventurers," Dernal pushed Knox forward. "Meet Knox, my E Ranked pupil. We need him registered as part of our group and I'll be covering his entrance fee this season, as well as sponsoring his entrance to the Guild."

"Finally taking another hopeful under your wings!" The attendant seemed surprised. "After what happened to Adam, I wasn't sure you'd be interested ever again. Good on you!"

"That's enough of that," Dernal said, his voice losing its friendly demeanor all at once. "Setting up in district D, send any request for additional information there."

Dernal threw a handful of translucent coins on the desk and stormed off. Knox took a moment to study the odd coins but was interrupted by Leo grabbing his arm and turning him to follow.

Knox waited until Dernal had put a fair distance between them, walking twice as fast as the rest of the group, before turning to Leo to ask him, "Who is Adam?"

"Who *was* Adam," Leo corrected. "The last hopeful Dernal vouched for some twenty years back. He didn't last very long after blowing out his essence channels by pushing himself too hard, too fast."

"You can blow out your essence channels?" Knox asked. "How?"

"Oh, I wouldn't worry about it," Leo said, slapping Knox on

the back. "It's very rare and only happens to those who gain power far quicker than their body and spirit can adjust. So, you know, find your balance and you will be fine."

"I thought the goal was to get to B Rank as fast as possible?" Knox asked.

"Well yeah, but, you know, not *too* fast," Leo said, chuckling as he pushed ahead to catch up with Dernal.

Dernal had rented them a tent and as soon as they got inside, he laid out his bedroll, then promptly fell asleep. There was enough room inside the tent to fit each of them comfortably, but Knox wasn't tired yet.

"Want to get something to eat?" Knox asked Leo. The blue-skinned man gave him a regretful smile.

"No, sorry," he said, glancing outside of the tent flap. "I don't mix well with these lower-Ranked Adventurers. They usually have too little brains attached to their mouths and I don't wish to explain my origins to every simpleton I encounter."

"Oh, uh, sorry about that, I didn't think anyone would care," Knox began to say, but Leo held his hands up grabbing his attention.

"It's fine, it's fine. Ask John, he loves to go out for a drink, just steer clear of Caleb. He can be nasty if he gets you alone," Leo said.

"I heard that," Caleb said, poking his head into the tent.

"So, you did," Leo shot back with a grin.

"I'll go find John," Knox said, slipping past Caleb and out to the forest of tents. To his relief, Caleb didn't follow. He wasn't ready to challenge the man's temper until he got a true under-standing of his own power. No point in picking a fight that wouldn't go well.

"And then I told him, no, you can't put it there!"

Knox followed the sound of John's voice and found himself in a large pavilion tent. He was sitting next to two heavily armored men. Realizing as Knox got closer, it was actually a man and a woman.

Knox stared up in awe at several small floating lights that lit the tent. There was some sort of persistent magic cast to provide illumination. Knox had never come across such casual use of magic. It did well to remind him he was finally an Adventurer, among whom such marvels were probably commonplace.

Before Knox was able to reach the table and sit down, he felt something. A familiar sensation, and it called out to his mind.

Victory, Victory, to the deep ones went the victory. Gone for now, we come again, victory, victory.

"Shit," Knox swore under his breath, moving to put a hand on John's shoulder. "Did you hear that voice?"

"Oh, hello there," John said, looking surprised. "This is Knox, he's new to the party. Knox meet the twins." He gestured to the pair of armor-clad warriors.

"What voices are you hearing, boy?" the female twin asked.

"What? You didn't hear just now, someone saying: victory something, something?" Knox asked.

"No," all three answered at once.

"Uh, Knox, you sure you weren't mistaken? I'm sure you didn't hear any voices... right?" John asked, looking worried.

"Right," Knox said, feeling uncomfortable. "Yeah, you're right. I misheard."

They had gathered more attention and Knox wasn't feeling up for a drink after all. He walked to the edge of the wooden palisades and made his way to the exit. He felt closed in, as if he was being watched.

Standing at the large gate opening, Knox looked out and saw something standing between two large trees, several hundred feet out.

As dusk approached, the silhouette of a small child holding a farm sickle emerged, shrouded in shadows so deep that they were almost impossible to see through. Even with his more enhanced vision, it was like looking into a pool of perfect darkness. Yet he was certain that the form of the child was not just a figment of his imagination.

Knox's hand went to the boomstick he carried on his hip, clenching his teeth. He took a step forward, toward the dark specter.

"Hey there, you leaving before your dungeon run?"

The voice caught Knox's attention, distracting him from the girl's faint silhouette. He turned to see a guard eyeing him, expectantly awaiting a response. Knox didn't answer.

He turned his attention back to the tree line, ready to investigate and confront whatever the entity really was.

Yet, the tree line was now empty. Steeling himself, he went out to check the spot where he had seen her, ignoring the guard's question. But he found nothing, not even a footprint.

Deciding he was tired after all, Knox returned to the tent and fell asleep moments after laying his head down.

He stood on a large hill. All around him, dark forms bled from the ground and attacked a legion of armored men and women. Somewhere in the back of his mind, Knox knew he was dreaming, but he was unable to wake up.

Huge cities emerged from the dust and the dark figures enslaved everything they encountered, building monuments for their dark gods. Then at the height of their power, something fell from the sky.

A golden light that drove back the darkness. The gold light seeped into six of the enslaved beings, setting them free but also binding them. Those six went out and forced their idea of order on the entirety of the planet. Until one by one, the lights went out.

The world returned to darkness, but the creatures from below didn't return... yet.

Knox awoke with a start.

"It's time for your first dungeon run," Dernal said, smoke puffing out of his mouth as he spoke.

"Suit up everyone," Leo proclaimed.

"Here we go," Knox said, trying to remember all the details of his dream, but too excited about his first dungeon run to take the time to write it down.

It only took ten minutes before the entirety of the dream faded from his mind.

CHAPTER 13
DUNGEON

It was still early, the sun barely cresting the horizon as their small group approached the inner walls, where the dungeon entrance awaited them.

"Let me see yer papers," one of the heavily armored men asked. Dernal pulled loose a sheet of paper and the guard took it, examining it intently.

Knox, meanwhile, examined the guard. His aura was being suppressed, so he was likely C Rank. The armor he wore shone from a heavy assortment of runic marks. And beyond even that, the man was a giant of a specimen. He towered over his guard companion and their entire dungeon team.

"Everything looks to be in order," the guard said. "We will credit your account, and as per the standard agreement, if you haven't made it out in two weeks, we will purge the dungeon iteration. You will find yourself right back here, dead or alive."

"We know the drill," Caleb said, he was in his regular surly mood.

"Come on in," the other guard said, motioning them through a six-foot-high door.

Stepping through the wooden frame, Knox found himself standing in front of a stone monolith. It was as wide as three men and twice as tall. The gray stone surface was polished to three perfectly flat edges and down the center of each side was a series of runes, only a handful that Knox recognized.

"Place your hand here, next to mine," Dernal said. He stepped forward and put his hand on the stone surface. Knox did likewise.

"Now what?" Knox asked.

"Now nothing, we are here," Dernal said.

Knox started and turned around to see what he meant.

He wasn't in the crowded walled-off space anymore but was now standing in a huge cavern. In front of them the same stone monolith stood like a dwarfed stalagmite when compared to the vast height of the cavern.

The dungeon's stillness was disturbed by the footsteps of the five Adventurers, each ready to take on the challenge it offered. Knox let his eyes roam across the open cavern before him and he felt his breath leave him. It was massive. The stories he had heard from passing Adventurers had led him to believe that dungeons were closer to their namesake: small, dark, and damp.

This place was none of those things. The vastness of the room they were in was highlighted by the brightness that shone above them. The room stretched out several hundred paces and ended in a curved wall with several large doorways placed at even intervals. From this distance, he could barely make out symbols carved into each door, maybe six per door, but it was hard to tell.

His eyes lifted and took in the globe of light at the apex of the ceiling. It was bright enough that he had to avert his eyes almost immediately after looking at it. The ceiling was smooth and curved to a point about twenty feet from the floor where it then leveled out.

Knox was knocked out of his awestruck trance by a loud fart echoing from beside him, followed closely by a chuckle from John.

"You're spoiling the essence with your shit-filled fart, John," Caleb said, punching John hard on the arm. The rogue-like man just laughed and put his pack onto the ground.

Dernal turned away from whatever he was looking at in the distance and gave the three his best sneer.

"Time to stop shitting around," he announced, setting his own pack down as well. "We will set up camp here and take the shortest run first. Bring only the essentials and don't get yourself killed."

Dernal's eyes ran over the group as he spoke and lingered on Knox far longer than he felt should be necessary.

Dernal beckoned him over.

"These three know what they are doing," he began, his words barely a concealed whisper. "You don't. I'll tell you why dungeons are so great, and you do your best not to die, got it?"

Dernal paused, letting the words sink in before continuing.

"Remember the essence training I gave you?" he asked.

Knox nodded.

"This is where it really comes into play. There is enough latent essence in this room for you to cycle for a bit, but after this, the amount of essence we get to draw in directly correlates to the number of monsters we kill, traps we disarm, and puzzles we solve."

"There are puzzles in dungeons?" Knox asked. He considered himself an expert on any gossip or stories to do with dungeons and he hadn't even heard of there being puzzles, just traps and powerful monsters.

"Hhmm. There are puzzles. Not in all dungeons, mind you, but a good number," Dernal explained. "We will get to that later. Right now, I want you to practice your cycling."

He did so, sitting in a position that he knew—from the knowledge he was given—was optimal for drawing in essence.

"Good lad," Dernal said. "You are already halfway there. Close your eyes and focus on breathing and my words, nothing else."

Knox did so, closing his eyes and trying his best to focus only on what Dernal said.

"You are the center of a mighty storm. You can feel the points of power throughout your body."

Knox's breath came in sharp gasps as one after another he felt pain shoot through his body. First his head, followed by his heart, stomach, hands and feet.

"Feel the latent energy all around you and pull. Take the threads of power. They know where they should go."

Knox did as he'd practiced and been taught. But instead of a specific type of essence, he got all types, even some he didn't recognize with mostly Pure essence. He added it all to the vortex around his Core and let the technique he'd learned do its job.

"Well done!" Dernal said, sounding genuinely excited. "You see how your spirit knows what to do without you forcing it into action? Dungeons contain all sorts of different essences depending on the Core that controls them, but what makes them special is the abundance of Pure essence. That is growth you can't get anywhere else."

"I feel..." Knox paused, trying to find the right words. "I feel stronger."

"That's the essence working," Dernal said, standing up and offering Knox a hand up as well. "You will get a little stronger every time you pull in essence until you break through your barrier and move to the next Rank. Within each Rank are ten Tiers, you will feel yourself strengthened each time you pass a Tier. Now it's time to clear the first room and release more essence."

"What will I be doing exactly?" Knox asked, his hand kept going to the boomstick at his side, but he knew he should keep that for emergencies, so instead he slung the shield off his back. He had put his pack down like the rest of them, and now had only his armor, the boomstick, his trusty axe, and the shield Dernal had given him.

"You are going to work the front line with Caleb. He will run in first and you will cover his back. If a monster tries to flank him, it is your job to run in and stop it before it gets an attack in on Caleb. Your armor isn't the best, but that shield should work to keep them at bay. Your weapon is going to be pretty useless, but hand it over to Leo and he will give it a touch of magic to give you a chance at killing something."

Knox walked over to Leo and reluctantly handed over the axe.

Leo held it up to his eyes and ran his hand over the shaft. A perplexed look came over his face and he shrugged, handing it back.

"It's already enchanted," he announced. "I had to focus and look very deep, but someone has inscribed the smallest B Ranked runes I've ever seen inside the wood and axe head. Where did you get this?"

"It was my dad's," Knox said, taking his axe back perplexed. "He isn't an Adventurer, though."

Had his mother somehow inscribed the axe for his father before she died? Knox's mind raced with possible scenarios, the biggest of which was that his mother had been an Adventurer after all, and a strong one.

"Hhmm. No matter," Dernal said, a look of confusion on his face as well. "Looks like you will be alright after all. Let's get the first room cleared. For this first pull Knox, I want you to stand back and pay attention to how the monsters attack. This is your only chance to sit out a fight, but it's important that you get a feel for the flow of combat."

Knox wanted to protest and tell Dernal that he was ready to fight on the front line, but he understood the benefit of studying. He had spent his entire life studying his mother's runes and it had helped him get to where he was today. But that wouldn't make him a competent fighter, so he accepted that he would have to learn and went forward, following the group from behind, to see what a dungeon had to offer.

There were six doors carved into the side of the massive cavern and they approached them casually. No one but Knox had his guard up. He wasn't sure when the monsters would come but given their relaxed stances, he guessed that it wouldn't be for a while, or perhaps these men were braver than he'd previously thought.

"Each door represents a string of challenges," John said, slowing his pace and pointing at the one on the far left. "From left to right they get more difficult, and each one can take a day to two to clear, depending on the complexity. See those runes above the door?"

"I see them," Knox said, his gaze sharpening as he tried to memorize each one. He'd left his notebook behind, figuring it wouldn't be safe to try and take notes during a fight, but now he wished he'd brought it. He'd likely have time later, after they'd killed all the monsters that lay beyond the different doors. Then a thought occurred to him, and he had to ask, "Are each of them filled with monsters?"

John shook his head as they stopped right outside the far-left door. "Nah, but the weaker ones almost always are purely monster halls. The harder the challenge, the more complex the door. See the last door on the right? I bet my share of loot that it is one of the scenario hallways. Like its own little pocket world and the risk is huge, most groups don't try to do a full clear, but most groups don't have a C Ranked Healer."

"Focus up," Dernal said, peering into the darkness of the unlit hallway. He pulled free a torch from seemingly nowhere, he did that often Knox noticed, and passed it to Leo, who promptly lit it.

Meanwhile, Knox studied the runes. He recognized one for Fire or Heat and several others that he could just barely pronounce because of his long study of his mother's journals, but their meanings were useless to him without more context.

"Drakar, Runeth, Gormin, Icendel, Farle, Ignis, Thundrak."

He read off the names of each one under his breath and caught Leo's attention. The blue-skinned man walked over to him and put a hand on his shoulder.

"It is wise to not utter the runes aloud unless you mean to enact them. Even focusing your mind on them too hard might begin to trigger their effects and without proper training, you'd find yourself on the receiving end of a terrible headache. I promise to teach you one technique before this dungeon run is over, just be careful to stay alive long enough to learn it."

Knox didn't know how he felt about that, as he'd been saying and thinking about runes his entire life without any backlash. But he reckoned that Leo must know something about it since he was the powerful caster of the group. His techniques would be focused around using runes to damage enemies.

Caleb cleared his throat and said two words, "Going in." And the group followed, with Knox in the back next to Dernal and Leo and John moving just behind Caleb.

Knox hadn't expected what their first encounter would be, but what was now before them wasn't it at all.

Rats.

Giant rats.

Now, giant may not be the most accurate word, but these rats were the size of Dire Wolves and snapped with the force of a falling tree.

They found themselves in a dimly lit room, though there was no light source, the dark hallway opened into a cavern-like room a hundred paces wide and four times as long. Just a quick scan with his sense told him there were at least twenty rats, if not a few more than that. They patrolled the area in small packs of two or three, some hiding behind large fallen rocks but most just out in the open.

Knox's first thought was what the correlation between the runes outside the door and the monsters found within must be. Could he assume that one or two of those runes indicated that they'd be fighting rats, or was it more likely that the runes indicated the level of difficulty? He almost forgot to pay attention as he tried to work out which of the runes might mean rat in the runic language.

Caleb, armed with his sword and shield, dove right into a group of three.

Knox turned his attention to the fight; he saw that one rat had already fallen. Leo was in the middle of a technique and, as usual, his incantations were a bare whisper, spoken too softly for Knox to pick up, but the effects were clear. A haze of Fire essence was being pulled from the torch and suddenly Leo pointed his palm at the rat to Caleb's left.

A pillar of fire shot down from above, killing the massive rat nearly instantly, its cries cutting off after only a moment. That left a final one, for which John appeared out of nowhere, stepping out of a shadow and driving his dagger into its neck from behind. This also had the effect of killing the target instantly and Knox wondered if he'd be able to learn a cool technique like that. Jumping out of shadows could have all sorts of benefits.

"That wasn't so bad," Knox said, seeing Caleb position himself to take on another pack. "Should I join him up there now?"

"Hmm. We got lucky today. Rats are the easiest monsters you

will ever face in a dungeon, but that means the far-right door will be harder than usual. Might even be too much for us," Dernal said, a troubled look on his face. "Get up there and show me you have what it takes to be an Adventurer."

The moment he made it to Caleb's side, he shot Knox a glare and snarled. "Stay out of my way or I might hit you, *accidentally.*"

Knox wasn't sure he believed that there would be any accidents, but he took the meaning well enough and took several steps to the side.

Caleb activated a technique of some kind, his voice rippling the air as he growled at a pack of four rats. Their heads snapped toward him, and he raised his shield.

Knox drew out his axe and raised his own shield, ready to block any rat's attack. However, all four came right for Caleb, scrambling over themselves to get to him. This left one wide-open for Knox to attack, so he imagined it was a tree in need of cutting, swinging with all the force he could muster.

His axe bit deep, and to his horror, got stuck in the ribs of the monstrous rat. Moving his shield between its nasty face and two rows of razor-sharp teeth, he blocked a bite and felt an odd surge from the shield. The rat bucked and thrashed, but Knox held tight to his weapon and with a final heave, got it loose.

This left a nasty bloody gash on the side of the rat's ribs, which gained one hundred percent of its attention on Knox. It slammed against his shield, skinny rat feet slashing at his legs, but met only his armor and left him unharmed. Feeling like he was finally getting the hang of the fight, he stepped backward and smacked the rat in the head with his shield.

Slashing at its face from over the top of his shield, Knox smiled as he cut its black beady eye to bloody bits. He wasn't killing it instantly like the others, but he was determined to down this beast by himself. Slash, and smash, back and forth, his shield applying a bleed effect and his axe strikes taking it down little by little, until finally the mighty rat fell at his feet.

He looked up, panting and out of breath, to see that the

others had killed the remaining three rats and were all watching him now.

"I killed it," Knox proclaimed proudly.

Caleb snorted and scanned the perimeter for more rats to clear, but John, Leo, and Dernal each expressed their approval in their own way. John held two thumbs up, Leo gave a nod of his head, and Dernal grunted. Sure, it was only a rat, but he'd done it himself and he was damn proud.

The pulls continued much the same as they cleared out the room, with each encounter Knox getting the attention of a single rat and slowly beating it down. John gave him a few tips on the best places to strike on a rat, which helped him kill one with four strikes instead of a dozen. Knox soon discovered that killing rats was less like chopping a tree down and more like striking specific locations for maximum damage.

It was a learning process that concluded as they finished clearing the room. On the other end of the long room was another door, no runes this time, but it led into a pitch-black hallway once more.

"Since the first room was rats, we can expect ratmen in the second room," Dernal said knowingly. "Which means the final room will have the Rat King. Don't let him summon any of the rat archers, they are a pain to deal with."

Knox wasn't sure what to make of his comments, would they really be fighting ratmen in the next room? That would increase the difficulty if they had the ability to attack the group strategically.

Caleb led the way, and they entered the next room.

CHAPTER 14
RAT KING

THE NEXT ROOM was nothing like what Knox expected and he immediately wondered at how useful he'd be. It opened up to a space twice as big as the last one, filled with small huts and cooking fires. Surrounding each fire was a group of creatures resembling rats, but had humanoid hands, legs, and proportions.

Some wielded swords and shields, others carried bows, and

several had daggers. Only a few had any semblance of armor, besides some rags and the occasional leather covering. It was as if they'd entered a village of rat people and now, they were expected to exterminate them. As Knox let his sense wash over the room, he was amazed at the number he counted. At least three dozen ratmen—some nestled atop wooden towers placed at seemingly random interval—occupied the room.

This wasn't going to be as straightforward as pulling one group at a time. They'd need to take care of the towers first, then hopefully not catch the attention of the dozens that surrounded the various campfires.

"Hmm. I hate this configuration," Dernal complained, shaking his head. "Here's the plan. John, you clear out the nearest tower, I sense only two inside, so you got it. Leo, I want you to use the fire around that group to scorch them, and Caleb, you taunt them the moment they run for Leo."

"What should I do?" Knox asked, immediately.

"Stay out of the way," Caleb said, sneering.

"Be ready to cut them down with your axe. We will teach you a technique after this path is cleared and you'll be more effective, I promise," Dernal said, putting a reassuring hand on his shoulder.

John left first, fading to near invisibility, though Knox could still feel him with his sense as he neared the tower. He flickered into sight a few times as he climbed, but none of the ratmen seemed to notice. The moment he made it to the top, Leo acted.

There was a campfire of ratmen only a stone's throw from the tower. Suddenly, the fire flared around them, and pillars of flame smashed into all three of the ratmen at once. Leo's hood flew back as if a gust of wind had blown past him, even though the cavern was still. A single bead of sweat ran down his forehead, but apart from that, the task seemed to take no toll on him.

Caleb used his growling technique again, which caught the attention of the three burnt ratmen, causing them to charge directly at him. Their rage was so apparent that the one with the bow seemed to forget its purpose and brandished it like a club instead. But stopping ten feet away, it seemed to remember its capability to attack from a distance and let its two comrades move forward as it readied its bow.

Knox took that as an invitation and he hurled his axe, launching it in a manner he'd done countless times for amusement. It turned end over end and hit the archer right in its exposed chest. But Knox wasn't done yet. He ran the moment he'd thrown the axe, and he dove atop the staggering ratman. Using his shield, he knocked the creature over and wrenched his axe free. Then, with as much ferocity as he could muster, he slammed his axe into its face, over and over again.

It died, but not before covering Knox in a splatter of blood and fleshy bits. Spitting out some blood that had gotten into his mouth, he turned to see that his team had taken care of the dagger, sword, and shield rat combatants.

"Quick thinking," Dernal commended Knox, earning him another friendly pat on the back. This seemed to piss Caleb off more and he walked so close to Knox that he knocked him over, his shoulder slamming into him like a stone wall.

Knox stood back up and rounded on the asshat of a man. "You mind not attacking a group member?" Knox asked, his shield and axe at the ready.

Caleb's face contorted into a mask of rage, but Dernal was at his side in an instant, a hand on his shoulder.

"If you can't play nice, then you will be replaced. Do you hear me?" Dernal whispered the words, but Knox heard them anyway.

After a tense moment, Caleb looked at Dernal and seemed to deflate. "Fine, but you better keep that worm on a leash."

"Hhmm," was Dernal's only response.

The rest of the room wasn't as difficult as Knox had initially anticipated. They ensured that any signaling towers were cleared out, and then dealt with the surrounding ratmen. Dernal explained that as long as no alarms were set off, this room could be easier than the first, given that these ratmen lacked the brute strength of their more primitive rat counterparts.

When they cleared out all the ratmen, Dernal stepped forward to speak to the group. "Enough essence has begun to fill the air, let's cycle for a few hours and then we can defeat the boss."

Knox knew what he meant by the air getting filled with essence, he could sense Death essence, Life essence, and even a fair bit of Pure essence in the air. With each kill, the monstrous rats and ratmen released more.

So, doing as the rest of the team, Knox found a spot and settled down to cycle through the essence available to him. It was so much easier than outside, where essence seemed thin in comparison. Here, he barely had to pull, and overwhelming waves of essence pushed in all around him. His cycling technique worked well to take the pure and feed it straight to his Core, while the rest was purified, adding more impurities that would later need to be expelled.

Even with his vortex and techniques working perfectly, he noticed that small traces of impurities were making it into his Core. He would have to speak with Dernal about this, because he did not like the idea of losing space to impurities. There had to be a better technique that would stop those little bits from getting in.

With that thought in his mind, he began to examine the technique and the memories he'd been given. He had six separate strands that weaved around his Core, each one adding a layer of filtration. Why couldn't he add another one and improve it even further? He decided to try, using his focus he split one strand and began to cycle seven. It was like something grasped his lungs and heart at the same time, then squeezed.

He immediately let the strand fall and went back to six. There had to be a trick to figuring out more strands than six, but something told him instinctively that his body wasn't strong enough yet to handle anything more than six. The best he could hope for was to grab as much Pure essence as he could, while not allowing any other essence in.

This proved to be nearly as difficult since the cycling he'd learned just pulled indiscriminately. He did find that if he opened his sight and focused on the waves of essence around him, and with great care, he could pull mostly the Pure essence. It was hard, and doing it slowed his gathering by a factor of ten, but it resulted in less corruption inside of his Core.

Feeling like he'd just discovered the most optimal method of progression, he opened his eyes to see Dernal eyeing him intently.

"You do that, and you'll advance so slow that even D Rank will be hard to reach before you die," Dernal said, shaking his head. "But for now, it might be worth doing. The higher you can get without corruption, the healthier your Core will be."

"I understand," Knox lied. He felt like he was grabbing plenty of essence, slow as it might feel, when he would only take in the kind he wanted. But Dernal had given him the okay to continue his strategy, so he did so, pulling only the Pure essence from the dungeon around him, until it faded to nothing. There was still plenty of essence around, but the Pure essence was gone.

Another drawback of his strategy, but then he had an interesting idea. Several of the runes he'd learned were all about purification, perhaps he could make a runic formation or script that would purify the latent essence? Surely, someone would have thought about it already, but he had to try. He knew of three runes that might work, so using the edge of his axe he drew them into the stone and waited to see if they'd work.

"That won't work," Leo said, glancing over at Knox after he finished the delicate work of drawing each rune.

"Why not?" Knox asked, frustrated that it had indeed seemed to do nothing.

"First of all, one of those runes is meant to purify water or liquid sources, and the other two don't so much purify as they do cleanse out impurities. You aren't the first to try and make a device to passively cleanse essence outside your body. It can be done, but it would take you years to learn enough of the basics to even begin to make the required device. Even if you could, the components are so expensive that it is hardly worth it unless you've got a noble family at your back financing your advancement."

"So, it is possible," Knox said; it was all he'd taken from what Leo had said, and he tucked away his other ideas for later. Perhaps he could use an empty Monster Core to hold the impurities like they did memories? He'd need to learn that process first, but it was a start. Then a thought occurred to him.

"Why haven't we been collecting Monster Cores?" Knox asked, glancing over at the bleeding corpse of one of the ratmen.

"Cores only form on stronger monsters, so, door three and above," John answered, and Caleb grunted angrily.

"Hhmm. Focus up and cycle," Dernal said, not even opening his eyes from his own cycling.

Knox decided he couldn't miss out on advancement, so he cycled in the elemental essences and focused on keeping his vortex of filtration as efficient as possible. Another hour went by before they were ready for the final room. The room of the Rat King, a boss level monster.

Entering the final room of the branch, sent a wave of nervous energy up Knox's spine as he tried to wrap his head around what a 'boss' level monster might be like. The team seemed prepared enough.

"We've faced the Rat King before, nothing to worry about," John assured him as they traveled down the long dark corridor, toward a light from an open doorway some hundred paces ahead of them. "Just watch out for his Charge and Roar, both of which can be deadly."

"Not to mention his bite. It's venomous," Leo added.

Knox knew they were trying to be helpful, but it just ate at his nerves. He hadn't truly tapped into the potential of his Haste ability yet, but he was going to try his hardest to use it during this fight. It sped everything up, so he could benefit from faster strikes or perhaps dodge some attacks.

When they finally reached the end of the hall, Knox was relieved and surprised at what they found. A single ratman sat upon a throne in the middle of the room. Pillars of carved stone depicting more ratmen in battle or going about their daily lives were positioned all around the massive, cavernous space. Though the walls were the same rough stone as the rest, they'd been painted red, along with a few white outlines of what must be additional ratmen.

The bottom of the room was flat, and the Rat King didn't stir on his throne as they entered. Instead, he lazily set his gaze on the group, looking at each of them in turn until he came upon Dernal and sneered.

The rat had a humanoid body with grey and black fur that could be seen on the exposed parts of its body, the rest covered in plate armor. Sitting beside the throne was a massive sword the same height as the six-foot tall rat. His tail was armored and as it shifted beside him, it clicked from the overlapping armored plates. The black beady eyes seemed annoyed at Dernal yet bored with the rest of the group.

"See the red ring on the floor," Dernal said, turning to look at Knox while pointing at the floor.

Knox, affirming with a nod, had only just noticed its presence. Roughly five feet ahead of them was a massive red circle spanning a hundred paces from its edge to the king.

"Once we cross it, the fight begins," Dernal said, all business. "You will be with John clearing the rat adds, they'll begin streaming into the room as soon as the fight starts. But don't worry, if my memory serves, they are much weaker than the first room."

Knox looked at John and they shared a brief nod, before turning toward the wall with their weapons out. This was it; the fight was about to begin, and he'd finally have finished a small part of a dungeon.

A thought suddenly came to mind, about when the loot came into play. They'd not received so much as a single gold coin and all the rumors he'd heard said dungeons were filled with coins and special magical items. Perhaps he'd ask after they defeated the Rat King.

Behind Knox, the remaining party walked over the line and the fight began with a roar from the Rat King. Suddenly, the forms on the red wall shifted and four rats, smaller than the first room rats, appeared rushing toward them.

Activating his Haste ability, Knox rushed in to meet them. John had already disappeared, so he would act like the tank. The speed at which he hit the first rat sent it flying backward a step or two, then he slashed out, before letting the technique fade. His single strike, infused with the speed of his Haste, had split the skull of one and his shield bash had broken the back legs of the other, rendering it immobile.

John appeared a moment later, stabbing another through the neck just as Knox slashed down on the fourth. John went for the easy prey next and finished off the injured rat, just as Knox did the same to his last opponent.

"Easy enough," John said, smiling as he cleaned one of his daggers off on his pants. "Oh look, Caleb got knocked on his ass, let's watch."

"What about the rats?" Knox asked, turning to look at the wall. Several painted figures moved but no new monsters appeared yet.

"They come every few minutes, with you helping me kill them, we have time," John said, sitting cross-legged to watch the boss fight.

Knox turned and decided he ought to enjoy the view as well. Caleb had already made it back to his feet and Leo rained fire down on the Rat King using a technique Knox hadn't seen before, shooting a slender beam of flames at him. Wherever the fire hit, it burned right through his armor, hopefully doing some decent damage.

Meanwhile, Dernal, for the first time since starting the dungeon, had to use one of his heals. He'd used his light palm strike a few times before, but no one had really taken any damage until now. Caleb wobbled on his feet as a blow came down hard on his shield, the room cracking from the sound of the two metals hitting.

Light washed over Caleb and his posture hardened and he straightened. Then, showing a crazy amount of speed and agility, he sidestepped another sword blow, using his shield to catch the glancing blow before striking with his sword at the Rat King's exposed side. Knox watched in awe as the fight progressed and the Rat King took hit after hit without going down.

"Focus up," John said, hopping to his feet.

Knox turned to see more rats on the way, but this time it was a squad of five ratmen. Two of which had bows, two had swords and shields, and one had daggers. John had already slipped into the shadows, so Knox raised his shield and readied himself.

As he closed the gap between him and the squad, two arrows slammed into his shield. He worried if he'd be a match for so many, but his concern was unwarranted, as most of them wore only cloth scraps for protection. John swiftly appeared between the two archers, his two daggers slashing open their throats simultaneously. Knox cheered and caught a blade from one of the sword-wielding ratmen and activated Haste to deliver a devastating blow with his axe.

His attack was caught on the shield, just as the other sword and board rat flanked him. Then, just as he realized how precarious his situation was, pain flared in his shoulder, and he turned without thinking of the opponent in front of him. What he found was a rat appearing out of the shadows, its dagger wet with his blood.

A sword strike fell on the plate covering his back, it hurt but nowhere near how much the stab to his arm had. He found that he couldn't even lift his shield, so he let it fall free and he forced his left hand up, palm open to the rat's face. Behind him he heard the other rat scream, hopefully John was taking care of the pair of them because this shadow rat was going to pay.

Pulling from his impurities he focused on pulling out only Fire essence, or the impurities left behind at least, and was happy when he felt it come easily. Filling the space in his arm he activated the technique but focused on the shadow rat's head. This all took moments, and the rat was beginning to fade into the shadows again, but it was too late.

A ball of fire flared to life around him and he began to scream as the rags on his body burst into flame. Knox wasted no time, swinging his axe and taking the burning rat across the throat. It fell silent, dying seconds later.

Pain lingered in his arm and just when he turned back to check on John, he felt a wave of healing wash over him. The pain receded and he got back the use of his arm, so he grabbed his shield and rushed to join John's side as he fought two on one. He'd moved them into a position that was easy enough to flank and his axe bit deep into the first one's back.

The second opponent turned as his rat brother fell and it was his last mistake, a dagger slashed open his throat the moment his shield was lowered even an inch.

Back on the main fight, the Rat King had somehow grown to twice his height and his weapon fit his size much better now. Caleb struggled to dodge or block the blows and Leo continued to smash tiny holes into the Rat King, who was finally slowing and staggering around like he was feeling the damage.

"Final wave," John yelled as the Rat King grew red and became even bigger.

A dozen of the huge rats appeared, perhaps even bigger than the first room's and Knox knew he was no match for them. John seemed surprised as well, turning back to the group and shouting, "Leo, some help to thin the ranks!"

Leo turned, the rats approached, and the air around them

grew hot. Suddenly, Knox knew he was going to see the real power that Leo was capable of, and he smiled eagerly. Out of a cloud of hazy red that appeared overhead, dozens of small beams of fire shot down, shredding most of the rats. Luckily for the pair of them, at least three made it through so they had something to do.

Knox's jaw hung open when he saw the nine rats that Leo had so quickly and casually destroyed, but this was no time to sit on his hands. He raised his shield and axe and prepared to fight.

Their three remaining rats fell at about the same moment the boss fight ended. John slapped Knox on the back, before jogging over to the Rat King's throne, saying something Knox didn't quite catch but sounded awfully close to 'loot time'.

"It's a silver chest!" John yelled to the group and then he began to pull free a chest the size of his torso from beneath the Rat King's throne.

"Time to see what loot we earned," Dernal said, rubbing his hands together, before waving everyone closer.

The chest was made of wood but had polished silver bandings around it and no lock. It opened noisily and a faint golden light emanated from within.

"About time," Knox said, leaning forward to get a look. What he saw made his jaw drop open.

CHAPTER 15
TECHNIQUES

"IT'S A ROCK?" Knox said, trying to wrap his head around what they'd found.

Within the silver chest lay a single box holding a grey, oblong stone. Surrounding the box were translucent coins, resembling the ones Dernal had used to pay for their passage into the dungeon. As Dernal began to scoop up handfuls of the coins, they disappeared each time his hand neared the pouch on his belt.

"Do you have some kind of bag that holds more things than it appears?" Knox asked, suddenly distracted from the mundane grey rock that seemed to be the main prize for defeating this branch of the dungeon.

"Hmm. I do," Dernal said, finishing picking up the pile of coins. There had to have been at least a hundred of them in total. "At the end we will split the coin up, but for now you can take the main prize."

Thrill built up within Knox, until he again looked at the case and the rock inside, and he began to wonder. What did it do? Even so, he reached out and took the box all the same.

"I've gotten a general feel for the rock's powers already," Leo said, smiling. "It appears to be an Everwarm Stone. It lets off a gentle heat that will keep your body warm in the coldest of climates. Very handy if you do any traveling in the winter."

"Oh, how handy," Knox said, repeating the word Leo had used to describe it but feeling pretty bummed out at the prospect of getting a magical warming rock. If anything, his armor made him warmer than he'd liked, so he didn't even want to use the stone right now. Instead, he put it away in a pocket, determined to add it to his bag as soon as they got back.

"I once got a Sparkstone—a stone whose only purpose is to light fires—as a dungeon drop in the first branch of another dungeon. So, don't fret about it. Since you got first pick, you'll likely get one more item or an item's equivalent in coin before we finish a full clear," John said, picking at his teeth with a toothpick while he talked. Where he'd gotten the small sliver of wood or what he'd eaten recently to need it, Knox didn't know.

"Quiet down and let's cycle," Dernal said, taking a cross-legged position in the center of the room.

Knox complied, focusing inwardly and trying not to be bothered by the weakness of his first magical item. There was, of course, something to be said about a rock that could help you survive the cold. It was a miracle when one took the time to think about it, but Knox had been hoping for something that would increase his combat abilities.

Even in the first branch, the weakest of the branches, he felt almost useless. True, he'd killed his fair share, or at least gotten hits in, but he had a feeling John could have held off all those additional mobs by himself. What troubled him most was that he didn't feel confident that he'd been able to face off against the boss at all. It had let off a serious amount of power and show of strength, enough to hurt several D Ranked Adventurers, if only a little.

But while his cycling went into full effect, he let all those thoughts fade away. He had to advance and get stronger, that meant pulling in as much of the essence as he could, pure or otherwise. So, he pulled as much as he could, getting that much closer to filling his E Ranked Core. He could tell, now that he'd done this a few times, that it would take weeks, if not months, just to fill up his Core at its current size.

Although the area was practically smothered with essence during the two sessions he'd done so far, it hadn't lent much overall essence. Perhaps there was a faster way, but Knox didn't know it and he wasn't ready to ask just yet. Dernal had a Pill that got him over the edge last time, perhaps he could save up his coin and purchase something like that in the near future.

His thoughts quieted again as he focused on pulling more essence, until his cycling was disturbed by a stray thought once more. Why was he in such a hurry to advance? Surely, even being as strong as he was now, was a blessing. He felt that if he were matched against an owlbear now, whether it was infected or not, he might stack up well against it.

The rest of the cycling lasted another hour, maybe two; keeping track of time was difficult when in such a state of concentration. Once they'd finally finished, they all got up and headed back for the base camp at the entrance of the dungeon.

It was while walking and turning his sense onto his new prize, that Knox allowed himself to grow excited. He could read runic formations inside of the rock and he understood several of them.

One such rune meant heat and it was one his mother had notes on, then there were two Fael and Foal that he'd heard from Dernal, though he was guessing at the formation versus the pronunciation. Most of what he'd learned about pronouncing runes came from his mother's notes and they weren't exhaustive. But, if he understood the use and formation of the rock, it was fairly simple. There was even the use of Resoria—smaller and not vital to the core runic formation—which, with the attached runes, meant that there was a healing aspect to the rock.

Perhaps it warded off too much cold by creating a restoration field around the wielder? Whatever it did exactly, he was already beginning to feel like he'd gotten a better deal than he'd first realized. If he could create armor with this runic formation and alter it to include heat, he might be able to resist any weather, good or bad.

However, he was getting ahead of himself. First, he needed a deeper knowledge of runic formations and perhaps a few tools that he could use to create basic formations himself. With that on his mind, he turned to Dernal with a request.

"Are there supplies that I can purchase to learn runes and perhaps crafting?" Knox asked, biting his lower lip in a nervous gesture as he awaited his response.

Dernal grunted and just looked at him for a solid three seconds before responding. "You remember what I said about learning to walk before you run?"

"I do, but," Knox began to say, but he was cut off.

"I told you I'd teach you a technique or two. These will inherently also teach you about the runic language. Be satisfied with this first, then after you've grown a bit, you can dive into runic theory and crafting. Promise me you won't try anything on your own until you're ready," Dernal said, his eyes narrowing. Knox chose that moment to avert his gaze, looking anywhere but directly at Dernal.

After another grunt from Dernal, Knox relented with an exaggerated sigh, saying, "I promise not to start anything until I'm ready." He just failed to mention that he meant when *he* felt he was ready, not when someone else did. That gave him sufficient wiggle room he felt and when they reached the camp, he pulled out his notebook and began taking notes on his ideas.

Dernal cleared his throat, and for a second, Knox thought he'd caught on, but Dernal's attention was directed at the entire group.

"That will be all for now, I need the rest of the day to teach Knox a few techniques and see if any of them line up with his confusing affinities."

Caleb grumbled but said nothing and the other two just nodded their assent.

Knox went back to his notes and even took a few pieces of his armor off to examine them more closely. What he found when looking at the armor gave him a punch to the gut. The armor bore countless runic formations; while some were layered atop one another, the majority stood alone, separated by mere finger space.

He squinted against the bright glow and could make out most of them, so he took notes on those as well. He made two lists of the runic formations: one with room for more notes where he hoped to ask crafters the meaning of the runes, and another where he speculated already at their meaning or function. For instance, he believed that one formation on his gauntlet existed solely to reinforce another runic formation whose purpose he didn't understand at all. There was another formation that worked alone, which he was fairly certain it controlled the size or scope of the object, whatever that meant.

His head was abuzz with information when Dernal, standing over him, cleared his throat.

"Time to learn your first true combat technique," he said, and Knox snapped shut his notes, standing immediately.

He didn't get chastised for his notes, so Knox figured that Dernal either didn't care about theoretical creations and notes or he hadn't seen what he'd been doing. Either way, Knox smiled and waited to learn his first real combat technique.

"My two highest affinities are light and life," Dernal said, sitting beside Knox in a cycling position. Knox followed his example and sat across from him, several paces away from the others. "This makes me a natural healer. You claim to have easy access to both light and life as well, so I will try and teach you a very basic restoration technique. I simply call it, Heal."

This dampened Knox's excitement a measure or two. It wasn't that he didn't appreciate learning the healing arts from Dernal, but when he pictured himself using powerful techniques, they were all offensive and powerful in nature. Something about standing in the back line and throwing heals at people doing all the work, seemed a bit lackluster to him. Not that he would tell Dernal that, as he clearly enjoyed his role and was good at it.

So instead, he just smiled and nodded his head. "I understand," Knox said. Then, not wanting to come across as rude, he added, "Thank you."

"We will use the left arm channels you've already cleared for this technique, though before you leave the dungeon, we will clear open several more pathways for you. But now isn't the time for that."

Dernal paused and Knox nodded.

"The words of power used in this spell, that is what healing and offensive expelling techniques are called, are simple. *Fael Thunkar Foal Resoria. Fael* controls the Light that is called on in *Thunkar*, while *Foal* controls the force of Life that is called forth by *Resoria*. Try saying them a few times."

Knox did so, repeating the phrases several times, but felt nothing. Then Dernal pulled out his dagger and cut his arm. It happened so quickly that Knox only had time to gasp and look to Dernal for an explanation.

"Watch now as I heal my arm. Your intentions are as important as the words now. I'm imagining the cuts closing up and the flesh knitting itself back together. But more than that I am thinking about the healing nature of life, the power of light to illuminate the mind of how it is done. There is a fair bit of abstract thinking required to learn new techniques, but this is my most basic heal and also my most powerful one."

He held a single hand over his arm and began to chant.

Fael Thunkar Foal Resoria.

A single chant turned into three. The blood in his arm moved and snaked back into the wound, then, just as quickly as it formed, the wound closed up.

"Now, pay attention because this is where it gets tricky. You will want to focus on taking both Life and Light essence from around your Core, unfiltered as it is, and force it into your pathway to your palm. It won't be easy but give it a try."

Knox nodded again and shut his eyes. He found it easier to imagine the internal workings of his spirit when he blocked out his own sight. He saw that he did indeed have a good measure of Light and Life essence flowing around the inner part of the vortex that surrounded his Core. The filtering process was so slow, but the vortex could handle a crazy amount of essence, so he wasn't afraid of it overflowing anytime soon. He found that there was a place just before entering his Core that the essence hovered and sat. In fact, he got the distinct impression that he was using barely a tenth of its capacity.

The only real issue being that he didn't have enough essence to feed it. With a measure of focus, he identified the different essence types and saw that he had much less Light essence than any of the others—this likely being because he added it to his Core so easily. Beyond that, when he reached out for some, it easily came, flowing out in tendrils and ready to follow his command.

Thinking perhaps he'd just gotten lucky; he moved to the Life essence and did indeed find that it wasn't as easy as moving Light essence. However, it wasn't nearly as difficult as Dernal seemed to think it ought to be, as both moved fine. It wasn't until he tried to combine them together into his pathways that he finally met some resistance.

He got the distinct impression that they were separate and that they shouldn't be mixed. So, he instructed them not to mix, but to weave together in a way that allowed them both to fit while remaining distinctly separate. Surprisingly this worked immediately, and he overcame another roadblock. Dernal must have been testing him with his words of caution because this task wasn't beyond him at all.

He focused on the meanings of the technique, light and life and how it worked to heal wounds or set things back to a state of equilibrium. It came much easier than he thought it ought to, yet he wasn't complaining.

Running down his pathways he felt a surge of power and looked up at Dernal. To his surprise, the weathered stout man had cut another line into his arm and held it out to him.

Knox took a deep breath; his left arm charged with powerful essence and he began to chant.

Fael Thunkar Foal Resoria. Fael Thunkar Foal Resoria.

After only two such chants and a warmth in his palm, Dernal's cut in his arm began to seal up. So amazed by the technique or spell, he was still unclear on what he ought to call it, he lost concentration and it faltered.

"So close," Dernal said, grinning ear to ear. "I'd say you definitely have the potential to be a great healer!"

Dernal held out his arm again and Knox restarted the process, almost all the essence in his arm had retreated back to the vortex, having not actually been expended much, if at all. So, taking it one step at a time, he repeated the process until Dernal's arm was fully healed.

"Techniques are hard when you first learn them, but the more you practice, the better you'll become. And remember they are much weaker both because your knowledge of them is weak and your skill at wielding them is weak. Of course, most will use three to five core techniques, which ones you choose is up to you.

Personally, I lean on three or four, but I've learned just shy of a hundred in my long life. Though, I am practiced with only a dozen well enough to do them in the heat of combat," Dernal said, his words almost running over themselves. This was the most excited Knox had ever seen Dernal, so he let him keep talking without interruption.

A part of him wanted to ask that he teach him a combat technique or spell, but the delight on Dernal's face was too much to crush so soon. So instead, he let Dernal run him through the same spell a dozen more times, each time Dernal cut himself and Knox healed it. By the time they finished, Knox could do the spell without even closing his eyes.

He'd learned his first real technique, and it was a healing one.

"Perhaps with how fast he is progressing, might it be prudent for each of us to try and teach him a technique?" Leo asked his question, facing Dernal's critical stare.

The night was still young, or so Leo said, so they hadn't bunked down just yet and Knox got the feeling that Dernal had thought the learning of the healing spell was going to take much longer.

"One technique each. But be wary, boy. A glass filled too fast is prone to break," Dernal said, turning his attention away with a grunt.

Leo looked positively delighted to pass on one of his techniques, his eyes running over Knox as he considered which would be the most useful.

"I feel like you could benefit from this particular attack. It can be used with any element, but the Death element is most effective if you have the aptitude to use it."

Leo went on to teach Knox, similar to how Dernal did, except instead of shooting from his palm, he had him stretch the path-ways to his fingertips, making the one to the index finger far greater than the rest. In the end, he felt like he could use the pads of his fingers just as easily as his palm to expel spells.

Next, he went over the words of power for his Ray of Fire spell, which required a different runic name depending on the element being used. He taught him each and Knox took notes but paid special attention to the runic name for the Death element, as it was the one Knox was meant to try. With all this done, now there was only testing it, so he squared his feet and remembered the simple focusing gestures Leo had taught him to make with his hands.

Focusing on the feelings Leo described and picturing the flows of power required to turn the element into a bar of devasta-tion, Knox built up to doing the technique.

Power welled up inside of him and it came when he called, filling his channels and zipping toward a quick exit. He controlled it enough that when it hit his index finger, it came out as a finger width bar of purple that seemed to warp the air around it.

"Another successful technique learned!" John exclaimed. "My turn!"

This is when things got difficult for Knox, as learning tech-niques meant for weapons was an entirely different bag of bones. John then explained what was required.

"To be successful here, your intent is far more important than anything else. You must see your weapon as an extension of your-self and see it as having pathways of its own. This is made easier when you have a magical weapon, but anything can be a conduit for the power." With that, he pulled out a sharpened stick and swung it through the air. Why he had a stick, or when he had sharpened it, was a mystery to Knox, but he watched in awe as the end lit up a dark black, leaving behind an afterimage in the air.

"I'll be teaching you the most basic striking technique I know. I call it Shadow Strike. Imagine a shadow striking out in the darkest night and flood the weapon with essence, then swing. Like

I said, the hard part comes in seeing your weapon as more than a weapon. It has to reach out from your hand as if it is another part of your body," John went on, enthusiastic about his chance to teach Knox.

"I think I understand," Knox said, pulling his axe out. This part might be hard for most, but Knox had spent years and years thinking of his axe as merely an extension of his own arm. He and Scarlet were one.

He followed John's additional instructions, readying himself for the strike and reinforcing pathways for a flood of essence. It took much longer than learning a few runic words, but after about an hour of reinforcing and meditation, he was ready.

Power flooded his arm, strengthening it, and it zipped up his arm and into his weapon, instantly making the head glow a dark black. He'd chosen the element John had suggested, Darkness, and it left streaks in the air where he slashed.

"Impossible," Caleb muttered, but Knox didn't even care at this point. He was thrilled to have three powerful techniques— well, four if you counted his Haste technique—to use when they took on the next branch of the dungeon.

Dernal glanced over at Caleb but said nothing until he walked over to Knox. "That's enough techniques for one day. Meditate on them, cycle what little essence you can and focus on building up your Core."

Knox looked over at Caleb, curiosity in his gaze. But, Dernal just nodded, and Knox understood: 'no, he wasn't going to learn anything from him today'.

Instead, Knox did as he was instructed, and began to go over each of the new techniques, meditating on them as hard as he could. There was a certain amount of peace that came with focusing on them, as if the more attention he gave them, the more ingrained into his mind they became. Now, he would be ready the next time combat began, that much he was sure of.

CHAPTER 16
PUZZLES

LEO APPROACHED after a time and Knox let his concentration lapse, looking up into his aged, blue face. For a long moment or two, no one spoke, but then Leo sat beside Knox and sighed before finally speaking.

"I don't think you realize the magnitude of what you've accomplished already, so I want to tell you," he said, his voice a low whisper. Not that he was trying to hide his words, but everyone was cycling, so it made sense to keep distractions at a minimum. Knox followed his lead and whispered back.

"It's only three techniques," Knox said, as if to minimize his accomplishments, although in his head he was already planning how he'd learn hundreds of techniques and their many variations, maybe even write a book about them to keep track of them all.

"There is an aspect of yourself that melds to each technique you learn, as you use it more it will become more powerful, however, it is very rare, almost unheard of, that someone has more than two affinities high enough to do what you've done today. In fact, I'd say we ought to not let you get tested for your affinities now, as that will just inform the Guild you are an affinity savant. That could give you much more social pressure than I think you want."

"Is it really so rare to be able to use the different elements?" Knox asked, truly confused at why anyone couldn't do what came so easily to him. *The process is simple,* he thought, *grab hold of the element that you want and push it down your pathways.* The hardest part came with visualizing the effects and remembering the right runes. Of course, he wasn't so naive to think that more complex spells and techniques didn't have increased difficulties, but those would come with time, he was sure.

"Extremely," Leo assured him, eyebrows raised. "You see, we are naturally inclined to an element at birth. Some of us with a strong affinity toward Life can expect to live long lives, while others with an affinity toward Fire or Water find their moods adjusted accordingly. Fire tends to make you more rash and quick to anger, while Water is soothing and calm."

A thought occurred to Knox, and he opened his mouth to ask a question. Leo stopped talking, allowing him to do so. "I've only ever seen you use Fire, but you aren't angry at all. In fact, I'd say you are one of the more relaxed people I've met."

"Thank you," Leo said, inclining his head. "However, I have a high affinity for both Fire and Water, a rare combination among my people. It allows for my natural mood to be in balance, however, not everyone is so ruled by their affinities." His eyes flicked toward Caleb, and he lowered his voice even further. "Caleb is a Water and Life specialist, but his mood has always been foul. He walks the Blood path, strengthening himself internally and uses very few external techniques."

Knox could swear he saw Caleb's head move just a measure toward them when his name was spoken, but he didn't open his eyes.

He took the hint from Leo's gaze to not discuss it any further, so instead, he asked about another thing that had been on his mind regarding affinities. "If I am able to access all the affinities, does that mean I can combine them as well?"

"Eventually," Leo said, putting a gentle hand on his shoulder. "More advanced techniques are difficult to master and often leave you torn apart inside if done improperly. For now, I just want you to know that you have a rare gift, and it will be wise to keep it a secret."

"I understand," Knox said, nodding. If he truly had a gift worth hiding from everyone, a part of him wished Caleb didn't know, but it couldn't be helped. What could he do anyway? Dernal surely had him under his thumb and he wouldn't risk his chance at reaching C Rank over a petty squabble that he started in the first place. "Thank you," Knox added as Leo went to stand, his message delivered.

"You are welcome, young friend. You have an epic path ahead of you and I am glad to have met you at the start of it," Leo said, smiling friendly at Knox.

Morning came swiftly and Knox held the warming stone in his hand, his entire body warmed by the mere touch of it. He dreamt about what amazing items they might encounter on their second day and how cool it would be to use the techniques that he'd learned. All around him, his companions checked their weapons and finished their breakfast.

Dernal had provided the food, part of his duties as the party leader John said, but the dried meat and heavy cracker he'd provided wasn't what Knox would call a delicious breakfast. They were both so dry that he drank nearly an entire waterskin before Caleb yelled at him for hogging it all. But they were well on their way to exploring the second branch through the next doorway.

Caleb complained that they should just go for the last door and end the run, saying the last branch always let off half as much as the entire dungeon, but Dernal rebuked him saying they needed as much essence as possible, not just enough to get him to C Rank. This had shut Caleb up, but Knox couldn't help but cut his eyes in the man's direction. At each chance he got to be a nuisance, the man took it.

Knox let the rock fall to the ground, it wasn't far, and he wasn't terribly worried he'd break it. This time it took a fraction longer for the effects to fade, and he made a note in his book. He'd been testing the length of time using it against how long the effects lingered after letting the stone lose contact with the skin. He found, surprisingly, that the longer one held the stone, the longer its effects would stick around. With his limited tests, only seconds or mere moments of difference, what did that mean about prolonged usage of the warming stone?

Would it be possible to use it for a year and have the effects last weeks afterward? What would the benefits of that even be? Many questions had been listed out in his notebook, but he didn't have the answers yet. More than anything, he was just fascinated at having an item he could study and learn about. What if he got an object that had a certain effect, and he could modify it to last longer without contact due to some runic formations inside the stone?

He listed out several more questions, each one building off the next.

When he was finished, everyone was standing and ready to move to the next door. While Caleb shot him a spiteful glance, Dernal appeared contemplative, hurrying Knox with a grunt.

Knox did so, stuffing his notebook away and checking that his axe and boomstick were in place. Mentally he went over the three techniques he'd learned, ready to activate them at a moment's notice.

"Move out," Dernal commanded, and they moved as a group to the second door. Knox glanced lazily up at the markings above the door, he'd already put each of them to paper and learned that they weren't quite runes, but a language based on them. Though, it was different enough that the markings didn't make much sense. Leo told him last night after he'd made a note of each of them, that legend says they tell you what you will face beyond, but without a translation, it was just anyone's guess.

In formation, Caleb at the head and Knox a step or two back and off to the side of him, they entered the dark doorway. It was like stepping through a cool breeze, and the moment they passed the threshold, a glow in the distance hinted at a room illuminated beyond. Behind them, Leo held up a torch and provided light for the group.

The room they entered at the end of the hundred-pace long hallway, was not filled with monsters. Instead, there was a perfect square with a cylindrical pedestal in the center with a flat top and lines of the strange runic language on it.

"Damn," Caleb spat the word, kicking at the floor in anger.

"What is it?" Knox asked, looking at the blank walls and seeing no door or way forward. "Did something happen?"

"It's a puzzle room," John said, shaking his head as if he, too, wasn't happy about it either. "It'll take all day and there won't be any monsters to kill, but the dungeon still releases a good measure of essence upon completion."

"So, what's the problem?" Knox asked and Dernal answered

after grunting at Caleb to move aside and walking forward to look at the pedestal.

"Puzzles are boring," Dernal said, shrugging in a very, not Dernal way.

"I love puzzles," Leo exclaimed, walking up to Dernal and peering at the pedestal as well. "And it isn't without risk. A dungeon of this level will have a final puzzle room beyond that will likely have a trap to keep us there until we solve it or..." He turned toward the door and sighed. "It will be a single room and we are already trapped."

Knox turned and realized the door, the one that had been only paces behind him, was gone and they were trapped inside of a twenty-five-by-twenty-five pace cube. Staring at the walls, he wondered if they'd start closing in or do something malicious.

"Let's get started," Leo said, pressing his hand against the words on the pedestal. It suddenly flashed white and the walls began to distort until each of the four walls had puzzles of different kinds on them. One particularly simple looking puzzle had tiles that were placed incorrectly.

Knox held out his hand to solve it, as the solution was simple enough, but he looked to Leo first, not wanting to make a mistake that could cost lives by triggering something.

"You can solve it," Leo said, waving a hand. "They get more difficult as we solve more and more, but we will be at this for hours, so might as well help on the ones that you can."

Knox reached out and removed a tile, pushed over another, placed back the one that lifted out and after only a few moments, solved the puzzle. Happy with himself, he grinned at the finished puzzle and began to turn to try his hand at another, but the wall shifted and changed.

The same kind of puzzle as before lay before him, but bigger and more difficult. Several pieces couldn't be moved off the board, only shifted around. But he went to work on this one as well. It took him nearly an hour to work it out, given the sheer size of the puzzle. When the next puzzle appeared, he had to admit it was beyond his capability. There were numbers on this one that had to do with other numbers, some type of mathematics, as well as matching up the larger symbol found on the pedestal.

He worked on it as much as he felt comfortable doing, then Leo took over, having solved an entire wall already. Meanwhile, the rest of the team just cycled, not even trying to solve any of the puzzles.

"Don't mind them, they know I enjoy the challenge, otherwise they'd help," Leo said. He had a wide smile on his face, and he truly did seem like he was enjoying himself.

"I yield to your expertise," Knox said. Then, after thinking about it and not sensing much essence in the room, he added, "Mind if I watch?"

"Not at all, I'll even explain what I'm doing," Leo said excitedly. Caleb groaned at that, but Leo ignored him, as did Knox.

"You see these numbers and the image here..."

And so went the rest of the day, puzzle after puzzle, Leo solved them when given enough time. Until finally, essence filled the room and two doorways appeared—one leading forward and the other back. Leo was surprised by this, having assumed that it might just be a single puzzle room. However, to say he wasn't ecstatic to continue would be a lie.

But first, they needed to cycle all the released essence. They did so, sitting in silence as they worked. Knox enjoyed every minute of cycling, as it felt like taking the deepest breath possible and filling oneself with pure joy. The essence worked slowly to fill his Core. Based on the current rate, he figured he might fill the first ten percent of his Core by the end, provided the essence continued to increase as the branches got harder—which Dernal assured him was the case.

There were two more puzzle rooms, the last one taking the longest. It ended only when Leo realized that the four puzzles had parts that required to be moved to different walls for resolution. It was way beyond Knox's puzzle skills, limited as they were, but he paid attention even when he began to tire. By their reckoning, they'd spent an entire day in the puzzle rooms before the chest finally arrived, allowing them to collect their loot.

Excited to see another silver chest, John explained that they came in various levels, Bronze, Silver, Gold, and beyond. But a dungeon of this level would only go up to Gold, maybe a level beyond, but he didn't say what they were and waved Knox off when he asked.

Leaning over the chest with the rest of the group, Knox saw what the silver chest provided and wished instantly that he'd gotten second pick of items. Though, he was sure they only gave him first pick due to the type of item that dropped, so there was nothing to be done but to feel jealous when Leo picked up the item and claimed it.

Dernal grunted before speaking, as he did most of the time. "Anyone else want to claim it? If not, it goes to Leo for fifty points."

No one said anything and Leo did a little happy dance. While it did not fit the elderly blue-skinned man's appearance, it perfectly matched his typical spirit.

The item in question was a necklace with a reddish orange rock hanging from it, and looked almost like a flame, giving off the impression of intense Fire essence. Knox didn't know what the necklace did, but it seemed like a prize to be desired. Seeing Knox gazing at the item, Leo filled him in on its purpose.

"I've seen one of these before. Diviners call it an Emberheart Pendant. It increases, if only slightly, my affinity toward Fire. That, matched with my Ring of the Deep, means I will be much more balanced than I was before. What a happy day!" Leo exclaimed, practically bouncing from foot to foot.

"Can I see it?" Knox asked. He could feel the powerful essence all around it but when he turned his sense on it, there were small runic formations folded into the metal and on the edges of the pendant.

"Just don't get too attached," Leo said, his voice almost musical as he spoke.

The Emberheart Pendant was a radiant amulet adorned with a gemstone that seemed to contain a flame flickering inside. He felt a draw toward it, but he didn't dare put it on or try to cycle the essence it gave off, as it wasn't his to do so. Instead, he merely studied the runic formations.

Where his warming stone had maybe a hundred total, some so small as to not be seen, this one had three times as many, some even smaller than before. It was a work of art and suddenly, Knox wondered if such a treasure could even be created by humanoid hands or if only the magic of a dungeon was capable of such crafting.

The thought was disconcerting, and he gave back the pendant a moment later. He'd recognized many of the runes, but he'd have to make note of some of the others.

They returned to the campsite, everyone tired and ready for a decent night's sleep. Despite spending most of the day waiting and standing around, everyone, except Knox, was asleep within what felt like minutes. Only Dernal sat awake smoking his pipe, a gentle ember burning at the tip.

Knox had noted that the grizzled man hadn't seemed to need to sleep last night either, so he decided to ask him about it. "Do you not require sleep?" Knox asked.

"I'm C Ranked, my body was reformed when I hit E Rank, my Mind strengthened when I hit D Rank, and my Spirit hardened when I entered C Rank. The combined might of all three changes has several benefits. I only need to sleep one in seven days, and I can survive on crumbs for weeks at a time. Besides that, the fatigue of Mind and Spirit don't weigh so heavily on me," Dernal said all of this barely above a whisper and Knox was surprised to get so much out of him.

His face was clouded with the smoke wafting up from his pipe, but Knox went to sit beside him anyway. "So, something will happen to my mind when I hit D Rank?" Knox asked, latching on to what Dernal had said and wanting to fish more information out of him.

"Hhmmhm," Dernal replied, letting out a mouth full of hazy white smoke. Licking his dry lips he continued, "It won't change you, just make things easier. You remember more, come to the same conclusions as before the change, just much faster, and you get a focus that you can only dream about. I've known some smart fellows who hit D Rank and can study for weeks at a time without stopping. For you, I imagine it might even remove the need for you to take so many notes."

Knox clenched up at that, remembering Dernal had told him not to try experimenting with runes or their meanings just yet. He hadn't really, but he had come up with a few designs that he wanted to test. One of which was a rock that used only half of the runic formations to do the same thing as the warming rock he had. It likely wouldn't work, but it was worth a try. He'd already begun to list out how he'd do it, just lacking a strong enough rock and tools to inscribe the surface or better yet, inside the rock.

He still didn't know how or if that would be possible, but so many of the runic formations he'd seen had been hiding under the material that it must be common enough. A huge part of him couldn't wait to get outside into the dungeon camp with all his new ideas and some coin to spend.

"That would be nice," Knox admitted, realizing he hadn't said anything in a solid four or five seconds.

Dernal put a hand on his shoulder and gave him an intense look. "You'll be tempted to do everything, experience it all and more, I'm sure, but promise me something."

"Anything," Knox said before thinking through what he'd said. Sure, he owed Dernal a great debt, but he wasn't ready to promise anything. However, he didn't backstep. Instead, he listened to see what Dernal would ask of him.

Dernal grunted, this one more of a chuckle than anything, before speaking. "Not sure you should say that, but I won't take advantage of you. I'm here to help. Promise me you will pace yourself and only reach as far as you can and not any further. I'll be here to help you when you fail at my promise, but some damage isn't as easily healed as you might think."

"I can promise that," Knox said. Then, thinking about how he'd phrased that, he looked Dernal in the eyes and said, "I promise to pace myself."

"Good boy," Dernal said, taking his friendly hand off Knox's shoulder and clapping him on the back.

Sleep didn't come very easy after that talk, but he laid in his bedroll all the same. He wanted to learn so much, discover it all, and more than anything else, he wanted to grow stronger. He now knew some of the benefits of reaching D and C Rank, but what lay ahead if he could reach B or A Rank? What about the S Rank that Dernal had mentioned in passing, what did that involve? The idea of being a true immortal scared him, but he didn't know why. Before he drifted off to sleep, he thought about Ramses and the journal, but he didn't want to explain it to anyone, so he kept it safely tucked away in his pack.

CHAPTER 17
BLIGHTED

THE THIRD DOOR was a much more promising start as the first room opened into an indoor forest. Even the ceiling had the look of a sky, though Leo said the illusion was only skin deep. Knox turned his sense on and oddly enough, was able to see through it. A rocky ceiling sat above them about two dozen times their height. The trees, however, seemed real enough. Knox ran his hand on the bark of one, identifying it as a pine tree if his judgment was any good.

The forest around Keenlen's Vale was made up primarily of old pine trees and newer ones that they planted to keep the wood coming in. It was a long process, as the trees took a good thirty years to grow before they were ready, but between fallen trees from storms and the ones that got marked for cutting for one reason or another, they kept a healthy forest around them.

Thus, seeing the dungeon creating an entire miniature forest that seemed to stretch on for miles, shook Knox to the core. Could this magic be learned? What else could the dungeon just create out of seemingly nothing? Was it really out of thin air or was the dungeon connected to something that gave it the raw power to create? Questions battered into his brain, and he looked at Leo to ask a few, but Caleb stepped roughly in front of him, knocking him to the ground.

Though, it seemed to be for good reason, because at that very moment, a rock whizzed by where he'd been standing, bouncing harmlessly off Caleb's shield. Knox's anger disappeared and he looked up to see what they were facing, ready to unleash his techniques.

A line of gnarled and ugly trees, their branches shifting and forming into the semblance of humanoid bodies, faced off against them, each with rocks raised, ready to pelt them from a distance.

"Treants," Leo said, then a moment later he slashed out with his beam of fire, hitting all four of the treant monsters. They cried out in a way that sounded like branches crashing to the forest floor. Their rocks were either dropped or were launched toward the team of five Adventurers.

Dernal stepped forward and began chanting a spell Knox hadn't heard before, his arms held out to the side, palms open.

Aeloria Vyndel Zyrinth Fyrion Aquyl Thunrak!

He got two chants of the new spell off before two rocks the size of his torso slammed right into him, or at least they would have if not for the spherical barrier he'd erected around himself. It was a dull blue, but as he chanted it began to grow more brilliant and brighter.

"Hit them with me," Leo called out, getting Knox's attention.

In the midst of battle, Knox had gotten lost in watching the events unfold, but now was his time to strike! He focused on the spell he'd learned: Ray of Death. Well, it had been Ray of Fire, but since he was using the Death element, he adjusted the name in his mind. Before forming the spell, he suddenly had a doubt cross his mind. He looked at Leo as if to ask, but his companion was mid-casting another spell as more treants appeared through the trees, bringing the total to six now.

Should he use the Fire element because they are trees or is Death universal enough to deal destruction upon them? He didn't know but he had no time to think about it, so he continued to cast Ray of Death.

The spell built up in him as he focused, and he stepped just to the side, next to Leo, and let loose a bar of purple energy into the closest of the treants. At the same time, fire washed down from above on each of them and he didn't get a chance to see what kind of damage his spell did.

Just as the treants fell, fire began to lick the other trees and suddenly, Knox was worried that they'd all die from the smoke and spread of flames. But Leo knew what to do, his hands went wide and his eyes closed shut for only a moment. The flames weakened and went out, leaving the steady glow of the illusory sun above as their only light source once more.

"Well, that sucked," John said, examining one of his daggers. The leather around the edge seemed darkened but intact. He must have thrown his daggers before Leo rained fire down on them.

"Hhmmhh," Dernal said, cracking his neck to the side. "Scout ahead and give us a good idea of their numbers. Treants are a pain in the ass, but they won't be the only foe. Three branches in, we can expect some fae or perhaps goblins in the next rooms. All depends on what the dungeon's cooked up for us."

"We need to close the gap immediately, otherwise I'm next to worthless," Caleb said, as he was pacing back and forth.

Caleb seemed to act like this after fights when he didn't get a chance to participate much. Leo reminded Knox that it had to do with his Blood path and how worked up it got him. Useful information that Caleb likely didn't want Knox to know, so Knox was grateful Leo shared it with him.

Knox averted his eyes, Caleb wasn't to be confronted or acknowledged when he was like this, especially since he was so close to breaking into C Rank. That would make him a bad enemy to have, if Dernal's power and strength were any indication.

John arrived back several minutes later, Caleb still pacing but had stopped muttering to himself.

"Not just treants," he confirmed. "There are a dozen or more Blighted beasts, mostly Dire Wolves, but there were also a few Dire Pumas that nearly caught me with my pants down. Stealthy bastards."

"Blighted?" Knox asked, catching John's eye, but to his surprise Caleb answered.

"Means they're tainted by Dark or Death elements, turning them into pathetic mockeries of what they once were. If this branch is Blighted, then expect a real challenge—not that I'd expect you to know," Caleb remarked with a sneer. He didn't even bother to glance in Knox's direction, instead locking eyes with Dernal.

"Hmm. I have faith in everyone here. We will take it slow and steady," Dernal said, looking over the group, but his eyes lingered on Knox.

Were they worried Knox couldn't keep up? Or that he was a liability? He had a guess or two about who thought which, but he kept his thoughts to himself. Something did occur to him, though; he leaned into Dernal to ask, "Could that be what was affecting the owlbear?"

Dernal looked up at Knox, he'd moved close enough that their height difference was noticeable. "Hhrrmm. Not likely, you will see once we kill a few."

That time came sooner than Knox thought it would, as a dark form blurred from a tree above and suddenly, he found himself on the ground with a several-hundred-pound cat atop him. Before he could so much as scream, the beast was pulled off him, claws cutting a line on his face as it was hurled into a tree. The sudden pain kept Knox from standing immediately, but eventually he had the better sense to get off his ass and onto his feet.

He turned and made it to his knees, looking up as he went the rest of the way up. The cat was dead, a predator Knox had only seen once up close, though something was different about this beast.

Instead of the usual golden-brown and white fur on the puma's body and face, it had dark brown and black covering most of its original markings. In some places, you could see where the color had originally been, but festering open flesh had done its job to scar the creature to near ruin. It was truly a Blighted beast.

"More incoming," John yelled as another appeared from the upper tree branches. The beast eyed them all, its yellow eyes settling on Knox. But this time, he was ready. Already, the head of his axe glowed a gentle white light, and he raised his shield. As the puma jumped, he took a step back and chopped with all his might. Scarlet, his axe, bit deep into the puma's chest and he turned with the blow to allow the Blighted beast to fall anywhere but atop him.

John cheered the successful swing, but his congratulations were cut short when two Dire Wolves, nearly the height of a horse, appeared between the trees. Caleb moved himself into a defensive position and Knox took his place at his right, giving him enough space to strike out and defend if necessary.

Letting his sense flow through the trees, he was sure that these were the last two within a half mile. However, they weren't the kind of Dire Wolves he'd faced off against before. These were towering beasts of muscle and rot. Purple eyes glowed with power as they stared down their group, each one running their eyes over them one by one.

Knox stood his ground with fierce determination in the face of utter demise. He was determined to get plenty of techniques off before they took him down, and his party members weren't sluffs either.

One of the wolves let out a howl, causing Knox's sense to tremble. Several more wolves appeared at the very edge of his sense's range, and he looked at Dernal to warn him.

Dernal caught his eye and grunted. "Let's do this," he said, pulling free his weapon for the first time since they'd arrived inside the dungeon.

The two Dire Wolves rushed in on Caleb, one catching hold of his shield and ripping it free from his grip, but he wasn't standing idly by. He slashed a line into the rightmost one, just as Knox cut into its backend. The strike held the power of his newly learned technique, but even still, it barely scratched the surface of the beast's hide.

Meanwhile, Dernal stabbed into the Dire Wolf to the left just as four more appeared. The newcomers were not nearly as big as the two they currently faced off. John smiled and disappeared, while Leo finished his long chant. Roots appeared out of the ground and grabbed hold of all the wolves. Just when Knox thought Leo had done all he could with that single spell, the roots holding the Dire Wolves in place burst into flames.

Howling from the lesser Dire Wolves filled the air, but the two largest weren't even close to being done. The one on the right turned its attention to Knox just as Caleb got his shield and slammed the left one to the side. With its fur on fire and its mouth dripping black fluid that turned into mist the moment it fell, the Dire Wolf advanced.

Before Knox could finish his Ray of Death, a huge mouth closed around his shield arm, ripping the shield free and yanking him to the ground. Axe still in hand, he chopped outward, forcing the wolf to release and retreat or lose a foot. Or so Knox thought had been the wolf's intent, but instead, it backed up to jump over him. Then, it grabbed Knox's foot and began to pull him away from the group.

"Save yourself," Dernal called, driving his weapon into a wolf. At the same time, he extended his hand, letting loose a heal on Caleb, whose arm was bleeding profusely.

Was this the end for him? Knox couldn't help but ask the question in a moment of panic, as he got pulled away from his group. But no, he had several techniques, though he only needed one. Pointing his finger right toward the face of the Dire Wolf as it pulled him further and further away, he readied his attack. Through the pain, he remembered what Caleb had said about Blighted beasts. It wouldn't do any good hitting a creature of Death and darkness with more Death essence, no, he had to think what would work against it.

At first, he considered weaving together Light and Life, as he had done for the healing spell. However, he realized that might inadvertently heal the damned thing. So, he decided that Light was the element he could rely on to do the most damage. It came on naturally, filling his pathways to bursting. So much so, that when he tried to shoot it just from his finger, as he'd been taught, it erupted from his entire palm and every single finger.

Luckily, despite the many directions the light shot out, a solid thick beam of condensed Light essence struck the Dire Wolf in the head. This time, he saw firsthand the damage the Ray spell could do. Even though he hadn't done it properly or cleanly, his attack bored a hole right through the Dire Wolf's head, killing it instantly.

His ability to use Light essence was insane and he didn't understand why. He got the feeling that even if it had been a normal wolf and he'd used Death essence, he'd have not done so well. Something was special about the Light essence and his connection to it; he just couldn't figure out what.

With much effort and pain, he got the maw of the dead wolf off his leg. Then, using the spell for the first time in actual combat, he healed his leg. It took two tries and he instinctively felt that he couldn't have mustered enough energy to do a third, despite having plenty of essence. There was a certain strain on the spirit that came with using certain techniques, and in that moment, he was glad to be part of a team.

Getting up, he noted that the rest of the wolves had been taken care of. So, he focused on the tiny holes in his leather armored legs. That wolf had cut right through, its teeth more razor sharp than any animal Knox had ever encountered before. But that was the nature of dungeons. Dernal had told him before they'd even left that he'd need to maintain the armor and that it was likely to get damaged after even a single dungeon run.

Knox had been suspicious of the notion, his armor seemed so powerful and sturdy, but he was beginning to realize that it wasn't perfect. Using his sense, he determined that none of the internal runic scripts down by his boot were damaged, which was a good sign. The armor, otherwise, had done its job, keeping him safe from the puma and mostly safe from the Dire Wolf.

The rest of the room was a cakewalk in comparison to the first few pulls. With John's help, they discovered pockets of resistance, as well as ambushes meant to test their abilities to the limit. But in the end, Knox and his team made it to the next room in a single piece.

This branch had five rooms in total, each one a bit worse than the last, with the fifth room containing the boss monster. The team weathered the attacks and Knox enjoyed the immense essence collection they got from so many fallen monsters. They were careful to clear out the entire room before leaving, so there wouldn't be any surprises on the way back.

There was much speculation about what the boss might be.

John figured treant, Caleb wolves, and Leo was sure it would be a puma. So, when they finally made it to the boss room, everyone tired and ready to call it a night, they were surprised by what they found.

A single figure stood atop a pile of animal bones, shrouded in black robes, and wielding a black staff with a skull at one end. The skull's eyes glowed with a haunting purple light. The room looked like a prison, skeletons chained to the wall, some broken chains, some not. There were also several rotting piles of flesh in square cages. On the furthest wall, and barely visible over the several feet high pile of bones, was a table with all manner of tubes and glass cups.

Knox took all this in within a moment, and then Dernal grabbed him by the arm and pulled him back through the door. The rest of the team followed, and purple eyes watched them leave. A cackling laugh followed their retreat, but Dernal kept a tight grip on Knox until they were clear down the hallway and back into the fourth room. Only then did he release him and say a word.

"Hrrmm. Couldn't risk it. We should rest before we take her on, she's a pain in the neck," Dernal said, shaking his head.

For once, Caleb had nothing to add about slowing down, and only nodded his head in agreement. They retreated all the way out, and Knox wondered if the branch would reset, so he asked as much.

"Not during the same dive," Dernal informed him. "This branch is oddly harder than it ought to be, which doesn't bode well for the remaining branches. Still, I want everyone to rest and I want to help you unlock the rest of your pathways. It'll help with the stress you felt using so many techniques so close together."

"I'm ready," Knox said, despite not knowing what awaited him. He was feeling pumped, despite their retreat. The feeling of pushing himself to the brink like that over and over again, it added an odd sense of thrill to the fight. He felt sore and every single muscle hurt, but more than that, his spirit felt worn out. Really, it was the only way he could describe the weight that pushed down on him from every angle.

Dernal took him aside once everyone got settled. Leo, John, and Caleb started playing a game of cards, though Knox didn't recognize the face cards they were using, so he made a note to ask them about it later.

The process of unlocking his pathways was the same as before, Knox just paid special attention to Dernal's instructions on where to connect and what to leave be. Several nodes were in places Knox could have unlocked, but Dernal instructed him to go around them as a certain amount of time should pass before opening a new node. Eventually, he was told by the time he hit C Rank, he should have them all unlocked, which would add to his abilities and power.

The task was slow and arduous, but he did it, unlocking what Dernal called phase one of his plan for Knox's pathways. He instructed him that there were many paths that could be followed, but this one Dernal felt suited him the best. It was a versatile path that would enable strong expelling, enforcing, and more. So, whether he found himself slinging spells, enforcing his own body, or slashing out with striker techniques, he would be in a position to leverage a good amount of power.

Thus, Knox began to feel what it was like to have his entire body truly connected, or at least as connected as it had ever been. Before going to sleep, no one was ready for that yet, he joined a game of cards with John and Leo. Caleb found a reason to excuse himself, shooting Knox a look before retreating to a space several paces away.

"What game are we playing?" Knox asked, not recognizing the setup of the cards.

Leo explained the rules and said that it was called Chronicles. The idea was to collect and arrange your cards to form powerful combinations, and when the cards ran out, the highest points won. The problem was, Knox didn't know any of the common combinations, so the first few games proceeded with him getting steam-rolled while Leo and John fought for first position.

"Let's make this game more interesting," John chimed in after Leo wiped the floor with both of them that round. Knox was just getting to the point where he thought he understood the game, and the idea of raising the stakes intrigued him.

"What did you have in mind?" Knox asked, he wasn't one to seek out gambling, but it did no harm if done to a limited extent. Plus, he only had so much coin to lose at this point.

"Shall we bet dungeon points?" Leo suggested and John made a face, then stole a glance toward Dernal.

"Not sure that's a good idea," John said.

Dernal walked over and John pretended not to notice him. "If you want to play for dungeon points, I will judge the next match. Let's say, everyone puts in five points, winner gets fifteen? Not such bad terms."

Knox was lost at this point, but he wanted to see where it all landed, so he said nothing yet.

"I've so few already," John complained but by the tone of his voice Knox could tell he was bending. "What about the kid, how many points has he earned so far?"

"I'll spot him ten," Dernal said, a wicked grin spreading over his face. "I'll even give him a few pointers, if that is alright with you both?"

Leo and John exchanged looks and it was clear they wanted to say no, but slowly they both nodded.

"What is a dungeon point?" Knox finally asked, seeing as they seemed to have no intention of letting him in on it.

"Oh right," John said, putting his hand on his forehead. "No one told the new kid about Dernal's dungeon points. Here's the short version. Each room that we defeat has a value based on the difficulty, each person is assigned points based on their contribution for each room cleared. For instance, Leo made a good many points clearing out that puzzle room. I bet you got a few as well, seeing as you were the only one to help him."

"Hhmm. He did," Dernal said, interrupting John. "But enough of that now, let's get back to the game. I'll explain points to him as we play."

And so, he did, while giving Knox pointers and helping him figure out the game more thoroughly. Dungeon points were a system used by most dungeon parties, where the dungeon group leader added value to points as John had explained. The harder you worked, the more points you could earn. Which meant Knox was earning very little as he did the least out of all of them.

This alone lit a fire under him to try even harder. He had no reason to fear death, he told himself, for they had a powerful C Ranked Healer. So, as he played, he thought of ways he could push himself further in battle, taking more risks for higher rewards. It wasn't until the game ended that he realized he had the most powerful combinations of cards and had won the game. Surprise and the thrill of gambling filled him, and he immediately asked for another game.

Unfortunately, everyone decided that was the time they all wanted to go to bed, so the game broke up and John took his cards back. Knox really felt like he was getting the hang of the game, each of Dernal's subtle suggestions really opening his eyes to what he could do. He decided he should get his own deck of cards, because he learned dungeon point contributions also reflected how many coins you got in the end. Now, if only he knew why the coins from the dungeons looked like translucent rainbow coins.

CHAPTER 18
HIGH PRIESTESS

PREPARATIONS for the Dark and Death-aligned caster went how Knox expected. Dernal spoke, and everyone listened. He said there would likely be adds—additional mobs that were expected to be summoned in—and the entire team would be on them, with only Leo and occasionally Knox throwing out ranged techniques on the boss to test its barrier. When the barrier went down, everyone would transition to the boss. He'd faced down a similar, if not the same, foe before, so they were confident that the plan would work.

The stone felt more solid underfoot as Knox headed for the door behind his team. This was only the third branch and already he'd been taken to his limits. What awaited them in the fourth, fifth, and sixth branches? Another stray thought tickled his mind, and he did some quick counting. One, two, three. They'd only been in the dungeon for three nights, but they had two weeks. Would the other branches be so difficult as to warrant all the extra time?

There was a particular scent to the forest branch and Knox took it in as they stepped into the first room. The ground beneath his feet went from the hard stone to the soft ground of healthy soil and brush. You wouldn't know by looking at the forest or smelling it that death and darkness roamed these halls. So it was with apprehension that he thought about the final boss and what secrets she might unleash on them.

Before too much time had passed, they reached the final room, and it was the same as before. The cloaked female figure stood on a pile of bones, while dead prisoners remained chained to the walls all around. The same mounds of flesh filled cages sporadically throughout the room. The only difference Knox could see was the purple glowing eyes of the cloaked female weren't on them.

Her robes were black with streaks of purple... showing her elements perhaps? It hung loose beneath her waist but cut tight around her bosom. The front of her dress-like cloak had a slit revealing white-grey flesh, sizable breasts, and a silver chain holding a blood-red pendant that glowed with ominous power. Knox couldn't remember seeing a necklace before, but they'd only been in the room for moments, so it was an easy detail to miss.

"Leo," Dernal said, turning to the tall, blue-skinned man. "Start us off, will you?"

Leo stepped forward with a glint of humor in his eye as he

readied his spell. Words ran over each other as Knox tried and failed to catch the specific runes he used, until finally the chant reached a crescendo. Clouds formed above the dark clad female, black rolling things with red lightning crackling around them. Then, just as the caster looked up to see what had been summoned above her, red lightning that burned with heat that Knox could feel from twenty paces away, struck out.

It crashed harmlessly on a transparent black and purple swirling sphere that formed around the dark caster. Her hood fell back from the blow, revealing an ancient face with grey skin and skeletal features. She began to cackle and laugh, before opening her mouth and speaking.

"You face the High Priestess of the Damned. I see that my minions were no match for you, nor the treants I corrupted to my cause. No matter. My experiments must be allowed to continue. Make ready, fools, for I am your death!" Her voice was like dried out parchment and she cackled the moment she finished, purple light swirling around her hands.

The same light surged, and more lightning struck down at her, but the barrier held. Her spell released and it struck the pile of bones beneath her. Several of the skeletal parts came together to form four bone warriors and two bone archers. It was fascinating really, Knox thought, the bones weren't put together perfectly. Instead, they looked like they were created by a person with a limited idea of how the humanoid shape worked and were thrown together haphazardly.

One of the bone warriors had a shield made of bones held before it and charged, while three others with massive bone clubs flanked both sides. The two archers held up bone bows with no string, but as they drew back, purple strings appeared with black arrows of pulsing energy forming out of the nether.

Red lightning crashed down on the one of the left, while a shadow beside the one of the right deepened and John appeared, daggers crashing into the skeletal creature's spine. Despite his weapons not being what would be traditionally considered effective against a fleshless target, it had a devastating effect.

With the spine severed, the bone archer fell into two pieces, but both kept moving. John quickly smashed the skull of the top half and both pieces went still. Then, just as quickly as he appeared behind them, he slipped into a shadow and appeared beside Knox once more. Just in time for the warriors to arrive.

Caleb caught the shield bearing bone warrior and a loud crack filled the room as its shield buckled under the power of Caleb's own. Knox wasted no time, infusing his strike, he smashed into one of the bone wielding warriors, taking only a glancing blow off his pauldrons. He followed up his strike by spinning, activating another infused strike and smashing his axe into the bone warrior's hip.

It had the desired effect, bringing the bone warrior down, however, he wasn't out of the fight. A sudden pain in the back of Knox's calves sent him tumbling to the ground and he rolled just in time to take another glancing blow to the shoulder. But his body had been reborn when he entered the E Ranks, and he could take more punishment than he'd been able to before. On his knees, he swung down his axe with all his might, blow after blow the head slowly began to cave in. Finally, he ended the bone warrior, but his body ached from several powerful blows from its club.

If only he'd had the concentration to infuse more strikes, but the closer he tried to do them together, the harder the infused strikes became to finish. He pushed the worry out of his mind, getting back to his feet to help his group. The more he could defeat, the more points he could earn. Unfortunately, they'd already finished off the first wave and now the High Priestess was busy casting another spell, her hands swirling, more black than purple this time.

"Now you will face my latest experiments!" the High Priestess called from behind her barrier. A moment later, more red lightning cracked down on it, but still it held.

Knox regarded Leo. He had sweat beginning to show on his brow and his forehead was clenched in concentration. He spoke another word of power and more lightning crashed down on the barrier. It clearly wasn't easy for him, but Knox noticed that finally a small line of cracks was beginning to form around the barrier. It wasn't impenetrable after all; it could be taken down.

Leo must have noticed as well, because his face turned truly iron, and he shouted the runic command this time.

"Pyroclast Thalos!"

Two more runes to add to the notebook, Knox thought as he took stock of the room. The High Priestess's spell finished, and black energy snaked out from all around her, filling six of the cages and obscuring the mounds of flesh within. She cackled some more, but it abruptly cut off when more lightning struck around her, drowning her out as her barrier shattered.

"That's got to be a new record," John remarked, elbowing Knox to get his attention, though he was already watching. "Last time it took twice as long; the easy part is over now."

"The easy part?" Knox asked no one in particular as they all made themselves ready.

Even Dernal had pulled out his daggers and they shone with a gentle white light, similar to Knox's axe when he infused it with an element. Caleb screamed at the room and the air trembled from his fury. Meanwhile, Leo fell to one knee, exhausted. John went to his side and offered him a bottle of something. Leo quickly took it and drank it down.

The cages began to shake violently, and the High Priestess began chanting a spell, purple light encircling her.

"Hhmm. Bad timing," Dernal said, his eyes going to the cages and back to the caster. "Change of plans. Knox and Caleb you handle the adds, John and Leo with me."

With that, Dernal shot forward with impossible speed toward the Priestess, John stepped into a shadow, and Leo stood and began to chant again. Caleb looked over to Knox and sneered, but

Knox wasn't about to disobey Dernal, so he stepped up and followed Caleb's lead.

Caleb led them to an open area, then stopped. "These fuckers have big teeth and if they touch your skin, it'll burn like hell, but it won't kill you, so keep fighting."

"Got it," Knox said, just as the black inside the cages faded and out walked mounds of flesh that vaguely resembled a skinned Dire Wolf, muscles and blood oozing everywhere. The heads were twice as big as even the biggest of the Dire Wolves they'd faced before. One of them made a keening noise, showing an impossibly wide mouth, filled with bone shards for teeth.

They were monsters of the worst kind and by the time the darkness had faded, six of them prowled toward the pair. Knox would have to do his very best if he wanted to make it out of this fight in one piece, but he had all the confidence in the world that he could do it. A part of him wished he wasn't fighting beside Caleb, but that couldn't be helped.

Caleb yelled into the air and all six of them turned their attention to him. He looked over his shoulder at Knox and cursed before saying, "Hit them from afar, now!"

Knox didn't need to be told twice, he held out his finger and focused like he'd never had before, calling Light essence into his pathways, and speaking the words of the spell. Together his channels ran hot, and power flushed through him. He managed to keep it within just his index finger, but upon releasing, it quickly expanded to nearly the thickness of his forearm.

He'd aimed his attack on the one farthest to the left. They'd gathered into a line as they approached with four in front and two trailing behind. As he attacked, he swept it to the right, hitting all four of the front targets. Then, just as the power felt like it was too much, he cut it off and saw what damage he was able to do.

The first fleshy wolf abomination withered on the ground, unable to hold its form any longer. The others were visibly slowed, and a line ran across their bodies, but they hadn't fallen.

Before Knox could congratulate himself, Caleb yelled at him to do it again.

He had bought them a second, maybe two, but he stepped to the right and readied to do the spell again. It didn't come as quickly as the first, and three wolves slammed into Caleb's shield before he'd gathered enough essence for another blast. This one came out much like the Ray of Death, a finger's width beam of energy. However, the Ray of Light still struck with deadly accuracy.

Aiming for the two in the back that were flanking Caleb, his Ray of Light struck the neck of one and punched right through it, striking the next one in the chest a moment later. This had the added bonus of getting both of their attention. Trying to ignore the fatigue of spirit that was beginning to settle over him, Knox charged the weakened masses of flesh, shield at the ready.

The one with the hole in its neck got to him first, opening its maw wide to catch Knox's shield. But he turned just in time, his sense aiding him when his back turned on his opponent. Then, with the momentum he'd gathered from the turn and a quick infusion of his strike, he slammed down his axe on the abomination's head. It cut deep and made a sickening squelching noise when it finally came free, but still, the beast did not fall.

Behind him, another battle raged, purple and black lights whizzing here and there, but Knox could pay no more attention to it than he could Caleb, so fierce were the attacks of the two abominations in front of him. He endured bite after bite on his armor, returning just as powerful blows, until finally the first one fell. His body ached already, and he knew he didn't have many more techniques left in him after the flurry he'd just done.

Suddenly, pain slammed into him as one of the bone teeth made it through a portion of his armor. It spread and threatened to lock up his body, and he then did something out of pure instinct, allowing him to move freely again. He flushed his pathways with essence, and he became stronger and sturdier. Without stopping to think what he'd done, he attacked, his swings coming faster and harder than before.

Within only seconds, he'd downed the final abomination, but he fell to his knees as his essence retreated. He was done, but the fight wasn't over.

"Get on your feet!" Knox hissed the words at himself, and his body obeyed. He rose to his feet and staggered over toward Caleb, who was still fighting two of the meaty wolf shapes. One fell before Knox could get there, but he raised his axe and swung it down with all his remaining strength. It glanced off the monster's back, doing almost no damage. However, it did get the creature's attention, and in that brief moment, it turned away from Caleb, its head then removed from its body with one swift movement.

"Good distraction," Caleb said, tilting his head to Knox.

Knox on the other hand just nodded, while struggling to stay on his feet. He was already feeling better, but whatever he'd done for that instant of strength had taken a great deal out of him, and he wasn't sure he should do it again. Now that his mind was clearing, he was sure it was some kind of body enforcement technique, but without any guidance, he knew he shouldn't try it again.

Caleb rushed off to help against the caster, but before he had taken a dozen steps, with Knox struggling to keep up behind him, bone warriors emerged from the heap of bones surrounding the High Priestess.

Despite this, the fight and its conclusion were set. The bone warriors were easily dispatched and only seconds after Caleb joined the battle against the Priestess, she fell as well. The room filled with her cackling and suddenly her necklace flared, a red, bloody copy of her appearing.

"Next phase," John announced excitedly.

Nearly twenty minutes later and so many minions slain, Knox collapsed, uncaring that he lay on an extremely dirty floor filled with bones and blood. He'd pushed himself further than he ever thought possible, and by his count, had killed a solid seventeen monsters himself. That had to add something to his dungeon points, he mused.

The chest appeared and it was gold this time, which got everyone's attention. It slid out of a space beneath the bones and if he wasn't so exhausted, he might have gotten up to see what it was. However, that was truly out of the question at the moment.

"I'll do a hundred dungeon points for it," John said; his eyes were as big as saucer plates.

"One hundred and ten," Caleb said, glaring at the rogue.

"One hundred and eleven," John countered.

"Who needs it more?" Dernal asked, looking at each of them.

Caleb huffed, but John beamed. "I do," he proclaimed.

"Fine," Caleb practically spat the words and Knox found the strength to stand, if only to see what they'd fought so hard for.

It was a small golden pin in the shape of a boot in the act of running. It couldn't be bigger than a coin or so in size, able to fit comfortably in the palm of a hand. But it radiated power like the pendant Leo had gotten.

"What is it?" Knox asked, clearly, they'd seen one before.

"An Evasion Charm," John said proudly, holding it up for Knox to see. It glimmered in the pale light of the room, but under his sense, he saw the runes at work, as many as had been on the pendant for certain. "It increases my natural agility, making it easier to dodge attacks and strike back swiftly."

Knox could see why Caleb wouldn't mind having it, despite it clearly being a more rogue style item. If he could dodge as much as he blocked, he'd be an even more effective bulwark against the enemy.

They made their way back and out of the branch, having completed it, and Dernal eyed the fourth door before shrugging.

"Hhmm. Take a breath, then we move on."

John pushed a piece of armor aside, and Knox watched as he put the pin on his shirt beneath the armor, where it might be slightly safer. He also noticed that John had another small pin, but didn't catch its design in the brief moment it was shown.

After everyone had settled down, Knox immediately approached Dernal.

"I did something during that fight," Knox began to say, trying to think of how best to phrase what he'd done.

"Hhmm. I saw," Dernal said, his usual grim expression on his face. "That was a body enforcement technique, similar to what Caleb does, but with far too much essence. You got the hang of the most basic kind; just reduce the essence you flood into it, and you'll be fine."

"How much should I reduce it?" Knox asked, ready to try it again, just to make sure he could do it still.

"Do one tenth of what you did before," Caleb said, walking up on the pair of them. "Body enforcement is a subtle touch, not like slamming an axe."

"Hhmm. What he said," Dernal said, thumbing in the direction of Caleb.

"Well, do it," Caleb said, looking annoyed. "Imagine yourself being filled and reinforced. Your mental intent is as important as where you put the essence. I call the technique, Hardy."

Knox did as he was asked, focusing on only putting a trickle of power into his pathways, but spreading it throughout all of them. It took time to carefully fill them instead of rapidly flushing them, but the results felt good. He was stronger, he swung his axe, and it was faster. It was noticeable, but not the overwhelming strength he'd felt before.

"There are techniques that rely on a flood of power like you did, but they are as deadly to the user as their opponent because it leaves your body weak and recovering moments later. So don't be stupid," Caleb said, then turned and left.

Knox let the power wane and his essence returned to his Core, slowly feeding his advancement.

John shot him a grin and Knox returned it. At least Caleb was talking to him now, that was an improvement.

CHAPTER 19
TRAPS

By Knox's count, he now had five techniques that he could call on to aid him in battle—six if you counted his ability to expel toxins.

These were Haste, Ray of Light—his light element being the most potent—Shadow Strike, Heal, and Hardy. Lastly, he had his toxin-expelling technique, which he liked to think of as Rough

Blast. He felt so rounded out now, able to call upon so many different techniques to bring down his enemies.

He was ready as ever when they finished their break and approached the fourth door. Their next hardest challenge and where Knox planned to finally earn some decent dungeon points. Perhaps he'd even get to bid on the treasure, instead of being assigned a weak item.

They took up formation and stepped through into the fourth doorway. The same as before: darkness, followed by a tunnel of light at the end. They reached the light, only to leave Knox looking around, confused. It was another hallway, though slightly bigger than the first, and was wide enough to have all five of them walk shoulder to shoulder. The floor and ceiling were cobblestone bricks loosely fit into place, with some jutting out at odd angles. On the floor, maybe twenty paces into the long hallway, were colored tiles set into the ground.

"Trap room!" John exclaimed. "Stay back everyone and watch the master work."

John stepped forward and Knox extended his special sense as far as it would go. He noticed several concentrations of something in the wall that glowed, not unlike runic formations, but it was blurry and hazed over. He was going to mention it to John, but the roguish figure stood, as still as possible, with his hands out, as if feeling for something. Then, he snapped his finger and dropped to the floor.

A moment later, he'd used his dagger to pry loose a cobblestone and reveal a switch. He pressed it to the side and sighed.

"I disarmed the first trap, but I can sense plenty more. Get comfortable and watch as I earn some dungeon points," John said, sounding a bit smug.

"Could you teach me?" Knox asked, aware that he wasn't likely to earn many dungeon points if he didn't try and get involved.

"He has a decent sense ability," Leo said, an amused grin on his face. John just looked flustered as he looked back from Knox and down the hallway.

Finally, he threw up his hands and let out an exaggerated sigh. "I'll teach you the basics, but I'm doing most of them."

He was just eager to gain more points for himself, Knox mused, coming to kneel beside him.

"Anyone can find and disarm basic traps," John began to explain. "Use that sight of yours to see why I chose this switch and not the two fake ones on the wall." He placed the cobblestone back into place and stepped back.

Knox focused his sense and looked again. The cobblestone beneath him was barely visible, so much so, that he'd passed it up at first. Meanwhile, the other hazy spots seemed obvious in comparison. "Is it because of how obvious the other switches are? They are torches compared to the tiny candle flame of this switch."

"Precisely," John said, raising a finger in triumph and patting Knox's back. "Now, tell me what kind of trap did this switch trigger?"

Knox used his sense again but found nothing. So instead, he used his eyes, scanning all around the space in front of the switch. It took him a solid three minutes before he found it, but on the left and right sides of the wall were tiny little holes where arrows or a projectile could be released from.

"Some kind of projectile, right?" Knox asked, smiling as John nodded that he was, indeed, correct.

"Now I want you to take five steps and start scanning for the next trap. Remember, only five steps. Any further and you'll likely trigger a trap."

Knox took three steps before he stopped mid-step on the fourth. John was shorter than Knox, so his steps would be shorter. Did John take that into account, Knox wondered? Deciding four steps was good enough, Knox halted and opened his senses up. Several locations appeared in his vision, both bright and faint, but no single target differed from its counterpart.

"I can't tell. It's like they are done in pairs this time around," Knox said, frustration bleeding into his voice.

"Ah, precisely the case," John said, stepping forward one more step than Knox. "See these two faint spaces on the wall? They have to be disarmed at the same time. Still simple switches, I'd wager."

Sure enough, when he got the stone pushed off the wall, inside were two simple switches that could be moved from one side to another. As one, he switched them, and Knox felt a pressure he hadn't noticed before release.

"Did you feel that?" John asked, his eyes scanning the hallway. "That pressure that released? There was a magical trap somewhere and if we can find it..." His voice trailed off as he began to examine the wall looking for whatever indicated a magical trap.

Knox tried to look as well, using his sense and his eyes, but still, it was John that spotted it first. One of the rocks had markings on it, but if you weren't looking, you'd think it was just the way the shadows fell on it. When John pushed the tile aside, he found a red gem. Carefully, he pulled it free from a mechanism with springs and an odd little glass container with some type of liquid inside.

"This is worth more than its weight in gold to the right person," John said, holding it up for everyone to see. Knox got the distinct impression of Fire aura from it and Leo leaned in close to examine it.

"Basic Fire Essence Gem," Leo said, then shrugging, he added, "Worth maybe two or three Runemarks at most."

"What's a Runemark?" Knox asked, immediately looking toward Leo, then to John, for an explanation. There was so much about the world of being an Adventurer that he didn't know, and he didn't want to forget to ask later.

"Currency that Adventurers use," Leo said, pulling free a translucent coin with a faint blue reflection within as it moved across the light of the hallway. He handed it to Knox, and it felt cold to the touch, a very odd coldness. "Dungeons drop only a single type of currency: Runemarks. They can be used for crafting, as they are pure crystalized essence. One Runemark is worth roughly six gold pieces the last time I checked."

"Seven now," Dernal said.

Knox looked at the coin with a new respect. He could earn a gold piece if he worked for several weeks at both his jobs, but the idea of getting a single coin worth seven times that was mind blowing for him. With the handfuls he saw in just the first chest, he'd be able to set himself up for years in a decent place in the city. With the coins from an entire run, he could buy the mayor's mansion in Keenlen's Vale.

He really looked this time and noticed a runic script on the surface, but it was the odd kind that he'd found over the door, so it meant nothing to him. Turning the coin over, he saw the likeness of a man he recognized from his dreams. Without thinking, he dropped the coin and took a step back.

"What? What's happened?" Leo asked, reaching down to retrieve his coin, and looking at Knox with a furrowed brow.

"Nothing," Knox said, shaking his head. But he couldn't shake the image of the Titan from his mind. His dream had suddenly become so clear, and he remembered everything, including the man who called himself Mah'kus.

Dernal was beside him, hand on his arm before he knew what had happened. He looked him in the eyes and up and down before speaking. "Are you sure you're okay?" he asked, his eyes reflecting concern.

"Do you know who that is?" Knox said, pointing at the coin.

"The man depicted on the coin? Plenty of people have given him names, different cultures and such, but no one knows for sure," Leo said, sounding almost academic in his speech.

"I do," Knox said, shifting uncomfortably under everyone's gaze. Dream or not, he had known the name of this Titan and in part his role in the creation of the world. "Gowlen." Knox tried his best to pronounce it as closely as possible to the name he heard in his dream. "He created this entire world, like a pocket of air just

TIMOTHY MCGOWEN

outside the vast sky of another." His head was beginning to hurt as his dream flashed through his mind.

"Sit and cycle," Dernal commanded, the weight of his hand bringing Knox down within moments. "You're becoming unstable inside; you need to keep your concentration up."

Sure enough, when Knox began to cycle, following the techniques pressed into his brain, he found his vortex had begun to lose stability. He vaguely heard the others speak while he cycled but he was too far into his meditation and concentration to hear a word. An unknown period of time passed before Knox opened his eyes, finding only Dernal sitting beside him and the rest of the party well down the hallway.

"Why do you think that you know the name of that being on the coin?" Dernal asked, his voice as gentle as a warm breeze.

Knox sighed and wished he'd kept his mouth shut. Dreams of the future were said to be something only very powerful Adventurers could do—not normal folk. Though, the dream he'd had wasn't necessarily of the future, he'd had it before becoming an Adventurer, so nothing was quite fitting together. He decided the best thing to do was to try and make the others think he was just having a silly dream.

"I had a dream where I thought I saw his face, maybe I saw one of those coins before and dreamt about it. Yeah, I'm positive that is what happened," Knox said, rubbing at the back of his neck in irritation.

"Dreams can be a window into fate for those with the gifts for it," Dernal said, his voice still gentle as ever. "If you truly saw this Gowlen, then perhaps you have a greater destiny than even I imagined. But if I can give you a word of advice."

"Of course."

"Dreams and knowing things you ought not to, will get you asked questions that you won't want to answer or worse, get you put into a position under the royal family in which you will be no more than a slave to their will. Not a thing I'd like to see repeat-

218

ed," Dernal muttered the last part to himself, but Knox fixed onto it.

"Repeated? Have you been forced to work for the royal family?" Knox asked, his eyes going as wide as saucers. He knew nothing about nobles or the royal family, only that all of them were Adventurers. That bit had made them intriguing to him, but gossip was all that filtered out so far and he couldn't even say who ruled what, besides the king over it all, King Wilham.

"What? No, forget I said that," Dernal said, standing and giving Knox a hand up. "Let's catch up, just remember to keep your thoughts to yourself, alright?"

"Alright," Knox said, giving Dernal an appreciative smile before following just behind him.

The rest of the fourth branch continued at a slow pace, taking a total of three days to completely clear. And in the end, Caleb got a new shield out of the ordeal since he was the only one that could really use it—Knox's own shield being outside the fighting style he'd hoped to adopt. Caleb's new item was a tower shield, longer than the one he had before, but with gems set into it that he hoped would inflict some damage to the enemy, but until he had someone who specialized in identifying items he didn't know for sure.

After a day of recovery, they set out to take care of the fifth branch, which turned out to be a giant maze. There were traps to disarm and monsters to kill, including a giant minotaur—basically a muscular humanoid body with a bull's head and temperament—and even a few puzzles to solve. Considering it was the fifth branch, it felt surprisingly easy all the way up to the final boss in the middle, a giant cyclops that crushed walls with every swing of its club.

It was because of this giant club swinging, that Caleb learned what his shield did. When a blow was coming down atop him and he didn't get the shield up in time, the gems flared to life and a barrier appeared, taking the blow and blocking a solid five-foot sphere area of any damage. Leo remarked that he'd need to fill the gems back up after several uses, but Caleb looked happy for the first time since Knox met him.

It took another few days to clear the maze and Dernal got a bracelet from the chest that would increase his connection to Life essence. All Knox could tell was that it gave off a heavy Life aura that he could almost feel without his sense on. So, with five days left they approached the final branch of the dungeon, ready for anything.

CHAPTER 20
THEMED BRANCH

THE LAST BRANCH had put them into a routine of challenging a room and then resting. If they kept up the same pace then by the time they ran out of time, they'd have completed the dungeon. There was only one problem with that, according to Dernal the final branch might be a bit different.

"I don't get it," Knox said. "What do you mean by themed branch, like the forest from earlier?"

John cleared his throat. "Not at all really. Think of it like a pocket world where there might be a narrative or an entire story the dungeon wants to play out in real time. So instead of rooms and monsters to kill, we'd have an entire world to work with."

His explanation didn't help as much as John likely thought it did, but Knox nodded finally getting a vague idea of what he meant. They were standing outside the entrance to the sixth branch and it didn't look like anything special, same dark entrance with words no one could read over the doorway. So as they had five times before they entered the hallway, torch in Leo's hands.

That is when the world around Knox began to spin and twist. It felt like someone grabbed firmly hold of his gut and began to twist it into knots. The feeling cut off and suddenly all around them was white light and flashes of color. Then the gentle roar of conversation filled his ears and his eyes adjusted to the dim light of a fireplace lighting up a room some twenty paces wide and a bit longer.

They found themselves suddenly and quite unexpectedly inside a tavern that Knox could swear looked vaguely familiar. Though the more he took it in, the more it appeared to be just an average tavern hall filled with patrons of various races. Surprisingly he even noted a few ratmen, though they didn't attack or act monstrous, instead just ate from plates of cheese and cups of wine.

"Hmm. That twisted my insides out for a bit there. Can't ever get used to that," Dernal said, taking a deep pull in the mug of ale before him.

Knox took his cue from him and also took a drink of his ale. It was frothy and had hints of a sweetness laced into it, overall satisfying. Meanwhile, John dug into a bowl of steaming stew and, based on his reactions, enjoyed every spoon full of it. Knox noted that he had his own bowl of stew and also dug in. His taste buds thanked him as the most delicious stew he'd ever put into his mouth filled his stomach.

Maybe it was the fact that he'd been on rations for nearly two weeks or maybe the dungeon just really knew how to make the best stew, but either way Knox couldn't remember a time he'd tasted better. Even Caleb started eating the stew, which mildly surprised Knox.

Once they'd all eaten and drank their fill, Dernal was back to business. "This is a new one for me, let's split up and talk to as many people as possible. These themed branches are also a bit on the nose about the quest they want you to follow, so at the first mention of a dragon to slay or a town to save, latch on and get as much information as you can."

A round of head nods followed and Knox joined in. He didn't like the idea of splitting the party, but what could go wrong inside a small tavern like this?

Knox stood from where he was and scanned the room with his sense. Several of the people inside had enchanted armor or weapons, but he decided that talking to the man behind the bar was the best place to start. Moving over there before anyone else could, Knox put up a hand to order another drink, "I'll take another drink."

"Right away, stranger." Came a low and pleasant voice from the rotund man behind the counter. He had a bushy mustache and friendly eyes, though his hands spoke of someone accustomed to hard labor—thick calluses and thin white scars ran up his forearms.

When he came back around after tending to another patron, Knox caught his eye and took the drink. "As you said, my group and I are strangers in this... land. Perhaps you've heard of some work that needs doing?"

The barkeep squinted his eyes at Knox and smiled. "Name's Bardsley, but you can call me Bard. If you are hearty lads, there is always work to be had. Just yesterday the foreman over the lumber yard told me they were in need of fresh blood for felling trees and cutting lumber. You've any experience in that kind of work?"

Knox inclined his head and suddenly wondered if these dungeons were self-aware or had this person just gotten lucky with his guess. Before Knox got too suspicious, the man inclined his head toward Knox's axe and Knox understood.

"Ah I see," Knox said, feeling a bit red in the face for assuming such a ridiculous thing. "We are Adventurers, looking for an opportunity to earn gold or renown. Any dragons nearby that need slaying?" He felt silly for asking for a dragon to kill, especially with how rare they were in the real world, near extinct if rumors were to be believed, but it was the example Dernal had given.

"Dragons? No dragons here," Bard said; then, looking around the room he leaned forward as if to say something, but suddenly a new patron entered, and the entire tavern became eerily quiet.

Bard stood and very purposely shut his mouth. Knox turned to see who had entered that was causing such a reaction. A tall dark-haired man with a short, trimmed beard and dark eyes stood just inside the tavern, a smug smile on his face. He wore armor, a silver polished plate that covered most of his body. A sword half his height sat at his waist, and he radiated power.

"My usual," he said, his head inclining toward Bard. The barkeep moved with swift resolve, pouring a drink, and walking it out to the still unmoving man.

Knox turned to see where the rest of his team had gone, Caleb and John were back at the table, talking with a light-haired man who had suddenly gone white in the face as if he were about to pass out.

"Now Gary," the man said, walking up to the light-haired man sitting beside Caleb and John. "Can you tell me why you've decided to sit at my favorite table? You know this is reserved, tell your friends to piss off and you," he pointed at Gary, "go get me some of Bard's famous stew for me."

Gary stood immediately and said two words that Knox barely heard. "Yes, sheriff."

John stood as well, looking amused at the plate-wearing sheriff, but Caleb remained sitting, his face a mask of barely contained fury. Knox suddenly wondered if the man was always a step away from losing it or if he could switch it on and off as he wished.

"Excuse us for intruding, but perhaps you can be of assistance," John said, his voice carrying throughout the room. "We are but humble Adventurers, seeking... well, adventure. Perhaps you know of something or someone in need of killing, helping, or maybe local legends of treasure nearby?"

At first Knox was sure that the sheriff was going to draw his weapon, his hand went there immediately when John began speaking, but slowly he relaxed his grip and a smile spread over his face. The room was still, and the only sound was that of Gary's footsteps as he returned with a bowl of stew. He sat it on the table and the sheriff sat where Gary had been sitting before. He shot a look at Caleb, but the burly man just glared right on back.

"I don't know," the sheriff said, his finger tapping at his chin as he appeared to be pondering over something. Then, as if struck by inspiration, he raised a finger and said, "Let me think it over while I eat. The name is Sheriff Paul Montgomery. What do you call your band of merry men?"

Caleb scoffed at that, but John was quick with a response. "Oh, we don't have a name per se, just five individuals traveling together to take on challenges and earn a living. My name is John, the surly fellow here is Caleb, the young-faced boy there is Knox, the man to your left is Dernal—he leads us—and lastly Leo is the blue-skinned fellow standing in the corner. See, all friendly here."

"Indeed," Sheriff Paul said, taking his first bite of stew. He seemed to be having the same reaction as Knox had, because he made a show of truly enjoying it.

Knox looked to his left, noticing the barkeep, Bard, shaking his head at him, but in a way that seemed suspicious. Knox opened his mouth to ask him what he meant, but he held a finger up to his lips. It was such a quick motion that Knox nearly missed it, but he took the hint. The barkeep wanted to say something and couldn't in front of the present company.

Before Knox could think of a way to get the barkeep alone to talk with him, the conversation at the table resumed and he turned his attention back to them.

"You know a little problem I've been dealing with lately could use the strong hand of an Adventurer or two. We've been having the worst trouble lately with a group of bandits in the eastern forest. If you were to root them out and collect the belongings they've stolen from the town, I'd reward you kindly and with a sizable amount of wealth. Of course, I'll need proof of their death, a collection of ears ought to be sufficient proof of death, unless you have a way to transport two dozen heads? No? Well then for each ear you bring me I can give you ten gold and if you bring me the head of their leader, I'll reward you with a great treasure beyond your imagining."

Caleb was suddenly interested in the conversation, nodding along, so was John, and from a distance even Dernal was paying sharp attention.

"Two dozen bandits and a powerful leader no doubt," John said, repeating back to the sheriff what he'd heard. "I would think fifteen a head would be more suitable, wouldn't you?"

He was haggling with the dungeon for additional gold? This was beyond interesting to Knox and with this fresh interest, he forgot about the barkeep and his attempt at communication.

Would they really be able to get more rewards from the dungeon? Was that how the themed parts worked, were they so mutable as to be shifted about by a mere conversation.

It appeared so as the sheriff began to nod his head, then said, "That is doable. We have a deal then. Venture into the eastern forest and find the bandits' hideout. Slay them and return with proof that their leader has been taken down. Kill and return, simple as that."

Dernal stepped forward with his hand extended. "You have

yourself a deal," he said, grasping the sheriff's hand as he extended it as well.

Just like that they found themselves on a quest to rid the forest of bandits. Knox joined his group as they headed for the door that the sheriff had entered through, still not remembering that the barkeep had wanted to say something to him.

The sun was low in the sky, early evening by the looks of it. The tavern was set atop a small rise and below was all manner of buildings in a town much the size of Keenlen's Vale by first glance. A small waterway worked its way through the town, a larger stream but not big enough to be called anything else. All around the edge of the town were trees, so picking out the eastern location, they headed in that direction.

"We trusting that asshole's word?" John asked when they'd moved a considerable distance from the tavern.

"Why not, it's just a dungeon puppet," Caleb said, shaking his head at John.

"We have a quest to complete," Dernal said, matter-of-factly.

The barkeep's actions filtered back to the front of Knox's mind, and he looked back. Too far to go back now, but worth mentioning perhaps. "The barkeep tried to tell me something but wouldn't in front of that sheriff," Knox said. "Maybe there is more to the quest than meets the eye?"

"Dungeons can be tricky, but themed branches are rarely more than they seem," Leo said, patting Knox on the back, then added, "But we can keep an eye out for suspicious activity. Who knows. There might be a greater reward to be had."

The forest was dark under the canopy of so many trees, but Leo lit a torch and they roamed into the unknown. At first, they found no signs of life in the forest or the forest floor, but the more they searched and the deeper they went the more noticeable certain markings on the trees were. A slash here or two slashes there.

"Some kind of code?" Knox suggested, running his hand over the most recent find.

"Not sure what it means, but if we continue this way, I'd wager we find more with two slashes. Some kind of directional guide perhaps?" John said. Why he assumed they'd find more of the two slashes Knox didn't know. Had he seen some sort of pattern that Knox hadn't?

"Hhmm. Let's keep going East," Dernal commanded. "Dungeon can't be too big. We're bound to run into something."

They continued east and sure enough more and more trees were marked with two slashes instead of one. Finally, they found a massive tree with three slashes on it and while they examined the tree, voices called out from above.

"You have trespassed in the people's forest," one voice said.

"Leave your goods and treasures behind and your life will be spared," another voice spoke out.

"Do not test our patience," yet another voice said.

There were at least three, Knox thought, but as he did, the light of Leo's torch swelled and the light reflected off of dozens of eyes above, as well as the glint of steel from the tips of arrows. This wasn't an ideal situation, but Knox wasn't worried until Dernal looked worried. So far Dernal's face was the picture of calm.

That is when Knox decided to reach out with his own sense and what he discovered made him grin. There were only three people up in that tree. Whatever else was being reflected back must be some kind of illusion. Right as he decided he needed to tell Dernal about it, he noticed the grim man smiling and looking at him. He nodded his head and Knox knew that whatever sense detection Dernal had from being a C Ranked Adventurer, must have allowed him to pierce the illusion as well.

"Why don't the three of you come down and we can discuss your surrender?" Dernal shouted the words and the entire team, save for Knox, acted.

Caleb threw his shield up, catching an arrow, Leo began to chant, and John tossed a dagger up into the tree before fading away into shadow. Dernal meanwhile put a hand on Knox's shoulder and spun him around. An arrow slammed harmlessly on the shield he'd been keeping on his back.

Knox blinked at the sudden exchange but wasn't going to be left out of the next volley of attacks. Pulling the shield free, but leaving his axe away, he prepared to cast his Ray of Light into the tree. A body fell atop his shield and stopped his cast midway through. Knox was thrown backward from the force, but he rolled with it, leaving his shield to lay on the ground and pulling free his axe with practiced ease.

However, his opponent didn't get up, groaning and holding his gut some three paces away. Knox raised his axe to deliver the killing blow but stopped when Dernal stepped forward and put a boot upside the man's head, knocking him out cold.

"We surrender," came a call from above, followed by weapons being thrown down, a bow and a staff. "We just wanted to help Big Don and the Hood clan."

"Come down, nice and quiet, if you have information we can use, then I'll heal your friend," Dernal said, despite the fact that Knox had seen a flicker of white light go off from his hand and the knife fall free from the man's gut. He'd healed him already, though Knox didn't know why as they had to collect their ears and that wasn't going to be fun for anyone if they were still alive.

Despite it all Knox had a moment of pause as he considered what he'd been about to do, kill a man. But wasn't it a man, the dungeon created it after all? What if it were a man and this situation were happening in the real world, would he still stay his blade? He wasn't about to be killed by bandits just because he was a tad reluctant about killing other people.

No, he decided, he had no qualms with killing people if there was a need behind it. These bandits were dungeon spawn, so it hardly mattered, but if someone attacked him he wouldn't hesitate to take a life. His life over that of another was a clear bet any day. He didn't know if he liked how that made him look to himself, but he pushed it aside and decided to examine it further when not in the midst of an enemy's surrender.

The man who'd been stabbed in the gut didn't look like any bandit that Knox had ever come across. He was well dressed and had a leather chestplate, though it hadn't done him very much good in blocking weapon attacks. The two climbing down from the tree wore similar brown outfits, almost like they belonged to the same organization of well-dressed but badly armored music troupe.

Dernal started the questioning immediately, his presence seemed to loom over them and suddenly there was a weight in the air that Knox didn't understand. It made breathing a bit harder and he had to really focus on keeping his cycling vortex together as an outside force threatened to push it apart. He pushed out his sense and immediately retracted it.

Dernal was blazing like the sun in his sense, harsh and unyielding. Caleb and Leo seemed unaffected, but John cringed back similarly to Knox. Was this what the full power and weight of a C Ranked Adventurer felt like? Then just as fast as it came the pressure lessened and Knox could focus enough to hear the two bandits' response to whatever Dernal had asked them.

"The marks are meant to lead you here," the bandit with the big nose and lanky form said. His companion gave him a hard look, but he kept spilling the beans. "We are part of the Hood clan, we help to steal back the unfair taxes the sheriff forces on the people in the surrounding towns, then we give it back whenever we have a chance. Please believe us, we aren't the enemy." He was practically sobbing at this point and Knox felt an uncomfortable itch in his brain.

Could this be what the barkeep wanted to tell them, but he failed to give him the chance to? Would it be worth seeing if there was another way to finish the dungeon branch or did they just need to kill this Hood guy and be done with it? Knox was suddenly glad he wasn't the one calling the shots, because he didn't know what he'd do.

Dernal did, however, his dagger flashed, and he knocked out

the larger of the two, leaving only the skinny one that spilled all the news.

"Take us to this Big Don and the Hood, we just want to hear the entire story before we decide what to do next. Your sheriff seems to think you are bandits out to kill and pillage the countryside."

"Yes, that Sheriff Montogomery would say that; he's a vile evil man who wants nothing but the suffering of all those around him," the man was practically squealing at this point and Dernal held up a hand to silence him.

"Show me the way," he commanded, and the man nodded violently, pointing to the south.

And just like that they'd found a guide to reach their quest's destination. But whether or not they'd take the easy path and kill all of them once they arrived or learn more about the potential corruption of the sheriff, Knox did not know.

CHAPTER 21
BIG DON

THE TRIP WAS SHORTER than Knox would have expected. Within half an hour, they met with some scouts demanding to know why they were encroaching on their territory. Dernal spoke up, saying that they only wanted to speak with Big Don and as easy as that, the group was let through. Of course, the hostage was taken and ran ahead, likely to spill the entire tale to the leader, but Dernal seemed fine and therefore, so did Knox.

The treetops were filled with little huts and contraptions to lift people up into the higher branches. The entire area was a tree fort builder's dream, not that Knox had ever been into that fascination. No, he'd been much better at bringing down trees instead of building on them. Now that he saw so many trees, some of which looked half dead, he wondered how well he could cut one down with his enhanced E Ranked body.

Dernal shot him a look and Knox thought there was a message there, but what he meant was lost on him. Perhaps it was 'be ready' or 'wait until I say to attack' or even 'be careful' but Knox had no way of knowing. They really ought to have talked about this more on the way over.

The rest of the group stiffened and seemed to prepare themselves at a glance from Dernal, so Knox laid a hand on his axe and mentally prepared himself to use one of the techniques he'd learned.

Ahead, a crowd had formed, much more than the two dozen that the sheriff had promised. Yet, there were women and children among the group, so Knox wasn't immediately worried. He did note that several of the women were armed, so they were very outnumbered.

"Greetings," Dernal said, his attempt at sounding cheery came up a bit dry, but a large man with rather tight leggings and leather chest armor, bowed dramatically in their direction.

"Greetings to you, fine sirs," the man said. "I am Big Don; how may I assist you this fine day?"

"We've been set upon you by the order of Sheriff Montgomery, however, we've been told there is more to your story, Don, than the killing and looting you've been doing," Dernal said, his words coming out confidently and powerfully.

"I can assure you there is more to the story," Big Don said, then looking to his right he took a cue from a smaller blonde-haired man, who nodded. "First of all, there has been no killing that we are aware of. Even the sheriff's men have been only wounded, if severely in some cases. We, the Hood, pledge our goals are fair and forthright. We take from the rich and untaxed to give to those who've been taxed beyond what is right. Of course, some coin stays to feed the hungry mouths you see around me, but who can fault me for that."

Dernal seemed to consider his words, his hand coming up to stroke his bearded face. After sweeping the crowd once more, he turned to the group.

"Thoughts?" Dernal asked.

"We have a quest, let's finish it," Caleb said, not even lowering his voice. Suddenly, several bows went taut, but neither Dernal nor Caleb flinched.

"Might be that we have a choice," John said, looking at the crowd before them with a hungry glint in his eyes. "Should we see what they'll offer for us to get rid of the sheriff?"

"This seems less straightforward than I'd have expected," Leo said, his dark eyes focused on Dernal. "I'd like to hear them out more."

Dernal looked at Knox, the only member who had yet to say a word. What did he want to do? It was clear they were being given a choice. Despite what had been said about these themed dungeons being straightforward, this was clearly not. There was a part of Knox that wanted to follow the clear chain of law enforcement by this sheriff character, but was it right?

"I'd be willing to hear more from them. Who knows, maybe they have a better treasure than the sheriff? Or we could just go wild and kill everyone? It is just a dungeon after all," Knox said, adding the last bit as a joke more than anything, but Caleb nodded his head and pointed at him.

"I could get behind that," Caleb said; Knox felt a knot grow in his stomach hearing Caleb agree with him.

"We will hear them out," Dernal said, then turning back to

the group he waved. "Convince us not to kill you all and report back to the sheriff. If you have treasure, offer it to us and we might be convinced to rid you of this oppressive sheriff."

Big Don's head shot to the side and the smaller blonde-haired man held a hand up, stepping forward.

"I'm afraid I've deceived you," he said, his voice elegant and smooth. "I am the true leader of this group known as the Hood. You may call me Sparrow, for that is the name I've taken upon myself when I took the role of protector of these people."

"Tell me, Sparrow, why shouldn't we kill you and collect the reward?" Dernal asked.

Sparrow laughed, then an oppressive voice clamped down on Knox, not dissimilar to Dernal's own aura. This man must be C Rank as well.

Another force joined Sparrow's as Dernal unveiled himself. The pressure of both nearly brought Knox to his knees, but he remained standing through pure grit. The majority of the onlookers weren't so lucky, several of the kids fainted and men and women alike hit the ground, going to a knee.

"You are outmatched," Dernal called out, his aura and Sparrow's released a moment later.

"So it would seem," Sparrow said; then, tilting his head to the side, his medium length hair fell over his eyes. "Lower your weapons and dine with us. Hear our stories and be convinced of our true intentions. It is as Big Don said, we only steal from those who deserve it and have thus far been able to refrain from killing anyone."

"Alright, lower your weapons but stay on guard," Dernal said over his shoulder. Knox put his axe back, only then realizing he'd picked the weapon up while the two C Ranked Adventurers let their auras flare.

The people recovered quickly and turned into a flurry of movement. Tables, chairs, dinner plates and cups were moved to the forest floor. It was as if they'd robbed a banquet, and suddenly, Knox and his team were the invited guests. He watched in awe as they moved, swift as ever, setting up an entire eating space within minutes.

Then came the food.

Everything from cooked birds to fancy desserts. They lined the entire table and soon Big Don waved them over to sit at the head of the table beside him and Sparrow.

The night wore on with limited conversation and many wary glances at the newcomers. Dernal sat closest to the pair, and they exchanged whispered conversations that Knox could only make out a word or two of. Because of this, Knox was entirely unprepared for the turn of events. Sparrow stood suddenly, nodding to Dernal and then pulled out a thin sword. He brandished it toward Dernal, who took out his dagger and turned to his group.

"Stay out of this, just some friendly sport. We've a new quest, kill the sheriff and his lackeys," Dernal announced.

Caleb grumbled, but otherwise the team seemed fine with this turn of events. Besides all that, it looked like he'd get a chance to see Dernal cut loose against another strong opponent, which was fun.

They walked a ways away, people coming to form a wide circle around them. Dernal looked slightly bored, but Sparrow's demeanor had changed from relaxed and harmless, to sharp and deadly. He looked as serious as death as he did a few practice swings of his sword.

"To first blood?" Sparrow asked, but Dernal shook his head.

"To surrender," Dernal said, flipping his dagger in his hand.

Sparrow nodded and lunged forward a moment later, though his action didn't catch Dernal off guard. His dagger came up and turned aside the thin blade as if the strike were sent out from a child. However, Sparrow was fast and only a second later he was back, striking with a speed that made his movements hard to follow. This time Dernal turned aside his blade, but a thin line of red appeared on his cheek.

"First blood is mine," Sparrow announced, his more flamboyant speech returning.

Dernal took that exact time to strike, flashing forward with equal speed he slashed the man across the thigh before his eyes could return from the crowd.

"Pay attention," Dernal warned, stepping back and hopping from foot to foot.

He may just be a healer, but Dernal had the body, mind, and spirit of a C Ranked Adventurer, and it showed. Back and forth they wove, leaving small shallow cuts all over any exposed flesh. Only when Dernal was forced to use some of his open palm light magic, did Sparrow finally show off a technique of his own.

Standing before Dernal, Sparrow rolled his neck. The tip of his blade began to glow with a blue light. Then, suddenly, his blade was copied by a dozen more, all poised to strike out. Dernal's eyes widened in surprise, and he began to chant just as the blades struck out.

Two made it through, one piercing his shoulder and the other slashing another line across his face. The rest, however, along with the actual sword Sparrow held, slammed against a barrier of Light and Life fueled magic. But Dernal wasn't done, he threw himself forward, the barrier shattering. Light exploded from all around him and some of the shards of the barrier slashed out, wounding Sparrow in the process.

Dernal closed the gap, his dagger flashing and the tip stopping inches from Sparrow's throat. Meanwhile, Sparrow had his sword ready to take Dernal in the gut.

"Shall we call it a draw then," Sparrow said, and Dernal laughed.

"Hhmm," was all he said in response, pulling back his dagger and helping Sparrow up from where he'd fallen. Then, chanting all the while, he healed Sparrow, then himself.

"Was that necessary?" Leo asked when Dernal walked back to the group.

"It was part of the deal," Dernal said, shrugging. "He says he knows a way into the storage house where the sheriff keeps his greatest treasures. If we play this right, we will get more than a single chest's worth of loot. I hope at least."

The tables had been cleared out during the fight, leaving no trace that they'd ever been there in the first place. This entire situation was odd to Knox, but he kept his concerns to himself. Instead, he focused on the upcoming plan, which Dernal had just begun explaining to them.

"Sparrow isn't okay with killing, but I doubt the dungeon will let us finish this sequence without spilling some blood. So, we are going to sneak into the sheriff's home and kill him. He has guards, so it won't be easy. Then, we bring Sparrow the sheriff's keys and he'll lead us to the hidden location. Easy as that."

There were many things that could go wrong with such a simple plan. The more obvious being they had no idea how many guards they'd face or how strong this sheriff might be. But Knox left that for the party leader to worry about, as he was going to kill whatever he was ordered to and grow as strong as he could. When cycling, he felt that he was close to making some sort of breakthrough, but he just needed more essence to reach it.

Already the vortex around his Core brimmed with potential essence, but it was so slow. What he wanted, or needed, was another one of those pills filled with Pure essence that Dernal had given him to help him break into E Rank. Not that he thought he was close to D Rank, more like, he'd reached a barrier within E Rank that required a concentrated effort or understanding to get through.

He knew he ought to worry about this later, but the walk back to the village was slow and they'd decided to make camp, attacking in the dead of night. So, they set up a fire and Knox worked on cycling until his burning question couldn't wait any longer.

He knew he ought to rely on Dernal's word, but he really

wanted to talk to Leo, who seemed the most knowledgeable about essence so far.

"Leo," Knox said, moving to sit on a log with the blue-skinned man. His eyes were closed, and he was likely focusing on cycling, but he opened them and returned Knox's words with a friendly smile.

"Yes, Knox," he said, giving him his full attention.

"I was wondering if I could ask you a question about my Core?" Knox asked.

"Go ahead," Leo prompted.

"I feel like I've filled my Core with enough essence now, but I'm hitting a wall of some kind. Like, soon I might have a break-through, but I don't know what that means," Knox explained.

Leo nodded sagely. "Within each Rank there are small hills you must crest; they are referred to as Tiers. You are likely reaching your first or second Tier. It is time for you to reflect on the nature of your power and the techniques you've learned, for as you grow stronger, so will they. With each Tier you pass, you solidify what you will be when you reach the next Rank. It is hard to explain, but the more you focus on what you want out of the power, the better that power will form. This is the nature of being an Adventurer and part of the process in which we advance. Does that make sense?"

Did it make sense? What did Knox want from the techniques and power he was gaining? Did he mean perhaps what role he wanted to fill within a party or as a solo Adventurer? That was something he hadn't spent a lot of thought on, so he nodded to Leo and decided to do just that.

"Thank you, Leo. It would seem I have much to think about," Knox said, leaving the man to continue cycling in peace.

He knew by experience that there were three primary roles for someone in a dungeon and that is what he wanted to focus on first. He had a shield, though he hadn't used it as frequently or wisely as he ought to. Would he walk the path of a protector, someone that enforced their body and pulled the attention of all the other monsters? He had a rudimentary understanding and use of a body enforcing technique, but he wasn't sure that was the path for him to follow.

Then there was the path of a healer. Dernal's role seemed almost boring at times, waiting for damage to be inflicted. Despite his attitude, Caleb was very good at what he did. In a less over-powered group, Knox could see himself straining his very limits to heal and restore people fast enough for the fight to continue. Hell, when he thought about it like that, it seemed exciting, but he just hadn't seen that excitement from Dernal, so it gave him pause.

Then there was the job of those dealing the most damage. John and Leo had two very different roles in a fight, yet they filled the same slot. One from range and the other from the shadows. Knox knew immediately that fighting from the shadows wasn't going to fit what he wanted to do, but maybe attacking from a distance?

But no, he liked the thrill of being right up in the melee, slashing out and using his axe. He also enjoyed the use of his ranged technique, so it left him puzzled but a measure closer to understanding where he stood in the group.

Could he be a hybrid between Leo and John? Someone with decent gap closing techniques as well as powerful melee strikes. Was there a name for such a role or did it matter? It didn't, he decided, forming a picture in his head of himself in the future. He'd focus on perfecting his fighting style so that he could be deadly in any melee, but also study up on techniques that could be used to close the gap.

No fight would be out of his purview with his hybrid meth-ods. Archers and swordsmen alike will quake and fear his coming. Armored to the teeth and wielding powerful axes, Knox saw himself not as he was, but as he would be. Magical knowledge mixed with martial skill. He pictured himself pitted against a powerful unknown enemy, adorned with magical armor summoned to protect him and bolstered by powerful runes enhancing his strikes.

It was while he visualized this and cycling that he felt a wall come down in his mind. Power flared through him, and he felt himself grow just a measure stronger. It wasn't a huge breakthrough, but it was enough to put a smile on his face. Power would be his and no opponent would be safe against him.

CHAPTER 22
SHERIFF

THE SHERIFF'S home was more like a compound than anything else. Stone walls and iron gates barred the way, but they weren't so well guarded to stop five Adventurers from scaling them and dropping down to the other side. Patrols moved here and there, despite the late hour, but they were lax and with John's help, they made it to an inner gate before anyone so much as saw their shadows.

It was when they approached the inner gate, that a figure appeared out of the darkness alongside two others, weapons already drawn.

"You are trespassing. Surrender or die," a gruff male voice said, his saber swishing through the air.

However, despite his words, he didn't call out an alarm, leaving the odds at five against three. Two of the three rushed forward with weapons ready, but the one in the back fled, likely to sound the alarm.

What the two expected from the fight, as unbalanced as it was, seemed unclear. However, the moment one of them got within range, Knox understood a little better. The first unleashed a line of black shadow from the tip of his blade while the other launched an arc of energy that crackled in the air. Both of these men were powerful Adventurers, with techniques to boost their chances of survival.

Though, they did not realize their opponents were just as powerful. Caleb caught their attacks on his shield without flinching and Leo launched a technique back in response. Calling on the technique he'd learned from John, Knox slashed out at the nearest man. The blow took him in the chest and cut apart his armor, the leather not able to withstand a reinforced strike.

John disappeared into a shadow and reappeared next to the fleeing man, a dagger sliding cleanly into the back of his neck as he fled. He didn't so much as utter a single word before he fell to the ground, his attempt at raising the alarm failing.

However, their battle hadn't been quiet, the exchange of techniques making enough sound that a nearby group was alerted, and a call of alarm went out.

The final man of the first group went down from an attack by Caleb, just as two new groups merged in their direction. The fights were simple and easy, though each of these men fought with the strength of ordinary men. Knox marveled at the difference in strength when he tested himself directly against a muscled opponent.

He was sure the burly man would take him right off his feet, but to his surprise, Knox's shoulder push took the other man off his instead. Then down came his axe, ending the dungeon created man's life. The thrill of battle filled him as he wove through opponent to opponent, testing his strength and dexterity. Only occasionally was his rhythm thrown off by an opponent that was clearly an Adventurer. In those moments, he stepped back, accepting aid from his team, locked in the heat of battle as they were.

Dozens fell that night as the battle waged on and any hope of sneaking into the compound was lost. It wasn't until a retreat was called on the enemy side, did they begin to move forward toward the house again, stepping to the side of so many fallen dead. The air reeked of blood, piss, and shit, but Knox ignored it, instead stretching his sense toward the building.

He could make out another dozen men just behind the door and four more men somewhere above and deeper into the compound. Knox turned to Dernal and informed him as much, but Dernal seemed to already know, only grunting an affirmative.

Several moons appeared between the dark clouds, their bright light illuminating the night. Knox's party continued forward, ready for battle. The towering manor stood before them; its silhouette prominent against the late-night sky. After easily passing through the inner gate due to the guard forces' retreat, they now faced the structure's defenses. Several wards were etched into its wooden surface. For a moment, Knox was worried about what they might do. However, Leo lifted a finger at them, and fire lanced out, destroying them one by one.

When he finished, he signaled to Dernal the 'all clear' and they continued forward. Knox on the other hand, set each of the runes into his memory and was determined to ask Leo what they did later. This dungeon had been such an eye-opening experience and now Knox found himself completely immersed in the narrative that the dungeon had created. Wicked sheriffs and noble thieves.

The four forms Knox had sensed deeper in the manor were moving closer to the front, and Knox looked up to a balcony on the second floor just as they appeared.

It was the sheriff and three others. He wore sinister black armor, and his aura gave off the impression of Death so thick that it made Knox take a step back. Yet, no one else in his party seemed affected. A woman to the sheriff's direct left wore purple flowing robes and wielded a staff that emanated a powerful sense of Fire essence mixed with something else. The staff crackled a yellow light with small barbs of lightning appearing every few seconds.

To the right were two figures in black armor similar to the sheriff's, but not as powerful. They wore helmets that covered all features, but their gaze was set firmly ahead as if staring at nothing and their hands were on the hilts of their swords, each had matching blades on their hips.

"Have you gotten lost?" Sheriff Montgomery asked, his tone mocking. He seemed amused by the turn of events and not at all as fearful as he ought to be.

Dernal turned to John and grunted. John stepped forward to speak for the group.

"It is with great displeasure that we must inform you that we've had a recent change of employment. It is now *your* ears and head that must be collected. Unless you can speak to the crimes you've been accused of? Murder, theft, and excessive taxes?"

Knox thought it was odd that John highlighted 'excessive taxes' in his little speech, but then thinking about the times he'd had to pay his own taxes, he quickly understood. Excessive taxes were exactly the kind of crime that deserved a potential death sentence. Damn bureaucrats milking people dry of their hard-earned coin just so that they can enjoy a small percent of increased revenue.

Knox recalled, not so fondly, a few years back when a war of some kind was being waged and taxes had increased to help pay for it. Of course, Keenlen's Vale was so far away that by the time they collected the damned taxes and they'd reached their destination, the war had concluded. But did the coin get returned? Of course not!

With renewed heat burning in his chest, Knox looked up at the cruel sheriff, wondering when the battle would resume.

The sheriff cleared his throat and finally responded. "I am no stranger to the pressure of taxes; I too must give my fair share. But you are strangers in this land, and I am the law. Disperse now and you can keep your lives but push further into my home and I will have your heads."

Despite his offer for retreat, Knox felt power building in the woman to his left and Knox's team reacted immediately. Knox pulled off his own shield, and raised it in a similar fashion to Caleb, ready to ward off the spell. Meanwhile, Leo began to chant as John disappeared into the shadows.

Dernal grunted and stepped forward, his own chanting beginning to form a barrier around the group. Whatever was coming must have been a powerful spell because the caster beside the sheriff continued to chant and power built all around her.

"Go help John," Caleb said, gesturing ahead where John had appeared by the door and seemed to be working on getting it open. Knox nodded his head and slipped forward, sticking to the shadows as best he could. Of course, he couldn't go invisible like John, but the night was dark, with each of the elemental moons only providing minimal light.

He reached John just as something clicked, and the door swung open. Perhaps the sheriff ought to have barred the door instead of just locking it, but it was too late for them now. John and Knox took on the group of twelve beyond the door with the confidence of seasoned warriors pitted against weak amateurs. These were not Adventurers of any Rank, so despite John and Knox being the lowest Rank of their group, they cut through the men with surprising speed.

One such man, moving as clumsily and slow as a child, swung

his sword for Knox's neck, but he easily ducked the attack. Knox countered with a swing of his own, bringing his axe into the man's chest with a bloody squelch. Then, turning, he caught another attack with his axe just as two figures appeared on a grand staircase just ahead.

It was the two black armored figures that had stood beside the sheriff, and with the final of the twelve slain below, Knox was able to get a good sense of their power. They were likely E Ranked Adventurers the same as John and Knox.

John turned to Knox and then looked over his shoulder outside. An intense exchange of lights and power slammed all around Dernal, Caleb, and Leo. They'd be no help for now, but Knox was confident in their ability to deal with the threat within.

"We've got this," Knox told John. Nodding, John promptly disappeared from sight, stepping into a shadow.

One of the figures let out a scratchy laugh before speaking. "Hah. You are alone now. Time to die, little fly."

With speed that was a match for Knox's, if not a bit faster than he could manage, they descended the staircase in a run.

Knox held out his shield in front of him. Then, with great difficulty, he raised it so that his finger had a clear shot at his targets. Unleashing the technique he'd learned from Leo, Ray of Light, he struck the one on the left, staggering him but not piercing his armor. It slowed him enough that Knox only had to deal with one at a time, at least in the first moments.

He caught a sword blow on his shield and bashed out with it, hoping that the effect would trigger, causing his opponent to have bleed damage. He felt the familiar surge when it did, and he smiled. The follow up strike of his axe was turned aside by the first fighter's blade, and Knox braced himself for the strike of the second, but it never came.

Instead, John appeared behind the man and cut deep into a gap in his armor by his arm. His right arm went limp, and his sword fell from his grip, however, he held out his left arm and it zipped into it, carried by an unseen force. The air around him began to stir and cuts appeared in several places on John's face and arms.

The attack wasn't lethal, but somehow the swordsman was able to lash out and cut without bringing down his sword at all, and that was worrisome.

But Knox had to turn his attention back to his own opponent as he slashed at his shield. He caught the blow, but it hit with such force that the shield let off a sudden cracking noise. The wooden form of his shield was damaged and several of the runic formations had been disrupted. Until he could get it fixed, his shield had just become far too normal for his liking.

His opponent took this opportunity to slam against his shield again with force equal to the first blow. His shield fell apart around him, and he was thrown backward from the blow, taking some of the attack against his armor. Luckily for him, his armor was built to weather such attacks and he barely felt it.

Rolling the moment he hit the ground, Knox was back on his feet within moments, though his opponent was already on him. Knox barely managed to slam aside one attack of the sword and he had to throw himself back to avoid another. Despite this fighter having the same speed as him, he was clearly a more skilled swordsman. Knox, on the other hand, had, until recently, cut down trees for a living.

This wasn't a fight he was going to win, and he knew it the moment his opponent's blade cut a line into his face. He had moved back just in time, narrowly avoiding a potentially fatal strike, yet couldn't fully escape the blade's graze. However, Knox hadn't played all his cards just yet. He still had the full body enforcement technique he'd recently figured out. The only challenge now was how to use it to make him fast enough to strike back, but not so fast as to blow through his energy reserves.

Taking two steps back he activated the technique, being as careful as he could, given he only had moments to think about it. Power thrummed through him and suddenly it appeared as if his opponent slowed ever so slightly. Knox cut forward with his axe, aiming to take the fighter's head off. But despite his slower reaction, a sword appeared, blocking the blow.

Knox didn't let up, strike after strike he rained blows down on the fighter. His opponent took steps backward, barely keeping Knox's attacks at bay. When finally, it looked as if Knox had the upper hand, he felt his energy faltering. He'd held on to the technique for too long.

It puttered out and a parry from his opponent nearly lost him his weapon, though he held fast and struck out one final time. His blow cut into the flesh of his opponent's leg just as his blade came down clumsily on his pauldrons. His opponent screamed out in pain just as a dagger cut across his throat, silencing his outcry and blood filled his lungs.

"Thanks for that," Knox said, seeing John appear from around the fallen fighter. "I had it but thank you." Knox added with a grin.

"You were doing fine, but Dernal and the team are coming so I wanted to hurry things along," John said, a smirk of his own appearing on his face.

Sure enough, Dernal, Caleb, and Leo came jogging into the room, Leo limping but everyone else looking fresh faced and ready to fight.

"Only the sheriff remains," Dernal said, looking to the staircase where they'd likely find the final boss of the dungeon. "Let's kill him and be done with this dungeon."

Knox and the others ascended the stairs leading up to the sheriff, each of them seeming ready to strike out against the dungeon's creation and eager to win the prize set forth. Knox was unsure if they'd be a match for the sheriff, but he knew they had to try.

They cleared the balcony, then proceeded to search each room until they stumbled upon a grand ballroom. There, below them on the main floor, stood their target. The sheriff's sword was drawn, shield at the ready, and a fiery determination evident in his eyes. Knox felt a knot in his stomach, realizing this would not be an easy fight.

Leo remained on the balcony, while Knox and the rest of the team descended to confront their opponent. The staircase was easy enough to find, and the sheriff waited patiently below, seeming indifferent to their preparations and how long they took.

Soon, they found themselves surrounding the evil tax collector, and the fight was on.

The sheriff struck out first, his movements a blur to Knox's eyes as several strands of black and purple, essence of Death and Darkness, shot out from him like many arms. Caleb caught several on his shield, Dernal turned some aside with his dagger, and John simply disappeared. Meanwhile, Knox was on the defensive immediately, his energy low and his axe strikes just fast enough to turn away any attack that might hit his flesh.

Though his opponent outclassed him, he was not alone, and that gave him hope. John appeared, striking for the neck, only to be battered away by a shield. Caleb charged forward next, the two clashing, shield against shield. But to Knox's surprise, Caleb was thrown backward. With Caleb being on the cusp of hitting C Rank and for him to be knocked back so easily, this had to mean that the sheriff must already be at C Rank.

That left only a single fighter in their group who could match his strength and power: Dernal. This must have occurred to Dernal at the same time because he shot forward, daggers raised to strike. But Dernal was primarily a healer, not an expert of the martial styles of fighting. The sheriff caught his attack and put a knee into Dernal's leg with such force that he was thrown to the side.

As Dernal went flying, he opened a palm and struck the sheriff with a technique that blasted him to the side as well. While he might not be the sheriff's match in martial techniques, he clearly surpassed him in spiritual techniques. Knox watched the exchange in awe, moving to attack the downed figure the moment he hit the ground.

John and Caleb had the same idea and before the sheriff could stand, they unleashed technique after technique on him. Dust and dirt billowed up around him as the ballroom floor gave way to the soil beneath it.

"Stand clear," Leo called from above and they did so.

A beam of fire and water, swirling around each other and filled to the brim with potent energy, slammed into the space where the sheriff had fallen. A scream erupted from the space as the D Ranked attack did its job.

When the dust cleared, the sheriff appeared on his feet and quickly moved toward them. He smashed into Knox first, his blade slamming into a small space where Knox's armor met his waist, then threw him to the side like a rag doll. Knox felt his blood pour freely, and he could tell he was suddenly on death's door. The pain became a secondary thing as he watched in horror and one by one his teammates were cut down.

John took a strike to the neck that would have taken the head from any lesser man. Caleb took a blow to the shield so powerful that his arm hung limp at his side afterward. Meanwhile, Leo took a slash to the chest from a casual swipe of the sheriff's blade, energy lancing off it in a well-formed technique.

As the world around Knox began to fade, Dernal appeared over him. Dernal's words were lost on him, but a familiar chant filled the air.

Fael Thunkar Foal Resoria.

Moments later, Knox felt the blood return to him and with it a new strength. He rose to his feet to stand beside Dernal, however, Dernal had already moved on to tend to the others. The sheriff's gaze landed on Dernal's healing efforts, but then refocused on Knox, charging toward him in a blur. Knox reacted swiftly, activating his own technique in defense.

His entire body vibrated with power as he overtaxed his full body enforcement. Suddenly, the sheriff moved to a crawl and Knox became aware that he had mere moments to act before he would be rendered useless.

His feet hit the ground and the air screamed around him as he raised his axe for a strike. The sheriff's eyes barely moved fast enough to track him, but his movements were much more sluggish. Slashing with all his might for the space behind the knee, Knox hoped his sacrifice would give them the upper hand.

Pain erupted all around him and he realized that the sheriff had somehow moved his sword in a way that Knox's path crossed it, a path that couldn't be altered with the time he had left. Holding on to the pain in order to stay alert, Knox smashed his axe into the back of the sheriff's leg and heard a satisfying crunch follow the attack.

The world spun back into normal speed a moment later and several things happened at once. Blood from the sheriff's wound and Knox's own sprayed out in a display of crimson. Then two more strikes fell home on Knox's armor, neither of them getting past his chest plate. Lastly, Dernal appeared before the wounded sheriff, dagger cutting deep into his throat.

Knox's sense of the room suddenly became one person less as the light inside of the sheriff cut out and he fell dead at their feet.

"That was risky," Dernal said, before chanting more healing to put Knox back together again. "But worth it. Good job on completing your first dungeon."

Knox smiled. They'd done it and now, like all good Adventurers, they needed to find the loot.

CHAPTER 23
THE LOOT

WITH THE AREA cleared of the sheriff's men, Big Don led a group to meet with the townsfolk, while Sparrow led their group to a treasure cache where they found not one, but five golden chests.

"Whoa," John said, running his hand over the first one, however, it did not open as they had before.

"Looks like the dungeon approved of our way of solving its little challenge," Dernal said, and even he couldn't keep a smile off his lips.

"But five?" Caleb asked. "That must mean diminished rewards."

"It won't open," John complained, now trying to pick at the chest with his dagger. It didn't budge or unlock.

Sparrow looked on amusingly but said nothing. Finally, John went to the next chest, he was supposed to be checking for traps but if he'd found any sign of them, he'd kept that to himself. When he touched the second chest the lid popped open as easy as can be and light poured out from within as it had before on other chests.

"I have a feeling the dungeon has given each of us an item. Go ahead everyone, touch a chest and see which reacts to you," Dernal said, stepping forward to touch the first one himself. It snapped open the moment he touched it.

Knox watched as the rest found the ones that opened for them, one by one, streams of light appearing from within. Finally, he walked up to the very last chest and placed his hand atop it. The lid shot open, and he peered inside.

Inside was a simple silver amulet, round and set with a polished clear gemstone. Upon closer inspection, the gemstone seemed to shimmer with a faint light, almost magical. When pressed by his sense, he saw that runes encircled the amulet, but they were far more straightforward than any piece he'd gotten so far. Though he couldn't decipher the amulet's effects, he guessed it would help him greatly in his pursuit of learning runes.

"An amulet of protection, a decent one at that," Leo said, looking over at the item Knox held.

Meanwhile, Caleb held up an ornate sword with intricately engraved runic formations on the surface. Upon closer inspection with his sense, Knox saw that there were many inner runes as well; a much more complex item than what Knox had gotten.

Stepping back and away, Knox admired the gifts the others

had been given by the dungeon. John held up a single night black dagger.

"It's an obsidian dagger," John said, when he saw Knox looking. "It takes Darkness essence in by the handfuls. And when reinforced, can strike through even the most warded armor. The sneak attacks I'll be able to do with this is mind boggling."

Knox then looked to Dernal to see what he'd gotten. Dernal stood, holding up a simple pendant featuring a four-pointed star as well as an odd symbol in the middle. It looked like a flame but with lines coming off it at every angle.

"Healer's Embrace," Dernal said, putting the pendant around his neck and tucking it under his armor. "Pretty common healing item for Life and Light healers. It enhances my healing spells."

"Fantastic," Knox said, his sense running over the pendant and seeing it was as simple as his own amulet. He would have to note down as many of those as he could during his downtime.

Next, he leaned around Dernal to get a good look at what Leo got. He held an object the size of his fist, in the shape of a many pointed star. It looked awkward to hold onto, but Leo held it, nevertheless.

"It's a casting crystal," Leo announced, lifting it so Knox could get a better look. Upon closer inspection by his sense, he recoiled. It was as bright as the sun but had no visible runic formations.

Seeing Knox's reaction, Leo smiled. "It is an arcane focus of sorts, so it might be difficult to look at with a spiritual eye. It takes in essence of any kind and magnifies it during the release. Basically, it empowers my spells as I cast them, but it can only do so a limited number of times a day. Not sure how powerful this one is, but I'd be surprised if it could handle more than once or twice a day."

"Fascinating," Knox said, reaching out to touch it.

Leo allowed it, handing it over. The edges weren't as sharp as they looked but it was still awkward to hold. He felt it as much as he could without the full attention of his sense, before handing it back. He'd need one of his own someday so he could study it. An object that naturally functioned without the need of a runic formation was indeed interesting.

After collecting their loot, they were presented with several bags of coins from Sparrow, who insisted they take it. Upon inspection, it was revealed to be the same translucent coin as they'd collected before. This amount alone doubled their pull of coin. Dernal grumbled about the Adventurer's Guild taxing them too much, which Knox found ironic considering the themed branch they'd just defeated.

After Sparrow gave them the coins along with a wisecrack or two, the world around them shifted into light and darkness until they stood just inside the doorway of the final branch. Inside the small room, they all sat and began to cycle the essence. It was so condensed and powerful in the room that Knox had to really focus to start pulling the Pure essence in first.

He'd learned so much during his first dungeon and he reflected on that as he cycled the essence into his Core. Just this last branch was providing enough essence that he felt himself approaching the next leg of his Tier advancement. He wished it was clearer which Tier or leg he'd reached or how to reach the next one, besides just collecting more essence.

The more he meditated on the meaning of essence and how it filled his Core, the more he felt like he could feel himself slowly growing stronger. He knew that the next Tier would require an understanding of this power and so he pondered on it for hours. It took much of their remaining time to finally finish cycling all the available essence, and none of them wanted to leave early. So, patiently and quietly, they kept on cycling.

At some point, the energy around Caleb shifted and began to glow a dull green. He'd broken into the C Rank! Knox expected him to announce it to the group or say something, but he just blinked and looked around like he was seeing everyone for the first time.

"He's unlocked his spiritual sight," Dernal whispered from where he cycled beside Knox.

Nodding knowingly, Knox wondered what his own spiritual sight might be like, seeing as he could already sense magic to a point. But he was a fair bit away from hitting D Rank, let alone even considering C Rank.

In fact, Knox did a touch of mental math. It would take seventeen more dungeon runs just like this one before he'd reach D Rank and who knew how many more before C Rank.

"How many times can we do the dungeon before the season ends?" Knox asked, interrupting his cycling and that of Dernal.

"Depends on the crowd, but we ought to get another two runs before we need to leave. We could get six or seven if we stayed year around, but I've got a standing appointment in the capital during the Fall and Winter seasons. Those runs will net double what we can get here, and they are a fair bit safer if you know what you're doing. Don't worry, we can get you to D Rank within a year or two, and C Rank before you turn fifty," Dernal said, as if his words would pacify Knox.

But something wasn't adding up. "Does E Ranked progression slow or does it stay consistent?"

Dernal looked at him confused for a moment and then his eyes glazed over. He must be looking at him with his spiritual eyes because they went wide, and he leaned in to whisper.

"You've already reached Tier 2, nearly 3? How is that possible?" Dernal asked, clearly shocked by this turn of events.

"I'm just doing what I've learned: cycle and draw in essence," Knox said, defensively.

"You have advanced much quicker than expected," Dernal said. "At this rate, you could hit D Rank within the year. If we had priority dungeon access, you could make it within a month or two. But be careful. Part of why it takes so long to reach the Tiers, is that your progress requires a certain knowledge about oneself that isn't easy to unlock for most."

Knox listened intently when something occurred to him

about his physical growth and suddenly, more Pure essence poured into his Core. He'd reached Tier 3. The not so profound knowledge he'd focused on was his inability to match every opponent through raw strength.

He'd been thinking about how his growth wouldn't be the end all be all for his advancement, realizing he'd need to learn so much more. His thoughts then switched over to his own ability to face foes. He understood the need to be able to match opponents through different methods, recognizing that physical strength and physical techniques wouldn't be enough. This had triggered a train of thought that led to accepting that he couldn't beat everyone.

His body reacted to the new Tier and Dernal, once more, went bug-eyed while watching him. His spirit surged, his mind sharpened, and his body hardened. He'd grown even stronger just like that. And along with that strength came a certain amount of freshness, though he was still very fatigued from the battle.

"How do your channels feel?" Dernal asked, his eyes sharp and his focus fully on Knox.

Knox ran his sense through his channels and shrugged. "They are just as sturdy and strong as ever," he said to Dernal. Dernal responded only with a 'hmm' and let the matter drop, returning to his cycling.

When the final bits of essence were absorbed, Dernal stood and announced, "We're leaving."

And just like that, Knox had finished his first dungeon.

Making their way back to camp, they collected their stuff and ventured to an obelisk not far from where they'd arrived. Placing their hands on it, the entire world swirled for a moment and then they were in a small fenced-in area. However, no one was there to greet them, only the cries of battle could be heard all around.

"Shit," Dernal said, his eyes closing for the briefest of moments as he focused. "We are under attack by a horde of monsters. Get ready to fight; we aren't yet done for the day."

Exhausted and worn out from the final branch, the entire

group readied themselves. They'd barely made it out of the small clearing when a cheer went up, and Knox looked about, confused.

"The day is won!" someone cheered from a dozen paces away.

Others took up the cheer, and Dernal shot away to find out more information. Smoke rose all around the camp and outside of it. Whatever had attacked had breached the walls, and several bodies, both human and monster, lay on the ground.

"Seems we missed quite a fight," John said, leaning down to check on the still form of a man next to what appeared to be a wolf, but uglier. John saw where Knox was looking and elbowed him. "Ever seen a Worg before? Ugly little bastards but as strong as a bear and as vicious as a wet cat."

"A Worg?" Knox asked, he had never heard of such a monster, but the longer he looked at it, the less wolf-like it appeared. If anything, it looked like a cross between a rat, a cat, and a wolf. Perhaps, Knox thought, he ought to start keeping a journal of the unique monsters he encountered. Or, at the very least, see about finding a list of commonly known monsters from another source.

There were several other types of monsters, each one John identified for him, though he recognized some of them.

A giant spider, a giant snake, a displacer beast, lizard folk, goblins, drakes, and lastly, a wyvern the size of a large horse. Dernal approached from a ways away, his demeanor grave.

"A horde of monsters and monster races is traveling through the area. They are saying only about half slammed against the encampment. Search parties are getting put together and they are saying it'll be an even split on the Cores collected if you pledge to help. I told them we need a day to recover, but it looks like we will only get that on the road. You all up for a Core hunt?"

A round of nods later and they were checking their packs, finding more food supplies, and being led to pay their dungeon tax.

"Present the items you earned that they may be identified and assessed for value," A nasally skinny man instructed them, his robes a vibrant blue and gold. He gave off the presence of a C Ranked Adventurer—which is to say, no aura at all.

Knox went last, watching as each of their items were identified and given a value. When it finally got to his turn, he was surprised at the low value each of his items were given. The first being called an "Everwarming Stone" and the other a "Protection Amulet Plus One". One was valued at three Runemarks and the other four. Which on its own with the gold equivalent would be enough to make Knox a rich fellow for a few months, maybe even a year.

Another fact locked in place when the value was given: Dernal had given Knox the deal of a lifetime when he'd sold him this armor. Sure, it had cost him several years of savings, but based on the common items and their values, it was worth ten times as much, if not a bit more.

Then came the tax on his items and gold, he only had to give up twenty Runemarks, but his haul was a massive forty-three Runemarks after all taxes were paid. According to John, this was enough to repair armor, buy a new piece or two, and live out the rest of the year in luxury while waiting for more dungeon spots to open up. John had only been with this group for a year and a month, but he was nearer to D Rank than he was away from it, or so he said.

When Knox looked at his aura, he was surprised to see how much blue had leaked into the mostly indigo aura surrounding him. It was proof of what he said, that he was nearing D Rank.

It was crazy to think how close Knox had gotten in such a small amount of time, which he shared as much with John.

"You got lucky," John insisted. "I bet it was that Pill Dernal gave you that got you so far."

John didn't have a spiritual sense, but Knox hadn't seen a point in hiding his progression from John, so he'd just told him that he was past the third Tier already. For his part, John was equal parts surprised and worried looking.

"My pathways are fine," Knox said, before John could ask. "In fact, they feel stronger than ever."

"Take care to keep them that way. And remember, if you go too fast, you risk letting too many toxins into your Core and that will slow you down further down the line. Be slow and smart now so that you have a greater future later," Leo said, putting a hand on his shoulder. Knox jumped a little, having not sensed or heard him approach. "It is time to rest."

Knox bustled with energy, but he knew that he needed at least a short rest if he were to be at his full potential. So, he followed Leo and John back to their tent, where they found Dernal and Caleb already sleeping.

"Three hours will be enough," Leo assured them, and he sat, taking a meditative position. "I'm lookout tonight, but I am fresher than you all."

Knox wanted to protest and offer his own services as a lookout, but suddenly the extent of his exhaustion hit him. He laid down and was asleep before his head hit the pillow.

What followed in the next two weeks was very little rest, much killing, and Knox earning himself a total of nine Monster Cores. He got the weakest of the picks, but he didn't complain, as he did so much less than everyone else present. Moreover, their journey took them closer to the Shadowfall Swamp, until on the final day of their hunt, they ended the horde in one final strike.

Scouts reported losing some of the strongest to the swamp, but no one wanted to venture into it, as it had a reputation of containing C Ranked and above monsters. Which Knox also learned was the max Rank that most Adventurers reached. In the entire small army of fifty-eight souls, not a single one was above C Rank. In fact, only nine, including Dernal and Caleb, were C Ranked at all.

Knox wasn't sure if he should be as surprised as he was when he found that out, but he imagined there should be more with how he was progressing. He'd taken half of his Monster Cores and done what John did with all of his, absorbing the internal essence. It wasn't as potent as a pill that could be made from them, but it was a quick and dirty way to speed your advancement. Like all monsters, their Core was filled with Pure essence.

It had brought John over the threshold and broken him through to D Rank by the last week and he hadn't stopped talking about it.

"These Cores provided as much essence as a freaking dungeon run, a dungeon run!" John said, his arms doing most of the talking for him, waving about here and there. "Speaking of which, aren't we up for our second run now?"

"Hhmm. Yep," Dernal said. He had put away all his Cores, the biggest haul in the group, as he'd done more than anyone else to keep the small army going with his heals.

Knox really saw the extent of Dernal's power when he had to push himself to keep so many targets alive at once. It had been like watching a fireworks show the one time the mayor had sprung to pay the expense for a festival. He was here, then there, then back over here in a flash. It was truly amazing to watch.

The dungeon camp was much the same, despite most of the Adventurers rotating out and in again to take on the monster horde. Before their next dungeon run—it was set to start the next morning—Knox wanted to see about making some purchases and learning more about runes.

So, with his mind filled with what he expected would be an adventure all of its own, he set out into the camp with John at his side as a guide.

CHAPTER 24
CHANGE

IT TURNED out that an entire section of the camp was laid out for the purpose of shopping, trading, and general identification of goods and services. Vendors called out their wares as John took Knox to the first place he wanted to visit: a book vendor. They found the woman easily enough, she had one of the smaller tents, but the biggest table of them all. Books were laid out and she held a wand in one hand that she wasn't afraid to use on people, or so her general demeanor said.

As they approached, she flicked her wand and a spark of white light hit the hand of someone that was reaching out to touch one of her tomes.

"No free reading," she hollered, before turning her glare to us. "Can you even read?" She directed her question at John, but Knox answered.

"All the time," he said, being careful to look but not touch as he went over the various titles. "I'm looking for anything you have on runic formations and monster lore."

"Those are two very broad subjects, my boy, and these tomes don't come cheap. Tell me what it is you want to learn, and I can help direct you, if you can afford me," she said, waving her hand at a sign that listed the prices.

Books started at fifty Runemarks each!

A Core was worth anywhere from ten to fifty Runemarks, depending on the quality, so Knox wasn't completely dismayed, but the fortune a book costs nearly took his breath away.

"I can afford you," he remarked; then, under his breath said, "If barely."

This was enough to shift the woman's demeanor, though, and she smiled at them. "The name is Nessy, and you are looking at Nessy's Bookshop, how may I be of service?"

Nessy was a petite female wearing robes befitting a caster, but black and gold in color. She had spectacles over her green eyes, which was rare enough, but seemed odd to Knox. Adventurers, or so he was told, were immune to normal wear and tear of the eyes. He thought that she must be very old to need spectacles as an Adventurer, that is, until he put his sense on her and saw that she was barely D Rank.

"Keep your scans to yourself," Nessy said, looking between the pair as if she couldn't tell who'd just scanned her. Interesting.

"I'm looking to learn about runes. I have a very basic education, but I want to know more," Knox said, being as simple and straightforward with his answer as he could.

"Just general learning, eh? Well then, you'd be best taught by the Grand Imperial Wizard himself, eh. Basic Runic Formations and their Uses, by Pen Fell," Nessy announced proudly. When neither John nor Knox reacted to her little announcement she'd so dramatically given, she huffed. "Uncultured swine don't know who Pen Fell is? Suggestion is the same, take a look."

She handed over a thinner volume with black binding and gold lettering. It was Volume 1 of four that she had on the table. Knox looked through the first volume and found many runes he knew, but something struck him immediately. Several of the meanings and uses differed from the ones his mother had said. For instance, there was a rune that was meant to reinforce spiritual structures in a spell, but this book had it listed as a basic enhancement to any spell, not just spirit directed ones.

Of course, it might be that it could be used by any such formation and his mother's notes had only spoken on the best uses of it, but Knox didn't know enough to say. He flipped to another page and found another such discrepancy. This book would be useful indeed, if only to highlight what he already knew and where his knowledge was suspect.

He reached for volume two, but a flash of energy hit his hand aside. "These are cheaper as they are mass produced, but still going to cost you twenty-five Runemarks per volume. All four I can give you a deal, only eighty-five."

Knox's stomach fell and he dug in his coin purse to reveal the coins he had. When Nessy's face went suddenly stern, he held up a hand and put half his Cores up as well. Suddenly, she looked happy once more.

"Deal," she said, but Knox held up a hand.

"Give me a fair value of each of these Cores, then we will make a deal," Knox said.

"I look like I specialize in Monster Cores, do I?" she said, raising her eyebrows. "Get those turned into Runemarks and then we can talk."

Knox looked to John who shrugged and led him away to find a Dungeon Core vendor. With such a huge influx of Cores, Knox was worried at what value his weaker Cores would have, but he was pleasantly surprised.

"Thirty marks for that Core, twenty-eight for that one, and twenty-five for that lot," a burly man said. He wore a single lens over his right eye attached to a chain, barely even glancing at the Cores before answering a question for another potential customer.

"That a good deal?" Knox asked, John nodded.

"Damn good deal," John said, looking a bit perturbed. "Wish I'd kept at least one or two to sell now. Damn the luck."

Knox wanted to say that if he'd done that, he wouldn't have broken into the D Ranks, but he knew that well enough so there was no point in pouring anything sour into the wound. Instead, Knox gave him a reassuring smile and agreed to the price the seller offered, selling five of his Cores for one hundred and seventy-five Runemarks, a fortune greater than he'd ever had before.

Heading back to the book vendor, he smiled as he approached, ready to buy more than just a single book now. "I'll take those four volumes and anything you have on advancements, reinforcing pathways, or general theory. Oh, and the price for a book on the different types of monsters."

"Got a good deal on those Cores, I take it," Nessy said, shaking her head as if she'd missed an opportunity herself. "Fine, look at this tome here and this one here, but only a few pages each. No free reading."

Knox spent a total of one hundred and fifty Runemarks on four volumes of 'Basic Runic Formations and their Uses', a book on crafting basic items and constructs while reinforcing them with runes, and a book on local monsters that even speculated at some species in the Shadowfall Swamp. It contained thirty-four species and subspecies, with drawings and descriptions.

"You're robbing me blind, but someone has to nurture the ones wanting to gain knowledge and not just power. You've got a deal," Nessy protested when she finally agreed on the one hundred and fifty amount, but Knox had remained firm on his price.

"You are blessed, Nessy, thank you kindly," Knox said, trying to be as friendly as possible, as he'd probably return here before the season ended and more books were always a welcome weight.

Speaking of weight, he needed to find one of those bags that held things without getting any bigger. He explained to John what he wanted, and John laughed.

"Yeah, me too," he said, still laughing. "You got a spare thousand or two Runemarks do you?"

And thus ended Knox's desire for a special bag that could hold a multitude of items. Instead, he bought a new backpack that was designed for Adventurers. It was three times the size of his old one, but he could carry it filled with rocks and still not be bothered too much by the weight. However, it could only carry the items you could fit into it.

He spent the rest of the night studying from his books on runic formations and making notes. Part of his most exciting study came from the crafting book, which was the thickest of all, even thicker than all four volumes on runic study put together.

It described how to make such basic items as fire starters, little devices that could light a fire and cost almost no essence to activate or how with the help of certain types of gems, a crafter could make it so anyone could use it. The gem would take a few runic marks that allowed for storage of essence, not nearly as well as Dungeon Cores, but enough for the striker to work several hundred times before failure.

After stealing out into the night to gather a few crafting supplies, Knox spent most of the evening trying his hand at it. It took him longer than he cared to admit, but he created a fire striker that would work with his own essence, then managed to hunt down a red ruby, and got it to work without needing essence directly each time. He even found putting in Fire essence directly made the flame bigger and much more powerful. However, the book warned against doing this as it would deteriorate the product faster.

However, Knox found that if he added a rune meant for reinforcing Flame essence scripts, according to his mother at least, the damage wasn't even noticeable. It was such a thrill to go from what his mother had taught him by leaving her journals behind to what the books taught, then finding a middle ground that appeared to work. The thrill filled him until the darkest of night came and he knew he needed to get rest before another big dungeon adventure.

The dungeon had various new monsters this time around and the themed branch at the end didn't give the amazing prizes it had the first time, nor was the adventure very difficult to figure out. Just a "Kill a Dragon" quest given to them at the foot of a mountain. They were to race another few groups to the top, which meant killing them, then killing a dragon. All in all, they got it done within a week and half, leaving another day to pull in the essence from the final branch.

Everything was progressing wonderfully, Knox had reached another two Tiers, putting him at Tier 6, thanks to using the rest of his Cores. He was within spitting distance of D Rank already, making Dernal that much more worried about him. He asked constantly about his pathways and how his nodes felt and prodded him constantly about if he'd opened one without first consulting him. He hadn't of course, but he'd considered it.

The others had gotten cool items, but Knox had spent his points on a single item drop, the very last one in a silver chest. It was a pair of communication stones that he wanted to see if he could replicate. He gave one to Dernal with plans of having him venture out and test the range. Until then, it would be safe. Plus, from what he could tell, they had identical Runic Markings, so he wasn't losing out by only having one to study.

It all progressed swimmingly, until they came back out of the dungeon to a deathly stillness. Two dead bodies lay in several pieces in front of the dungeon, one with an arm near to the dungeon. One of the dead Knox recognized as the Guild man who'd registered them in the first place, though his name eluded him.

Dernal went to a knee beside the man. "Damnit Chad, what got you?"

Knox remembered now, the man named Chad had been close to Dernal, though he didn't know how close until he saw how dark Dernal's expression had gotten.

"He was on the cusp of B Rank, if something tore him apart, we've no chance. We are going straight to the Guild Charterhouse two days from here to report this incident. I can't sense any life, monster or otherwise, which means whatever they faced can either veil itself or its dead. Either way, we run as fast as our legs will take us," Dernal explained, his eyes checking each of them before landing on Knox. "Don't fall behind." Was the last thing he said before they left the inner walls surrounding the dungeon.

Knox wished he could close his eyes, fire and death surrounded him, hundreds of bodies lay in pieces, some charred by fire and others eaten at by something with a maw greater than any monster he'd encountered. They didn't stop to check their tent, the entire area a mass of fire. Knox was glad he'd taken all he owned with him, his books included.

The stench was almost too much to handle, Knox held his nostrils shut against it. The walls around the entire camp were obliterated, but somehow the gates were left untouched, barely standing on their own while the rest of the wall had been laid low.

Knox let his sense go out and it brushed against a whole lot of nothing. No signs of life among so many dead, just the sense of Fire essence and Death essence heavy in the air. He had the oddest random thought: because of the two heavy amounts of essence, they ought to cycle it in and not waste it. But he quickly pushed the thought aside. He knew it wouldn't be right, plus, Death essence left his stomach in knots as much as Dark essence.

Dernal was true to his word and the moment they hit the road they were off running. Knox found that he could now use Haste pretty continually if he filtered it down, similar to how he did with his full body enforcement technique. So, despite him being the slowest one, he ran beside Dernal and pushed them all to go faster. Which they did, eventually making him the one in the back and losing ground to them. They never let it get too far, which Knox was glad for.

Several times during their run, Knox felt the presence of something closing in on them. Each time, Dernal would adjust their path to move them directly away from it, then correct their course later. Dernal could obviously feel it, so it wasn't masking itself, which meant it might be a target they could deal with. However, Knox trusted Dernal to make the right decision.

It was on the second day of running that everything came to a head and Knox's life changed forever.

His sense flared and he felt it come only a moment before it appeared, both Caleb and Dernal turning as one a second too late. Caleb was the first to fall. The massive, black, and terrible form slammed into him, and blood splattered everywhere. If he survived the first hit, then Knox would have been surprised.

"RUN!" Dernal yelled, his voice almost more a command of power than mere speech.

John disappeared, Leo blurred and suddenly he was several paces away and running at a full spring. But the beast, whatever the hell it was, wanted Dernal next. Knox readied a technique, unwilling to leave behind his friend to such a fate. Dernal caught his eyes and shook his head as the monster slammed against him. The next thing Knox saw was Dernal on the ground, an arm missing and his screams blocking out the raging roar of the nearby river.

They'd only barely crossed a bridge and suddenly Knox had a plan to save them all. He ran, pumping himself full of essence, toward the bridge. He felt a terrible power focus on him, and he ran all the faster. It was after him now, which meant... but no, he reached out with his sense and a flicker of life remained in Dernal. He could still help him!

Then everything went black, and he felt water wash over him.

His dreams were filled with despair. The moment of Caleb's likely death repeated over and over again, each time a new member of his party dying in his place. He dreamed that he lived to see them all die, his own corpse a bloated thing filled with water that would be discovered later. Death, it seems, would find him no matter what actions he took, but he had refused to run, refused to be prey in the end. If he'd just made it to the bridge and gotten the dumb monster into the water, it might be washed away.

It had been some kind of dragon, that much he was sure of. Though, how a dragon of such power, most likely a wyvern or drake his mind suggested, made it to the dungeon and killed all those Adventurers? How? Why? So many questions poured through his mind and only then did he feel the weight of his pack and the water flowing all around him. He was awake, the terrible nightmares had ended.

He was sure he'd open his eyes and find that it was all just a terrible nightmare, that he hadn't in fact been nearly killed. Pain on his neck, arms, legs, everywhere told him otherwise. Painfully, he opened his eyes and struggled into a sitting position, his pack still on his back, the top still shut tight keeping even the water out.

He was on the bank of a river, but he didn't recognize any of his surroundings. Carefully he stood and opened up his sense to all around him. Dozens of monsters were within his sense and he pulled it back, worried he might alert them. Carefully and as quietly as possible, he lowered his pack and checked that it was still closed tight. He tried not to think about the books he'd packed near the top or what a loss they would be if they were ruined by any water. At the very bottom of his pack was his mother's journals and his notes, so he at least knew those were safe.

The trees around him looked dead, and the ground was wet. Even the sky had a gloomy purple haze to it, like death itself hung low in this swampy area. Then it hit him where he must be, Shadowfall Swamp.

He was a dead man walking.

But walking was all he could manage at the moment. So, ignoring his sense as best he could as it screamed at him that threats approached from every possible angle, he picked a direction and hoped against hope it was the right way out of this death swamp. He walked at first, but as his strength began to return, he ran. Several times he narrowly avoided running into monsters, but surprisingly very few even approached.

It wasn't until he heard a mighty roar in the distance that he figured out what was happening. He'd been marked, that was the odd scent he'd been smelling, by a monster of Death itself. None of the monsters wanted to be the one to take the prey of such a mighty beast from it. So, while he'd thought he'd gotten away, it appeared that he was just awaiting Death, as it were. This didn't slow his pace, merely forced him to increase it until he felt like he was truly safe.

First, a night went by as he continued to run without rest. Then a day, then two. His pace had turned to a crawl, but he kept moving. There was a pleasant smell of salt in the air now and he thought perhaps he was getting near civilization. Then, through the haze of it all, he came to a damning realization.

The Endless Sea's coast ran right up to the Shadowfall Swamp; he knew this because he'd seen a map of the area before. Despite the coast being marked well enough, boats never ventured too close due to the monsters lurking in the waters and along the coast.

He'd gone deeper into the Shadowfall Swamp, not out. Still, no monsters had attacked him, so he kept walking toward the coast. Perhaps he'd find a boat and they'd help him. Perhaps he was a dead man and didn't know it yet?

Finally, on the fourth day, he collapsed and lost consciousness. He awoke sore and starving. So, he did what he ought to have done days ago, he made camp. It was eerie to do so when just out of sight he could sense monsters easily his match, but they kept their distance, despite the scent on him being noticeably fainter than it had been. He still heard the occasional roar in the distance, but it was so far off that it could be anything.

He drank deeply from his waterskin, leaving plenty for later but draining at least half. Then he bit into his rations and couldn't remember ever not thinking they were the most delicious things in existence. When he'd finally finished, he sat and cycled. The essence around him was primarily Light, Death, and Water but it was stronger than even a dungeon and if anything, he knew getting stronger only helped his cause.

Getting stronger? He almost laughed as he suddenly dropped out of cycling. That beast, dragon, whatever the hell it had been, cut through Caleb like he was a bag of rice. The man never stood a chance and Knox hadn't even gotten a solid look at it.

No, getting stronger wasn't going to help him now, but he'd be damned if he'd waste a chance to cycle the essence either way. It was amazing to him that in a place as gloomy and dark as this swamp, that Light essence would be the strongest type of essence around. It was almost like Light essence poured out from the very ground around him. He cycled and grew stronger for hours and hours, until his body succumbed to sleep once more. On the second day of such cycling, he felt himself pressing on the edge of the next Tier and that much closer to D Rank, but he had no idea how to push through.

It required a revelation of the mind, or so John had said, but what that meant, Knox was too tired to even try to imagine. Breaking his camp, he began to walk toward the coast some more.

The scent of Death on him had all but disappeared and he could feel monsters getting closer and closer to him. Soon he'd be fighting off powerful monsters and he could use the advantage of being a D Ranked Adventurer. Just a few more days with this much essence in the air and he was certain he could reach the D Ranks.

He had to figure out what insights he needed to gain or die.

CHAPTER 25
DEATH

IT TOOK several more days of traveling before he began to make progress with breaking through, getting ever closer to the D Ranks. Each day, he'd taken in as much, if not more than enough, essence that he could get inside a dungeon. If this area was so rich in essence, why weren't more people here claiming the prize? Of course, Knox knew why no one did, though he was currently immune to the effects.

Monsters by the dozens stayed just out of sight, coming closer with every passing hour. The dragon-like creature that had pursued him left a mark or scent of some kind on him and it had to be that mark that kept the monsters at bay, he guessed. A signal to them that their prey belonged to another. However, the signal was fading, and the great beast hadn't reached him, though his few hours of sleep were filled with nightmares of it doing so.

The fact remained that for now he was protected. If he could reach the seashore in time, he might be able to get a signal to a boat before he got eaten. There was no way he could go back now, nor would he want to travel closer to the great monster waiting for him.

He found that in the quiet hours of cycling and meditation, his mind often traveled to the friends he'd left behind. Would they be safe with a monster, such as that, only days away from the town? Of course, he knew they wouldn't, if an entire camp of Adventurers had fallen, then their little village would be destroyed, and the people slain.

This motivated him to push hard and try harder, he had to figure out an insight about his mind. He knew so many things, he studied so hard all his life, he was sure that his mind would have been the easiest of the insights he'd uncover. So many of the Tiers had fallen before him, insight after insight about his physical limitations and lack thereof if he kept training.

But his mind was something different, something special to him. What did he know about his mind that would trigger an insight into it?

"I know that I know nothing," Knox jokingly said, but he felt a stirring inside of himself as what he said neared a deeper truth. This shocked him and he pondered on his words, said so casually and without thought.

I know that I know nothing.
I know nothing.

Just like that, he felt his mind grow, expand, his Core began to burst from so much essence. He took hold of it and began the process of refining it, crushing it down from its new larger size. One moment at a time, each second, progress was made. Then, by sheer instinct, he reached out with his pathways and made a connection with a node in the middle of his head.

Suddenly, pain filled him, and thoughts turned dark as he struggled to contain it all. Had he done wrong by opening this eye? For he knew now that it was an eye of sorts, an eye of under-standing, an eye of knowledge, an eye into the world around him. Then the pain lessened, and he fell into a cycling rhythm.

He was a D Ranked Adventurer now, after only months of being an Adventurer. This alone was an accomplishment that he couldn't believe, but so thick was the essence around him that he was sure he could go even further given enough weeks. However, there was a limitation of his vortex: the filtering technique. If not for how quickly Light essence seemed to add itself into his Core, much like Pure essence, then it might have still taken him so many more months to reach D Rank.

Could he find a cave and hide until he reached the C or even B Rank? He didn't know what was possible or how fast his insights might take for each Tier, but he dreamed about it to take his mind off the seriousness of his current situation.

Dernal was likely dead, Caleb was for sure, and what of Leo and John? Were they dead as well, from the attack of the monster? He had to accept that was the likely possibility and move forward. Now the best he could hope for was rescue by sea and perhaps he could warn the Guild Charterhouse so they could send a more powerful team of Adventurers here to slay the dragon.

A dragon in this part of the world was so surreal as to be unbelievable. But he'd gone over his limited sighting of the monster and decided that it had to have been a dragon, and a powerful one at that. It was nothing like the small dragon the dungeon had presented them to kill, but even that memory felt like it was months old instead of barely a week.

Testing his sense, Knox was surprised at the clarity in which he could see the approaching threats now. He made out several wolf-like creatures, a wyvern, several unknowable humanoid shaped figures, and an owlbear. Each of them thrummed with the power of a C Ranked Adventurer but in the advanced Tiers, based on their auras.

He could also judge the slow decay of whatever scent kept them away, each minute taking away a step from his safety ring. If only he could figure out what about the Death aura that they feared, then he could empower it. But that was far beyond his skill as an Adventurer, and he knew it. Instead, he focused on getting as close to the distant sea as he could, without walking in circles.

Step by step, the ring around him closed, but fewer monsters followed him. The strongest taking charge and ownership of the soon to be prey. He knew this as much as he knew he was a dead man, but still he walked, still he tried to work out a way to save himself. He'd lost the remains of his shield, but he still had his axe. Despite being alone and only a newly made D Ranked Adventurer, he was armed and ready to try and defend himself.

It was another day or two—he was beginning to lose track of time as he marched—when the aura around him failed altogether and all at once. His slow walk turned into a sprint as three monsters came for him at once. His luck held and they began to fight among themselves, ripping and clawing until only the strongest would survive. Then his time would come.

His run was fast and furious, aided by his almost instinctual use of the Haste technique. He'd used it so much in the past month that it was as easy as breathing to enhance himself if he only used a tiny trickle of essence. It wasn't as fast an improvement, but it made him consistently faster. He grabbed hold of his use of the technique and pulled harder, ramping it up to put some distance between his potential attacker and himself.

Step by step he shot through the endless swamp, splashing up water and soaking through his boots. He had a continuous number of blisters form on his feet from the pace he'd been setting, but his body healed minor injuries quickly enough that he wasn't too worried. Whatever won the fight and pursued him now was faster still, he felt it gaining on him and he was helpless to stop it. So instead, he looked for a place to fight it.

There was a rocky patch not far and he made for it. Atop it, he could see the endless sea and even make out the tiny dot of a boat in the distance. He was so close to freedom and yet this would be where he died.

He pulled out his axe and readied his full body enforcement technique. It didn't matter that it took everything out of him when he used it at full power, he would need all the strength and speed of a C Ranked or even a B Ranked to survive this, so he'd flush his pathways to bursting if it meant one more day of living.

What appeared before him was the very same foe that had killed Caleb and torn Dernal limb from limb. Except, it was smaller and more compact. It looked like the dragon they'd defeated in the dungeon, a C Ranked Monster for sure, but not undefeatable. If only he had his entire team to help him. The beast had four powerful arms and intelligent eyes. The scales were the blackest of night with lines of purple running down the length of its body to the tip of its tail. Spikes adorned it all over and it opened its mouth, sharp teeth and a thin tongue showed from within.

For a moment, Knox was sure it was about to speak, but it only hissed in his direction, opening its wings wide. It buffeted him several times, but he managed to keep his footing. Then, all at once, it struck.

If Knox had been only a moment slower to activate his technique, he would have been dead already. Fortunately, he wasn't, and so he slid to the side, the dragon moving slowly enough that it appeared to be at normal speed. Nevertheless, it was still faster than Knox could deal with, and he was depleting energy every second he held onto the technique.

He struck out as the small dragon snapped at him. His axe barely left a line on the powerful scales, but he kept attacking.

Back and forth they went, but it was clear that even filled with essence and reinforced as he was, the dragon was clearly the stronger opponent. The battle wasn't long or epic, it just ended seconds after starting when his technique failed.

The dragon bit into his chest, its teeth easily cutting through his armor and piercing him. While this happened, Knox's sense shot out from him and he felt something... odd, below. The rock he stood on was thin and perhaps, if he broke it—

The dragon released him, and Knox swung his axe as he fell, cutting the flesh on its left wing and laughing at the success. The dragon struck again, throwing him clear of the rock. Bloody and on death's door, Knox struggled to move closer to the rock, a plan formed in his mind. All the pain in the world settled on him, but his mind was reinforced, and he could handle such pain.

Striking with his axe as if attempting to fell a tree in a single strike, it bounced off the stone harmlessly. The dragon neared him, walking right into the center of the thin, rocky covering. Knox infused his technique—as painful as it was to do so—with the one he'd learned from John, driving down his axe into the stone. The stone shattered and the dragon fell.

Just as Knox smiled at his short-lived victory, a tail slashed out and pulled him down as well. If not for the rock, debris, and the cut in the dragon's wing, it might have flown away. Instead, it slammed right atop a sharp stalagmite. Knox, meanwhile, slammed into it and crunched hard on the rock beneath, his mind going black.

He came to, in pain and with blood flowing from everywhere, but something warm flickered at the edge of his vision. He felt it pull at him and he approached it, dragging his broken body forward, one step at a time.

Before him, sat an armored figure of gold and blue swirling light. Each step of a small staircase got him closer and closer to the figure, it called to him in a way he couldn't express. The sun shone above, filling the dark cavern with light and illuminating the skeleton within the armor.

Why did he feel the need to touch even a part of it, a boot or a toe? It called to him and if it took his dying breath, he'd reach it. So, inch by inch he crawled, leaving behind him a trail of blood.

Finally, after what felt like hours, though it may have been mere minutes, he reached out and touched the golden boot. Something blue and translucent appeared before his vision—words! He struggled to read them at first, they were alien and unknown to him, but after staring for a moment they became readable.

-Do you choose Life or Death?-

"I choose Life," Knox managed to say, though to whom he spoke he didn't know.

-System Activation of Titan Engine, Code Named: Clockwork Titan, Essence Type: Light-

-You will be remade as a Titan Born-

-The Age of Chaos has ended. Order has once again been restored, the Age of the Titans has returned.-

-Are you ready to walk the Path of the Titans?-

"Yes," Knox said with his final breath, and his body could take no more. He died, just as the Path of the Titans grabbed hold of his body, mind, and spirit, reforging them anew.

-System Activation Commencing in 3... 2... 1-

-System Activation Complete-

-Host body renewed, rebuilding commencing... estimated time of completion of Tier 1 Reconstruction, 303 days-

Knox didn't realize that in death one could dream, but he was dreaming, and he knew for a fact he had died. There was just no other explanation for the memories he had or the dreams that now filled his mind. He watched as a cloaked figure known to all that he met as 'The Clockwork Titan', go throughout the land and spread the light of knowledge and healing. Where his influence went, so did enlightenment and growth. Then, something flashed in Knox's mind amidst his dreams, and he focused on it.

. . .

-What is your name?-

That was easy enough. *'Knox'*, he thought the words and felt them become pressed into being.

-Name: Knox, Level: ???, Essence to next Level: 0/400-
    -Health: ???, Mana: ???, Stamina: ???-
    -Body: ???, Mind: ???, Spirit: ???-
    -System initializing, please stand by...-
    -You are Titan Born. Welcome to the Titan System, Titan of Light-

CHAPTER 26
TITAN ENGINE

"ARE you ready for your first quest?" An extremely distinct voice spoke, so high-pitched and sharp that it jerked Knox right out of his sleep.

He woke expecting pain and anguish, all the memories of his fight against a monstrous dragon-like creature still fresh in his mind. However, instead of pain, he felt... well, good was the only way to describe it. Even his breathing, coming in slow and steady, felt powerful and healthy. Blinking sleep from his eyes, he glanced around in search of any sign of the voice he had heard. Yet, the cavern remained dark, and the moonlight from above wasn't at the right angle to provide sufficient light. He could make out little more than the giant armored figure seated a few paces away from him.

So, doing the only thing he could, he sat up and looked at the armored figure. The armor that had once fully adorned it was now diminished and faded. Previously, it had shone brilliantly bright—a detail he had managed to observe even in his weakened condition.

Whoever the figure was, it hadn't been the one talking; he knew that much for sure. Stretching out his sense like fine fingers of silk, he took in what he couldn't see with his naked eye. The dead dragon's remains were still there, though they felt odd. Without seeing them, he wouldn't be able to tell why. The figure before him radiated a faint glow, but as the clouds above shifted, Knox began to see much more.

The massive figure, now revealed to be nothing but a skeleton, sported numerous decorative gears on its armor. It also wore a crown of tooth-like gears, sitting horizontally atop its head. On that crown were runes that Knox had never encountered before, and he felt an immediate urge to find his notebook and record them.

Turning, he found his pack wasn't far, but upon reaching it, he discovered it half buried in the ground and covered in a thick layer of dust. Brushing it off, he dug inside, checking the contents and retrieving his notebook, ink, and pen. There was some water damage, but the pages didn't stick so he went to work writing down the runes. While doing this, he noticed behind the throne a circular gear with runes on the teeth as well, so he marked those down on the next page.

So enthralled by the exciting discovery of new runes and the armor that was clearly magical in some way or another, he'd nearly forgotten about the voice that had spoken. Penning a final note under the moonlight, he resolved to ask a question of the disembodied voice.

"Where are you?" he asked, raising his voice only a measure, as he remembered he was still technically in the Shadowfall Swamp. It wouldn't be wise to attract more monsters, especially when he'd been so lucky to deal with only the small dragon.

No answer came, and Knox continued his study of the armored skeleton. He realized it had been stabbed, seeing a massive sword sticking out of the tall, armored figure. It was so tall, in fact, that it likely stood twice his height, he reasoned. Knox wondered what manner of man this creature had been, but he didn't get to think on it much longer, as a voice cut through the silent darkness.

"It is I... well, I don't quite recall my name now that I try to think about it. But I do know one thing. I am here to serve the Titan Born, or Clockwork Titan, or a Titan of Light... I'm pretty sure I know stuff too, but my gears are a bit rusted at the moment, bear with me." The voice came from behind the throne. With a quick expansion of his sense, Knox felt he'd located whomever it was, though it gave off a feeling and glow unlike anything he'd encountered before. The aura around it was red with a touch of silver.

Finding his axe, dusty but in one piece, Knox turned his attention to the voice behind the throne of stone. Walking cautiously around, he was prepared for anything. Yet, he was still surprised enough to gasp when he saw what he found.

The upper torso of what looked like intricate armor and gears attached to a head with glowing eyes wobbled back and forth awkwardly before swiveling to look in his direction. It smiled and Knox let out a gasp. It was some kind of metal man, but it had only a single arm and its upper chest, along with most of its head left.

"What are you?" Knox asked, completely taken aback by the appearance of this half-destroyed armored thing.

"I'm MIC or rather I am a MIC. Which stands for Mechanical Intelligent Construct. Hey, I do know who I am. Call me Mic," Mic said, scratching at his dented head in a very human-like gesture.

"You're some kind of golem created by that dead armored guy, aren't you?" Knox asked. He'd heard about golems before, but most were elemental by nature and controlled by powerful Adventurers to help them do whatever they wanted.

"Call me Mic," Mic insisted, then, pushing himself up a bit, he continued. "I'm supposed to direct you to your first Quest, so pay attention. I'm sending you the Quest request now."

Before Knox could ask what he meant, a blue translucent screen appeared before his face and he fell backward in surprise. He'd thought that part had been a dream, not reality. What did this mean if the words he'd heard were real, then was he a 'Titan Born? But what did that mean? He practically screamed the words inside his head as he swiveled his head left and right. Though, no matter the direction he turned, the blue words stayed directly in front of him.

He tried reaching out to touch it, but his hand passed right through the translucent blue screen. Finally, with nothing else to do about it, he read it.

-Quest Received!-
-Learning the Basics-
-You are a newly reborn Titan. As such, you must learn the ropes and figure out what that means. To do this, start by locating the Titan Engine and inserting an Essence Core. Then you will have the ability to pick your first three Core Titan Born Traits. If you do not have an Essence Core, then go out and kill one of the local fauna to retrieve one of C Rank (Level 40+) or better.-
-Objective: Unlock 0/3 Titan Born Traits-
-Reward: Unlock a Path, 400 Essence Toward Next Level-

. . .

288

So many questions filtered through Knox's mind at that point, but he settled on one to ask the mostly ruined mechanical intelligent construct.

"Where is this Titan Engine?" Knox asked, turning to feel his way as best he could toward the monster. He was D Ranked now, or at least he had been when he fell down here. If his dream was right and the process of making him a Titan Born had truly taken 303 days, then who knows what he was now. Nearly a year had gone by in the blink of an eye and yet all he could think about was getting his hands on the Core that this Dragon must have had to see if he could complete his first quest.

This wasn't at all how Knox thought his time as an Adventurer would go, and deep down, he knew that he was still freaking out. He needed to latch onto something to do to maintain his sanity. Change was hard for everyone. If he could focus up and see where this quest took him, perhaps he could avoid losing his mind over the ridiculousness of his current predicament.

Using his sense as best as he could to aid his eyesight in the darkness, his hands found the rough dried-up carcass of the dragon. He carefully cut away dead flesh in search of the Core within. There was an expectation of wet, bloody flesh or rotting stink, but the dragon had been drained of blood via the way it had died, and what was left had dried out months ago.

What he was looking for he found in its chest, just beside where the heart would have been. It had narrowly missed being destroyed by the rock the dragon had been impaled on, but as he pulled it out, he could feel the powerful thrumming the Core gave off. It felt as if there was enough Pure essence inside to give him his first Tier or two in the D Ranks.

In that moment, he decided to take a look inside himself and he lurched backward in shock from what he found. In place of the few pathways he'd built and the two node connections he'd had before, was a vast network of smaller and seemingly infinite pathways connecting every single one of his nodes and limbs. Even his eyes had countless little connections built into them. What in the hells did this mean for him?

Before he could think much about it, Mic responded to his question he'd asked nearly a minute ago.

"Titan Engine located ten floors below our current position. Calculating safe route... route calculated. Uh, can you pick me up and I'll show you the way?" Mic asked, sounding a tad sheepish at his request.

Putting his axe away, Knox stepped back to Mic and scooped him up with one arm. "Show me the way," Knox said, looking around and wishing he had some way to light up the room. As if he could read his thoughts, Mic lifted his one good arm and a ball of light appeared in it, illuminating the room around them.

It was nothing more than an overgrown cavern, but following Mic's directions, Knox found a hole in the ground that led to a staircase leading further down. It twisted and turned downward for some time before finally letting out in a shiny metallic room absolutely filled with runic carvings. Enough to keep Knox busy studying for several lifetimes.

Reining in his sense, he saw with his natural eyes.

Despite the lack of dust within the room, unlike the rest of the complex, Knox's eyes were drawn to a singular, massive piece of machinery in the center. It lacked the gears and clockwork style present elsewhere and instead featured six smooth, interconnecting humps, emitting an audible thrum of power.

Not a single speck of dust had settled on it, and it shone even in the dim light provided by Mic. Knox didn't dare bring his sense to bear on it, as even with it so withdrawn as it was, it ached to look at it.

"The Titan Engine," Mic proclaimed, waving his one good hand toward the object.

Walking up to it, the height of the Titan Engine became apparent, towering over Knox's head. If he held his arms out full spread, he might encompass half of the engine's length. He then reached out his hand toward the metal surface, which felt cool under his touch. However, before he could explore it further, Mic's sudden words startled his hand away.

"Now feed it," he commanded, his voice practically squealing with glee.

Knox fished out the Monster Core and pressed it against the machine. It began to thrum rhythmically, faster and faster, until the Monster Core turned to dust in his hand and all that precious essence was lost. Feeling a touch of regret as he moved his hand away, Knox waited to see what would happen next.

-Titan Engine engaged. Titan System Aura activated Base 1, Tier 1. Current spread of aura, one cubic mile. All targets within aura will be added to the collective Titan System... Current subjects within the Titan System Aura: 1 Soul.-

The words spoke directly into his mind and a screen appeared before his eyes, showing him the words and listing the same '1 Soul' as part of the current system. What was the point of this system and why was it being activated, Knox wondered as a new notification flashed over his screen.

-Welcome to the Titan System.-
-As a Titan Born you have access to both a basic Path and the Path of the Titans. Do you wish to see a Path? Yes/No?-

"Yes," Knox spoke the words aloud and more text followed.

-Which Path do you wish to access? Basic or Path of the Titans?-

. . .

"Go for the Path of the Titans, that way you can complete your quest!" Mic said, his voice still eager.

Knox shrugged and responded, "Path of the Titans." This was all so strange to him, yet he had to admit a certain amount of excitement to see what the Path of the Titans held.

-Processing Request, Request Rerouted...-

-Before you can pick from the Path of the Titans, please pick your starting three Titan Born Racial Traits. Reminder! You get to pick 3 Traits for Tier 1 Traits, but only 1 Trait per new Tier, at Levels 25, 50, 75, and 100-

Unbound Sight (0/1): (Racial Trait Passive) Grants the User the ability to sense their surroundings, both physical, mental, and spiritual. The longer the Trait is practiced, the more effective it will become. This is a base Titan Born Trait, and as such, taking it will affect you from the beginning of your natural life.

Path of Iron (0/1): (Racial Trait Passive) Grants the User stronger than normal pathways, physical recovery, and baseline strength. The longer the Trait is practiced, the more effective it will become. This is a base Titan Born Trait, and as such, taking it will affect you from the beginning of your natural life.

Titan Born Advancement (0/1): (Racial Trait Passive) Grants the User increased essence gains and decreased essence requirements per Level when leveling, as well as increased base affinities. This is a base Titan Born Trait, and as such, taking it will affect you from the beginning of your natural life.

Titanic Resilience (0/1): (Racial Trait Passive) Grants the User the capacity to withstand and reduce the effects of status ailments, mental afflictions, and elemental imbalances. This is a base Titan Born Trait, and as such, taking it will affect you from the beginning of your natural life.

Mystic Resonance (0/1): (Racial Trait Passive) Allows the User to harmonize with the elemental forces around them, granting easier access to elemental energies and natural elemental control.

This is a base Titan Born Trait, and as such, taking it will affect you from the beginning of your natural life.

Knox read, then reread the entire list several times. If he understood this all correctly, he'd be picking out traits that he'd always had since the very beginning of his life. Which suddenly made a hell of a lot of sense, seeing as he could think of at least two of the traits that he knew he had. But it also presented him with a conundrum of sorts. What would happen if he picked a different three than he knew he must have already picked? Would he break the world if he never truly had Unbound Sight?

"What happens if I pick wrong?" Knox asked Mic, setting the metallic remains of the golem aside for now, and fixing him with his best stare.

Mic, for his part, didn't seem intimidated or worried in the least. Instead, he just smiled and answered Knox's question. "You can't pick wrong, that's not the way this works. Just focus on which choice you want to take, and it will be as if you've always had the skill."

"So, I know for a fact I have Unbound Sight, what happens if I don't choose it now, will I lose all memory of having used the skill?" Knox asked, clarifying a bit more what he meant by his question.

"Oh, hmm I'm not sure, why don't you try, and we can find out together if you break the world," Mic said, his smile widening to odd proportions, considering the metallic nature of his face.

Knox wasn't about to just throw away such a cool skill though. In the end, he decided he knew which three he would take.

"I choose Unbound Sight," Knox said; and just like that, the screen updated with a one out of one instead of the zero out of one. It was listed as a passive ability, but it was by far the most active of the five skills listed, so Knox was sure he made the right decision to go with it.

"And what next?" Mic asked, seemingly too eager for Knox's taste but with all the strange occurrences happening lately, it was hardly the worst thing he'd encountered.

"Path of Iron and Titan Born Advancement," Knox declared, picking the two that made the most sense when he thought about how his life had gone and his quick advancement with essence when everyone else said it should take much longer. These had to be the right choices, he thought, and a part of him waited eagerly to see if the world came crashing down around him because of some time-related snafu.

All was still and quiet until a loud ding and whooshing of golden light surrounded him, and he nearly fell over in surprise.

-Congratulations! You've Leveled up to Level 2!-
-All Resource Pools have been filled, all negative ailments cleansed, and you are one step further on the Path of the Titans.-

That text took up the whole of Knox's visual space with bolded gold lettering, but as it faded away and became smaller text, he saw that he had several new messages regarding his quest.

-Quest Complete!-
-Learning the Basics-
-You are a newly reborn Titan. As such, you must learn the ropes and figure out what that means. To do this, start by locating the Titan Engine and inserting an Essence Core. Then you will have the ability to pick your first three Core Titan Born Traits. If you do not have an Essence Core, then go out and kill one of the local fauna to retrieve one of C Rank (Level 40+) or better.-
-Objective: Unlocked 3/3 Titan Born Traits-
-Reward: Unlock a Path, 400 Essence Toward Next Level-

. . .

Next came some confusing bits about 'personal status'. Knox looked it over, but what the values meant, he wasn't certain at first glance.

-Personal Status-
  -Name: Knox-
  -Level: 2 (F Rank, Tier 2)-
  -Essence To Next Level: 0/500-
  -Health: Common Tier 9-
  -Mana: Common Tier 9-
  -Stamina: Common Tier 9-
  -Mind: 36 (Wisdom: 12, Intelligence: 12, Charisma: 12)-
  -Body: 36 (Speed: 12, Strength: 12, Endurance: 12)-
  -Spirit: 36 (Willpower: 12, Attunement: 12, Resonance: 12)-

Knox had to blink and rub his eyes several times before he could believe what he was seeing. Somehow, he'd been knocked down all the way back to F Rank, Tier 2—or rather, Level 2, as the system called it. What in the actual hells was going on here?

CHAPTER 27
SYSTEM UNDERSTANDING

HE DECIDED to ask as much to the only thing he could currently get any answers out of, the metallic man known to him as Mic.

"What the hells man?" Knox asked, then taking several deep breaths and focusing himself, he tried again. "Why is this system listing me as an F Ranked and not D Rank?"

"Oh, I have an answer to that question!" Mic said excitedly.

Taking his time to answer, he shifted around and readjusted his position on the floor beside the Titan Engine.

"Well, out with it," Knox said, then added a 'please' at the end because he didn't want to be rude.

"You've been through a very dramatic shift and change, the process to make you a Titan Born took all the essence you'd gathered, plus much of the latent essence in the air around the complex. Well, much further than that if my memory serves. But that isn't important. What is important is that you've been remade from the top down. You are new, and as such, so is your advancement. You start at Level 1 like a newborn babe."

"A newborn babe!" Knox exclaimed, flexing his muscles just to be sure he had any kind of strength left in him. To his surprise, he noticed that he definitely felt weaker than before, but not by a huge margin. He was stronger than a child, that much he was certain about.

"I don't feel as weak as a baby," Knox finally decided on saying, to which the construct nodded vigorously.

"Well, obviously, that has to do with your new body. You are as strong as a baby Titan, which is to say, stronger than an average sentient race even at the peak of their advancement. You are also technically already max Level; you've just had several restricting bands placed around yourself to keep your body from being ripped apart from the inside out."

"Restricting bands?" Knox asked, not understanding his meaning.

"Yes," Mic gestured at his hands and Knox looked down to see that he had a simple golden ring on each finger, so thin and tight that it might have been missed if he didn't know to look. "Those bands, when kept on, will restrain your Mind, Body, and Spirit to levels that you can cope with. For every ten Levels you earn you can take one off, growing substantially stronger when you do. You are on the Path of the Titans, and as such, you will find greater power than you've ever imagined before. But only if you survive long enough to claim it. Do you have what it takes?"

Knox thought on his words for several minutes, letting the silence stretch between them as he took every bit of what he was saying and turning it over in his mind. Was he ready to walk this path, and if not, was there any turning back? No, he decided. He'd been at death's door and he took the opportunity presented to him when it came. It would do no good to start looking backward now. His future was set, in a way, but that didn't mean his life was over.

In fact, it meant quite the opposite, he figured. He had the potential to become the strongest Adventurer in the world. Suddenly, his thoughts went to the journal he'd found and realized that he'd been reading about someone going through the same process as him. He'd have to go over the journal now that he was alone, but first he had a quest to finish, as well as more questions he had to ask.

He decided to start with a few more questions before jumping into the Paths. "Mic," Knox said, getting the construct's attention. Mic had been focused on an orange beetle nearby, making several attempts to squish it, yet failing each time.

"Uh huh?" Mic said, slowly turning his gaze up to Knox, towering over him from where he sat on the ground.

"What happens if I take off one of these bands, do I die instantly?" Knox asked, fingering one of the rings now that he'd become aware of them.

"Do not do that," Mic exclaimed, waving his one good arm in alarm. "When you are stronger you might be able to handle releasing a single band, eventually even two, but at this point in your progress you are more likely to just explode from the sudden burst of power. Even when you grow stronger, you will lose progress on your path each time you remove one. A mere minute with it off and you could see yourself lose a Level, maybe even two!"

Knox removed his fingers from around the ring and blinked rapidly in response. He would lose multiple Tiers at a time just for a quick power boost that could only last a minute or less? *No thank you*, he thought grimly.

Going over his next question in his mind, he fixed Mic with a look and asked, "Health, Mana, and Stamina, what can you tell me about each of them?"

"I don't need to tell you anything about them, just focus on your Personal Status Screen and it will elaborate on each for you," Mic said matter-of-factly.

Sounded easy enough, Knox thought. Focusing on the idea of the translucent screen caused it to reappear and he found the area he was looking for quite easily. Next, as he focused on each one at a time, additional text filled his view.

-Health: A measure of your general physical wellness.-

That was simple enough, but what about the Common part, he wondered, focusing on that part in particular.

-Common is Rank 5 in the overall count of 14 Ranks that you can achieve to increase your physical wellness.-
 -Status Pool Ranks-
 -Poor: The equivalence of a sickly man of twenty years old.-
 -Weak: The equivalence of a man suffering a debilitating illness.-
 -Subpar: The equivalence of a healthy man of 20 with lower than average wellness.-
 -Average: The equivalence of a healthy average man of 20 years of age.-
 -Common: The equivalence of a healthy man of 20 who shows himself to be slightly above average in wellness.-

. . .

The descriptions continued on from there, but Knox just skimmed through. It went from Fair, Good, Great, Excellent, Exceptional, Extraordinary, Peak, Transcendent, to Godlike as the very last one. Each of them gave the same vague descriptions that really said nothing—most even using the names of their Rank inside the description. Common didn't seem so bad now but Knox wondered what it would take to get it to the next Level.

He then put his attention toward the Mind, Body, and Spirit sections, each with subcategories beneath them. None gave descriptions that really told him too much. The 'Mind' section said something to the effect of 'Strengthening your overall Mental abilities', and the breakdowns beneath it being the three ways you could increase it through 'hard work and practice'. What really caught Knox's attention, though, was that they all seemed to be the same value.

"What is the deal with all my attributes being the same across the board?" Knox asked Mic, who had gone back to trying to murder the helpless golden beetle.

"Oh yeah, you will find you are rather unique when it comes to attributes and even your resource pools. Each one will increase to the maximum allowed value for the Level you obtain," Mic said simply, as if it were the most straightforward thing they'd talked about so far.

"Why?" Knox asked the obvious question. Stepping forward he batted away the beetle before Mic could smash it.

"Rude," Mic said; then, turning his attention back to Knox, he finally answered. "Because, as a Titan Born you have already been advanced to Level 100, but your body's being suppressed until your Mind and Spirit can withstand your new power. It's basic procedure with a new Titan Born."

"How many are there of us?" Knox asked, thinking about Ramses and his journey.

"I don't have that knowledge," Mic said, his head drooping as if he were sad to admit the fact. "More than one I'm sure, and with you, that makes at least two."

"I could have told you as much," Knox grumbled, but the excitement of everything quickly brought his mood back. He guessed he'd understand more as he grew and got stronger, but... suddenly, a nasty thought occurred to him.

"How in the hells am I going to get stronger in a place like the Shadowfall Swamp?" Knox asked, directing his question more to the air around him than to Mic. "This place is crawling with C Ranked Monsters, there is no way I stand a chance now that I've been pulled all the way to the F Ranks!"

With that, he opened himself up to the air around him, eager to pull in essence to add to his Core. Though, with an odd realization, he found he couldn't. Even sensing the essence around himself was difficult, much less using the knowledge he'd learned to pull it in and add it to a vortex that no longer existed around his Core. In fact, his pathways were so thick and jumbled by his Core that he didn't see space for a vortex at all.

"Oh, I can see what you are trying to do, and that won't work. The Titan System will take care of all essence processing automatically, including optimal essence purification and advancements. That wild vortex you built around yourself was fascinating but ultimately flawed to failure. The way of the Titan System is much better," Mic said confidently.

Mic shifted in his place and tried to get a better look at Knox, his glowing eyes sympathetic.

"So, everything I've learned is, what? Worthless now?" Knox asked, then suddenly remembering his techniques, he picked out the very first one he'd learned and tried to do it.

He found his ability to move essence around inside of him was practically impossible and the pathways so complex that he didn't honestly know where to start. Not wanting to give up, he closed his eyes and tried his best pulling from his Core. There was a very tightly packed bit of essence there and it answered his call as he reached for it. Then, spreading it out over as much of the complex pathways as he could, he felt his body respond and felt that the world around him might have slowed just a bit, but it was hard to really tell.

"Fascinating!" Mic exclaimed. "You are using a skill without unlocking a Path. This is very odd; I'd suggest just looking at your Paths and see if there is a skill you can unlock. It'll be much easier as well."

"Fine," Knox said, the effort of what he'd been doing taking a toll on him, forcing him to find a place to sit or risk falling over.

He decided he'd go ahead and see the normal Paths first, then go to the more advanced Path of the Titans next. The last time he'd tried to open the Path of the Titans, he'd been waylaid and told to first pick out traits, but when he tried to pull up the normal Paths, it went right to it.

-Basic Paths-
    -Body Paths-
    -Warrior: Warrior comes with three specializations available at Level 10.-
    -First: Mystic Templar: A warrior who has blended the raw power of physical combat with elemental or arcane magic.-
    -Second: Berserker: A warrior who taps into primal energy, gaining immense strength and rage during battle.-
    -Third: Guardian: A protector, focusing on defense and safeguarding allies.-

-Rogue: Rogue comes with three specializations available at Level 10.-
    -First: Shadow Walker: Master of stealth and darkness, they can become nearly invisible and use shadows to their advantage.-
    -Second: Assassin: Specializes in quick and precise strikes, eliminating targets without a sound.-
    -Third: Trickster: Uses cunning, deception, and agility in combat, often employing traps or illusions.-

· · ·

-*Ranger: Ranger comes with three specializations available at Level 10.-*

-*First: Beastmaster: Bonds with and commands animals or mythical creatures.-*

-*Second: Marksman: An unparalleled expert in ranged weapons, especially bows or crossbows.-*

-*Third: Warden: Merges the wilderness skills of a ranger with druidic magic and up-front fighting.-*

-*Mind Paths-*

-*Scholar: Scholar comes with three specializations available at Level 10.-*

-*First: Arcane Theorist: Delves into the intricacies of magic theory, enhancing spell efficiency or discovering new spell combinations.-*

-*Second: Historian: Accesses and utilizes knowledge from ancient times, perhaps even reviving forgotten techniques or spells.-*

-*Third: Strategist: Master of battlefield control, able to predict and maneuver troops or allies to ensure victory.-*

-*Mentalist: Mentalist comes with three specializations available at Level 10.-*

-*First: Telepath: Can read or influence the thoughts of others, and establish mental links.-*

-*Second: Illusionist: Creates and manipulates illusions to deceive or trap foes.-*

-*Third: Cognitive Bender: Warps perceptions and memories, altering how foes perceive time and events.-*

-*Diplomat: Diplomat comes with three specializations available at Level 10.-*

-*First: Ambassador: Builds connections and alliances with other groups, races, or even otherworldly entities.-*

-Second: Silver Orator: Persuades or manipulates crowds, essentially charming or pacifying large groups.-

-Third: Truthseeker: Can discern lies and hidden motives effortlessly, making them indispensable in negotiations.-

-Soul Paths-

-Elementalist: Elementalist comes with three specializations available at Level 10.-

-First: Pyromancer: Specializes in fire magic, manipulating flames to do massive amounts of wild damage.-

-Second: Aquamancer: Controls water and ice, allowing for both fluid offense and solid defense.-

-Third: Geomancer: Draws power from the earth, summoning rock barriers or causing earthquakes.-

-Necromancer: Necromancer comes with three specializations available at Level 10.-

-First: Soulbinder: Binds souls to objects or constructs, creating powerful artifacts or golems.-

-Second: Spiritcaller: Summons and communicates with spirits or ghosts, drawing upon their knowledge or power.-

-Third: Death Knight: Blends dark necrotic magic with martial prowess, siphoning life force from enemies.-

-Mystic: Mystic comes with three specializations available at Level 10.-

-First: Celestial Adept: Channels the power of the stars and cosmos, using astral magic and summoning celestial beings.-

-Second: Druid: In tune with nature and its creatures, harnessing the power of the natural world for spells and transformations.-

-Third: Arcanum Scholar: An expert of arcane lore and esoteric rituals. The Arcanum Scholar commands spells lost to time, deciphers ancient scrolls, and can even rewrite the arcane rules temporarily to suit their needs.-

It took Knox a good while to not only read but re-read and study each of the options. It was during that time of study that he realized if he focused on one of the base Paths, like Warrior for instance, he would get an expanded list of abilities he'd learn at Level 1. It wasn't much more to go on, but it at least allowed him to make a more informed decision. Looking over each of them in turn, he pondered over their potential.

-Path Abilities-
  -Body-
  -Warrior-
  -Level 1-
  -Charge: Dash rapidly toward the enemy, delivering a powerful initial strike. Useful for quickly closing distances.-
  -Power Strike: Focus power into the weapon, delivering a blow that deals amplified damage.-

-Rogue-
  -Level 1-
  -Stealth: Hide yourself in plain sight by infusing yourself with magical shadow energies. In broad daylight, you will be hard to focus on; in the dark of night, you will be physically invisible for a short period of time.-
  -Backstab: Deliver a swift and deadly strike from behind the enemy, dealing significant bonus damage.-

· · ·

-Ranger-

-Level 1-

-Aimed Shot: Take a moment to focus and fire a precise shot, dealing increased damage and having a higher chance to hit critical areas.-

-Nature's Mark: Mark a target, making them more susceptible to damage and easier to track.-

-Mind-

-Scholar-

-Level 1-

-Arcane Blast: Release a burst of arcane energy at a target, dealing magic damage.-

-Mystic Barrier: Erect a temporary shield around oneself or an ally, absorbing a certain amount of damage.-

-Mentalist-

-Level 1-

-Mind Crush: Target an enemy's mind directly, causing mental strain and damage.-

-Telekinetic Push: Use psychic force to push objects or enemies away from yourself.-

-Diplomat-

-Level 1-

-Mask Emotion: Conceal target's true feelings or intentions, making it difficult for others to read or predict the target's emotions or intent.-

-Silver Tongue: Charm or convince people for a short duration, making them more receptive to the Diplomat's words.-

-Soul-

-Elementalist-
-Level 1-
-Flame Blast: Blasts the enemy with a burst of fire, causing burn damage over time.-
-Water Lash: Lash out from a distance with a powerful stream of water that can cut and ignores a small amount of enemy armor.-

-Necromancer-
-Level 1-
-Raise Dead: Summon undead minions from nearby corpses to serve for a limited time. Time and type of undead increases with level.-
-Plague Bolt: Launch a bolt infused with decay, damaging the target, and infecting them, causing them to spread the decay to target's nearby allies. Decay deals a small amount of damage every few seconds.-

-Mystic-
-Level 1-
-Arcane Pulse: Send out a wave of raw arcane energy in a single direction that damages and disrupts enemy abilities.-
-Void Grasp: Summon tendrils from the void of space to immobilize and drain the energy of enemies caught within.-

There were nine Paths in total, each one having three specializations, making it a grand total of... Knox counted on his fingers and calculated the number to be twenty-seven. While his basic math skills were decent, his formal education had ended when he was old enough to work. Fortunately, he had a natural curiosity and had taught himself quite a bit beyond the limited schooling available in his town.

Knox knew for certain that he had no idea which Path he

ought to take, nor was he ready to make a decision until he'd seen what the Path of the Titans already offered him. For all he knew, it could be very Warrior-centric, and he'd want to pick a more Soul-based Path to balance it out. With that in mind, he focused once more and brought up the final path: the Path of the Titans.

-Path of the Titans-
  -Titan Born of Light-
  -Level 1 Abilities-
  -Luminous Surge: Unleash a powerful beam of light, damaging and blinding enemies in its path, while also healing friendly targets for a small amount.-
  -Radiant Glyph: Inscribe a rune in the air, which will activate, depending on the runes' intended purpose, to either heal, damage, or even explode once target reaches it. This ability is only as limited as the Titan Born's knowledge of Runecraft.-

-Titan Born Specializations-
  -Luminous Vanguard: As a champion of the Light, Luminous Vanguards embody the raw physical might of the Titan. They can harness light to fortify their bodies, making them nearly indestructible. Their blows radiate with energy, and they stand as pillars on the battlefield.-
  -Arcane Luminary: Luminaries delve deep into the ethereal essence of Light to craft spells of unparalleled brilliance. They weave the raw magic of the Titan with their own soul, resulting in dazzling displays of magical power that can both mend and obliterate.-
  -Illuminated Sage: Drawing upon the vast wisdom and knowledge of the Titan of Light, the Illuminated Sage is a master of strategy, foresight, and mental manipulation. They can anticipate enemy moves, decipher the most cryptic of patterns, and even influence the thoughts of others.-

. . .

Knox reeled a bit at the immense power that each specialization seemed to promise. Even the two abilities listed for Level 1 seemed more powerful than the basic paths. A thought occurred to him as he looked over the information once more. He was Level 1, he was a Titan Born and he was supposed to already be on the Path of the Titans, so why didn't he just automatically know these two abilities?

Clearing his throat he asked, "Mic, I'm on the Path of the Titans, right?"

Mic looked up from where he lay and nodded enthusiastically.

"So why don't I know how to do Luminous Surge or Radiant Glyph?" Knox asked, even taking a second to try and draw a rune in the air before him to see what might happen. He drew out the runes for the spell of healing that Dernal had done so many times before. Nothing happened, not even a tingle of something.

"You need to learn them first. You didn't think you'd just automatically get them inserted into your head or something, did you?" Mic asked, chuckling to himself at the idea of it.

Knox let out a steady breath before asking his question. "And how does one learn his Path abilities?"

"Simple," Mic proclaimed, then, with his one good hand, he tapped the Titan Engine. "Normally, you'd need someone who already walks your path to teach you, sort of like a Path Trainer, but all Paths and abilities can be learned from the Titan Engine as well. Think of it as a master repository of knowledge and so much more."

Knox reached out his hand and touched the Titan Engine once more. He'd had to touch it to get all the information he'd been acquiring, but he hadn't thought to ask it how to learn his skills yet. He decided to do so immediately.

What happened next surprised him more than a little bit. The world around him shifted and swirled and he stood before a metallic figure he recognized from his dreams: the Titan Gowlen.

"Welcome to the Ranks, Titan. What do you wish to learn today?"

CHAPTER 28
ECHO

FOR SOME REASON, Knox was riddled with fear by the sudden appearance of the Titan and the dark, shapeless void all around him. However, he mastered his emotions and fixed his gaze on the towering ten-foot figure made of golden metal. The Titan stood there, passively waiting for Knox's response. He glanced around one last time and, not seeing Mic, proceeded to address his inquiries to this new figure.

"Where am I?" he asked, the most important question currently on his mind.

"You are in the training simulation room where you may learn and train Path Abilities—skills or spells—and unlocking both passive and active abilities. You may leave by simply sending the thought request or perhaps you'd prefer to learn one of your three abilities available to you?" Titan Gowlen spoke in a low rumble of words that conveyed a voice weathered by time.

"Who are you?" Knox asked next, knowing the answer but wanting confirmation.

"I am a visual representation of the Titan who created this realm, Titan Gowlen. However, I am not the Titan, but a mere echo of his presence left to aid those that walk the Path of the Titans," the echo said.

"Can I call you Echo then?" Knox asked, a weight of fear leaving his chest from the knowledge that he wasn't actually dealing with the immense presence he'd encountered in his dreams.

"You may," Echo said, a gentle smile gracing his face.

"You said I have three abilities to learn. I know of only two, Luminous Surge and Radiant Glyph, what is the final one?" Knox asked, remembering what Echo had said.

"Passive Ability, Titan's Insight. It allows you to gain an innate understanding of Arcane Patterns, such as the ability to hear a runic incantation and know its pattern or vice versa. It will also strengthen some of your Titan Born traits, such as Unbound Sight," Echo said as he shifted his stance, placing his hands behind his back, much like Knox's father did when he had something important to say.

"How come I learned or got the Titan Born traits automatically and not abilities?" Knox asked, the thought suddenly occurring to him.

"Traits change your very fabric of being through magical alteration. Abilities are something anyone can learn; however, it would take years and years of study or a simpler node and pathway formation to accomplish even the most simple abilities," Echo lectured.

"But I learned like four abilities before I ever found my way here," Knox said, then thinking about it he added, "in fact, my pathways were much less complex than they are now. How'd you change my internal pathways without me participating?"

"It is all part of the Titan Born Process and the Titan System enacting its will upon the territory that has so far been claimed. You will find that even the local fauna has been remade and reduced from within the territory of the Titan System. As you grow stronger and assist the Titan Engine in growing stronger, the influence that it exerts will become more potent. All will succumb to the Titan System."

Feeling that the topic was getting a bit eerie for Knox's liking, he decided to change the subject and learn an ability. "What ability should I try to learn first?" Knox asked.

"It is recommended that you first learn the passive ability, as it will aid in your learning of active abilities. Prepare for Tier 1 knowledge transfer of Titan's Insight," Echo said. Removing his hands from behind himself, he reached forward and touched Knox's forehead with a massive finger.

A sudden rush of images hit Knox and he struggled to understand them. It was the Titan Gowlen outlining which pathways within Knox that ought to be flushed with essence and permanently changed to give the desired passive effects. After the fifth time of seeing the images, Knox tried to make the first few changes. It was a long process, but he learned that he could slow down and focus the images as he wished.

He remained completely focused on the task, and after an undetermined amount of time passed, everything finally clicked into place. He felt a rush of mental fatigue wash over him and all around him he saw the tiniest of runes that made up the organization of the room. It was truly like his eyes had been opened and he knew at once that he'd unlocked his first ability, Titan's Insight.

It took a measure of focus to shade his mind from the constant barrage of runic formations and their meanings. Most of it was just too complex for him to begin to understand, but some of it made sense to him.

"I'm ready for the next skill," Knox managed to say as the fogginess left his mind. "Teach me, Luminous Surge."

The images hit hard and fast, but Knox was ready for them this time. After several minutes to gain his bearings, he realized this particular ability wasn't far too different from the technique he'd learned called Ray of Death, except that it used exclusively the Light element and required an immense amount of focus and care to initiate and control.

It felt like he was at it for weeks before he got control enough to do anything remotely resembling the example that was being given to him. He also found out that he could ask clarifying questions of Echo while in process and he'd answer. In the end, he'd learned his two abilities and Echo bid him farewell.

Returning to the normal world hit him as hard as going to the void space had been. He stumbled back, gasping for air and twirling his hands about as he regained his balance.

"Ten seconds," Mic could be heard saying, though Knox barely paid him any heed. "Was wondering if you'd ever finish."

Then what he said hit him and he had to ask, "What do you mean ten seconds? I've been there for weeks at least. I should be starving but I feel as normal as I did going in."

"Ah, you've discovered one of the many boons of the Titan Engine being used as a trainer: time dilation. I'd say it took you ten weeks to learn the most basic forms of those abilities. You'll want to check in every few levels for more abilities and to enforce the learning you've already started with your first few skills."

Knox scratched at the back of his head. "That's a neat trick," he finally said, not knowing what else to say.

Mic made a show of clearing his throat by making a coughing

noise. Knox regarded him in confusion, knowing he didn't even have the ability to breathe based on the missing section of his torso. "What?" Knox asked.

"Will you be picking a path now? Because, I have a quest for you if you are. Here, let me send it to you," Mic said, then suddenly words flooded over Knox's vision.

-Quest Received!-

-Pick an Additional Path-

-You've gained access to an additional path. This is a rare gift—unless you are a Titan Born, then it's par for the course. Either way, you have been given the chance to learn more than those around you. Find the balance between your two paths and choose wisely, as this choice cannot be re-made.-

-Objective: Pick an additional Path-

-Reward: 500 Essence Toward Next Level-

"Any tips on which Path would work best with my own?" Knox asked, finding a fallen rock to sit on to get more comfortable for what was likely to be a fair bit of studying that lay ahead.

"None at all," Mic said a bit more proudly than should be necessary.

Knox sighed and began to think over the specializations available to him on the Path of the Titans. Whatever he chose there, would dictate what other path he'd choose to help either bolster that choice or pick one to give him more flexibility in the role.

First, there was the Luminous Vanguard that seemed to focus on melee combat and raw physical might. It had the benefit of making the body stronger, which was never a bad idea, but what would the drawbacks be like? If he focused on a more physical-based specialization, he was likely to be weaker in the magical or ranged means. But he could offset that with a ranged focused Path or specialization if that was the only issue.

Next, he considered the Arcane Luminary. It was heavily focused on magic and casting, that much was clear. It also seemed to give the ability to heal or at least that was part of what he'd gleaned from the description. It could be handy to both wield powerful spells and heal allies. With this specialization alone, he might be able to connect both Dernal's type of magic and Leo's.

The idea of his two friends potentially being lost pained him, and he found himself distracted by thoughts of where they might be if they made it out alive. Knox knew he needed to finish this and pick a path, so he could wield his new magics in the defense of those he called friends. According to the system notifications, it had been long enough that he might already be too late, but he had to try and get home to see if he could help them. He had to.

One thing at a time, he told himself, looking at the final path specialization, Illuminated Sage.

There seemed to be a heavy emphasis on strategy and foresight, both of which Knox knew could be massively useful in any engagement. However, he just didn't see himself as the sneaky strategist. This surprised him a bit, as he'd always considered himself a bit of an intellectual, but he'd learned a bit about himself in the two dungeons he'd run as an Adventurer.

He enjoyed the front line, but he also yearned for knowledge and understanding. So, if he could pick a path set on learning and one of physical focus, that would be the way forward. But which one was best?

Because he wanted to survive and have at least a fighting chance against the monsters he'd soon be facing above, he was instantly drawn toward the Luminous Vanguard. It wasn't the best fit for him intellectually, but it sounded like it was the path of the most survivability and that spoke to him more than anything else. If he'd been harder to kill, that would have solved much of his problems right away.

Now that he'd chosen the path he'd walk when he achieved Level 10, the Level when the specializations would unlock, he looked back to the basic paths. These paths would give him a few new abilities and be instantly useful, even if the specializations wouldn't open up till Level 10.

There was the Warrior, but with his specialization he'd decided to pick up on the Path of the Titan, would it be wise to double down on the physical paths? There was a certain draw toward the Mystic Templar, seeing as it was all about mixing magic and physical force, but he wasn't sure. So, moving to the next few Paths, he disregarded both the Rogue and Ranger out of hand, as he wasn't the sneaky type nor did he want to take up a bow, though he did still have his boomstick.

Moving to the more magically based Paths, he first looked at the Elementalist. This seemed like a natural choice if he wanted to add a bit of ranged power that was magically focused. However, the specializations seemed a bit lacking, as they focused more on elemental choices and not the actual mystical side of it all. He marked it as a possibility and moved onward.

Necromancer. There was a sickness in his stomach just thinking about it, however, he couldn't dismiss it offhand, as the specializations really spoke to him. The Soulbinder spec called to him like no others; the ability to make objects and infuse them with the power of souls. But it made Knox curious, causing him to ask Mic a question.

"Can only Necromancers create constructs and golems like you?" Knox asked, wondering if the construct had been created by a Soulbinder.

"Not at all, although Necromancers with points into the Soulbinder talent tree are much more naturally adept at doing it. There are no true limitations, even if it might seem that way at first, in the Titan System," Mic said, giving Knox his signature smile. Knox was beginning to find it creepy, but he said nothing about it, instead nodding his thanks for the answer.

If anyone could do what the class focused on, then it wasn't a route Knox wanted to take. The spirit caller and Death Knight specs weren't of much interest to him, not if it meant his base Path had to be Necromancer. He moved to the next Path: Mystic.

This one really called out to him, but he decided to take it one at a time, like he'd been doing.

First, he looked at Celestial Adept. This very much reminded him of Dernal—at least the idea of using magic to heal. He missed Dernal, but he also didn't want to walk the healer's path. So, he moved on to the next spec: the Druid. This was a bit more interesting, as it harnessed the natural world and Knox had always been an outdoorsy kind of man. However, in the end, he moved on to the spec he'd been most excited about, the Arcanum Scholar.

-Arcanum Scholar: An expert of arcane lore and esoteric rituals, the Arcanum Scholar commands spells lost to time, deciphers ancient scrolls, and can even rewrite the arcane rules temporarily to suit their needs.-

This spec spoke to Knox in a way none of the others could. It was all about learning, spells, runes, and scrolls. What was more, the base two abilities that came with Mystic, Arcane Pulse and Void Grasp, seemed quite powerful. One that could damage and disrupt enemies and one to slow and ensnare them.

Of course, Knox was ignoring the fact that there was an entire Path named after his goal that he still needed to look over. The Scholar Path with its specs: Arcane Theorist, Historian, and Strategist. He discarded the idea of either Historian or Strategist and instead focused on Arcane Theorist as it drew him in the most.

-Arcane Theorist: Delves into the intricacies of magic theory, enhancing spell efficiency or discovering new spell combinations. -

. . .

This particular Path and spec had Arcane Blast and Arcane Barrier as the starting abilities. These spells, one for direct damage and one for shielding, could be helpful. Even without knowing more about the specs, Knox was confident he'd made his decision after all.

"I am ready to pick my next Path," Knox said, nodding to himself as if he needed to reassure himself. "Yes, I'm ready."

"Place your hand on the Titan Engine and make your choice," Mic said.

The world shifted and this time Knox didn't feel like he'd lose his lunch, though he was still a bit dizzy from the shift. Regaining his balance and looking around, he saw Echo waiting for him, this time with arms crossed.

"You're ready to pick an additional Path and learn the skills?" Echo asked when he didn't speak immediately.

"Yes, I pick the path of Mystic," Knox said, confident that his choice would balance well with his Path of the Titans spec, Luminous Vanguard.

"Very well, it is done, Mystic," Echo said. Then, putting his hands behind his back, he added, "Are you ready to learn your next three abilities?"

"I am," Knox said, standing tall and ready for the flood of mental information and images.

In the end, he learned Arcane Pulse, Void Grasp, and Mystic Insight. The two active skills presented themselves much as he'd guessed they would. Arcane Pulse appeared as a barely visible pulse of power rushing out from Knox's outstretched hand, while Void Grasp shot out from the ground like black tentacles. What was most surprising and amazing, was Mystic Insight.

It took his sense and increased it even more, specifically making it easier to spot certain patterns and traps that Knox might encounter.

. . .

-Mystic Insight: Enhance the ability to perceive hidden magical patterns, traps, or objects in the environment.-

Having not mastered any of his new abilities but having enough grasp on them to use the very weakest versions of them, Knox felt as ready as ever to go find some monsters and kill them. Furthermore, all the practice in learning the abilities made it that much easier to figure out how to use his old techniques. Though, not to the full extent that he'd learned before. They felt off when he tried to use them in the void space and doing so had gotten him a grimace from Echo, but he'd remained quiet.

"Only four seconds that time," Mic said as Knox left the void space where time moved differently.

"These abilities were much easier to master than the Path of the Titans' ones," Knox said by way of explanation. Either way, he felt tired and collapsed on the rock he'd chosen to sit on, thinking about what was next. He had a notification about his quest being complete, but he brushed it away, accepting the essence but not reading it over again.

-Personal Status-
   -Name: Knox-
   -Level: 3 (F Rank, Tier 3)-
   -Essence To Next Level: 0/600-
   -Health: Common Tier 9-
   -Mana: Common Tier 9-
   -Stamina: Common Tier 9-
   -Mind: 39 (Wisdom: 13, Intelligence: 13, Charisma: 13)-
   -Body: 39 (Speed: 13, Strength: 13, Endurance: 13)-
   -Spirit: 39 (Willpower: 13, Attunement: 13, Resonance: 13)-

CHAPTER 29
EXPLORING

"So, I have two paths and four active abilities, now what?" Knox asked, picking up Mic and deciding to go explore for a bit. He'd passed several floors, darkened as they were, when coming down to the lowest Level of the complex to interact with the Titan Engine. He made it to the stairs just as Mic activated his light orb once more.

"Now explore and I will search the system for additional quests," Mic said.

"Sounds alright to me," Knox said, moving to the next deepest floor and stepping through. To his surprise, a dim set of lights above turned on as they entered, illuminating a vast complex of buildings.

"What is this floor?" Knox asked, staying at the edge of the perimeter and examining the many hundreds of dome-like buildings built into the very stone around them.

"This is housing, though it's not been used for a very long time. I'd suggest skipping your exploration of this room and heading straight to the fourth floor. I have a quest that I think you might like," Mic said, and a quest prompt appeared before his vision.

Knox ignored it for the time being, heading straight for the fourth floor. The staircase twisted up as they went, and the smell of dust and rock filled his nostrils. This place, whatever it truly was, had been abandoned for some time. There must have been life here at some point, but it had been overgrown by rock and debris.

"Oh, here is a prime quest that you ought to work on," Mic said just as Knox reached the fourth floor. Whatever it was, it was lost on him as the view before him took his breath away.

Rows and rows of golems, covered in dust, yet still somehow gleaming, stood before him. It was like a vast army had been built and he'd just stumbled upon it.

"Whoa, these friends of yours?" Knox asked, laughing nervously as he wondered if all of these constructs were alive or not.

"What? No. These are all mindless empty vessels waiting to be filled. Check your quest and you'll know what I mean," Mic said, a hint of frustration bleeding into his voice.

. . .

-Quest Received-

-Activate a Golem-

-The Previous Titan of Light created a massive army of Clock-work Golems meant to help the spread of the Light and the influence of the Titan System. Continue his mission by taking charge of the Soulstone collection and gathering souls to inhabit the golems.-

-Objective: Active 0/3 Golems-

-Reward: 3 New Golem Companions, 2,000 Essence Toward Next Level-

Then, seeing as he had another quest that needed his attention, he peered at that one as well.

-Quest Received-

-Reach Tier 2 of the Titan Engine-

-You have just begun walking the Path of the Titans, but you must not forget to feed the Titan Engine. The more essence you feed it, the stronger you become, and the stronger the Titan Engine will also become. Go fetch additional Monster Cores.

-Objective: Add 5 C Ranked or Above Monster Cores to the Titan Engine-

-Reward: 10,000 Essence Toward Next Level-

While that quest had a nice reward, it wasn't Knox's main focus for the moment. No, instead, he was moving to examine items hidden in chest lockers at the feet of each and every one of the golden armored golems. Inside, he found a gem on a cushion and when he focused on it, he got a surprise as information filled the translucent screen that kept appearing before him.

. . .

-Soulstone: Can be used to capture an A Ranked Soul or below.-

How or where that extra bit of information had come from, he didn't know, but it didn't really give him any new information short of confirming what he'd already assumed. He went to three more of the lockers and pulled four walnut-sized gems out, pocketing them each in turn. He still didn't know how he'd face the monsters outside the safety of this cave, but he wanted to find his notebook and take notes.

Turning, he picked up Mic where he'd placed him, and they headed to the mysterious room at the top with the giant armored skeleton. Though, something odd awaited them above and he looked at Mic in surprise.

"Where'd the armored guy go?" Knox asked, the seat where he'd sat was now empty. Gone was the sword, the armor, and the skeleton.

"Oh, that," Mic said as if he wasn't a bit surprised. "The Titan Engine likely took what was left and converted it into usable essence when you activated it. No worries, he was dead after all."

Knox couldn't help but groan a little. He'd wanted to look at all those rune marks and possibly even try to use the left-over metal. Instead, it was all gone, just like that.

Eventually, he got over it, pulling free his notebook and going to work recording all that he could remember about it. Next, he went over strategies on how to defeat stronger monsters, whether it be from traps or other means. He came up with surprisingly little and, before too long, felt the call of sleep beckon him. The sky was now lit only by moonlight after the sun had slipped below the horizon.

While he lay on his back with his pack under his neck, he thought about all he'd likely missed. The system had said that he was unconscious for 303 days, this being the 304th day. His thoughts went first to Dernal, Leo, and John. There was a chance they were still alive, though he wouldn't have given them good odds. If the monster had taken after him like he'd thought, then perhaps all three made it.

The amount of blood pouring from Dernal's wound was worrisome, but Dernal was a healer. If anyone could survive such an interaction, it was him. But what of his friends and family back in his hometown?

His mind quickly passed over to his father, despite the time that had gone by, his anger still glowed red hot when thinking about him. But Terrim, Fred, Murdock, and Beth came to his mind and put a weight in his gut. If that monster attacked his town, they wouldn't have stood a chance. Once more he felt compelled to go check on them, to somehow escape the Shadowfall Swamp and see for himself.

Sleep came shortly after that and to his dismay, he dreamt of shadows. Each one whispering the words to long forgotten rhymes and children's songs, and with each passing note they drew ever closer. Morning woke him from his slumber, but he was surprised to find himself covered in sweat and breathing hard.

"You alright?" Mic asked from where he sat a few feet away. "You were screaming about shadows coming—uh oh, here comes another shake!"

Before Knox could ask what he meant, the entire complex around them began to shake and stones fell from the ceiling, narrowly missing him.

"What the hells is happening?" Knox finally managed to say as he stood and dodged a falling stone the size of his head.

"Been happening all night, but this is the worst one yet, ah dang, my good arm just got smashed," Mic said, and Knox looked over to see a rock the size of his torso crushing the golem's remaining arm.

Grabbing hold of the rock, Knox heaved, and to his surprise, it moved rather easily. The arm, however, had seen better days. It was leaking some blue fluid, and the metal was crushed.

"Any chance I can put you in one of those golems downstairs?" Knox asked, seeing the lights begin to flicker in Mic's eyes and not wanting to be left alone in this place.

"My Soulstone is cracked, bring another one up to my chest and I'll move over to it. When I enter, I won't be able to talk, but you must go downstairs and place it within the chest. There is a release switch that will open the cavity. You got this!" Mic said, sounding less assured than he was trying to appear.

Knox took out one of the walnut-sized gems he'd taken and held it up to Mic. Suddenly, the light in his eyes flickered and went out, but the Soulstone instantly glowed with a gentle blue light.

Next, Knox went down to the army of golems and chose one of the ones he'd taken the Soulstones from, feeling about in the dim light for a switch or lever to release the chest armor. After several long minutes of searching, he found it on the left side under an armored ribcage. Inside the chest was the perfect sized spot for a Soulstone, so he pressed it in gently.

Nothing happened.

Thinking perhaps he'd done it wrong, he tried to take the gem out and try again, but it stuck fast, flashing each time he touched it. Giving up and feeling like he'd just condemned himself to a lonesome existence, he closed the chest and took a step back.

Immediately the eyes flashed, and a familiar voice spoke out. "I knew you could do it! No doubt in my mind! Okay, perhaps a little bit of doubting, but you did it! I am whole again and ready to serve!" Mic spoke in such an excited tone that Knox almost wondered if he'd messed something up. Yet, he appeared fine, even summoning the globe of light to illuminate the stairwell better as they climbed toward the surface.

Knox walked in mostly silence as a plan began to form in his head. Now that he had a fully functioning companion that seemed to know a touch of magic, perhaps he'd have assistance in defeating the foes above.

"You are going to help me kill some monsters, you think you can do that?" Knox asked, shooting a wry smile over his shoulder.

"Negative," Mic said. "I am here to serve the Titan Complex; I cannot venture out of it, even for the defense of said Complex."

"Do all golems have that restriction, and if so, what is the point of you all?" Knox asked, feeling the frustration of another dashed plan falling apart before he even had a chance to work out all the details.

"Depends on the type. I am a worker-class; however, you have placed me within a combat-able vessel. I am just not programmed to do such violence. I can, however, begin repairs to the complex now that I am fully functional once more," Mic said, a rigidity to his words that hadn't been there before.

"Fine, get to work and I'll go out and get myself killed," Knox said, his frustration boiling over. He felt strong, he didn't need any help, regardless of his Level and Rank.

Finding his axe and going over his abilities in his mind, he looked around for an easy way out of the hole. In his frustration, he failed to notice a ladder on the far wall until Mic pointed it out to him.

Upon reaching the surface, he was surprised to find himself in a completely different environment. The once open swamp had transformed into a vast forest. There were also odd cracks in the ground here and there, likely where water had gone if not out to sea.

Birds began cawing in the distance and he turned toward the water. He was already so close; he might as well check out the shore and see what he could find. His special sense spread out before him, more powerful and keen than ever. He felt no monsters, well, he felt no monsters any stronger than him. There were a few wolves, even an owlbear, but all of them gave off the presence of low-Ranked beasts.

As the first wolf approached him, he almost didn't take it seriously, throwing his axe the moment it cleared the trees. It easily dodged the attack, leaving Knox without a weapon. Idiot! He thought to himself as he prepared to use one of his new abilities.

Figuring he'd start off by trying to slow its approach, he held out a hand and cast Void Grasp. Shadowy tendrils of black grabbed at the wolf and Knox felt the smallest bit of something leave him, likely either his Mana resource or Stamina, perhaps a mix of both. Next, he used his other Mystic ability, holding out his hand and speaking the runic words, he did the cast in half a dozen seconds, the wolf was nearly on him by the time he finished the cast.

The attack lashed out from his outstretched hand and smacked right into the wolf's open maw, cutting the top part of its head off in a gruesome display of raw power. Knox was unsure if it was because of how close the cast had gone off or if that was how it was meant to work, but either way, the wolf was done fighting, its body twitching on the ground as the rest of it came to terms with its demise.

-Wolf Level 2 Killed-
  -Gained 33 Essence-

Knox just about laughed out loud at the small amount of essence the wolf gave off. It was better than nothing but at this rate it would take twenty wolves just to get him to Level 4. That didn't sound so bad when he thought about it, but still, perhaps he could find a Monster Core inside of it.

Retrieving his axe, he began to dig around in the wolf's leftovers. If he had any kind of knife he might skin it, but as it was, he wasn't even sure he wanted the meat this wolf had to offer, it was so scrawny and weak. Guided by his sense, he found the Core easily enough.

-Weak Wolf Core Level 2: Contains 50 Essence-

. . .

Unbidden, a system notification gave him more information when Knox focused on the small gem he'd collected from the base of the wolf's spine. The outdoorsman in him hated to leave waste on the forest floor, but there must be stronger predators out there or at least scavengers that would enjoy the meal he was leaving out. With that in mind, he pressed on toward the endless sea, curious to discover what lay ahead.

CHAPTER 30
PIRATES

IT WAS ASTOUNDING to him that there were so few threats in the area that presented much of a challenge at all. He faced several more wolves, an owlbear that presented more of a challenge, and even a creature called a Nolic, a spiky being with three-fingered claws and two massive eyes. Having just defeated one such creature and bringing his essence gains to a total of 527, including the

Cores he'd found intact, Knox happily slurped up the essence of each Nolic since they were too low for the Titan Engine's consumption. As he did this, a group of weaker Nolics appeared through the trees.

Of course, Knox had sensed them coming, and based on the fight with the first one, he hadn't been concerned. But now that he could see them, he let a small trickle of worry fill him. They were twice the size of the first one and as he focused on them, the system filled him with more information about the group.

-Nolic Level 5-

It wasn't much, but that meant they were two Levels higher than Knox and the previously challenged Nolic, which meant with three of them before him, he might be in for a challenge. Throwing his hand up he cast Void Grasp; he'd gotten good enough at the spell that it encompassed all three this time, dragging them toward the ground and sucking away some of their energy.

Turning, Knox put a bit of distance between them, not out of fear, but in knowing that his next cast had a decent range and took a second to get going. Pulling from within himself, he felt the power build as he readied his most powerful ability, Luminous Surge. He'd previously used it on the owlbear that had been Level 3, to a devastating effect and now he was going to see how well it dealt with Level 5 monsters.

The air around him crackled as he gathered the tendrils of the ability for a powerful strike. The lead Nolic broke free from his snare and, with surprising speed, raced toward him, claws at the ready. After taking a final deep breath, Knox unleashed his spell.

Light poured from his palm in a cascading swirl of illumination that left him blinking against the brightness. Knox wasn't sure the spell would hit its target, as he'd lost sight of his attacker and felt a sudden drop that he now recognized as a substantial amount of Mana loss. That was the biggest drawback to the spell, it took time and cost a fair bit of Mana. It was frustrating that the values weren't more concrete, but he could feel himself drop to about half of his potential, not all of that was from just that attack, seeing as he'd just used abilities to take down the first Nolic.

Something he realized from the many times of casting, was that it wasn't just his Mana pool that took a hit; his Stamina pool was getting hit each time he used any ability as well. Over time, he knew he'd get a better feel for it, but until then, he was just hoping he didn't push himself too hard before he got stronger.

His eyes cleared in a flash, and he saw the damage he'd wrought, readying another spell for the remaining Nolic. Two piles of steaming flesh were all that remained of the two leading Nolics; the first must have been joined by another in the seconds he was focused on casting.

His Void Grasp faded and the third sluggishly came at Knox, clawing like a madman. It was at that moment that Knox decided he was a match for it in speed. Instead of finishing it off with an Arcane Pulse and leaving himself even closer to zero Mana, he readied his axe for the beast's incoming attack.

He nearly closed his eyes as his sense stretched out around him, focusing on the incoming attacker, but he managed to keep his eyes on it. Turns out he wasn't actually faster than it, but he had something better than speed; he could feel where it was going before it arrived. Leaning hard on his sense, he dodged and weaved the attacks until he finally saw his perfect opportunity.

It took one swing of his axe to remove the Nolic's head from its shoulders and end the fight. As he had with every other fight, he pulled out the Soulstones to capture the souls of the defeated monsters, but just as before, they were too weak, and the transfer process failed.

. . .

-Congratulations! You've Leveled up to Level 4!-
   -Personal Status-
   -Name: Knox-
   -Level: 4 (F Rank, Tier 4)-
   -Essence To Next Level: 323/700-
   -Health: Common Tier 9-
   -Mana: Common Tier 9-
   -Stamina: Common Tier 9-
   -Mind: 42-
   -Body: 42-
   -Spirit: 42-

Knox blinked at that and flexed his muscles. He felt refreshed and renewed since the leveling, as if all his resource pools were filled to the brim. Beyond that, this time he literally felt stronger, whereas the previous levels it hadn't been so noticeable. Still, his Health, Mana, and Stamina remained Common Tier 9. He'd have to ask Mic about it more when he got back, but for now, he pushed it from his mind and looked for more monsters to help him get to Level 10.

His new goal, besides exploring and whatnot, was to get to Level 10 so he could see what the specs on both his Path of the Titans and his Mystic Path held. Maybe then he'd have what it took to go explore and find his friends.

Considering how long it had been, the weather ought to be snowy by now. Yet, for whatever reason, the Shadowfall Swamp, that was more a forest than a swamp currently, was the picture of summer. Warm rays of run pierced the canopy, providing warmth and light as he moved through the trees in search of more prey.

As his steps took him closer to the coast, Knox began to pick up the faintest distant call of voices and swept his sense as far as it would go until he came across three individuals, humanoid by the feel of them.

He approached with caution but even so, he wasn't built for

stealth. Neither was his armor, several damaged pieces clinking in odd ways and announcing his approach.

Three figures sprang to their feet, weapons drawn. They wore loose fitting pants with different color wraps around their waist and each of them were shirtless. They held curved blades and had brands on their cheeks, each of them with a matching P seared into their flesh.

Knox had heard enough stories to know he was dealing with pirates. He was instantly on edge, his own weapon raised and ready to strike. If these pirates were operating inside the Shadow-fall Swamp, then they must be powerful indeed. However, based on the impressions he received, they couldn't be much more powerful than he was, though Knox knew his sense wasn't a perfect gauge of strength.

"Look at what we have here, Boris," the tallest of the men said. He sported a black beard, ragged and untrimmed, as well as a row of yellowing and black teeth, with dull brown eyes to match. "It's a lost little boy."

"Uh, he don't look like no boy to me," another said, presumably Boris. He had dirty-blond hair, no beard, and a short, stout, muscled build. With sparkling blue eyes, he regarded Knox, before speaking again. "I'm thinking he be some kind of Adventurer."

"Both of you shut it and let's grab him before he runs," the final pirate sneered the words, getting to his feet in a flash and running toward Knox. He had long brown hair and a long beard to match. He wasn't even as fast as one of the Nolics Knox had just killed, so he readied an ability without fear of being overwhelmed just yet.

To his surprise, the lead pirate suddenly accelerated, catching Knox halfway through casting Arcane Pulse. Knox was knocked to the ground, but not before he managed to slash in front of himself with his axe, intercepting the sword that was descending toward his chest.

Despite the distraction, he finished his preparations and was able to cast Arcane Pulse just as he hit the ground, and it went off in the pirate's face. The wave of energy slammed into the pirate's nose, cutting a deep swath of red into his face. He reeled back screaming, but Knox had already begun working on Void Grasp while simultaneously kicking out with his feet to throw the wailing pirate back and out of the way.

Tentacles of black reached up out of the ground, grabbing hold of the two pirates. One of them had already halted, perhaps thinking of fleeing, but that wouldn't happen today!

Knox released an attack of Luminous Surge and a powerful beam of light cut into the two remaining pirates. With more screams filling the air, he got to his feet and readied his axe. He watched them squirm in their own blood, living the last moments of their wretched lives in blood and agony. He then knelt over the first pirate and slammed his axe into his head, putting him out of his misery.

After he'd done the same to the other two pirates, the battle rush began to subside, and the gravity of his actions began to sink in. He had just murdered three men. Granted, they were pirates, likely murderers themselves. And they did attack first, he reasoned, so he only acted in self-defense.

He reached his hand in his pocket and felt the three Soulstones within. They had not worked for any of the monsters he had killed, their souls being too weak. Then an idea began to form. What about a human soul? These men weren't exactly deserving of a second chance. But he did need to figure out how the Soulstones worked. As he pressed each of the Soulstones to the pirates' heads, a notification popped into view.

-Unrecognized Sentient Being Outside of System Control killed-
    -Calculating proper Essence reward... calculated.-
    -130 Essence Per USBOSC killed-
    -Three Souls Captured in Soulstones-
    -Congratulations! You've Leveled up to Level 5!-
    -Personal Status-

-Name: Knox-
-Level: 5 (F Rank, Tier 5)-
-Essence To Next Level: 13/800-
-Health: Common Tier 9-
-Mana: Common Tier 9-
-Stamina: Common Tier 9-
-Mind: 45-
-Body: 45-
-Spirit: 45-

Knox had barely broken a sweat taking down those pirates and already he was halfway to Level 10. Now that he had the Soulstones filled, he could take care of the quest that rewarded 2,000 essence and get that much closer to Level 10. So, with that on his mind, he finished clearing out anything he could find, including going through the pockets of the dead, but finding precious little other than an odd black orb.

As he left the camp, an eerie feeling settled over him, and the forest around him seemed to visibly darken. His sense began to pick up a presence unlike anything he'd felt before. It was reminiscent of the time he had felt a living being, but it was colder, sharper. A chill ran down his spine as he continued to move in the direction of the Titan Complex.

For nearly a mile, nothing approached him, but still, he knew he was being watched. Sure enough, as he rounded another cluster of trees, there was a small dark figure standing directly in his path with a small sickle held outward as if ready to strike.

"Who are you?" Knox asked, prodding and attempting to sense the being. However, where she stood, he felt nothing, yet all around her, he felt a powerful presence bearing down on him.

The figure didn't answer, her face a mask free of emotion, and her eyes were as dark as the darkest night. Her mouth opened as if to speak, but no words came out. Instead, the ground trembled, and suddenly Knox looked away as he felt a powerful presence close in around him all at once.

Then it was gone, along with the young girl and the shaking ground. Knox blinked several times, his breathing deep and ragged as he struggled to understand what had just happened to him. With newfound haste, he headed toward the Titan Complex and what he hoped would be safety.

Before long, and after having to kill another four wolves, two Nolics, and another owlbear, Knox made it back to the safety of the Titan Complex.

With less than a hundred essence needed to reach Level 6 from his trip back, Knox almost considered staying out longer. However, he would soon have 2,000 essence coming in, so he dismissed the idea out of hand. As he descended back into the complex, less concerned about being attacked or killed, he began to contemplate. While he usually welcomed having his head filled with thoughts, these particular thoughts were dark and brooding.

He'd just killed three men in a more vicious and brutal manner than ever before, and not dungeon constructs either. Yet, he found himself looking at the situation from the outside in. He knew that he ought to feel bad, ought to be worried that he ended three lives with passions and paths of their own they were meant to follow. But he couldn't help feeling a bit numb to it all.

Much like when he had brought down his axe on each of them, putting them out of their misery, there was just a dull awareness that what he was doing might be beyond what others would call right. Yet, here he was, feeling the dark thoughts about what he'd done, yet now not being bothered by them in the least. As he reasoned before, these men were evil. If they had his powers, they would have killed him just as quickly and easily.

And now that he knew that Soulstones worked easily enough on human souls, he might even consider going back to look for more pirates to capture and kill. It wasn't like they were using their leftover energies the Soulstone captured when they died, right? It was a thought for another time. For now, it was time to go and finish his quest.

Knox was greeted by Mic the moment he had descended the ladder that led into the first sunlit room of the complex. Sunbeams filled the room with enough light that Knox worried they might be easily spotted from above. He made a mental note to ask Mic about it.

"Greetings," Mic said. "I sense you've grown in power and have captured several weak souls. I would warn against creating golems with inherently weaker souls, as it will hamper their growth and progress. I'd recommend you capture Level 30 or above to have the best outcome. My own soul was first captured as a Level 58 creature, though what I was before I couldn't say. My memories don't extend much further than meeting you and a mix of other random flashes."

"Greetings to you," Knox said in response to the long-winded greeting Mic gave him. "I think we have enough golems that I can activate these three, get the essence reward, and find stronger ones later. Do golems grow in power or learn cool techniques such as your light spell?"

Mic nodded along as Knox spoke and immediately answered when Knox finished, "Oh yes, these particular golems are able to progress and Level up the same as someone connected to the system. They have three paths, and thus, there are three types of golems: Maintenance, Physical Defense, and Elemental Defense golems. I've already told you I am a Maintenance golem; thus, I get abilities that assist me in my duties."

Knox nodded, understanding. "Yes, then Physical Defense and Elemental Defense golems would cover the two main types of damage dealing."

Mic nodded this time, adding, "However, it gets more nuanced as they grow. Some might take skills better suited for utility or support as they see the needs you have, but it is their choice to walk the path they choose."

"I understand that. What do you say we make you three new friends?" Knox asked, pulling the gems out of his pocket.

"They might not be much help at that Level, but let's get it over with," Mic said, smiling in his odd, slightly creepy way.

A sudden thought occurred to Knox, and he caught Mic's arm to get his attention. He was surprisingly warm, considering he was made of metal. "Is there anything we can do about the giant hole above us, I'm worried that predators or creepy little girls will find us and ruin what safety we have down here."

Mic's head went to the side a bit and he said, "Creepy little girls? I'm aware of no monsters who take the form of creepy little girls. Nevertheless, I can work on covering the hole. My earth mover ability takes time, but it is effective in making temporary or even permanent coverings. However, I must warn you that the covering will likely fail when the Titan Complex is lifted out of the ground and takes its rightful place on the surface."

"What's that?" Knox asked, then elaborated when Mic just gave him a perplexed look. "The Titan Complex is going to lift out of the ground?"

"Once you reach Tier 3 of the Titan engine, it will have enough energy to accomplish the feat, yes. Did you think that the enlightened and powerful Titan of Light would hide in the darkness?" Mic asked the question as if it were the silliest thing he'd ever considered.

"I guess not," Knox said, pocketing the Soulstones and leading the way to the fourth floor where the golems awaited.

Mic had been busy during Knox's absence, as far as the eye could see, dust and debris on this level had been cleared out and even several dozen golems had been polished to a shine far greater than the dull luster they'd had the first time Knox had come across them.

"Good job," Knox said, slapping the warm golem on the back in congratulations. "You clean up fast, pretty soon this entire complex will look brand new. Oh, quick question, you say the golems pick their own path, but can I request for them to be maintenance like you?"

Mic shifted from foot to foot, a very living humanoid expression that once more looked odd on the mechanical man. Eventually he answered, "Each golem has been created with certain limitations in how far they can disobey you—their creator—including myself. However, I'd recommend not pushing those lines too hard at first. Despite coming from the creation of other beasts and monsters, we are, in fact, sentient beings that enjoy having a sense of freedom. Though, our entire being speaks toward our actual imprisonment."

There was a tone of sadness in his speech that Knox almost didn't notice, but it was there, overlapping his words as he spoke about his lack of freedom.

"Are you sure there isn't anything I can do that will allow you more freedom?" Knox asked, feeling grateful to his only companion, and wanting to help him if he could.

"I'm afraid your current knowledge and understanding is severely lacking for the task of creating golems. Perhaps, in the future as you learn, you might be of more assistance," Mic said, then gesturing to the golems he added, "Shall we get started?"

"Let's do it," Knox said, pulling free the Soulstones and taking a deep breath.

Soon he'd be one step closer to reaching Level 10 and finding a way to check on his friends.

CHAPTER 31
BORIS, VLAD, AND EDGAR

THE ROOM SMELLED LESS dusty now, and instead, a new, sharper smell that Knox couldn't put his nose on filled the area after Mic's cleaning spree. Standing before the first of the golems, Knox almost stopped to ask him what he'd been using to clean and polish, but thought better of it, deciding to stay focused instead. He had three golems to bring to life and hoped that at least one of them wanted to be combat oriented so that they'd be able to help him fight mobs and grow stronger.

All the golems looked similar, metal bodies made thick and armored. Their faces had the semblance of eyes, but really what Knox had been figuring as eyes were more of a 'V' shaped visor with a darkened section at the dip of the 'V'. Each of the silent and still golems lacked any light in their eyes right now, but he knew that would soon change when he put the Soulstones in place. He wondered absently what type of personalities or paths these new golems would fill.

So far, Mic had been a bit strange, but mostly mild in his expressions of emotions and speech. Would all of them have the same willingness to serve and be helpful or would he have to compel them to follow his orders? So many questions filtered through his mind, and he couldn't help but hesitate before placing in the first stone.

Slowly and with much apprehension, Knox flipped open the chest armor and gently placed in the gem. At first, nothing happened, and Mic placed a hand on his arm, getting his attention in much the same way Knox had only minutes before, it was as if he was learning to copy Knox's own mannerisms.

"The first awakening is difficult and sometimes can take a while. I would suggest placing all three and then we can watch them for signs of failure or activation," Mic said, his lights dimming to a gentle glow as he spoke.

Knox nodded, saying nothing, and swiftly began flicking open chest plates and placing the gems into three golems, then retrieving five more just in case he encountered more pirates or stronger monsters. Surely, the Shadowfall Swamp still had some strong monsters left, otherwise, where had they gone?

It was a thought that had crossed Knox's mind several times while above ground hunting the weaker monsters he'd found, but no answers came. What was worse was that pirates had moved into the area, which was beyond odd to him. It made sense that they'd want to operate in an area without law and was avoided by most, but shouldn't they be worried about powerful monsters as well? His thoughts went to the black orb he'd found on the lead pirate and the odd feelings it gave off.

Perhaps it had something to do with the lack of stronger monsters around. Pulling it free from the pack he'd taken from their camp, he turned toward Mic, ready to ask him about it. But just then, the lights on all three golems flickered and their eyes blazed to life at the same time. Pushing the black orb back and setting down the bag, Knox pulled out his axe, ready for anything. It was never a bad idea to be prepared for something to go wrong.

"Welcome, brothers," Mic said, speaking first. "This is Master Knox, he activated you, and as such, you must obey his commands. Do you understand?"

"We do," all three said at the same time and Knox was surprised to find that their voices matched the ones they'd had in life.

After looking around for a bit, one of them stepped forward and leaned toward Mic, cupping his hand beside his metallic mouth. "Say, what the hells is happening here? Is this some kind of dream?"

Mic reeled at the question and turned to Knox. "You used a human soul for this golem?" His words were those of utter and complete shock; there was no masking it.

"Yeah, three pirates attacked me and the Soulstones finally worked to capture something. Is that bad?" Knox asked, suddenly worried he'd messed up and would need to put their souls to rest.

"No, it's just unusual. These golems were created to hold monster souls, taming them, and giving a certain amount of knowledge. However, sentient beings can't inherit that knowledge, and short of the binding scripts to keep them from harming you, they'll have an unprecedented amount of freedom."

"You knows we can hear you, right?" one of the other golems said, while looking at his metallic arm and then suddenly down at the space between his legs. "You stole my dilly wanker!" he cried out abruptly while pointing at Knox.

"Let's get him boys," said the clear leader from before. But as they all stepped toward Knox, their eyes suddenly flickered, and he spoke again. "On second thought, how bouts you explain what in the hells is going on with us and then... uh... maybe we will let you be."

"They can't harm you or even themselves," Mic said flatly. "Listen up new recruits, please introduce yourselves and then I will walk you through picking a path."

Knox was grateful that Mic was taking the lead because he was unexpectedly stunned and unsure how to proceed.

The one on the far left stepped forward. "My name's Vlad." Then the middle one did the same, answering as if compelled to do so.

"Name's Boris," he said, pointing a thumb at himself, as if speaking weren't enough to identify him.

"And that leaves me," the last one said, pausing for several long moments. Then letting out a very human sigh, he spoke. "I'm called Edgar, or at least I was before you killed me, master."

"Don't call me that," Knox quickly said, the very idea of them calling him master had his gut turning.

Several emotions came crashing down on him at once and he felt sick to his stomach. Not only had he killed these men, an action he still reasoned with himself was necessary, but now he'd enslaved them? Slavery wasn't something to be taken lightly, and it had been outlawed in the country for as long as Knox could remember, possibly from the start of the kingdom. Sure, there were prisoners confined and forced to work, but that was always as a way to pay back some debt or as justice for laws broken.

Perhaps, they could see this as an imprisonment, instead of outright being enslaved. He decided to offer it to them as such and see how they took it.

"I've got to clear the air," Knox said, holding up his hands to silence Edgar who'd been talking nonstop while Knox thought through his options.

They silenced and Knox continued. "You are all pirates, and you were going to kill me, do you deny it?"

As one, they said, "No."

"Then, think of this as your prison sentence. For attempted murder, you will serve me for as long as it takes me to figure out a way to grant you your freedom from the compulsion to follow my orders. Until then, I expect you to behave and be productive, do you understand?"

"You killed us," Boris said, looking down at his metallic hands.

"And now he is forcing us to pay for crimes he isn't even confident we've committed," Edgar said, he seemed the smartest amongst them and the most talkative. "Surely, you can see why we'd want to take any chance to kill you now that you've done us such a great disservice. However, I do admit to feeling the compulsion to protect you, so I suppose we are all in agreement. Now what?"

Knox looked to Mic who folded his arms and addressed the newcomers. "You will see that you've got system messages, go over them and tell me which path interests each of you."

Boris raised his hand and looked toward his comrades who just looked flatly back at him.

"Yes, Boris?" Knox asked when Mic didn't respond to his raised hand.

"Can't read," Boris explained, then put his hand down.

"Reading isn't required to understand direct system messages," Mic said, again, his voice flat and uncaring.

"Oh, well in that case, I want to be a wizard. Shooting spells and all," Boris said proudly.

"There are three choices, you dolt," Edgar said, shaking his head at his comrade. "Maintenance, which by the sound of it means we'd just be swabbing the deck some more. Physical Defense and Elemental Defense. I'd bet my arse that elemental is what would make you all wizard-like. Looks like we'll be learning techniques after all."

"I'm taking Physical Defense," Vlad said matter-of-factly.

"Good and what path will you follow, Edgar?" Knox asked, doing his best to come off as friendly, and not as a killer who enslaves his victims.

"I'm not one to clean when I have a choice for another option. I'd say I'm more inclined to wizardry than our friend Boris, so I will walk the path with him, assisting him as best I can," Edgar said, his tone a bit snootier than it had been before.

"Wonderful," Mic said, though his voice lacked any enthusiasm. "Now, make your selections and you will be given the knowledge to unlock your first two abilities. Since you are directly connected to the Titan Complex and Golem under its purview, you can learn and adjust your talent trees—once unlocked at Level 10—on command while within its walls. Any questions?"

"Uh, sure. So, how do I do the picking of the path?" Boris asked, stealing a glance toward Edgar who put one hand over his face and shook his head.

Before Mic could answer, Vlad did, his voice low and rumbling. "Just think it, got mine easily enough."

"Thinking ain't my strong suit," Boris complained, but he lowered his head and put a hand to where his temple ought to be. "Got it!" he exclaimed a solid minute later.

"So, what'd you learn?" Knox asked, eager to hear what new abilities his temporary allies had.

"Thunderclap and Whirlwind," Boris said, struggling to say each word. He held out his hands and suddenly a vortex of wind, small and pointless, appeared before him. It lasted all of three seconds before it faded away. Before Knox could say a word, Boris held up a finger and said, "Now, check this out!" He slammed a foot down and sparks of yellow energy shot out from all around him, hitting all of them, but doing nothing.

"Didn't even tingle," Edgar declared, shaking his head. "Let me show you what I learned. Mind if I target one of your many things?" Edgar gestured with his hand at one of the nearby golems, Knox nodded his assent and fire appeared in Edgar's hand.

He hurled it forward, and it slammed bodily into the construct, knocking it over and leaving a blackened scorch on it. "Fireball," Edgar announced as all eyes went from him to the scorched golem. Then, just as Knox stepped forward to tell him he probably shouldn't damage what was likely extremely valuable constructs, Edgar held out his hand and the room grew cold.

Chains of ice shot up from all around the fallen golem, wrapping and tangling it up further. After roughly six seconds, they faded into nothing, leaving icy marks all over the golem.

"Wow," Knox said, unable to put words to how impressive Edgar's spells seemed when compared to what Boris had shown. "That will be useful when fighting monsters. What did you learn Vlad?"

Vlad walked over to the golem and picked it up. The thing was as stiff as a board, so he took a second to balance it just right before stepping back. Then, Vlad reared back a fist and punched it. Just as his fist was moving through the air, a barrier of rock or something similar to rock formed over his fist, and the golem went flying, smashing into two others and knocking them all down.

"That was effective," Knox said, but suddenly Vlad was moving with extreme speed toward a new golem, passing two others and knocking them aside as if a force of energy surrounded him.

Knox cringed at the now half a dozen golems knocked over and scuffed. Stealing a glance at Mic, he couldn't read the golem's emotions, but he figured, as the only maintenance golem, he likely wasn't happy about the mess.

Sure enough, he spoke up with a cool and calm anger a moment later. "Combat golems or not, you will be picking up each of those and polishing them back up to a shine. Do you understand me?"

"Yes, sir," they said at once, each of them looking around afterward as if shocked that they'd responded in kind like that.

Figuring it must be a part of the compulsion that Mic knew much more about than Knox, Knox just smiled at the show.

"What are those abilities called?" Knox asked, wanting to make sure he could accurately record all of this in his journal later.

"Boulder Punch and Rampart Rush," Vlad said, his words the usual rumble.

"As you grow stronger, your abilities will evolve and more will become available to you. For now, I'd say try not to overdo them by using them too frequently while coming back to recharge. Shall I escort them to the armory to make them battle ready?" Mic directed the last bit toward Knox.

Eyes wide, Knox sputtered a few times before finally getting the words out. "A-armory, are you saying there is an armory here and you didn't tell me?"

"You have both arms and armor, though it looks to have seen better days. I assumed correctly you'd be safe above, seeing as most of the essence has been pulled from the land, forcing the stronger monsters to flee to more rich essence areas," Mic spoke matter-of-factly, but Knox grumbled all the while.

"Fine," Knox said, frustrated but ready to see this armory Mic spoke of. "Take us to the armory."

CHAPTER 32
ARMORY

THE TRIO TALKED ALL the while as the group moved from floor to floor, Mic leading the way to the armory. It wasn't so bad, but the three of them started to test how much pain, or the lack thereof, that they could feel, and Knox almost put a stop to it.

"Alright, alright, now kick me right between the legs," Boris declared excitedly.

Vlad took the opportunity without question, kicking him as hard as he could right between the legs.

"Felt nothing," Boris said, proudly knocking on his nether region. Then something seemed to dawn on the new elemental defender, and he spoke again, but this time sounding dejected instead of proud. "I felt nothing."

"Take cheer," Edgar said, cutting off whatever Boris was about to say next. "We are alive when we ought to be dead. I'm sure once this fine gentleman learns the ropes, he will endow us with all sorts of gifts, just like the captain always promised us but never delivered. Ain't that right, Sir Knox."

"I'm not a knight," Knox said flatly, then not wanting to totally shoot down Edgar's attempt at being civil he added, "But yeah, as I learn more about the golems, I promise to improve you guys and eventually set you free."

"Hear that, Boris," Edgar said, smirking. "He's going to improve us and set us loose."

"They won't ever be truly free," Mic said, a sadness in his voice that Knox didn't like hearing. He felt bad for the golem, and Knox didn't know why. "We depend on a charge that accumulates from exposure to the Titan Engine. Unless another power source is worked out, they could go, at most, a month away before they'd need to return."

"I'll figure it out," Knox said, before anyone had a chance to respond. "Just give me time."

He missed what floor they stopped on, but the staircase opened up to a pitch-dark room, with only the light from Mic revealing any details.

A door was set into the wall and came into view as they grew closer. Knox's sense tingled when it came in contact with it, so many runes glowing over every possible section of the door. It was by far one of the most complex pieces he'd seen, besides the Armor and Titan engine, which remained a complete mystery to him. Reaching out, Knox touched the door and found it oddly cold, almost as if it were sucking out the warmth from his body.

"Careful," Mic said, pulling Knox's hand away. "I've not yet keyed all the doors to you yet. Give me a second and then place your hand here when I say." He gestured at a circular area where the runes were less dense than the rest of the door.

The door appeared to be made from a mix of gold and a blue iron Knox hadn't ever seen before. The gold color was used more as an accent, with the rest of the door being the almost iridescent blue. Beyond that, Knox could see nothing really, just golden bands of metal over a massive blue iron door.

"Imagine if the captain knew about this place?" Edgar said, his eyes running over the door and, Knox guessed, dreaming of what lay within.

"What can you tell me about your captain and why you guys are in Shadowfall Swamp?" Knox asked, taking the opportunity to see what information they'd give up.

"You can screw right off," Vlad said, his gruff voice startling Knox at the sudden hostility.

"Oh look, we can tell him to screw off," Boris said, laughing. "Screw off, you cock-faced pickled peanut."

"Ah, refreshing," Edgar said, joining the fun. "You are a worthless slug whose existence has no worth. Also, you smell, or at least I remember you smelling before you blew my face off. And fuck you sir, we will not betray our captain so easily or give you intel so you can create more slaves out of our old comrades."

"Mic?" Knox asked, but the golem was bent into concentration over the door and didn't seem to be following the conversation.

"I order you to tell me why you are in Shadowfall Swamp," Knox finally said, seeing if the phrasing would do the trick.

"Don't know, just where Captain Dread and the Dreadbone fleet harbor has always been," Edgar said, the words spilling out.

Vlad, and even Boris, looked at Edgar with hands raised up in confusion. Edgar put his hands over his mouth and Knox realized he'd been looking at Edgar when he spoke, so the command must have forced him to comply.

"I'm sorry, I won't do that... uh... often," Knox said, feeling bad that he'd had to force their hands.

"You dimwitted ninny muggin," Edgar said, stepping forward threateningly but then, suddenly taking twice as many steps backward.

"Place your hand," Mic said, his voice interrupting in perfect timing.

Knox stepped forward and did as he was asked. "Now it will open for me and you, what about them?" Knox asked, trying to keep his voice at a whisper and failing to do so based on Boris's scoff.

"Only maintenance constructs and you have the permission to enter the vaults, same for all the sub doors leading to the treasury, armory, and the like," Mic said loudly enough that all who were present could hear. Another round of groans sounded, but Knox ignored them.

"Treasury?" Knox asked, putting a hand on Mic and raising his eyebrows.

"Yes, as well as an Arcanum Vault for dangerous magical items, a Memory Chamber to store critical information, a library, and several critical workrooms that require additional defense or security. I believe there might be more, however, my memory is still fragmented, and I can only barely recall the last Titan that ruled here and created much of what you see," Mic said, his words washing over Knox. Knox stopped hearing much of what he said after 'library', but he kept nodding along.

"To the armory, then the library, and maybe that Arcanum Vault," Knox said, his mouth beginning to salivate.

"Unfortunately, you currently only have access to the armory until you advance further down the Path of the Titans. However, at Level 30, much of the complex opens up to you. Here is a quest to remind you," Mic said, as the door in front of them began to open, a dull light leaking from within.

. . .

-Quest Received-
  -Complex Controls-
  -You are required a certain understanding and distance down the Path of the Titans before the fullness of the Titan Complex will be opened up to you. Reach the first milestone by reaching Level 30 and unlocking much of the Security Level.-
  -Objective: Reach Level 7/30-
  -Reward: Access to Security Level, 10,000 Essence Toward Next Level-

The quest alert made Knox aware of something he hadn't noticed. Looking up in his log of information, he saw that he'd completed the quest 'Activate a Golem' and got 2,000 essence, bringing him up to Level 7 and almost to Level 8. Now he was only 2 Levels away from his first major goal. Doing a quick little fist pump, Knox followed the four golems deeper down a massive hallway lined with doors similar to the one that had split right down the middle to allow them access. The door was now shutting ominously behind them.

Looking through his log, he saw that he'd completed three quests so far, 'Learning the Basics' and 'Pick an Additional Path' being the other two. Knox would have to bother Mic for more easy quests, as they seemed to be a quick way to get essence directly from the system. If he could have gotten one for killing the local wildlife and monsters, then he would have been golden.

"Here we are," Mic said, stopping outside a door that looked no different than the dozen others they'd passed so far. Without Mic, Knox wasn't sure he'd had survived this long.

"Put my hand here?" Knox asked, reaching forward after Mic nodded in agreement.

The door split open, each of the halves going into the wall like some kind of hidden pocket door that Mr. Tome might make for the mayor. Except, the metal itself seemed to fit together in a complex array of shapes and gears. A self-operating door was a wonder to behold, but Knox's eyes immediately went over the room in surprise and confusion.

The walls of the room were lined with metal stands holding countless spears—literally hundreds of them. Above them, on the wall, were fine-looking short swords, long swords, axes, and all manner of other weapons. However, Knox's sense left him feeling confused; not a single weapon in the room was enchanted. Stepping in further, he saw that the room was about two dozen paces deep and half as wide. Toward the back, bows, arrows, and even a few crossbows were neatly arranged.

"Where are the enchanted weapons?" Knox finally asked, turning from the back of the room and regarding Mic with raised eyebrows and a deadpan expression.

"The armory holds weapons, the Arcanum Vault holds the weapons created with runes, both weak and terrible in power. Unfortunately, you aren't yet strong enough to lay claim to that room. However, one of the workshops is open to you and it has several books on basic crafting, as well as Runic formation, that I believe you will find useful for your Radiant Glyph ability," Mic said, unphased by Knox's facial expression.

"Where's the armor?" Knox asked, looking around and seeing only weapons.

"Right here," Mic said, reaching down and touching the floor. The empty space in the middle of the floor moved up, shifting out of the ground, and revealing rows and rows of armor from leather to cloth to plate. Even some several layered types that Knox wasn't familiar with. They had scales that layered over each other like the flesh of a dragon.

"Scale mail armor," Edgar said, running his hand down one such suit of armor.

All the armor was plain and nondescript, though none showed any sign of age, rust, or wear. Which was odd to Knox, considering there wasn't a single rune in this room attached to a weapon or armor. However, the exterior walls, floor, and ceiling were stuffed with plenty. Knox made a note of a few he didn't recognize, but he'd come across enough already that he'd likely be spending weeks going over them when he had the time.

"Suit up and grab weapons you are familiar with," Knox ordered; then, turning to Mic he said, "Take me to the workroom you mentioned, I'd like to try and fix up my armor as best I can before going out again."

"Right away," Mic said, turning toward the trio. "We will return shortly, you won't be able to leave, so stay put."

All three protested loudly, but Knox and Mic slipped out the door, which automatically shut behind them, drowning out any other objections they might have had.

"What do you think of the three new recruits?" Knox asked as they walked down the hallway toward the workshop.

"I'm disappointed in you and them. But I understand you made your mistake in ignorance. Though, why they don't just request death as a release, I cannot understand. Being a sentient being and having yourself so thoroughly changed seems to me a sentence worse than death."

"I hadn't thought of it like that. Should I offer to... put them out of their misery... do you think?" Knox asked, genuinely not sure what to do next regarding the trio.

"No," Mic said, making a sound very similar to a sigh, though Knox didn't think he even needed to breathe. "They've taken to it better than I could imagine; for now, let them live out their new lives and when their usefulness has ended—end them."

"That's a bit harsh, don't you think?" Knox asked, surprised at the ruthless words of his companion.

"Would you set upon the world three evil men gifted with powers directly created by the Titan of Light? It is your job to spread enlightenment and truth, not set evil upon the world," Mic said, stopping in front of a door five down from where they'd started.

Reaching out, Knox put his hand on the door, and it opened. "I guess that makes sense. If the need arises, I'll end them and be sure they aren't a threat to the world. Thank you for your guidance, Mic," Knox said, though it pained him to do so. He truly wanted to be free from the burden of his actions, but now that Mic had brought it up, Knox knew it was the right thing to do. Setting loose metallic pirates gifted with magical and physically enhanced powers would only end in additional loss of life.

The room before them was the same size as the armory, yet it was filled with all manner of machines and tools that Knox didn't recognize. He could see what he thought may be a forge, and definitely could see a few anvils, but otherwise, he felt that he was more likely to injure himself here than he was to fix his armor.

"I'm not familiar with many of these tools," Knox admitted.

"Allow me to demonstrate them," Mic said, moving toward what Knox assumed was a forge. He pressed several buttons on the flat surface and then placed a block of blue iron into a small space that opened up. Inside, was the familiar glow of red-hot embers. How it had gotten so hot or if it was always hot, Knox was unsure.

"This is the blacksmithing station. That over there, works with hides, and here we have an all-purpose station with a variety of tools you can use," Mic went on, describing in more detail the workings of each, and how they would respond to Knox's pressing of certain buttons. The buttons were infused with Arcane circuits to facilitate the passing of energy from one place to another.

Luckily for Knox, he was familiar with working with many tools in Mr. Tome's workshop and was a quick learner. It only took a few explanations for him to get right to work—first, heating and bending the metal back into place, and then, using a special tool designed to cut into the middle of an object, he inscribed some runes that had been damaged. It was work that filled Knox's soul with joy and before long, after a trip to retrieve his notes and release the trio, he'd finally done it: the armor was restored to its original quality.

Sure, it had a few tarnished areas where Knox had used some

scrap blue iron to patch the missing metal, but all in all, it came together wonderfully.

-Personal Status-
    -Name: Knox-
    -Level: 7 (F Rank, Tier 7)-
    -Essence To Next Level: 947/1200-
    -Health: Common Tier 9-
    -Mana: Common Tier 9-
    -Stamina: Common Tier 9-
    -Mind: 51-
    -Body: 51-
    -Spirit: 51-

CHAPTER 33
GRINDING AWAY

"So, how'd you all become pirates in the first place?" Knox asked as they made it back to the top level and out onto the surface to find more monsters to kill for experience.

"Fuck off," Vlad said, but Boris laughed and began to speak freely.

"I was a wee orphan and made a living on the streets when the captain picked me up, with the promise of gold and women," Boris said, nodding vigorously to his own words.

"Our stories are much the same," Edgar said, waving a hand about. "But forget our tales of adventure, how'd you find yourself out here and alive in such a dangerous place?"

Knox saw no reason to hide information from them, seeing as they were bound to follow his orders. "Got attacked by a C Rank or higher Monster and it chased me all the way out here. I got lucky and fell into the Titan Complex."

"Aye, lucky indeed," Edgar said, eyeing Knox curiously.

"You ready to tell me how you all stayed alive in such a dangerous place?" Knox asked, his hand going for the black orb and pulling it out.

"Ah shit," Boris said. "He's found our bobble."

"Quiet you," Edgar said, reaching out for the black orb. Knox held it back, eyeing them with apprehension.

"So, this has something to do with it?" Knox asked, smiling. "Tell me more."

"Well, we don't know much to be honest. We had just gotten promoted to scouts and Captain gave us the orb. It apparently wards off strong monsters, but that's all we know," Edgar said, shrugging.

Putting the orb away, Knox motioned for them to follow. "We are going to test out your abilities, get ready for combat."

They traveled through the forest in a single file line, Knox in the front with his sense guiding them, Edgar taking the lead of the three, with Vlad at the back.

Their first encounter happened to be the most difficult of the day. A dozen Nolics appeared from atop some trees and set upon them with fierce determination.

"Boris and Edgar, you hit their flanks; Vlad, you take the middle and I'll support you from behind," Knox cried out, giving rapid orders, and sighing internally as none of them were followed.

Edgar stepped forward, wearing scale armor—the same Vlad

and Boris had chosen as well—and brandishing a too-big sword. He managed to land a hit on one Nolic, but Boris threw aside his short sword altogether and held his hands out to cast. A small wind funnel appeared, but it had no effect on any of the Nolics. Instead, it only drew the attention of four Nolics at once, and they all swarmed Boris together.

The largest of the Nolics slammed into Vlad just as he reared back a punch for it, knocking him on his ass. They'd each chosen a different colored scarf that they'd found inside the armory, so it was easy to tell them apart now. Vlad wore blue, Boris red, and Edgar yellow.

Currently, Boris's red scarf was being used to drag him out into the woods by three Nolics while one sat atop him slashing and beating him. Knox took in all the sights and sighed one last time before springing into action. With a quick Arcane Pulse, he blew off the one atop Boris and staggered the remaining three, giving Boris the opportunity that he needed to make it back to his feet.

With Boris now scrambling for his short sword, Knox turned to help a struggling Vlad. Activating his Radiant Glyph ability, Knox drew into the air a combination of runes that, if he remembered correctly, would react with explosive force. The runes hissed and sparked as he worked, releasing forward the moment he finished.

The attack slammed into a Nolic with deadly force, blowing an arm off and flinging the body like a rag doll. This Radiant Glyph ability was terribly useful!

Next, he lined up a Luminous Surge to help Edgar against the half dozen he was managing to keep at bay with wild swings of his sword. Two went down, three peeled away, leaving Edgar fighting against a single Nolic. Dropping his sword at an awkward angle, Edgar began to cast.

A ball of burning fire slammed out from him and took the Nolic full in the chest, leaving a blackened scorch mark and dropping it to its back. Retrieving his sword from where he'd stuck it in the ground, Edgar slammed it down on the first, and then onto the other two downed Nolics for good measure.

Meanwhile, Knox had cast Void Grasp, panting for the effort of using all of his abilities so close together. It was having the desired effect, though; slowing and draining the enemy enough that his pirate golems could take them out.

After only a minute or two, the battle was over, and they were no worse for wear. Sure, they were as tired as they were going to be already, but as long as another dozen didn't try to attack them all at once, it should be alright.

Looking over his system notifications, Knox realized that the essence he'd gotten was much less than it ought to be. Until he focused on it, and it showed that the essence was being split four ways evenly. More than ever, Knox was ready to find all the Cores intact, as he'd be guaranteed that essence if he did so.

What he found was only half of the dozen had Monster Cores that hadn't been cracked or broken from the combat. Still, he greedily sucked in the essence and felt a surge of energy as he Leveled once more. Now at Level 8, he needed 1,400 essence to Level up again. He had a solid chunk already, which meant he only needed slightly more than a thousand. Consequently, he needed to kill nearly a hundred more monsters or significantly less if they had Cores that could be harvested. And that would only get him to Level 9; they'd have to keep on grinding out essence for several days if he wanted to hit Level 10.

Looking over the quests he'd been given by Mic, he smiled inwardly thinking about how easy it might be after all. He'd asked for some more basic quests and Mic hadn't let him down.

-Quest Received-
   -Clearing the Way-
   -There are monsters above that need to be thinned out in order for the safety and secrecy of the Titan Complex to remain intact.

Kill fifty such monsters and return with their left ears to prove their death.-
   -Objective: Kill 12/50 Monsters and Collect their ears-
   -Reward: One Magically Infused Item, 2,000 Essence Toward Next Level-

-Quest Received-
   -Pirate Trouble-
   -There are pirates in the area, and they risk bringing more trouble down on your head than you can handle. Kill off as many as you can and bring back their left ears as proof.-
   -Objective: Kill Pirates and Collect their ears-
   -Reward: 25 Essence per left ear returned, repeatable-

Knox wasn't sure how the golem pirates would handle killing their own kind, but there was too much essence on the line not to try and find some more pirates. If the ones he found were anything like the three he'd killed, he wasn't worried about them presenting a challenge to him at all. Unfortunately, Boris, Vlad, and Edgar were still being tight-lipped on the subject and Knox didn't want to push his authority too hard on the matter.

But as the day progressed, no pirates were encountered, despite Knox taking them in a beeline direction toward the coast. Instead, they fought Nolic after Nolic, whatever the hairless bastards were doing breeding must have been at the top of their list. By the time Knox turned them around to walk back toward the Titan Complex, they were only ten shy of hitting 50 monsters killed. Because half of those had Cores on them as well, Knox had jumped into the next Level.

He was stronger and more able to cast spells, but still, the gains seemed negligible compared to the vast changes he felt when going from one Rank to another. He was just over a hundred essence into the next Level that required 1,700 in total. If they could kill just ten more monsters on the way back, he'd be set to reach Level 10 by way of turning in the quest to Mic.

It was while they walked and talked, that Knox's sense caught hold of something in the distance to the east. It was an all too familiar feeling of half a dozen humanoids—not Nolics this time.

"I order you to stay here while I go take a look at something," Knox said, being sure to get a head nod from each of them before setting off. They had to obey direct orders as far as Knox could tell, so this should keep them from getting too close to the other pirates he'd sensed.

As Knox neared, the forest began to fill with the distant smell of burnt wood. Sneaking as best he could and sticking to the shadows, he saw smoke rising from a recently extinguished fire. Five pirates walked about an open area in the trees, some talking while others were busy breaking up a small camp.

Knox got as close as he dared and settled down to listen and spy on them. His sense told him that one among them was stronger than the rest, but with the numbers so far skewed against him, he wasn't going to be the first to strike out.

"Can't believe those morons got themselves eaten up. Captain says that we will be pulling double teams and scouting missions for the next few weeks just to be safe, can you believe that?" a black-bearded man said, his accent odd enough that Knox barely understood the words he spoke.

A more articulate man began to speak next; he was also the more powerful of the bunch. "Keep your head down and do your work. If Captain hears you belly aching, he'll put you in the boo box, and you don't come out of the boo box."

"I just don't see the point of this, we've captured a bunch of weaklings, recovered almost no treasures from fallen Adventurers, and I hear Gensile island is bursting with babes this time of year. With winter coming on soon, we ought to make out to open waters and warm the beds of some fancy ladies," the black-bearded pirate said.

"You know damn well what the captain plans on doing with those captives," the stronger of the five said. "Each one of them, down to the lad that got himself run through, is dressed in fancy attire and you know only nobles or rich merchants can dress themselves so well. The ransoms we get for their skins will make the entire campaign worth it. But to do that, we need to keep the lands cleared of beasties, otherwise we might have some good for nothing Adventurer sneak his happy ass on to us and take away our prize."

Suddenly Knox's sense went wild, and he felt someone approaching from behind him. He slipped into the deep brush just in time for a sixth pirate to appear out of the shadows, daggers held ready. He looked about, seemingly confused by the lack of finding someone and Knox kept himself as quiet as he could. His sense ran over the man, and he was stronger even than the loudmouth sitting around the fire. By his aura, this man was well into the D Ranks.

Knox had to make a choice, and quick. He could lash out and begin fighting, possibly taking out their strongest member in the surprise rush, or he could sit still and hope he wasn't discovered in the thick brush.

His choice was made for him when he heard Boris call out from a distance. "Hey, is that you George? Guys, look, I found George!"

They'd slipped Knox's direct command and came after him. Damnit to the all the hells.

Standing straight up, Knox brought his axe down on the surprised and distracted rogue. However, he had tricks up his sleeves, because right as his axe was to smash him in the head, he lurched, and his daggers caught the weapon.

Using his not-as-effective version of Haste, his technique flared to life and brought him into a position to strike out once more. However, the rogue jumped back and out of reach. This was fine, Knox thought as he held out his left hand and let loose a Luminous Surge. Whatever the rogue had expected, this obviously wasn't it, because the blow took him full in the chest and threw him back like a rag doll.

So bright was the light that Knox found himself blinking rapidly to recover for the incoming crowd. His three not-so-loyal golems approached then, Edgar surprising him by stabbing down into the rogue's chest, finishing him off.

"Time to go to work boys," Edgar shouted, Boris and Vlad ran forward into the onslaught of five pirates, weapons raised, while Edgar shared a look with Knox before casting his Icy Chains attack.

Chains of ice lashed up at the pirates, taking two of them to the ground and slowing the rest. Seeing the opportunity, Knox held out his hand and smashed into the group with an Arcane Pulse, then ran into the fray with his axe up and ready.

The strongest of the remaining five met his axe with a curved blade, and for several long moments Knox matched his strength. Suddenly, his opponent grew stronger, throwing him back and slashing low. The pirate's attack on his magically reinforced plate armor did nothing but surprise Knox.

Back and forth they danced as chaos reigned around them. Each time Knox would get a decent hit in, the pirate would come at him with two of his own. Knox grew tired, but remained uninjured thanks to his armor, however, his attacks had done a number on the pirate, each shallow cut bleeding him out more and more.

It was due to this combined and cumulative assault that Knox finally found his opening, smashing his axe into the neck of the unsuspecting pirate. Blood spurted and poured out all around the mortally wounded pirate and a part of Knox almost pulled out the Soulstones to collect their souls. But Knox thought better of it, preferring to grab monster souls whenever he encountered some strong enough.

Looking around, Knox was glad to see his companions were in one piece and the remaining four pirates were not.

"Time to loot!" Boris exclaimed, reaching into pockets and

packs to clear out whatever items they might have. Knox joined them, each of them taking a pack and filling it to the brim with food, coins, another black orb, and an assortment of odds and ends.

On their way back to the Titan Complex, they killed a total of fifteen monsters: wolves, Nolics, and an owlbear. But it wasn't until they were near the entrance that Knox finally stoked up a conversation between the trio.

"You disobeyed a direct order," Knox said, his face stern and emotionless.

"Technically, we didn't," Edgar said so fast that Knox knew he must have been planning to have this conversation.

"How's that?" Knox asked, eager to hear Edgar's take on it.

"We stayed put as you asked, however, you didn't say for how long, so we continued our duty, protecting you," Edgar said as if it were the simplest of things. "Trust me, we don't like it as much as you do. It's been burnt into our very being that we have to keep your silly ass safe, no matter what. So, we did our duty and killed our brethren. The least you can do is give us some credit and congratulate us on reaching Level 5."

"We Leveled up?" Boris said, seemingly as surprised as Knox felt.

"We will surpass you I think, given enough time," Vlad said, a bit more proudly than Knox cared to hear.

"Doubtful, but your ability to Level up does certainly help matters," Knox said, smiling at the trio. They weren't the most ideal companions, but they were all he had at the moment. A thought occurred to him, and he put a hand on Edgar's shoulder. "Tell me about the captives you all took?"

Edgar didn't hesitate to fill Knox in this time, telling him how one of the scouting groups had found a group of five would-be Adventurers and the captain himself had gone out to capture them. He didn't know much more than that, but he reinforced the tale of one of them dying by the captain's hand when he wouldn't surrender. They were in the Titan Complex by the time

Edgar finished and Mic sent over a new quest after hearing only part of his tale.

-Quest Received!-
 -Saving the Day-
 -Some Adventurers have been captured by pirates and need to be helped! Do what you can to free them and bring them back to safety.-
 -Objective: Free Captives-
 -Reward: 10,000 Essence Toward Next Level-

"Really?" Knox asked, thinking about how impossible a task freeing them would likely be and what he'd have to do to pull it off, all for 10,000 essence.

"Quests are a great way to advance," Mic said, nodding his head knowingly at Knox. "Congratulations on hitting Level 10 by the way. It is time for you to learn about the Talent Tree Path System."
 -Personal Status-
 -Name: Knox-
 -Level: 10 (F Rank, Tier 10)-
 -Essence To Next Level: 993/2,000-
 -Health: Common Tier 9-
 -Mana: Common Tier 9-
 -Stamina: Common Tier 9-
 -Mind: 60-
 -Body: 60-
 -Spirit: 60-

CHAPTER 34
TALENT TREES

INTERNALLY, Knox felt like he was right on the cusp of something, similar to how he felt when he'd gone from one Rank to another. But this time was different, as it was in the Titan System. He looked at his system messages and pushed aside all the ones about Leveling up and his personal updated status, until he found what he was looking for.

. . .

-Path of the Titans Talent Tree Unlocked-
-Path of the Mystic Talent Tree Unlocked-

Knox focused on the messages until, just like that, the first of the talent trees appeared: the Titan one. Looking over what he found there, he was surprised.

"How many talent points do I have?" Knox asked, while trying to find the answer for himself in the system. Right as he found the right place where it told him, Mic answered his question.

"One for your normal path, and two for your Titan Path, although there is nothing preventing you from using the points on either path," Mic said.

Figuring this might take a while, Knox went and sat on the massive throne, surprised at how comfortable it felt to do so. With his feet dangling like he was a young child sitting in an adult's chair, he looked over what he had available to him, starting with the Path of the Titans.

-Luminous Vanguard-
 -Tier 1-
 -Radiant Endurance: (0/5) Enhance your physical endurance and Health by 5% per point.-
 -Illuminated Strikes: (0/3) Infuse your strikes with radiant energy, increasing physical damage dealt by 5% per point.-
 -Radiant Ground: (0/1) Smash your foot into the ground and infuse it with light, bolstering friendly targets' speed and slowing enemies. Does a small amount of damage per second to enemy targets and heals a small amount to friendly targets.-
 -Tier 2-
 -Blinding Resilience: (0/5) Bolster your resistance to debilitating

effects, reducing the duration of stuns, silences, and slows by 3% per point.-

-Titan's Aura: (0/3) Emit a radiant aura that inspires allies, increasing their physical damage by 2% per point while in your vicinity.-

-Ethereal Step: (0/1) Learn to perform a short dash, leaving a trail of radiant light that boosts ally speed and harms enemies.-

-Tier 3-

-Lightforged Armor: (0/5) Forge armor infused with light, reducing incoming damage by 3% per point.-

-Searing Strikes: (0/3) Infuse your attacks with searing light, causing your targets to take 3% increased damage per point from all sources for a short duration.-

Knox could tell that the Tiers went down further to Tier 7 at least, but they were blurred out and he could only see three deep. Shrugging, he moved to the other talent trees, as all three seemed to be open to him, despite him making up his mind before that he wanted to focus on the Luminous Vanguard build.

"Can I place points in either of the three talent trees?" Knox decided to ask before going back to looking over them.

"That is correct," Mic said, then added, "Although, it is recommended to put all points into a single tree as it will be the most effective. Eventually, you will earn enough points that putting some in other trees might make sense."

"Interesting," Knox said, turning his attention back to the system messages.

-Arcane Luminary-

-Tier 1-

-Radiant Surge: (0/5) Amplify your magical prowess, increasing the potency of your light-based spells by 2% per point.-

-*Soul Infusion: (0/3) Learn to infuse your spells with a fragment of your soul, reducing their Mana cost by 5% per point.*-

-*Tier 2*-

-*Illuminated Recovery: (0/5) Enhance your healing abilities, increasing the effectiveness of your light-based healing spells by 3% per point.*-

-*Ethereal Harmony: (0/3) Attune your soul to the harmonious flow of magic, reducing the cooldown of your light-based spells by 7% per point.*-

-*Tier 3*-

-*Resplendent Burst: (0/5) Empower your magical bursts, causing your light-based spells to have a 5% chance per point to explode on impact, dealing additional damage to nearby enemies.*-

-*Soul Channeling: (0/3) Master the art of channeling your soul's energy, increasing your maximum Mana pool by 4% per point.*-

-*Illuminated Sage*-

　-*Tier 1*-

　-*Enhanced Luminosity: (0/5) Increased damage and range of Luminous Surge by 10% per point.*

　-*Rune Mastery: (0/5) Radiant Glyph persists 20% longer per point.*

　-*Tier 2*-

　-*Solar Grace: (0/5) Solar Wings grants an additional 5% movement speed per point when active.*-

　-*Refraction Mastery: (0/3) Prism Ward increases ally movement speed by 5% per point within its vicinity.*-

　-*Tier 3*-

　-*Predictive Harmony: (0/5) Reduces cooldown of Chronicle Resonance by 2 seconds per point.*-

　-*Chain Fortification: (0/5) Lustrous Chains reduce damage dealt by bound enemies by 5% per point.*-

-Beacon's Call: (0/1) Summons a luminous beacon at your location, pulling enemies toward it for 2 seconds.-

Again, Knox found that he couldn't see past the third Tier, no matter how hard he focused. Though, what he did find in those three Tiers of each of the specializations really drew him in.

It was mostly as he'd thought, the Luminous Vanguard focused on increasing the body's ability to be a more front line fighter, even giving him the option of unlocking a really effective area of effect ability and a mobility move not so different from the Warrior's Charge or the golem's Rampart Rush.

But the other trees were all too tempting as well, increasing magical damage in general or enhancing the damage output of key abilities. It even mentioned abilities that Knox hadn't encountered yet, like Solar Wings or Prism Ward.

Next, he looked at his Mystic talent tree, leaning forward and staring into the translucent blue screen of information. Knox decided to just look at the first Tier of this tree and skip the second and third Tier for any useful abilities.

-Mystic Path Talent Tree-
  -Celestial Adept-
  -Tier 1-
  -Star-Bound: (0/5) Increases the potency of all star and cosmos-related spells by 4% per point.-
  -Celestial Guardian: (0/3) Allows the summoning of a minor celestial entity to aid in combat. Each point increases the guardian's Health and damage.-
  -Druid-
  -Nature's Touch: (0/3) Increases healing effects by 5% per point.-
  -Thorny Defense: (0/3) Upon being hit, reflects 5% damage back to the attacker per point.-
  -Arcanum Scholar-

-Arcane Study: (0/5) Increases the Mystic's Knowledge of ancient spells, reducing the preparation time required for rituals by 2% per point.-

-Scroll Mastery: (0/3) Enhances the effectiveness of scrolls created by the Arcanum Scholar, extending their duration or effectiveness by 10% per point.-

-Arcane Enhancement: (0/5) Increases the damage and spread of Arcane Pulse by 5% per point.-

"I'm Level 10, are there any new abilities that I could learn from the Titan Engine?" Knox asked, the realization hitting him that it probably was the case.

"Yes, I believe you've got a few abilities ready to be learned on the Path of the Titan and the Path of the Mystic," Mic said, already turning to walk to the staircase and summoning his globe of light. Meanwhile, the trio just sat around joking amongst themselves.

"How often will I learn new abilities?" Knox asked as they wound down the stairs to the lowest floors of the complex. The staircase had been recently dusted and polished, as well as debris removed from it. Mic continued to be hard at work while Knox wasn't around.

"For the first 20 Levels it's fairly often, but it slows down and all but stops around Level 40 to 50. Then it's all about how you can use or alter your own abilities, so they suit you the best," Mic said, but something about that caught Knox's attention.

If the Level system was the same as before, or not really the same, but had a certain level of equivalence, then reaching Level 40 meant reaching B Rank and Level 50 meant A Rank. He suddenly wondered if the essence would increase vastly on higher Levels or was the major block into the B and A Ranks gone with the Titan System in effect? He also really wondered if others joining the Titan System would have to give up all their powers and start from the beginning.

"What happens when others are joined to the Titan System, will they also start at Level 1?" Knox asked, as they entered the Titan Engine room.

"Not at all," Mic said cheerily.

Knox's face fell a bit. "Why not, I mean, I know you said all my essence was used to aid in my transformation and as a Titan Born I'm different, but that doesn't seem fair to me. How do they learn their paths and abilities?"

"Once you've increased the potency of the Titan Engine, the system will be able to directly teach individuals their skills much as you've learned, but from a distance. However, the Titan Engine is on low essence usage and cannot currently perform that function. Remember, the stronger you grow and the more essence we can feed into the Titan Engine, the stronger its influence will become. You are directly tied to the success and spread of the Titan System, so try to keep yourself in a single piece," Mic said, tilting his head toward the Titan Engine.

"So, as I naturally grow stronger so will the Titan Engine?" Knox asked, trying to read the subtext of Mic's words.

"More or less," Mic said, nodding.

Knox nodded and placed his hand on the Titan Engine. At once the world swooned and before him stood Echo.

"Welcome back, here to learn more about your path?" Echo asked, but Knox had a few questions he wanted to try and get information about before they started.

"Yeah, but first, what can you tell me about the Titan Gowlen and why the Titan System was created?" Knox asked, hoping that Echo would be friendly enough to enlighten him.

"I can answer a limited, few inquiries. However, they must be more specific. I know much about the Titan Gowlen, as I am a copy of sorts of him as he was when I was created. As to why the Titan System was created, it depends on what you mean. The Path of the Titans was a personal project of Titan Gowlen and an attempt to do as his creators did, creating beings able to create life as they do. If you mean why the Titan System that rules over reality here, all I can say is that it is the will of your creators that you have a certain amount of Order to ward you from the Chaos that travels through the vastness of space," Echo said, his words running together as he spoke, almost as if he were excited to get the words out.

Knox blinked several times, surprised at how forthright Echo was being. "Thank you for that information," Knox said, smiling. "Why did Titan Gowlen create a pocket world for us and what lies outside of it?" Knox thought back to the dreams he'd had; more and more they were returning to the forefront of his mind.

"Titan Gowlen endeavored to create a new way or approach to raising mortals into immortality. His siblings were a distraction that he deigned to ignore by using his specialty in dimensional pockets to create a space separate from the rest of reality where he could run his experiences in secret," Echo said, then putting his finger to his chin he added, "As to what lies without, everything else of course."

Knox's head hurt thinking about the possibility of what Echo was saying. But in the end, he determined that he shouldn't let himself hyper focus on it, with so many other mysteries currently taking up his time. "What can you tell me about what will happen to me as I grow stronger and follow the Path of the Titans?"

"You will grow to become that which Titan Gowlen wished, a true successor to his people, the Titans. If all happens as he planned, you will wield the power of a true Titan, being able to shape reality and bend fate around yourself. You will also have the ability to leave this section of space that has been pocketed off, should you reach the apex of your power. However, out of 32 Titan Born through the ages, none have reached the apex of their power. You could be the first, if you can survive long enough and not become stagnant. Good luck. Shall we look at what abilities you have available now? I've limited energy and this conversation had already taken more than I ought to spend on such tasks."

Knox sighed, but there was no helping it. "Yes, show me first what Mystic abilities I have available."

PATH OF THE TITANS - SYSTEM ACTIVATION

. . .

-Mystic Abilities-
-Level 8-
-Mystic Armor: Craft Basic Armor that shields the wearer from physical and magical attacks. The more powerful the Mystic the more powerful the armor.-
-Level 10-
-Mystic Veil: Cloak allies in a shimmering aura, making them harder to target and reducing incoming damage for a short period of time.-

"Now show me the Path of the Titan abilities," Knox ordered and soon his vision was filled with the Titan abilities.

-Path of the Titans-
-Level 8-
-Lustrous Chains: Conjure chains of radiant energy to bind and burn adversaries, preventing them from using abilities for a short time.-
-Level 10-
-Prism Ward: Craft a shimmering barrier that refracts and dissipates incoming attacks, converting a portion of them into healing energy.-
-(Passive) Luminous Resilience: Every spell you cast has a chance to leave a protective afterglow, reducing the next incoming damage by a half.-

Knox could see some potential and synergy between his two paths, but a part of him now wondered if perhaps he should have picked a more physical-based normal path. His Titan path was turning out to have very magical-based heavy abilities and tools.

He knew something for sure, he was definitely going to be going down the talent tree of the Luminous Vanguard now.

As he'd done before, he spent the time required to learn each new ability to the smallest degree, each one being only the most basic understanding. But he knew that as he learned more about the Runic system and used them more and more, they'd ingrain themselves deeper into his mind. It was enough that he was able to do them, even in their most limited capacity.

Giving Echo a thankful wave, Knox returned back to normal time and nearly went to a knee as he did so. The world around him swam more than usual and Mic was at his side at once, helping him up.

"Nearly thirty seconds," Mic commented. "You spend far longer than what is considered normal, you should be more careful."

Knox believed it, as he had so much to learn that it took weeks and weeks, even with the compressed time within the Titan Engine. But it was done, and his stomach was unknotting itself from the time within the Engine.

"I need to place my talents now," Knox said, pulling up the talent trees and looking them over once more.

He had three points to place and unfortunately, he couldn't currently place points deeper than Tier 1. He tried several times, as he wanted Ethereal Step, but it wasn't meant to be. A quick question to Mic revealed that each Tier had to have at least five points in it before the Tier below opened up. That meant he'd need more Levels. Of course, that was always the answer.

With three points to place and the Mystic tree being a bit lack-luster, Knox focused on the Path of the Titans tree. Of course, he'd be taking Radiant Ground, which took up one point, but where to use the next two? He decided that for survivability's sake he should take Radiant Endurance, so he added two points to it.

-Luminous Vanguard, Tier 1 Talents-

-Radiant Endurance: (2/5) Enhance your physical endurance and Health by 5% per point. (Currently at 10%)-

-Illuminated Strikes: (0/3) Infuse your strikes with radiant energy, increasing physical damage dealt by 5% per point.-

-Radiant Ground: (1/1) Smash your foot into the ground and infuse it with light, bolstering friendly targets speed and slowing enemies. Does a small amount of damage per second to enemy targets and heals a small amount to friendly targets.-

Power swelled within Knox, and he felt the talents begin to work. Suddenly, his mind reeled as knowledge crashed into him and he then knew the basics of Radiant Ground as if he'd known how to do it his entire life. Abilities learned through the talent tree hit different. Flexing his muscles and examining his body, Knox felt strong and sturdy. He was ready to go kick some pirate ass.

"Time to get back out there," Knox said, turning to Mic, but Mic held up a hand.

"Let me show you to your quarters so you can rest. I've spent time getting it all cleared out for you and you need sleep, regardless of how you feel from the constant Level ups," Mic insisted.

Knox felt nothing other than energized, but he had been going for a bit, and it was probably dark out now. Nighttime would help with stealth but also potentially bring out stronger monsters. Finally relenting, he allowed Mic to show him the way to his quarters.

CHAPTER 35
WARDS

THEY WERE a grand affair on the same floor as many of the other buildings Knox had seen during his previous tour of the facility. When Mic had first brought them through, it was like entering a small village. Just like back home in Keenlen's Vale, where the mayor's house overlooked the town from a hill, the round hut given to Knox had a similar setup.

On the outside, it screamed 'stone hut' with nothing too special about it, although it was clear that it was built using Mic's or another maintenance golem's rock-moving ability. However, that impression changed when Knox stepped inside. The entry room was furnished elegantly with wooden dressers, tables, and even some chairs.

However, it was the wooden doors and the runes around them that gave Knox pause. He'd seen these same patterns before at his house. Though, as he looked more closely, he noted a few differences, the purpose was the same. It warded off and protected, or at least that was what Knox understood from them.

He explored the space and determined it would do just fine. The hut had two rooms. One featured a stone bed, an odd thing without blankets or the usual bedding. The other room had a tub with warm water being fed into it... warm water! Knox marveled at having his own little bathhouse inside his house. He wasn't sure about the mechanics of how the water got there with just the turn of a valve, but he wasn't about to second-guess such a wonderful luxury.

He found that, despite the bed being made of stone, he became comfortable lying on it after only a few moments. His new body was sturdy and such niceties as soft beds or blankets, weren't things that he really required.

After such a long time without having his own personal space, he gladly put his pack aside and pulled out many of the books within. It was time to study and learn!

Upon seeing the old journal, he decided that first he'd read a passage; perhaps the stranger's own journey would shed light on his path.

Journal Entry #5 – 0001-02 Risen Titan Standard Time

I've had a chance encounter with a power beast of the sea and though my limitations are vast in my new form, through wit and guile I've slain it and taken its Core. Instead of giving it to the

Titan Engine as my promptings have encouraged me, I sucked in the essence myself and have grown powerful enough to choose several Paths.

It is because of these Paths that I find myself able to learn abilities that will allow me to venture out into the sea to gather more Cores and grow in power. From what I've been able to gather about the previous Titan and the Paths available to me, he was a Titan of Water. Walking his path gives me access to marvelous abilities such as water breathing.

I will return in several weeks with my new findings and perhaps begin to work out a way to reconnect with civilization. I've several teleportation spells I'd be willing to try if I trusted the new network of paths within myself.

Knox immediately tried to go for another page but found that nothing would appear. Closing the book he set it aside, he'd learned no great insights from it and now it was time to get into his study of runes. He had so many ideas he wanted to test out and combinations that he might be able to use offensively if he could only work out the right runic formations.

To start, he wanted to master a specific runic formation used to set wardings on an individual. He figured that perhaps if he could work out how to do it to himself and others, he might be able to lessen blows or prevent harm altogether at some level. He pulled out the first book and began to study. He had his notes ready, as they had the specific runic formations his mother had used for his door, but he also took note of a few that were used on the doors here in his private residence.

According to his book on runes and formations, you had to layer effects using certain runes that acted as bindings, but Knox wondered if he could get away with just making a longer, more complex single string, thus avoiding the more complex runes that interlaced the different formations. He spent hours working out what that might look like exactly, but found he had no one to really test his theory or those others he'd already formed.

What he needed was a place where he could inscribe them and then test whether they did what he expected. But the wards were sort of generalized and didn't stop anything overly overt if he was understanding it right. For instance, the protective ward on his door had five main properties that he had identified so far.

Firstly, it strengthened the structure to which it was attached. Next, it warded physical damage by repelling force outwards. Essentially, if people in his old town had thrown rocks at his house, they would have done next to nothing to damage it. The final three properties were a bit more abstract: one shielded it from elemental damage, one shielded it from mental assaults— which confused Knox a bit, as it was used on inanimate materials, but perhaps there was mental damage that could do real harm to even material constructs—and lastly, a shielding of the spirit.

Knox got up and made his way through the complex to the armory level and let himself in. It was dark but the low light that filled most of the complex now was enough to see by until he would make it to the workshop where powerful white light filled the area. But he wasn't quite there yet, so he walked down the armory in the dim light, when an idea began to form.

His Luminous Surge ability let off a crazy amount of light, perhaps he could half cast it and use it to brighten the room. But how would he go about that, he wondered. Thinking about how he activated the ability in the first place, he began tracing each step and what effect it had on the end product. The infusion of Light essence was key, obviously, but the large buildup of essence in general throughout his system probably wasn't. What if he took the smallest thread of Light essence and had it linger at the edge of his palm, not forcing it outward, but just keeping it controlled?

His first attempt failed, the essence dissipating back into him faster than he could trickle it to his palm. So next, he increased it and got a few flashes of light, but the sensation burnt at his hand a little and he had to cut it off as he felt his flesh begin to sizzle.

What was he missing? He decided to try one last thing before giving up. He wanted to do basically what he'd done before, but this time slowly release the essence so it couldn't burn him.

Pulling the Light essence around was easily done, it was like the essence was made specifically for him to control. The trick was how fast to release the essence from his left out-held palm so that he didn't start an attack of some kind. It turned out that a small rush in an interval of one burst per two seconds was the key to success.

His left hand pulsed brightly and before it could fade, he let loose another little pulse and soon he had a steady bright light emanating forth from his left palm. Moving it around he marveled at the flexibility of the system. Despite it not being an official ability, the methods to do almost any technique could still be learned and used. He also noted that he'd been focused on creating light, which he knew from learning other techniques mattered. Intent was as important as the methods you employed to do the various effects.

Reaching the correct door, he was pretty sure, he cut off the light and put his hand on the door. Sure enough, when the door swung open, he was inside the workroom that Mic had shown him only hours before. Inside, the lights bloomed, and he had his space to work.

Picking out a sheet of thinner metal he took up the inscribing tool and did as Mic instructed to use it, feeding a small amount of essence into it. It took him a dozen scraps of metal before he finally inscribed it well enough that he could feel it begin to pull in latent essence and activate. He had to push a tiny bit of essence to get it started, but it was off within seconds. Of course, he could have left out the pulling nature of the script to save a bit more space, but he wasn't practiced at infusing runic formations to activate them, so this method was going to have to work for his first attempt.

Next, he had to test if it was actually working, so he got a hammer and a test piece of metal that looked similar to the inscribed one. First, he smashed down on the normal metal, leaving a slight scuff. Next, he slammed down on the warded metal and to his amazement, no scuff or dent of any kind. Using the same hammer he increased the strength behind it, putting a severe dent in the first metal.

Tightening his grip, he tried to match the same power into the next blow. Instead of a hearty dent, it only had a slight scrape, similar to the damage done to the first sheet of metal with the lesser blow. Fantastic! It worked!

Now to test the other aspects of it!

Knox stepped back and looked around the room. There was an empty wall space to the left, so he moved a worktable over and leaned the items against the wall so he could hit them from a distance. Then he took ten steps back and readied himself to strike out on the first damaged piece of metal with Luminous Surge.

Focusing his mind, he imagined the beam of light being as condensed as possible so as not to do more damage than it needed and activate the ability. A beam of light, basically the same as all the other times he'd cast it, shot out and struck the metal with a resounding clang. The metal had folded into two as if a powerful force struck it dead center, doing significant damage and scorching it.

He repeated the process on the warded metal and was surprised by what happened. The metal bent and was scorched, but not nearly as much as the first. But it had done a decent amount of damage, so the warding was weaker than perhaps he'd first thought. Or was it something else...

An idea struck him, and he went back to the drawing board, using the traditional stacking method that would be much more time-consuming and doing the runes in the way he'd first seen them. Once he'd put them down on a piece of metal, he was ready to begin. Luckily, there were dozens and dozens of scraps lying about in bins.

He started with the hammer test, finding the results to be

much the same as before, but he thought this might be the case as the physical wards came first in his altered runic script. So, he moved on to the Luminous Surge test and laughed out loud when he saw the results.

The first piece took significant damage, as he'd expected, but the second piece had barely a dent and small bits of scorching. Satisfied that he knew what had happened, he made notes on the subject.

From what he understood now, he was certain that the layering had a renewing effect on the runes and their warding capabilities. So, stringing them all out in one, failed to renew them, which meant those runes that allowed for layering weren't just connecting them, but strengthening them as well. That would mean that the further down the wards went, the stronger the ward. So, if he wanted Spirit to remain the strongest, he'd keep it at the bottom, but if he wanted Physical to be stronger, he could lower it on the layers.

This started him on a path of making every single combination of the five lines, which if he did it correctly meant he now had over a hundred unique combinations. Really, he didn't see the point of writing out so many, but he'd gotten carried away and used up far too much of his precious paper doing so.

He tested five more times using physical resistance and the hammer as the test subject. His findings excited him. By the time he reached the final test with Physical at the bottom, it took him using a technique to strengthen himself to even scratch the metal, meanwhile, the control piece of metal was obliterated. Now he had one more test to do, but it required help from a golem, though not necessarily an activated one.

Mic found him as he entered the floor filled with golems.

"How goes it?" Knox asked, cutting off whatever Mic was about to say. The golem huffed and made a show of clearing his throat.

"I'm wondering why you haven't decided to rest?" Mic asked, his hands on his hips.

"How do you know I haven't?" Knox shot back, a wry smile on his face. He was far too excited to sleep, and he was so close to getting what he wanted from this experiment. Hell, he was close to unlocking the full potential of his Radiant Glyph ability, something that might just turn out to be his most flexible and powerful ability.

"Because I've been monitoring you," Mic said simply.

"Well, now that you are here, you can help me," Knox said, pointing at one of the golems. "Bring that over here and out of the way. I've got a few tests I'd like to run."

"What kind of tests?" Mic asked, but he moved to obey regardless.

"Are you familiar with the ability Radiant Glyph?" Knox asked, then continued when Mic didn't immediately answer. "It allows me to draw runes into the air using Light and activate their effects."

"I am familiar with it," Mic said, then pausing a moment he added, "What does that have to do with this golem?"

"I'm going to test warding it from damage," Knox said excitedly.

"Won't work," Mic said immediately, and Knox scrunched his brow at the golem with so little faith in his abilities.

"Why do you say that?" Knox asked.

"The effects of Radiant Glyph are short-lived, and the primary use is meant for offensive or defensive runes, not warding. However, when you unlock ritual bindings, you can do what you are planning. Rituals allow for runic effects to be scribed onto spirits instead of material, for reduced essence cost and shorter time periods."

"When do I learn ritual binding?" Knox asked, carrying over another golem to act as his control, he was still going to try his plan no matter what Mic said.

"I'm unsure of the exact Level, sorry," Mic said, placing his golem beside the one Knox had moved over.

"That's alright, try moving the golem about three paces to the left and let's begin," Knox said, smiling slyly.

"I already told you; it won't work. Why do you persist in trying?" Mic asked, seeming perturbed by the notion.

"Until I've tried it myself, I won't truly know," Knox said simply. "Now, stand aside so I can get started."

Mic made a grunting noise, but stepped aside as he was asked. Raising his finger like a writing pen, Knox activated his ability and went to work trying to scribe out all the lines.

His first attempt failed, as did his second, but not for the reasons Mic had outlined. He was finding it hard to keep his focus long enough to accomplish all the repetitions of the runic formation.

"Any tips on keeping the flow of essence going long enough to do this?" Knox asked, breathing hard from the effort of trying only twice.

"You just don't have enough Mana for such a complex attempt, you'd best wait until you reach Level 11," Mic said, crushing Knox's dreams in a single sentence.

"Well, damn," Knox said, then a thought occurred to him. If he couldn't manage the full set of the runic scripts, what if he just did a single line? It would at least give him something to test and not make this entire attempt a failure.

With Mic still standing out of the way, Knox readied himself for another attempt, going over in his mind the runic formation for physical warding. When he felt refreshed enough to try, he made his attempt. He focused his mind on what he wanted it to do: ward the golem on the right. The runic formation went off without a hitch and Knox had to blink several times as his vision suddenly swam.

"Are you alright?" Mic asked, but Knox was already recovering. He picked up the hammer he'd taken from the workroom and smashed it hard against the golem's chest. It left a scuff on the unwarded one, so next he smashed into the warded one. To his surprise and chagrin, it left no mark.

"It worked," Knox said, eyeing Mic with an eyebrow raised.

"Impossible," Mic said, walking forward and examining the golem.

Meanwhile, Knox examined it with his sense and sure enough, just in front of the metal was his ward, quickly losing its light. By the time he looked away it had already faded to nothing.

"It did work, how strange," Mic said, then looking at the scuff mark on the test golem he set his sights on Knox. "I'm going to have to polish that off, you know."

"I know," Knox admitted. "Sorry."

CHAPTER 36
NOLIC DEN

THE NEXT FEW days passed with Knox studying runes and testing a few of them here and there. He'd begun modifying his armor as well, not messing with any runic placements as he didn't truly understand them yet but adding new ones in empty spaces. His armor now had an additional warding and would keep him warm, like the stone he had. He had another stone, the communication stone, but what use was it going to be with one half of it lost along with Dernal.

It wasn't like he hadn't tried to communicate with Dernal with it, he had several times and would continue to do so, but so far nothing but silence accompanied the attempts. He still remembered the excitement that had filled him when he'd first thought to try several days earlier, but it was all for naught.

If Dernal had survived, he was out of range or had lost the stone during the attack. A thought occurred to Knox suddenly and he wondered if maybe he could extend the natural range of the communication stones? But no, that would have to wait, for now he needed to find stronger monsters to kill and souls to capture.

"Ready to go hunting?" Knox asked the three pirates-turned-loyal-golems.

Edgar made a show of clearing his throat. "I heard you've been experimenting with the golems? Have you learned how to grant us freedom or any improvements yet?" Edgar asked, but suddenly Boris blurted out.

"Jus' ask him already," Boris said.

"I'm getting to it," Edgar shot back, turning his back to Boris. "You see, as we have been adjusting to our new bodies, we have begun to feel sensations and even some pain, so it goes that we ought to be able to feel pleasure as well. Along that line, the boys and I were wondering." It was all too much for Boris, he stepped forward and blurted out what they wanted.

"We wants to know if you can make us wankers? Well, can ya?" Boris asked.

Knox's eyes went as wide as saucer plates, and he sputtered his next words as he struggled to find a proper response. "W-well, I-I mean to say, that I uhm, I don't know if I have the expertise to accomplish such an action just yet. But perhaps, with some study and trial and error, I might be able to do it, but I'm not sure what the point would be?" Knox formed his statement as a question at the end, finally finding some of his sense. What were they thinking of asking him to do this for them? These pirates were a bunch of perverts! Though Knox didn't say as much, he needed them to be amenable to his requests, not wanting to force their hand at every turn.

"Told you," Vlad said, he looked the most disinterested of the three of them.

It was funny how Knox was beginning to be able to tell them apart just by the way they stood and moved about. Vlad had a swagger to his step and stance that spoke of uncaring gruffness. Meanwhile, Edgar kept a tall and measured posture, always making his movements sharp and precise. Boris was the easiest of all three to identify as he slouched and had a sort of slow stutter to his movements, as if he doubted what he should do as he did whatever it was he was doing.

"I promise to look into it," Knox said, not sure if he was lying or not. The idea of recreating body parts was intriguing, but he was years away from understanding golems well enough to do anything of the sort, or so he figured.

"And we promise to remind you," Edgar said, then clearing his throat again he spoke. "You planning on taking care of the Nolic den or did you want to see how infested these woods will get?"

"I've never encountered Nolics before finding them here, do they breed frequently?" Knox asked, intrigued to learn more about the spiny sharp clawed little monsters.

"I can give you a quest for that!" Mic declared and suddenly Knox's vision was filled with a quest alert.

-Quest Received!-

-Clearing a Nolic Den-

-You've been tasked with clearing out a Nolic den before it becomes problematic. Nolics are creatures known for their endless appetite and greed. They collect shiny objects or things that give off magical auras, while consuming the more powerful items they find

to grow stronger, gaining unique abilities depending on their affinities. Nolics have a queen monster structure, kill the queen and clear the den.-

    -Objective: Kill 0/25 Nolics, Kill 0/1 Nolic Queen-
    -Reward: 2,500 Essence Toward Next Level-

Knox read the quest aloud and looked at Edgar. He nodded.

"That tracks from what I know," he said.

"The system borrowed knowledge from you to fill in the blanks. Thus is the life of a servant of the Titan System," Mic said, throwing his arms wide and making a sighing noise.

"How rude," Boris said, looking from one of his companions to another.

"Let's move out," Knox said, pulling their attention away from the fact that the system was clearly inside their head and perhaps inside of Knox's as well.

They made it to the surface easily enough, but just as they did, the ground rocked, and a fissure opened up some dozen paces away. From those fissures came a black ooze. It rolled into a ball and rolled off into the forest as if it were the most normal thing ever to do.

"What the fuck was that?" Vlad asked, pointing at another ball that rolled off in a different direction.

"I don't know," Knox said; however, he did have an idea as it seemed awfully familiar to the black goo that had taken over that owlbear all those months ago. Was the same outbreak starting here and it was coming from under the ground?

Knox almost went back down to warn Mic, but instead he took a deep breath and decided their quest was still the most important thing they could do. Though, what if the Nolics got infected and became harder to kill? They'd already been finding stronger and stronger Nolics while encountering less and less Dire Wolves and owlbears.

Going in the direction that they'd encountered the most

Nolics, Knox bit his lip, as it was the exact same direction the ball of black goo had gone.

It was late afternoon, but Knox figured they had at least four or five hours of light if he was any judge of time. So, they set out, Knox in front with his sense spread out like the tendrils of a spider's web and the three pirate golems behind him, ready to strike out on his command.

Whether because the goo had them spooked or they were just blessedly done with their normal chit-chat, the group stayed surprisingly quiet.

Knox on the other hand had his head filled with ideas, worries, and plans. He had several ideas of how to improve the warming aspects of his armor, which currently kept him nice and warm despite the chill in the air. He worried that he'd never see his friends and family again. And he planned on wiping out this den of Nolics as fast as possible, because another plan was stewing in his head at the moment.

He wanted to save those captives and get that sweet essence that was promised. It wasn't that he was only greedy to advance but he really needed to be stronger if he had a chance of getting back to his village and out of the Shadowfall Swamp. What were his long-term plans, he suddenly wondered.

While walking in the silence, he laid out what he'd like to do if he could. First, he needed to be stronger, how strong he didn't know yet, but stronger. Then he would seek out his friends, then perhaps find out what happened to Dernal and his group. What if he found them alive; would he go on with his life as he had before, running dungeons and the like? Certainly, he would like to, and his ambitions hadn't changed, but now he had an extra responsibility.

He was the Titan of Light and an emissary of the Titan System. There was a certain responsibility he held toward advancing the Titan Engine and seeing that it spread. It was odd to him that he felt so passionate about it, but it must be a part of what he was now and therefore not something that he could easily ignore. So, he supposed when he finished finding his friends and dungeon group, if they could be found, he'd see if they wanted to return with him.

They could select a Path and join him in advancing the Titan System to all corners of the world! Yes, that was what he wanted, he decided. That is what he'd do.

Knox didn't consider himself a great tracker, but the blob of black goo had left a trail that was easy to follow and continued in the direction he had been planning to go, so he decided to just follow it instead. After some time, they finally encountered some Nolics. However, Knox noticed that the blob had skirted around them and had not engaged. Odd...

"Vlad, you and I will lead the charge. But first, Edgar, throw a fireball ahead of us, and Boris, try to use your Whirlwind to distract one of them. We'll go in after the fireball hits," Knox said, addressing Vlad directly as Edgar nodded and began to cast his spell.

The Nolic hadn't noticed them yet, the brush being extremely thick between them, but Vlad and Knox flanked to the left, ready to attack when the fireball hit.

Three Nolics stood fairly close to each other, when the fire slammed down on the lead one, scorching it but not bringing it down. *Odd, these must be stronger than the ones we'd faced before,* Knox thought as he ran forward, axe at the ready.

Knox made it there first, his superior speed and reflexes out striding the golem. With a massive thump of his foot, he activated Radiant Ground, light poured into the ground like so many cracks. All three of the Nolics seemed to react to the area of effect talent ability at once, reeling back as if struck. The biggest one— also the one that got hit by a fireball and was still kicking—came at Knox.

Massive, clawed hands swiped for him, but he easily stepped back and out of reach while swiping with his own weapon. His axe bit into the flesh of the swiping arm but didn't take the limb off like Knox had been prepared for. The sudden stopping of his axe sent him reeling forward and into the Nolic's reach.

Pain erupted on his neck as claws found purchase and ripped into his soft flesh. Thinking fast and blocking out the pain, Knox used Lustrous Chains, hoping not only to pull back the larger Nolic but to help his pirate companions as they engaged the other two. Chains of light ripped out of the ground and wrapped the larger Nolic. If they did anything more, Knox couldn't see and was too distracted by the claws coming right at his face.

Luckily for him, the claws stopped mere inches away. Already he could feel the wound and pain lessen from around his neck, so he stood and took another swing with his axe, this time using the technique—or as much of it as he could—that John had taught him. He felt a trickle of power fill the weapon and he struck with the full force that he could muster.

Chains broke from his swing, releasing the larger Nolic but the strike arrived right where Knox had planned, taking the Nolic's arm off at the elbow. It shrieked a terrible cry and Knox could hear Vlad struggling against the other two, the sound of nails across metal as they tried to tear into him. Focusing on the Mystic abilities he'd learned, Knox cursed himself for his stupidity. He had both Mystic Veil and Mystic Armor now and he hadn't taken advantage of either.

No time for it now, he thought, as he jumped back to avoid another strike. He leaned into his sense and let it guide his steps, narrowly dodging as another Nolic jumped into the fray on his left. Weaving through the attacks, he waited for the right moment to strike. When it came, he was ready with an Arcane Pulse.

The attack ripped out of him hitting both the Nolics but he wasn't done, he began writing in the air in front of him with Radiant Glyph. Using the fire stream runes he'd learned from the trap, simple and deadly, he finished the sequence.

Out of seemingly nowhere, fire gushed out and covered both Nolics for a solid three seconds before it sputtered out. The damage was too much for them and Knox was easily able to finish them off with well-placed axe swings.

Looking around, he saw that Vlad had several new dents, but he'd killed the other Nolic. Meanwhile, Knox heard Edgar and Boris arguing somewhere behind them.

"Job well done," Knox said. "Now let's find the Cores and get back to searching for that Nolic Den."

There were a few more small fights with other Nolics along the way, but nothing they couldn't handle. Until finally they came upon a cave that Knox was sure must be the Nolic Den.

There was only one small issue, the Nolics all around the cave, maybe ten of them, were all dead. The mouth of the cave was wide and short, but if they bent down, they'd fit well enough. However, as they examined the corpses that lay outside, Knox had an uneasy feeling settle in his gut.

"I think the black blob did this," Knox announced, his worry transforming into a small fear. "We might be going into a trap or at least something we might not be able to handle. Anyone got a problem with that?"

Boris began to speak but Edgar raised a hand to cut him off. "We got this," Edgar declared, and Vlad nodded along to his statement.

Surely, this kind of courage from the three ex-pirates was something to marvel at, Knox thought. However, he didn't dwell on it too long, as there were monsters that needed to be slain. Moving deeper into the cave, he was forced to use his light palm technique to brighten the path.

The inside of the cave was much as it appeared from the outside, filled with dead Nolics and several winding paths leading this way or that. They'd gone around the cave for nearly ten minutes before they approached a sound ahead. The ceiling began to rise, and light poured out from ahead.

Cutting off his light spell, they approached slowly and sneaky-like toward what lay ahead. Knox took it all in within a moment before raising his weapon in defense.

The cave opened up to an open-air cavern much like the top layer of the Titan Complex. In the middle, surrounded by dead Nolics, was the mother of all Nolics, or so it seemed. It was huge, nearly twice Knox's height and as wide as he was tall. It had massive, clawed hands and rows of jagged teeth.

It had a gut so large that Knox wondered how easily it could get around. Not well, he ventured to guess. But worst of all was the black goo that surrounded it and covered most of its body. It seemed to be in the midst of a fight against the goo, and it was losing. However, it was clear the goo wasn't out to kill this Nolic but try to take hold of it as it had the owlbear and the Dire Wolf before it.

"We strike now while we have a chance. Edgar, Boris and I will hit it hard from a distance. When it takes notice, we all rush forward to slice it apart. Understand?" Knox asked. It was a simple plan, but simple was the best he could do considering the circumstances. If they could kill it before it became a goo-infested corpse, then they might have a chance at winning this fight.

Deciding to focus on his Mystic abilities, Knox stepped forward, planting his feet, and began to cast Mystic Armor. The cast was quick and easy, for his level of understanding of the spell at least. Blue translucent armor shimmered into existence around his body. Next, he turned to his allies and cast Mystic Veil over them, giving them a bonus to damage reduction. Finally, still feeling fresh despite the two casts, he narrowed his vision on the foe and began to cast Arcane Pulse.

This was a more difficult cast if he wanted to maximize the damage, so he focused his mind as best he could and... bam! The spell went off, shooting a wave of force just as Edgar and Boris let loose their own spells.

A funnel of wind tore up around the Nolic, distracting it but doing very little damage. A fireball then smashed into it and it took a step backward, stunned by the sheer force of the attack. As it was on its back foot, the Arcane Pulse hit and doubled it over in an earth-shaking fall.

While it was down, Knox cast Void Grasp to slow its movements and as one they ran forward to engage the monster. Knox could feel that he'd tapped out most of his Mana, the slight headache and the feeling of pressure on his head being the easiest way to tell, but he wanted to do one final cast before giving in to swinging his axe.

As he reached the fallen Nolic, he slammed his foot down and activated Radiant Ground. Luckily, this was an easy cast that required Stamina as much as it did Mana, so it went off without a hitch and the ground ignited in a golden glow.

The ooze hissed and suddenly tendrils of black came screaming through the air toward Knox and his party. Knocking away the first strike, Knox smiled as he saw a piece of it hit the Radiant Ground and dissipate in a hiss of writhing pain. It was weak to the light!

Using the technique he'd learned from John, he infused his axe strike with Light essence. Striking down, he smiled as his axe cut through the ooze like a hot knife through butter. Except in this instance the butter screamed out in pain, twice. One scream from the ooze and one from the Nolic.

The Nolic struggled to its feet, finally making it just as the three pirate golems began a 'wack fest' on its body. Smashing it with mace, dagger, and sword. Vlad came in with his signature punch, blood splattering out in a wave before he turned and put distance between the pair of them. Thinking at first that Vlad had decided to run, Knox turned to scold him or encourage him at the very least, but Vlad activated his rush ability, slamming forward into the Nolic and knocking it back on its ass.

Next, he used an ability Knox hadn't seen him use before. Slamming his foot down, the ground cracked, and damage radiated out from him. Just as Knox turned to use another ability of his own, he saw Boris raise his hands and water shoot forth. Even Boris had picked up a new ability. The water came out in such a rush that it cut a line into the Nolic, damaging it and spraying blood.

Ready to see what Edgar had learned, Knox turned to him just in time to see him finish a spell. A torrent of wind kicked up, but it was ten times as intense as anything Boris had ever conjured. It ripped away pieces of the Nolic's flesh while at the same time seemingly leaving the four of them alone, barely even pushing them back.

The black ooze around the Nolic began to writhe and squirm violently. Then, before they could do so much as take a step back, it began to enter into the Nolic's mouth. To say that the Nolic wasn't a fan of this would be the understatement of the age. It clawed and ripped away at its own throat, effectively killing itself, but where it lost flesh, black goo replaced it.

Knox slashed out several times during this slow and painful process, but the attacks had very little effect. So instead, he gave up and stepped back, waiting for his Mana to replenish just a touch more before he tried what he had planned next.

Edgar and the crew weren't so idle, each of them slashing out and using abilities as often as they could. Whatever their pools of Mana and Stamina, they had increased severalfold since first being created. Knox decided he needed to ask them what Level they'd reached when they made it out of this fight.

Fireballs slammed down, water screamed through the air, and the ground shook from Vlad's attacks. Finally, as the battle began to draw to a close between the ooze and the Nolic, Knox's Mana had replenished enough that he felt ready to rejoin the fight. The Nolic moved with unreal speed suddenly, and Knox found himself flying through the air.

It had punched him in the chest and shattered his Mystic Armor into motes of light, but other than that, he'd felt almost nothing. Suddenly, the momentum that had him flying through the air met the back of the cavern, and he lost all the air in his lungs. Gasping for air, Knox looked forward to see each of his companions get through around the room similar to how he'd just been struck.

However, the burst of speed it had shown was lessening, that much Knox was sure of as he got to his feet and prepared his next spell. Chanting the runic words and moving his hands in familiar patterns, he began to weave together Luminous Surge. It took only seconds, but in that time, the Nolic infused by the black goo took notice. It began to cover itself in thick webs of its black goo until it was a giant ball of the stuff.

Undeterred, Knox let loose his spell and grunted from the force of it. The spell came out stronger than ever before, his mastery of it getting better and better as he used it more. Light washed over the area between the pair, some of it washing over Vlad who was in the middle of them. Vlad was left unharmed but also the healing effects didn't appear to affect him either, as he remained dusty and dented.

It struck the ball of goo, and the cavern was filled with a terrible hissing sound as the attack melted through its defenses to strike at its Core. Knox kept the spell going, pushing as much of himself as he could into it. But the ability had a limit and eventually it cut off. The ball of goo had melted, leaving a half burnt up Nolic standing where it had been, smoke rising from all around it.

It turned its attention to Knox and began to charge, moving like a ravenous beast seeking its next meal. Its claws dug into the rock, leaving large divots, and kicking up rocks. Vlad made it to his feet just as it slammed into him, denting his chest heavily and pushing him aside with ease. A ball of fire, much smaller than when Edgar first began to cast only minutes ago, slammed into it, but it ignored it.

Knox closed his eyes for just a second to let his sense take full control. He sensed every part of the ooze and the movements of the Nolic as it charged. Opening his eyes in a flash, he was ready to meet it strike for strike.

It came in high and fast, slashing downward to remove Knox's head in a single strike, all the while several tendrils of black swooped in from the side to strike and hold. Knox slashed with his axe, focusing on the tendrils, before moving just a hair's width enough to dodge the slash. Back and forth, he moved with speed and foresight beyond what he thought he'd had access to as the Nolic continued its attack.

Knox couldn't help but smile as he dodged the fourth strike and returned one of his own. He wouldn't win this fight by strength of blade alone, but already the Nolic was slowing down as it used all it had to try and strike Knox. So, focusing on moving as little as possible, Knox found his eyes closed once more as he gave himself fully to the sense. Strike out here, dodge there, cut loose tendrils here, the battle went on and on.

All the while, his companions weren't idle, throwing in their most powerful abilities or just striking out with their physical weapons as often as they could.

The battle ended pretty quickly; Knox's Mana refilled enough that he could strike out with another Luminous Surge. He twisted and turned, releasing the ability right into the monster's chest. The impact sent them both screaming, Nolic and ooze, but as it reeled backward, the light in the Nolic's eyes went dim and the ooze lost its form, falling to the ground like the wet ooze it was.

"That hurt," Vlad said. Knox looked up to see he had a massive dent in his chest and his eyes were flickering.

"Time to get back to the Titan Complex, I need to learn how to fix you lot," Knox said, then thinking it over he added, "Thank you, all three of you performed marvelously. So, thank you."

"This mean you going to make us some d-," Boris began to say, but Edgar elbowed him into silence.

"Not now," he hissed at him, and Knox smiled at the ridiculousness of the situation he found himself in.

"Let's get back," Knox repeated, and they left, but not before searching out the cave for loot and finding a fair bit of odds and ends, including a magical sword that had seen better days. The blade was in fair condition, but the leather on the handle and sheath had all been destroyed.

Knox was confident he could fix it though; despite the damage it had undergone. He was more than willing to do a little tinkering if it meant he could arm one of his companions with a sword able to do more than annoy the monsters around here. Then a thought occurred to him, he had the tools and now two examples of enchanted weapons, perhaps he'd add his own enchantments to the weapons they already carried? Yeah, he could do that, he was sure of it.

With one last check of the corpses, Knox was disheartened to find none of the Cores were intact, including the larger Queen Nolic. Knox was sure it had something to do with the black ooze, but what it meant or why it was taking over monsters, he couldn't say. Just another mystery he needed to figure out.

-Personal Status-

-Name: Knox-

-Level: 12 (E Rank, Tier 2)-

-Essence To Next Level: 180/2,400-

-Health: Fair Tier 9-

-Mana: Fair Tier 9-

-Stamina: Fair Tier 9-

-Mind: 66-

-Body: 66-

-Spirit: 66-

CHAPTER 37
MAINTENANCE

KNOX EXPECTED something different when he reached Level 11, as it had to do with him going into the E Ranks, but after turning in his quest and the experience from killing the Nolics he found himself at Level 12, and finally, his Health, Mana, and Stamina had changed. It wasn't until he did a few practice casts and a bit of physical endurance, running around the complex, that he started to feel that his body had definitely changed.

It was like he could not just do twice as many casts as before, but nearly four times as many. His body must be more resilient and sturdier as well, because the aches and pains from the fight had all but gone away after Leveling. He was still nowhere near as powerful as he had been, but he was getting closer with every passing day.

The final strange thing that had happened was the ring on his left thumb had disappeared into a mote of light as he entered the E Ranks. Mic had been busy when they'd returned, but he found him now and meant to ask him about it.

"What's the deal with one of the rings disappearing?" Knox asked, then continued before Mic could answer. "I thought they were meant to keep me safe or whatever, am I in trouble now that I've lost one?"

"What?" Mic asked, then looked at Knox's hand and nodded. "Ah, no that is to be expected. Each ring is meant to hold back your Body, Mind, and Soul from each progressive Rank. So, the one you lost was keeping you from the body of a peak E Ranker. Now that you are in that Level bracket, you don't need it."

"So, when you say I could take one off, it would literally make me stronger just like that?" Knox asked, understanding what Mic meant but also thinking about how he might use it if he were to find himself in over his head.

"But you shouldn't do that, or you'll find yourself back at the lowest Level of the newest Rank you've achieved. So, at Level 12 you would buy yourself maybe thirty seconds of D Rank Mind, Body, and Soul, before you found yourself weak and powerless and back at Level 11. It isn't worth it 99.99% of the time, especially at lower Levels," Mic said, and he seemed very adamant about what he was saying.

Knox nodded along, but already he was forming contingencies about when to use it. He'd been smart not to use it against the Nolics, as he was already so weak that it likely wouldn't have helped much. But now that he could tap into D Ranked power... he had to consider it. What was more, once he hit the D Ranks, he'd be able to tap into C Ranked power or could he even do that now?

"What would happen if I took several rings off at once, like, let's say I wanted to tap into B Ranked power for a time," Knox asked, just as Mic turned to leave. Mic stuck him with a stare and silently shook his head no.

"At your Level, taking two rings off would be the max you could achieve without instantly killing yourself. But even then, you'd have less than ten seconds of power before you found yourself useless and at Level 11 once more," Mic said, shaking his head some more to really push his point home.

"I understand," Knox said, adding this additional information into his bank of knowledge.

It was time to work on the golems now, he'd had all three go and meet him at the workshop. He just needed Mic before they could get started.

"Come with me to the workshop, I need to fix the three golems, they've been damaged," Knox told Mic, who nodded and followed behind him.

"As a maintenance golem, I am fully capable of doing such work myself, but I know your curious nature will insist you come along," Mic said, and he was right. Knox wouldn't miss a chance to learn if he could help it.

They reached the workshop in minutes and the trio awaited them outside the main vault area. Knox reached out and touched the door, it retracted into the wall as it had before. No matter how many times he saw it, the door amazed him with its design.

"This dent is very uncomfortable," Vlad complained, and Knox felt a bit guilty that he had tended to his own things before thinking of helping the injured golem. But it wasn't like he was mortally wounded; he just had a dent and Knox had to deal with his Leveling first.

"Let's get to it then," Knox said, turning to Mic, ready to learn how he did it.

Mic picked up a hammer with a rounded end and walked right over to Vlad, hit a switch on the golem's chest and it swung open, dent and all. Then, without so much as a 'stand still', he went to work hammering out the dent. There was no special chanting or magic at work, he was just hammering the golem back into shape.

Knox did note that the hammer he'd grabbed, like almost all the other tools, had an enchantment on it. Stepping up, Knox held out his hand, ready to try his skill at fixing some of the dents.

What followed was about two hours of finding metal plating releases and hammering it back into shape. It wasn't perfect, at least Knox's work wasn't, however, Mic really knew what he was doing. He went back over the work Knox had done and got it to a perfect shape, even going back to polish away any smudges and scratches.

After a while, Knox gave up and went to examine the sword he'd found. He'd also gathered up the weapons each of the pirates had chosen and planned to add a few enchantments to them. It was hard to make out the tiny, almost invisible inscriptions on his axe, but with his improved sense, he could. So, he wrote out all the ones he could find, then did the same with the sword—a much easier process due to the size and straightforward nature of the sword's runic formations.

The sword had three basic runic formations. One for preserving the blade, which Knox was sure included the edge. Another for increasing the cutting edge specifically, and a final one that pulled in latent essence from around the sword to power the first two and give the blade a touch of essence damage. Mic assured him these were the most basic of basic runic formations and Knox's own personal studies reinforced it.

So, using the basic formations, he took up the first weapon and began to work on it, using the inscribing tool that could cut into the inside of the metal. He ruined his first attempt, but the next two went much better. After a quick trip to the armory where he got a replacement weapon for Boris, he inscribed it successfully. Now they would each have a basic enchanted weapon.

Next, he wanted to try and identify some of the formations on his axe so that he could transfer it to a new weapon if he ever found something worth replacing Scarlet.

The first and easiest to identify runic formations had to do with stabilizing the weapon from physical damage. This was a more advanced version of what the sword used, having several layers to it. Next, he had a combination of five runic scripts that ran into each other, but what they could be used for, Knox wasn't sure.

It was odd because one line looked similar to the Speaking stone he'd gotten, but it lacked the part that would allow for communication. So basically, it could listen or perhaps it allowed someone else to listen in? It was confusing the more he got into it, but he wasn't a fan of some of the stuff he was discovering. If someone was able to listen to him or watch him because of his weapon, what was the reason?

They'd know he was in trouble and did nothing, or perhaps it was built out by his mother before she died. A way to watch over them but she never got to use it? It was hard to pin down, so he left the combination alone and went to check out a few others.

The sharpening runic formation made enough sense, though it was overly complex and had redundancies that Knox found a bit over the top. Like, why have a line that ensures that it stays sharp, then also have one that sharpened the edge after each strike? The first one took care of the second's job, making it useless. But there had to be a method to it, so he took note of the entire process.

If he was right about his axe and its many redundancies, then it had been made by a master and his mother, perhaps one and the same, so he'd learn one way or another why they'd chosen this path forward.

After several hours of studying and replicating parts of the enchantments on a broad sword he'd found in the armory, he cursed himself for his clumsy hands. The size and delicate nature of the runes were such a different beast than anything else he'd worked on before. If he were to replicate even half of what his axe had, he'd need to learn to write significantly smaller than he was currently doing.

Mic came over, watching him work over his shoulder and interrupted him while he was trying to fit a sizable portion on the blade and failing to get it all.

"You should look into the runic formation for shrinking and transferring runes. It allows you to write them as big as you need and then with a touch of essence you can transfer them into much smaller areas," Mic said, filling Knox in on something he would have liked to hear hours before.

"So, I don't have to write super small?" Knox asked, deadpanned.

"What? Of course not, let me get you a book on it from the library, which you've unlocked by the way," Mic said, turning and leaving the workshop.

The trio of pirate golems had left already, doing whatever it was they did when no one needed them. Knox wasn't too worried about them, mostly because Mic didn't appear worried.

"Can we also get a book on golem creation? I need to read up and learn how to capture pirate souls without all the pirate memories attached," Knox said. He'd decided that he had a good supply of souls, and he ought to use them. None of the monsters, not even the Nolic queen, had a strong enough soul so far to be captured in the stones Knox had taken with him.

"If you could find some C Ranked Monsters, Level 30 or above, you'd have souls aplenty. Monster souls work best, though I might be biased, as I am one such soul," Mic said, leading the way down the vault hallway toward what Knox hoped was a vast library.

"Do you know what kind of monster you were?" Knox asked,

curious about what Mic could still remember. His memory seemed to come and go, so Knox didn't expect much from him.

"A Dire Giant Spider," Mic said without hesitation.

"From around here?" Knox asked, curious why he hadn't encountered any giant spiders if they were from the area.

"I believe so, though I only remember flashes," Mic said, stopping in front of one of a dozen or more similar looking doors.

Knox gave him a look and Mic nodded, so he reached out and touched the door. It swung open and Knox tilted his head to the side in confusion.

The room was empty, or at least it looked empty at first. The walls were odd, and watching Mic, Knox realized why. Mic moved with familiarity, walking to the far-left corner, and pulling a stone tablet from the wall. What Knox had assumed was an odd texture to the wall was in fact hundreds, maybe thousands, of stone tablets stored in the very walls themselves.

"Let me show you how to read the tablets," Mic said, bringing it over to Knox. "Place your hand on the surface and you will see the information unlocked."

Knox did as he was asked, placing his hand on the tablet's surface and taking it off a second later. The smooth surface with a few unrecognizable runes on it went blank and suddenly the surface was filled with runic formations. The trouble was, it wasn't anything that Knox could understand.

"I can't read this," Knox said finally when Mic kept looking at him expectantly.

"Oh right, here, let me get you a tablet on the Titan System standard language. It allows for picking and detecting of languages, so you'll be able to learn the language, with time."

Knox pinched the bridge of his nose, of course it wasn't going to be so easy. "Fine, get me the tablet and I'll start learning the language."

Mic went to the far back wall toward the bottom and pulled free another tablet. He handed it over and after pressing his hand on it, Knox found that he could understand half of what the tablet said. It was detailed instructions on learning a basic alphabet.

"To turn the page forward or backward, press your thumb against the bottom corner, left or right respectively," Mic said, and Knox followed his instructions.

It turned to another page, well, not really turned, but it sort of shifted and the words changed. He pressed the bottom left and it went back to the first page. Ingenious!

Left to his own devices, Knox began the study of the Titan System basic language. It turned out that it was the same runic language used above the dungeon doors and soon he'd be able to translate what they had said. It also shared similarities to the Runic Language that allowed for magic, except it was distinctly different despite sharing many symbols or very close symbols.

It was almost like the Runic Magic system was a system within the Language Runic System, similar but different. His understanding of the characters grew with each passing hour, but it would be weeks before he had even a basic understanding locked down. Luckily, he found that he could use the two tablets together and get a decent understanding of other subjects through slow translation.

Thus went the next week, with little need for nourishment—Knox found that a single small ration of food would keep him energized for days on end—he studied and studied, all the while thinking about his friends and family he'd left behind, even his father occupied some of his mental space.

CHAPTER 38
PIRATE HUNTING

Knox worked out enough about golems and Soulstones by the end of the week that he saw a single formation in the stone that could be used as a filtration system but had been left dormant by default. All he had to do was connect a part and it activated an entire sequence of runes that should, if he was understanding it right, filter out personality and bestial tendencies.

He could see how by default they probably wanted to keep some of the monster tendencies, but Knox didn't want to capture any more human souls unless he could filter them. This would allow for only the capture of the special essences required to give life. It was still technically possible, Knox knew, that he might be stealing their souls away. But the more he was understanding about Soulstones, it wasn't really the soul that was being captured.

Which also meant that he hadn't really captured the souls of the trio, but merely their essence of self and the special essence that gave them life. But the actual soul as the runic language described, would be sent to the Titans for judgement.

Of course, Knox had no idea if that was just dogma or fact, but he was willing to lean into it being a fact if it helped clear his conscience. Sure, that might not have been the most moral approach, but he had limited resources to work with and he needed more golems if he was going to stand a chance against more powerful foes. The sheer power of numbers might be enough to tip the balance for him.

Either way, it was time for pirate hunting. Plus, he figured he might be able to make some headway on the quest he'd gotten to save the captives. He had to admit to himself that he ought to have been more proactive in trying to save the people, but he had learning to do, and it often dominated his better sense.

"Let's go hunting," Knox announced. The trio had found some cards and dice, their attention fully encapsulated by their current game. But they must be getting stir crazy as well, because at the first mention of leaving, they all jumped to their feet, ready to go.

They followed Knox wordlessly as they traveled out into the wilds above. It wasn't until they were a mile out from the Titan Complex that Boris spoke up, breaking the silence.

"So, you from around here?" Boris asked, his question taking Knox completely off guard. Around here? Did he mean in general or was he having a malfunction of some kind. Then it hit Knox, he'd never really had a heart to heart or any kind of information exchange with them. He'd just enslaved their minds and put them to work. Knox felt like a terrible person at that moment.

"I'm local," Knox said, turning and gesturing toward the general direction of his town. "More or less. Obviously, I didn't grow up in the Shadowfall Swamp, but I'm only a week or so travel away, or at least I was before the Titan Complex got me."

"It got you?" Boris asked, it was his turn to look confused.

"Well, you know how I'm basically a Titan now?" Knox asked when they all looked at him as if he were speaking nonsense. He realized just how much in the dark he'd kept them. "Fine. Let me tell you a little story."

And he did, starting from his time back in his village and his time in the dungeon, growing stronger, to his fleeing with a monster on his heels. They listened intently, as they stopped and sat on a fallen tree while Knox spoke. While he explained everything, he remembered that he'd told them a bit about how he got here, but not much. This time he held nothing back, explaining it in full and trusting they couldn't give away any of his secrets. When finally, he'd finished filling them in on his life, he turned to Boris.

"Tell me about yourself now," Knox said, trying not to make it a command, but genuinely wanting to know more about them. "I mean, there has to be more to it than a promise of gold and you all being orphans?"

It was Vlad that spoke up this time, surprising Knox. "Where we are from you either got with a crew or you ended up being chewed up by the city. No matter the details, what Boris said is right. Captain Dread offered us a place, a family of sorts, and we took it. We aren't and we weren't good men, but we tried to be loyal and now we have to be. Life is a twisted bitch."

"What my friend of few words means to say, is we know our place and we will serve loyally, but if you should find a way to remove the bindings keeping us loyal," Edgar said, pausing as he seemed to consider something. "I'm afraid we might be too tempted to slit your throat and take all you have. I tell you this because I'm beginning to like you and a part of me can't stand the idea of harm coming your way, as out of character as that feels inside. It is what it is."

Knox didn't know if he should laugh or cry or well, he just didn't know how to react to such an admission. He was obviously being sincere, that much Knox could tell, but hadn't he just admitted that he'd kill Knox the first chance he got?

"I'm going to be killing more pirates, you all still good with that?" Knox asked with a round of nods in response. "Good. Let's move out."

The first pirates they found were another small group of three; they were walking through the woods and Knox sensed them from a mile away.

"We have three targets ahead about a mile out. Vlad and Boris, go left and flank them; Edgar and I will go right, and we will pinch them between us. Go for quick kills and don't let yourselves get injured," Knox said. They answered with an affirmative and Knox and Edgar left to flank and pinch.

Edgar moved quietly enough for a man made of metal and wearing additional metal armor, but it was loud enough that they'd give themselves away if they didn't rush in at the last second. Knox just hoped that the others came to the same conclusion or that they didn't get there too soon or too late. Though, he was more worried about them showing up early and being overwhelmed than he was about them showing up late. Edgar was easily their strongest and Knox had double the power than any of them had so far.

As they drew nearer, the sound of battle rang out and three more pirates snapped into view on his sense. Some type of rogues, no doubt! Knox felt another one, then another came out of hiding until they faced eight total pirates.

"Time to move," Knox said to Edgar, who nodded his head. They ran as fast as they could, and Knox had two thoughts enter his mind as he did so. First, he hoped that Boris and Vlad could last long enough, and second, he wished he'd brought more Soul-stones; he had picked up a few extra but only had six.

Rushing through the trees, they closed in on the original three and Knox raised his axe as he ran. Then, as he came through the trees, he slammed it down into the back of a red-haired pirate. "Ambush!" they cried as Boris and Vlad battled against five dagger-wielding foes at once. Lucky for them, they'd only taken dents and scratches, the weapons the pirates had not having the desired effect.

Just as Knox made that observation, one of the rogue-like figures used a technique and put a jagged cut down Boris's chest armor, sending scale mail flying in every direction. Knox had no idea how that technique would do against their golem armor beneath the armor they had, so he had to act fast.

Removing his axe from the dead redhead, he swung backward to avoid a strike from a massive, curved blade, cutting upward as he did so. The arm of the offending attacker went flying in one direction and his weapon another.

The last of the original three went down in a blaze of fire from Edgar, who burnt a literal hole through him. Checking the Soul-stones, he grinned. He'd collected three new potential golems.

Rushing forward, it was now five to four, and Knox felt bad for the remaining pirates. For all that awaited them was death. Boris slashed upward with a dagger and caught one of the rogue types with a surprisingly powerful attack. Vlad followed up for him, smashing his empowered fist into the rogue's back with an audible crunch. Four against four.

The remaining four put up a bit of a fight, but the outcome was a foregone conclusion. One of the rogues must have realized this before the end of the fight because he disappeared before the group and winked out of Knox's sense.

"Let's move fast. Strip them of any goods and let's double time toward the pirate stronghold or whatever, to see if we can catch the guy," Knox ordered and the trio moved with efficiency, gathering coin, food, and even clothing from one pack.

Edgar spoke up as they began to move in the general direction where Knox was sure the rogue had gone. "Turn more to the east, we have an outer camp and an inner camp, then further down the coast is where the city of Shadowfall Swamp and our fleet of ships sleep. He'll be heading for the outer camp, as they have the means to communicate with the city."

Knox did as Edgar suggested, moving to a full out sprint that the golems were easily able to match. A fact that surprised Knox, as he didn't know the full extent of their capabilities. Onward they went, closer and closer to the destination that lay ahead. It was while running that they came upon the rogue, first in Knox's sense, then in sight, sprinting forward with reckless abandonment.

Knox exchanged a look with Edgar and without saying a word, the pirate knew what was expected of him. While running, Edgar began to cast a Fireball. It took three times as long, but it went off all the same. The ball of flame slammed into the back of the rogue and sent him sprawling downward. The rogue cried out in pain as he was sent end over end down a hill leading into a large natural basin.

This was unfortunate because in this basin lay a mostly hidden camp filled with pirates. Two dozen such pirates appeared from makeshift tents and lean-tos. Knox wasted no time in calling a stop to their charge.

"Fire at will!" Knox screamed, readying his Arcane Pulse spell.

Fire, Arcane, Water, and mean looks slammed down on the pirates below, killing them as fast as they appeared. Knox threw out another Arcane Pulse, taking out three at a time with every blast and his Mana reserves felt as fit as ever. After three more Fireballs and two more water streams, both of Knox's ranged golems were tapped out until they could regen some Mana.

"Ready weapons," Knox called out as a dozen of the survivors of the massacre began to edge closer to the incline. Then, several of them leveled crossbows and Knox scrambled back before remembering he had a spell for that.

For the first time out of the Titan Engine, Knox cast Prism Ward. Using an extra measure of Mana, he spread it out to cover the trio as they huddled closer together behind it. Just in time, it shimmered golden into existence, bolts passing through but slowing to a harmless speed. Each bolt 'tinked' off the golems leaving them safe and sound.

The crossbow-wielding men ditched their weapons and pulled swords, joining the crew making their way up the hill. Really, they ought to have brought crossbows themselves, but it was too late for that now. Knox called for a short retreat, giving the incoming men space to die properly.

Vlad wasn't so ready to give them a fair chance, though; as they cleared the edge, huffing and puffing, he stepped forward and slammed his fist into the middle one, bowling over three others in the process. Even Boris tried to be sneaky, summoning a wind funnel that whipped with more force than ever before, throwing another man over the edge.

The battle, if you wanted to call it that, ended as quickly as it had started. The high ground won them the day, and not for the first time, Knox wondered why they'd hid themselves in a basin as they had.

"Let's go down and check it out," Knox suggested.

"We should hurry, that small of a force means over half of the crew is out scouting for treasures," Edgar said, looking around and kneeling low to take treasure from the fallen pirates.

They each had packs filling up with supplies now, but still, they filled them further. The ground smelled of blood and shit, but Knox pinched his nose against the smell and leaned into his sense to search the lower area. He was surprised to find a single target still alive, somewhere deeper in the camp, and whoever it was, they were strong.

The aura shone as someone E Ranked, on the cusp of D Rank. Still, Knox went forward with his trio and signaled that they should be ready, each step drawing them closer to the strongest target Knox had faced since becoming a Titan Born.

A voice echoed out from within the small tent city that had been erected by the pirates. "You walk to your death, powerful or not, I am the Jailer, and you won't make it past me."

Around Knox, the three golems stopped, and Knox turned to see what the matter was. The Jailer was still out of sight and barely within shouting range, but the trio looked like they were about to turn back.

"What's the matter?" Knox whispered his question.

"The Jailer is one of Captain Dread's lieutenants. He will capture us and torture out any information he needs," Edgar said, his head looking longingly back up the hillside littered with bodies.

"We've just killed two dozen pirates with ease, one man won't stand in our way," Knox assured them, and they straightened. His words appeared to be enough, because the trio brandished their weapons and looked toward the Jailer. It was difficult to make out facial expressions on golems, but Knox was sure they wore angry expressions.

All around them they had to bend low and duck beneath ripped and tattered tents, so it was only Knox's sense that gave him warning when the first attack came. A tendril of power snaked out from the Jailer from several dozen paces away. Knox moved to the left and an ethereal chain slammed down into the ground where he'd just been standing.

This also had the effect of clearing their view and ripping down several lean-tos and finally showing their foe to them. The Jailer was a tall bald man with a square jaw and a scar-covered face. He wore chains wrapping up his arms, legs, and bare chest. His left arm's chains recoiled around his arm like a snake as he cracked his neck to the side and spoke.

"You survived the first blow, but don't think you'll be lucky enough to survive the full power of my attacks," the Jailer said, lifting both arms up and whipping them down.

Two sets of chains tore out from him, the air snapping from the sudden movement. Knox stepped aside, but only one of the attacks had been meant for him. Boris took the strike right on the chest, but it glanced off his armor and wrapped around his arm. Suddenly, the Jailer pulled and off went Boris's arm in a sudden screech of tearing metal.

Edgar and Vlad were done sitting off to the side, Vlad ran forward with his weapon ready, and Edgar began to cast a Fireball. Meanwhile, Knox kept his attention on the Jailer, beginning the workings of a Luminous Surge. Before he could finish, the chains shot out again. Knox let his incantation end and he slashed out with his axe, while pivoting around to avoid the chains meant for him.

He stuck the chains, causing them to move just enough that they didn't take Edgar's head off. This was going to be a difficult fight, but if he focused on diverting attacks, they might stand a chance.

Vlad reached the Jailer and struck out with his punch attack, followed closely behind by a slash of his sword. However, the Jailer just smiled, showing blackened teeth, and kicked outward. Chains left his leg and smashed into Vlad's chest, sending him reeling backward.

Knox realized then that he'd have to take the fight in close if he had a chance of defending each of the trio. Boris stood dumb-struck but upon catching Knox's eye, he nodded.

"Take it in close," Knox shouted, and they all ran to get closer to the Jailer.

This had the added effect of making it harder to predict where the chains would go as Knox had less time to react, but one chain attack at a time he began turning them aside.

One, then two, then three, and Vlad got a hit in, sending the Jailer reeling backward and blood dripping down his broken lip. After all that, all they'd managed to get was a bloody mouth.

Back and forth they fought; Knox could feel his Stamina beginning to flag as he struggled to move fast enough to keep the chains back. But it wasn't one-sided, the Jailer was slowing as well, his techniques coming less frequently until finally they stopped coming altogether.

The Jailer let loose both chains on his arms and began to twirl them, making the air scream in protest. As Vlad came in for another strike, the chains slammed into him, leaving several dents on his head, and staggering him backward.

"Circle him and strike as one," Knox called out, they'd worn him down enough that they finally had a decent chance of taking him out, stronger foe or not, everyone had their limits, and the four of them had found the Jailer's.

They circled the Jailer, the trio taking blows but remaining upright as Knox took position behind the Jailer. He cast Lustrous Chains, grinning at the ironic use of chains to take down the Jailer.

Golden chains shot out of the ground and bound the Jailer fast. He wore leather armor on his arms and legs, but it did little to protect him from the coming onslaught. Blow after blow rained down on the Jailer until his screams went silent, his life ending in a spray of red.

-Personal Status-
  -Name: Knox-
  -Level: 12 (E Rank, Tier 2)-
  -Essence To Next Level: 1,427/2,400-
  -Health: Fair Tier 9-
  -Mana: Fair Tier 9-
  -Stamina: Fair Tier 9-
  -Mind: 66-
  -Body: 66-
  -Spirit: 66-

CHAPTER 39
RESCUE

"LET'S BE QUICK," Knox said, rooting through the Jailer's pockets and finding a ring of keys.

"You going to free the prisoners now, aren't you?" Edgar asked, seeing the key ring.

This caught Knox off guard, and he looked at the golem in

confusion. "Where are they being held, do you know? Do you think we could get them out?"

"The inner camp is where they are being held, supposed to be watched over by the Jailer," Edgar said, pulling a golden tooth free from the Jailer's mouth. "I suspect they are not well guarded now; we might be able to fight our way through the hundred or so pirates, but I'd suggest we fix Boris first."

"How are you doing Boris?" Knox asked, picking up the golem's missing arm and handing it back to him.

"Been better," Boris said, somberly taking his arm and regarding it sadly.

"I have a plan," Knox announced, the beginnings of a plan forming in his head. "You three go back and see if Mic can repair Boris while I do something sneaky."

Knox went looking for the least bloody pirate outfit he could find, stripping out of his armor and putting on the attire. Finding headwear and an eyepatch he finished the look.

"How do I look?" Knox asked, handing over the bundle he had that included the Soulstones and his armor to Vlad.

"Like a shit pirate, you should fit right in," Edgar said, laughing.

"Right, well I'm going to sneak in and free the prisoners and sneak out," Knox announced.

"Good luck," Edgar said, though his words were obviously laced with sarcasm.

"Point me in the right direction?" Knox asked, realizing he had no clue how to find the inner camp, despite his fairly good sense of direction.

Edgar explained how to get there and gave him some tips on how to get in. He told Knox to say he was part of Edgar's team, and they were ambushed by monsters, Knox being the only survivor. Despite his sarcasm, Edgar assured him that they didn't know every pirate by name and a new face wouldn't be all too out of place. Then, he spread some mud on Knox's face before giving him his approval.

"I'm Talon," Knox growled, practicing his fake name and voice. Boris laughed this time, but Edgar just shrugged.

"See you in death," Vlad said as they turned and left toward the Titan Complex, weaving through the piles of dead bodies they'd searched and stripped of useful items.

Knox scoffed, turning toward his own path and starting down it.

The path forward turned rocky and soon Knox's pace slowed considerably. It was enough to give him a moment to think about what was happening and the risks he was putting himself in for simple essence. But then again, it wasn't just about the essence, he wanted to do right by the people who'd been captured. He didn't know them or even know if they were people worth saving, but he'd grown up with certain beliefs and he couldn't cast them aside so easily.

Every man, woman, and child deserved to be free. He wasn't sure if he'd be able to save them all, but he would try and be damned the risk.

But what would he do after rescuing them? Could he trust them enough to show them to the Titan Complex? Would he even want to do that? He knew the answer to the question as he thought it; no, he couldn't trust them, but he had to get them to safety somehow. Unsure and a bit wary, he moved forward until he began to sense people at the edge of his range for sensing.

The rocky terrain gave way to the coast, just ahead and nestled into several large caverns was the grouping of pirates he sensed. Among their numbers were five or six dozen blurs of Violet auras —F Rankers. But there were also several Green and even a single Yellow all gathered together. That meant C Rank and even a B Ranker! However, something odd about their auras caught his attention. They seemed diminished or smaller than they ought to be for their strength. There was also the fact that they weren't being suppressed completely like all the other C Rankers he'd met, although he suspected that they'd want to show off their power in a pirate camp.

Knox nearly turned back right away, there was no way he could deal with a C Ranked pirate, much less a B Ranked one. But his feet kept moving and soon he was being flagged down by a lowly Violet aura.

"Name yourself," the dark-haired, scraggly looking man commanded.

"Talon, I was a part of Edgar's group, we were ambushed by monsters, and I was the only one to escape," Knox said, rehashing out exactly what Edgar had suggested he say.

"Hah, so that pompous ass is dead, eh? Good riddance, go on in. The Jailer went to deal with the disappearances in the forward base, so just report to him once he gets back in," the pirate said, lowering his sword and letting Knox pass.

Well, that was easier than he thought it would be, Knox mused. The camp, it could rightly be called a small village, lay within a massive cave filled with wooden shacks and canvas lean-tos. At first, Knox avoided the higher Ranked auras, no one gave him as much as a second look while they went about their business, most just playing cards or dice around one of a dozen campfires.

He roamed as much as he thought he could get away with before deciding he'd have to talk to someone to find where the prisoners were kept. His sense told him the only logical place was in the largest of the wooden huts, but it was filled with a few E Rankers and half a dozen C Rankers, as well as one B Ranker, if just barely—the yellow still having the tiniest amount of green to it. None of the C Ranked or higher were masking their auras very well, color seeping out of them that was easy to detect.

Checking the coin he'd gathered from the other pirates, Knox decided it was time to play some cards or dice. Finding a group with only three others, Knox went and sat down next to one of the players who sat on a larger rock. He got a grunt for his trouble, and without even asking, they dealt him in on the next hand.

"You with Kenny's lot?" Grunted out one particularly gravelly voiced individual.

"Nah, I went out with Edgar," Knox said, one of the men nodded knowingly but the other didn't react at all.

"That the scrawny talkative bastard that keeps company with Vlad and Boris, right?" asked a new voice; it was low and rumbling. Knox looked up and took him in, he had a bald head, no shirt and was missing several teeth. But despite this, he had the demeanor of someone who wanted to break something in half.

"That's right, got connected with them not long ago, but if I had to guess, they are dead by now, along with a good number of others," Knox said, hoping to see what the pirates' reactions to this might be.

"Heard as much," said the rumbling low voiced bald man. "Jailer went out to take care of whatever monster is wiping us out, you're lucky to have made it out. You ran the first chance you got, right?"

Knox made a show of looking ashamed, looking away and toward the ground. All three laughed, but no one said a word against him for it.

"I'm alive, aren't I?" Knox finally asked, to which they all grunted in affirmative.

Knox let them win, despite knowing he could win several times and the more gold they won, the more talkative they became. He learned that Captain Dread was meant to be visiting the front lines in the next week or two, and that he'd be taking the prisoners with him when he did. Without Knox having to ask, he learned that the reason the captives had been taken out of the seaside city was because other captains, ones meant to be under Captain Dread's thumb, had conspired to take the prisoners. So, he spirited them away and set his lieutenant, the Jailer, to watch over them.

During the back and forth, they directed their thumb over toward the larger building many times, indicating the location of the prisoners. Then, when he thought he'd have to give up and just leave, one of them gave him some key information.

"Crazy that those manacles work to suppress those strong Adventurers. I even heard that Captain Dread nearly lost his head when fighting them. He had to call in every one of his twelve lieutenants to beat them back, killing the strongest of the group. I bet he got a pretty penny from their armor and weapons, though; every single one was enchanted!" The third of the pirates spoke with a sort of whine in his voice, but the others didn't seem to mind it, so Knox pretended not to either.

Knox focused on the wooden building once more, and despite the auras he felt within, he realized he might have a chance after all. If he was understanding everything right, then the Violet auras were the guards and the Green and Yellow auras were the prisoners but they were having their powers suppressed, which might be why their auras seemed smaller than normal.

This was great news on many fronts, with as strong as they were, he could be fairly confident that they'd be able to make it out. Plus, he had a black orb tucked away that would help them keep most of the stronger monsters off them. Knox still hadn't had much of a chance to examine the powerful items that the pirates seemed to have in abundance, these black orbs.

Losing one last time, Knox pretended to be out of gold, holding his hands up in defeat. They all laughed and told him he could come back any time if he wanted to play, each of them sharing a drink from a canteen, then passing it to Knox before he left. This was the first time they had, and Knox didn't hesitate to stay in character, grabbing it and taking a long pull.

Whatever vile concoction lay within, it took all of Knox's self-control to not spit it out immediately. Instead, he swallowed and tried not to gag. He coughed a few times, gaining him a few more laughs, before he left. He roamed around a few more times, then went behind one of the adjacent buildings, pulling his pants down as if to pee.

After several seconds of peeing on the backside of the building and trying his best to block out the smell of others' piss and shit, Knox shimmied his way behind the building and toward the larger wooden construction.

It was a single-story affair, all the buildings were, but this one looked like it had been put together by an actual builder and not just a group of... well, pirates. There were windows with open shutters and a roof with a straw top, instead of just a panel of wood. Peeking in a back window, Knox breathed out a sigh of relief. The window let into a storage closet of some sort, and he easily slipped into the pitch-black room.

Light in the cave was almost exclusively from torch light and very little of it at that, so the chances that someone saw him sneak back here was very little, or so he hoped. Using his sense, he took in first the entire cave system; no one seemed to be following him, just going about their normal business. Then he narrowed it to the building, his hand going to the keys and hoping he had the right ones.

The two guards were on the far side of the building, away from the room he was in now, while the prisoners—or who he dearly hoped were the prisoners and not some powered up pirates —were right outside his door. He'd need to deal with the pirates first, but how to do it without drawing an alarm? He'd left his axe behind, instead, switching it for a set of daggers, a common weapon among the pirates.

Deciding that there was no way to get in and dispose of the two before it was too late, he left the room and made his way back into the crowds. He'd wait for them to go to sleep and then sneak in at night when they least expected it.

Finding another game, he began to lose more gold, but he let himself win a few hands this time, much to the disappointment of those he played with. It was while he did this, waiting out the night, when the pirate that had let him into the cave approached.

At once everyone began to look away and pretend to be interested in anything else but the approaching pirate. Knox didn't know any better and waved at the man as he approached.

"Good, you haven't left to the city yet. I need someone for the night shift watching the prisoners. You and Berk are going to do it," the man said, surprising Knox.

A man, who must be named Berk, groaned and shot Knox a look that would kill if it could. How had he gotten so lucky, he wondered as the man left after telling them to report immediately for duty.

"Those shits never shut up, you've just ruined my night, punk," Berk said, glaring at Knox hard. "You better hope I don't slit your throat when we finish this damned watch."

Knox raised his hands in his defense but said nothing, just putting his cards aside—he had a winning hand—and following after the nameless pirate that had let him into the cavern complex and was now giving him exactly what he needed.

He'd come up with all manner of ideas for distractions, each one more dangerous than the last, but this would be much better and safer. With this new turn of events, he'd only need to overpower a single person, and an F Ranker at that. He had as good as freed them now.

The double doors opened as he approached them with Berk, and two guards left looking as infuriated as Berk. Were they upset that they had to leave or just upset at the entire situation like Berk, Knox wondered.

"A pretty lass will call me crass, but don't..." A baritone voice sounded from within the room and Berk cursed then yelled, drowning out the singing voice.

"Shut the hells up or I'll take your tongue!" Berk screamed the words.

"Oh, new meat," the baritone voice said, and Knox turned to regard the caged individuals. "You can cut the act, I heard directly from your Captain that anyone that so much as lays a hand on us will be skinned alive. You don't look like someone that would want to be skinned alive. And who is this lovely change of color? Is that a Red aura? Finally letting stronger peons guard us."

"Not as powerful as he appears," a whisper of a voice said, feminine and coming from a disheveled blonde-haired woman in the back of the cage that held six of the seven.

Knox looked at them, trying to communicate with his eyes that he was a friend, and to his surprise, the man in a cage by himself, a massive man with arms as thick as Knox's waist, took notice and nodded his head to him. He had the strangest orange eyes with an odd birthmark on his forehead, a sapphire diamond shape that almost seemed to lift off of his forehead.

Berk pulled out some dice, and despite his attitude toward Knox only moments before, basically demanded that he play with him. Knox did his best, but his attention kept being drawn toward the larger fellow in his own cage. It felt as if he knew him or at least felt drawn to him, and he couldn't say why.

There was a power in his gaze, which made sense as he was the B Ranked yellow aura individual, but it was more than that. They remained quiet for only another ten minutes or so until the baritone voiced fellow began to sing again. It wasn't bad, if Knox was being honest, but the songs he chose left much to be desired.

Four hours later and deep into the night, even the baritone voiced man had begun to sleep. Looking over at his guard mate, Knox realized he'd dozed off as well. Now was the time to act, but first he had to do something unpleasant.

Reaching to his belt, he drew out his dagger and stood as quietly as he could.

"Hold," said a deep rumbling voice. It wasn't loud but in the silence of the night it made Knox jump nearly out of his skin. Turning, he regarded the brawny B Ranker, giving him a look but saying nothing.

"Release me and I will deal with them all. There is no need for there to be more blood on your hands, honored Titan. My name is Aetex, release me and allow me to do my duty," Aetex said, the stranger with the blue diamond shape on his forehead stared

Knox down and despite the ridiculousness of the idea, he found himself walking over to release him.

Coming closer to the man he saw that while most of his features were those of a human, he had pointed ears like an elf and skin a few shades greyer than any Knox had seen before. Then there was the gem set into his forehead. It hadn't been a birthmark after all, but a gem cut into the very skin. It seemed to shine for a moment from an internal light and Knox took a step back.

"What are you?" Knox asked, pulling out the keys and trying them on the cage door. Aetex looked to the wall over by the other pirate and there Knox saw another set of keys. Walking over, he took them and opened the cage with the single key on the ring.

"I am a Ki'darthian, or well, I am a hybrid now, thanks to Mah'kus, but don't worry about that for now. Use those keys and free my wrists," Aetex said, the strange *Ki'darthian*, whatever that was, looked intense as hell up close.

Going from key to key, Knox found the right one and released Aetex, his aura suddenly disappearing completely, which was a good thing because a sudden rush of its power had sent Knox stepping backward.

"Free the others," Aetex ordered as he slowly freed himself from the cage. Once free, he moved with impossible speed, his hand clasping over Berk's throat and with a gentle snap, the body went rigid.

Knox looked wide-eyed, but did as he was commanded, freeing the others and waking them in the process. They were all wide-eyed and silent, which was good because there were still several dozen, if not a hundred more pirates between them and freedom.

"Name's Draven, this is my sister Mareth, and our cousins, Liora, Elsire, Vyren, and Calix. What do we owe the pleasure of our escape? Do you wish to claim the ransom yourself?" Draven asked, his baritone voice much more pleasant to the ears when not singing profane melodies.

They were all blond-haired, some darker than others, and had purple eyes. The only one that didn't fit was this Aetex character. Turning, Knox noticed that Aetex had gone missing, not making as much as a whisper while doing so.

"Name's Knox and no, I'm just a concerned citizen who had to rub pirate shit on himself to be passed off as one of them. We can go over the details after we've escaped. Where is your friend Aetex?" Knox asked, a heavy feeling building in his gut.

"We don't actually know that man, he was already captured when we got here, though how they managed to capture a peak B Ranker, I don't know. That Captain Dread fellow took out my brother and he was a low Rank B, barely powerful enough to deal with some of the stronger monsters in the swamp. He assured us, of course, that we'd be fine, and he'd get us all to B by the time we finished here. Instead, we got captured by fucking pirates. Pirates who, mind you, somehow survive out here in the most dangerous place I've ever visited. We should have listened to our father and his stupid advisor, she will be so smug to hear about our troubles," Draven droned on, his voice getting more animated as he went.

Knox held up a hand and silenced him, then put a finger to his lips. "I'm going to go take a look and then we will get going," Knox said.

Going through to the backroom door where he'd snuck in before, he slipped out to get a look at who was keeping watch. What he found when he cleared the back wall made his eyes go wide. Bodies, dozens and dozens, lay out dead as Aetex moved from campfire to campfire, ending lives.

Then, as he worked, he turned and regarded Knox, looking right at where he stood in the deep shadows.

"Never fear, for I am here!" he shouted, and suddenly the camp was in a frenzy of motion.

This monster of a man was going to kill them all! Knox turned and went back into the room, checking all six of them to be sure he'd gotten all their manacles off. Then he collected them and put them into a sack he was carrying around, putting the keys in as well. Wouldn't hurt to take a look at the formations later.

"Time to go, Aetex is killing all of them," Knox said, looking to each of them for any sign that they were as worried as Knox was beginning to feel.

"Oh damn," Draven said, sounding concerned. Finally, someone with a little sense. "We are missing the fun." With that, the six strong Adventurers left the room in a rush, one picking up a dagger, but the rest just rushing out to fight.

It was a massacre of the worst kind. Knox had felt a bit guilty about taking out a few dozen pirates, but that was nothing compared to the hundred and ten pirates these overpowered Adventurers killed. All of them killed with such ease and ferocity that a part of Knox worried he might be next. At first, he'd been helping, but after nearly getting his head smacked off by a girl several heads shorter than him, he decided to stay out of the way and stripped off as much of the pirate attire as he could, even cleaning his face off as best he could.

"All clear," Aetex called out and Knox came out, breathing steadily so as to keep his nerves in check.

"What now?" Knox asked, looking between Draven and Aetex, the de facto leaders in his mind.

"We are going to flee as fast as our feet will take us back home. Please feel free to visit us and claim a reward," Draven said, pulling off a patch from his shirt and handing it over.

There was blood and grime on it, so much so that it was nothing more than a brown smear, but one of the girls reached out and touched it. Suddenly it cleared and showed what lay beneath. It had a magnificent silver phoenix with its wings spread wide and encircling a crescent moon. The moon was partially eclipsed with a sapphire color representing the shadowed part.

This was the crest of the city Lumisar, one of the noble families of the kingdom... it had to be. Knox knew very little about the different noble houses and such, but this one in particular was famous for producing talented Adventurers. Dernal had mentioned it many times, and from what he'd told him, this particular family, despite being weeks of travel away from his little town, was the one that owned the land their town lay within.

So, in part, they were meant to keep it safe from monsters and such, which they hadn't, and suddenly Knox felt a little resentment toward them. Why could they live so far away and have any kind of control over their lives? It made him feel sick to think about, so he pushed it aside and took the gift for what it was, a great boon if he ever tried to turn it in.

"Thank you," Knox said simply. He caught the eyes of each of them and imagined the Celestial powers they could likely wield, or so Dernal had said on the few occasions when the drink untied his lips.

"What of you, large stranger?" Draven asked Aetex, even going so far as to clasp a hand on the massive man's shoulder. Aetex stood at least two heads taller than Terrim, and that was saying something because Terrim was tall as hell.

"I am where I am meant to be," Aetex said, looking at Knox as he spoke. "Excuse me while I clear the path ahead. I will find you when the time is right, Knox."

A thought occurred to him at that moment, and he did a double take at Aetex. He had introduced himself after Aetex had already left, so how did he know his name? Before he could get too worried about it, he decided he must have just heard him with his B Ranked ears.

"Okay, bye," Knox said, the words coming out a bit awkward as he didn't really know how to respond to the powerful man. They all turned and left, running at speeds Knox couldn't hope to match, so he went on his way, ready to turn in the quest and get his sweet ten thousand essence reward, plus how much he was going to get from each of the ears he'd collected. He'd had to collect another few backpacks, but he managed to get all the ears and some good loot.

On the way back, he came across several five-man teams of pirates, all dead, so he collected their ears as well. It was a great haul, if not a bit morbid. Getting back to the Titan Complex, he turned in his quests and pulled up his new status screen.

-Personal Status-
    -Name: Knox-
    -Level: 18 (E Rank, Tier 8)-
    -Essence To Next Level: 787/4,300-
    -Health: Fair Tier 9-
    -Mana: Fair Tier 9-
    -Stamina: Fair Tier 9-
    -Mind: 84-
    -Body: 84-
    -Spirit: 84-

CHAPTER 40
GRINDING

GETTING to Level 18 had opened up several things for Knox, not the least of which were talent points that he hadn't been taking advantage of. So, he saw to that first, adding two points to Radiant Endurance, bringing it up to four out of five or twenty percent enhancement of endurance and Health. The effects were immediately noticeable, so much so that he decided to make it to a total five out of five. Now, with fifteen more points and a new Tier open to him, at least to see if not to add points to, he looked over what he had.

-Luminous Vanguard, Tier 4-
    -Luminous Surge: (0/5) Amplify the power of your Luminous Surge Ability, increasing its damage and blinding effects by 5% per point.-
    -Aegis of Light: (0/3) Harness light to enhance the effects of Prism Ward, absorbing an additional 5% of your maximum Health per point.-

Both interesting choices that in the future Knox knew he'd have to take, but for now he refocused on the Tier 2 talents and next, the talent tree of the Mystic. First, he took Ethereal Step, as it only cost a single talent point, leaving him with fourteen. Then, he put three points into Titan's Aura, a passive skill that radiates an aura around him that 'inspires allies, increasing their physical damage by 2% per point while in your vicinity.'

Ethereal Step was a bit cooler, allowing him to perform a short dash, leaving a trail of radiant light that boosts allies speed and harms enemies who cross it. The knowledge of how to do it came slamming into his head as he confirmed his talent tree picks.

With eleven points left, he looked toward the Mystic tree to see what benefits he might gain. They all seemed a bit more abstract and not as straightforward as the Path of the Titans' trees. Eventually, he decided to put five points into Arcane Enhancement, which increased the damage and spread of Arcane Pulse, leaving six points to assign. This unlocked the fourth Tier to view, so Knox took a look.

-Arcanum Scholar, Tier 4-

-Sigil Mastery: (0/5) Enhances the potency of sigils and symbols, boosting the effects of buffs and debuffs by 3% per point.-

-Arcane Resonance: (0/3) Increase the effectiveness of Mystic Veil, reducing incoming damage by 5% per point added.-

It was interesting for sure; Sigil Mastery seemed like it might be able to enhance his Radiant Glyph ability, boosting the effects in some way. He'd have to start making a list of effective runic formations for combat, though most took too long to be used in the moment, it did give him an amazing range of utility potential.

Switching back to his Titan tree after taking a solid look at the Mystic tree, Knox decided to add five points to the Luminous Surge talent, increasing damage by 25%. With five more points added into the tree, he unlocked the next Tier. Taking a look, he held tight to his final talent point.

-Luminous Vanguard, Tier 5-

-Titan's Fortitude: (0/5) Strengthen your physical resilience, reducing the duration of crowd control effects like stuns and roots by 5% per point.-

-Radiant Rush: (0/1) Fill yourself with radiant energy, dealing increased damage to enemies and gaining a short burst of movement speed for five seconds.-

Knox placed a point into Radiant Rush and smiled to himself. With this new ability along with Ethereal Step, his mobility issues on the battlefield would no longer be a problem. He imagined himself shooting from one part of the battlefield to the next, a true terror to behold.

With his talent tree items taken care of, he made his way through the complex heading toward the Titan Engine, ready to learn whatever new abilities his last six Levels had earned him. As it turned out, he only had two to learn, he studied the descriptions as he waited to begin his training with Echo.

-*Solar Wings: Manifest wings of pure sunlight, granting brief flight and emitting rays that harm adversaries below.*-
    -*Ethereal Step: Step through the ethereal plane, instantly teleporting a short distance away.*-

Though it ought to only have taken him a short period of time to learn these two abilities, he found that they were difficult enough that he spent nearly as long as when he had an entire host of abilities to learn. Ethereal Step was no cake walk to learn and it took him weeks to master just the basics enough to enter into the ethereal plane and out again. Then there was the immense amount of focus and skill it took to manifest wings of light.

He got it to the point that he could activate the wings for barely a second or two, but it was enough to say he learned it. Before leaving the training time dilation, he tried to combine the two, stepping into the air and using Solar Wings to slow his descent downward. It was mostly effective, but each time he hurt himself just a little from the attempts.

Slipping out of the realm where Echo lived and back into reality, Knox stumbled but righted himself a moment later. It was a tough transition, the longer he was there the harder it felt to leave.

"Welcome back," Mic said, a familiar voice greeting Knox as he settled himself down in a comfortable sitting position.

"Hey," Knox said, taking a good look at the golem but seeing nothing out of place.

"You've grown stronger, yet you've not collected any C Rank or above Cores for the Titan Engine. It is required that you find some so that the influence of the Titan System can be spread," Mic said, looking down at Knox.

"I'm barely at Level 18, I'd need to be Level 30 before I could kill C Rank or higher without issue," Knox said, pinching at the bridge of his nose.

"Actually, I believe Level 21 will put you at peak D Rank, which in turn makes you very able to deal with C Ranked, or low Level 30 mobs," Mic said as if he'd expected Knox's response.

"Then I guess I better get out there and start killing more monsters, eh?" Knox said, struggling to his feet and making his way toward the staircase.

Mic made no move to stop him and soon Knox was back on the surface, looking for monsters to kill.

The first monster he came across was some sort of reptilian creature that looked to be related to a dragon but had no wings and the biggest maw than anything he'd encountered so far. It came in quick, too quick, but Knox's new abilities gave him the edge he needed.

First, Knox activated Ethereal Step, moving himself a short ways to the left and behind the beast. Next, he charged in with Ethereal Step, raising his weapon to strike down and activating Radiant Rush, cleaving open a bloody gash. Next, he used the increased movement speed that Radiant Rush granted him to put some distance just as the monster's tail came around to smash him.

With space created, Knox began casting Luminous Surge, its power increased by 25% from his talent tree points. He just got off the cast before a tail slash took him in the chest, throwing him backward and lancing pain through his lower stomach.

Remembering that he ought to have cast his Mystic Armor, Knox rolled several times before making it to his feet and hiding behind a rather thick tree and casting his armor spell. Mystical translucent blue armor appeared over him, and he was ready once more.

Just in time too, as the monster came around the side of the tree, maw open and ready to strike. It spat forth some green liquid, which Knox only dodged because he cast a panicked Ethereal Step, appearing in the air above it.

Casting Solar Wings, he turned direction and flew toward the ground, but not before the wings' second effect came into play, slashing out at the draconic beast with rays of powerful light. The tree crashed down a moment later, the acid spray eating through it with ease.

Before the lizard of enormous size could turn, Knox cast Lustrous Chains, followed by Void Grasp. Chains of golden light wrapped the lizard followed by void tendrils grasping and draining it.

With it incapacitated by the chains and tendrils, Knox began to write out the most powerful runic formation he could think of. It took time, but he'd given himself enough. Just as he finished his slowing spells broke and the beast came for him, but not in time. A torrent of flame and brimstone came spilling out, smashing right into the lizard and ending its life.

Sweat poured down Knox's face from the effort, but he'd done it. Searching through the remains, he found an intact Core, it had been Level 27, so a D Ranked Core.

Because he'd gone alone, he hadn't had to share the essence with any of the new golems or the trio of pirates. That had netted him a cool six hundred and fifty essence and the Core, well he'd keep the Core for now, but it likely had just as much inside if not a bit more. Thinking better of it, as it wasn't even C Rank, so the Engine likely didn't want it, he took in the essence and was surprised to find it contained a thousand.

He spent the rest of the day hunting solo and killing monster after monster, growing stronger and stronger. He knew he had to get back and see to the new golems, but for now, he wanted to grow stronger, because he had places to go and things to do.

"You ready to meet the new troops?" Edgar asked, a hint of annoyance in his voice that Knox couldn't help but hear.

"They're ready?" Knox asked. He'd provided the Soulstones and let Mic do what needed to be done, but he'd been told it would take a while.

"Got'm names an' everything," Boris said, walking up to one of the six new golems that stood silently before them and placing a hand on its shoulder.

Mic stepped forward and gestured to each of them in turn, giving them their names. "Prime, Sek, Tertan, Quartheon, Quintar, Sextor."

"Which ones are what?" Knox asked.

"Prime is a Physical Golem, Sek is an Elemental Golem, Tertan, Quartheon, Quintar are all Maintenance Golems, leaving Sextor as another Physical Golem."

"Very good," Knox said, walking up to Prime. "Prime, how do you feel about all this?"

"I am Prime, first of my kind. I live to serve the Titan Born and spread the will of the Titan System. Give me a target and I will see to its destruction," Prime said, his voice oddly similar to Mic's if not a bit more rigid in his speech.

Addressing them each in turn, Knox got similar responses and the same voice coming from each of them, it was odd in that sense, like he was dealing with a complete blank slate instead of a soul with its own personality.

"I command you all to grow stronger and do your best not to attract the attention of any remaining pirates. I'm going on a trip and will return as soon as I can," Knox said, deciding it was best to just get this part over with.

"Where are you going?" Mic asked first, but the trio had all stepped forward to speak as well. "With the additional maintenance golems, we will be able to grow crops and be sustainable."

"I've got friends and family I've left behind and I need to check on them. But don't worry, I'm strong enough to get through and with this handy dandy black orb the pirates provided me, I should be safe from the strongest monsters," Knox said, though he could tell his words weren't reassuring them as much as he'd hoped they would.

"Why can't we go with you?" Vlad asked, surprising Knox with the eagerness he heard in his words. Vlad had remained the quietest and least interested in Knox's accounts.

"Because you need to be charged by close proximity to the Titan Engine and I don't want you dying on me halfway through the journey," Knox said simply.

The discussion continued into the night, but finally he assured and reassured them enough that he felt comfortable slipping into the night and out toward his town and the unknown. It was the first step on many into the mysterious and unknown landscape that he'd have to travel, but he was ready. Empowered by the strength of the Titans and nearly as strong as he had been before, there was little he feared now, except maybe the dragon that caused him to flee here in the first place.

But what were the chances he'd encounter it again so soon?

CHAPTER 41
C RANKED MONSTERS

AT HIS CURRENT LEVEL, Knox had access to the max resources of someone at peak D Rank. He had to remind himself of this fact as he traveled through the swamps in the direction of his home. The trees and forest that had gone up around the coast gave way to much of the wet and swampy area that he'd seen when first traveling into the Shadowfall Swamps.

He could even feel the monsters at the edge of his sense, none of them wanting to come too close because of the trusty black orb he'd obtained. He'd almost brought two with him just in case, but he had limited space with all his supplies and wanted to keep the others someplace safe. So here he was, walking slowly but surely through a swamp heading in the direction that he was fairly certain would lead him to his home eventually.

Emotions played through him as he traveled, and he tried to process them all but kept coming back to one that was more persistent than the others: hope. He hoped against hope that his friends were okay, that somehow even Dernal had made it out in one piece. But dread and uncertainty played their cards as well and he wondered if he was making the trip for naught.

Should he have just stayed around the Titan Complex and grown stronger and stronger? He'd already done the seemingly impossible twice now, growing to C Rank, then reduced to a Level 1 in this Titan system, only to rise once more to the low D Ranks, or Level 21 as they'd put it.

So much had changed in his life and the direction he'd hoped to take it, but the Titan System gave him an edge that no one else would have, at least no one that wasn't also a Titan Born. He touched the rings on his fingers; he'd lost two rings so far, they just kind of got absorbed into his skin when he'd passed certain thresholds. It was such a quick and painless process that each time he'd not even noticed it happening.

However, when the new wave of vitality hit him, it was obvious what happened. His power was growing to unbelievable levels, and given enough time, he'd be an unstoppable force on the battlefield. He yearned to test his strength against more powerful foes, so he did something stupid. He'd been studying the black orb, and he was sure that with the right surge of power toward a certain pair of runes he'd be able to turn it off and back on again.

Really, he ought to have tested this around weaker monsters, but they didn't seem affected by the orb as much as the stronger ones. So, doing what he had to do, he pressed his Mana into a set of runes and just as he'd guessed, a pressure in the air lessened, making the orb go dim.

Immediately, Knox felt a predator begin to close in and he reached out with his sense to get a feel for what to expect. What he felt surprised him, a lone humanoid figure approached. It came into view only a minute later and focusing on it, the system provided additional information that Knox quickly pushed out of his vision with a mental command.

-Bugbear Level 31-

What stood before Knox was a hairy bear of a man, with large pointy ears, a massive maw with two rows of sharp teeth, wearing primitive leather armor and wielding a wooden club. It swung mightily at a nearby dead tree and shattered it on impact, the wooden club not so much as bending from the effort.

It lumbered at a consistent speed, but Knox was clearly the fastest of the pair and he planned on using that to his advantage. Knox rushed the bugbear, using Ethereal Step to go behind the lumbering man-thing. His axe bit deep into the hide as he activated Radiant Rush to enforce his strike and give himself an edge to escape the coming blow then swung around with surprising grace.

Throwing up Solar Wings, Knox took off from the ground and out of the reach of the eight-foot-tall bugbear. The moment he was high enough he began to cast Luminous Surge, getting the cast off just in time for his Solar Wings to fail. The beam of light smacked into the roaring bugbear and took it right off its feet. Ten levels ahead it may be, but Knox was working with two Paths and resource pools equal to that of a C Ranker, or pretty close.

He wasn't even feeling the familiar pressure of low Mana or Stamina yet, so as he slammed into the ground, he activated Radiant Ground. Next, he activated Ethereal Step, zooming forward and under a swing of the bugbear's club. His axe cut across the leather armor, cutting a piece loose. However, in his haste to run through the bugbear, he turned his head away from it too long and a strike smashed into his armored back, sending him sprawling forward.

The lights of the day flashed in his vision as his head collided with the only damn rock within miles as he fell. Wet swamp water filled his armor and boots as he lay there, but his sense wasn't idle. He felt the bugbear approach, raise its club and swing downward with a strike that would kill even Knox's reinforced body.

He rolled and activated Mystic Armor as he came to a knee. His axe was up and ready to deflect the next blow, but he misjudged the strength of his opponent, and his weapon went flying from the attempted parry. Using Ethereal Step as it came off cooldown, the subtle feeling of the spell loosening in his mind being his only indicator, he activated it and put himself as far away as he could.

This was going to be a battle that would take a while, he'd need to slowly whittle down his foe and keep a good distance. It wasn't going to be his most heroic looking bout, but he needed to stay alive more than he needed to look epic.

Casting Void Grasp, then Lustrous Chains just ahead of it, Knox was able to slow the bugbear and give himself enough time to cast Luminous Surge again, knocking it on its ass.

He continued the game of running away using Solar Wings, Radiant Rush, and Ethereal Step when it was ready, to keep his distance from the bugbear. Whatever this creature was capable of, it had slow speed, high strength, and a crazy high Health pool.

After several long minutes of battle, Knox's own resource pools began to flag, and death was looking to be a near certainty. Using a final Arcane Pulse—it took significantly less Mana to cast than Luminous Surge—Knox's spell smashed into the bruised and bloody bugbear. It fell almost as if in slow motion and for several seconds, Knox was sure he'd imagined his victory. That any moment it would rise and strike him down.

But as he slowly approached and nudged the beastly humanoid with his toe, it didn't move. So, he stripped it down and began to cut into it looking for a Monster Core. The bugbear awarded a cool thousand essence, but if he could find the Core it would bring him that much closer to Leveling up once more. He already had three new Levels worth of talent points to spend—nine total—and while he searched the bugbear he thought about where he ought to spend them.

He could keep going down the Luminous Vanguard tree, but he had access to both the Arcane Luminary and Illuminated Sage trees, not to mention the three Mystic trees. Something inside told him he ought to explore down those trees as well; since talent points seemed to come so readily and in abundance, what would it hurt?

He found it and it was intact. Resisting the urge to immediately suck up the essence, he remembered that the Titan Engine required five of these, so he held off for now. Activating the black orb again, Knox rested for several minutes, eating and drinking his fill.

After he'd recovered enough, he began his trek forward, turning off the stone and ready to fight another C Ranked Monster. However, what came at him next had him wishing he'd waited till he was stronger to face off against such terrible foes.

A massive reptilian appeared in the shallow waters and eluded Knox's sense right up until the last possible moment. Only his quick activation of Ethereal Step saved him from losing a leg.

-Dire Alligator Level 33-

Fighting humanoid monsters was a different game entirely than when pitted against bestial creatures. Alligators, for instance, will fight in sudden and amazing spurts of speed and aggression that humans can't hope to match, so it was that Knox found his leg clamped down between the teeth of the alligator and being pulled under the water. Knox had been caught in a death roll that was going to be his end if he couldn't focus his mind long enough to escape.

Flashes of light and pain became Knox's reality as he struggled to focus his mind enough for an Ethereal Step, hoping it might free him of his fate. His pain reached a crescendo and in that moment of desperation he found the focus needed to cast Ethereal Step. Instead of the smooth transition he was used to, he and the alligator were flung bodily into and out of the ethereal plane.

Luckily for Knox, the shock of traveling so suddenly allowed him to roll free. Blood poured from his leg, but he wasn't about to give up just yet. He let loose his usual combo of abilities, tying the alligator up with Void Grasp and Lustrous Chains. Next, he placed a hand on his bleeding leg and used the technique that Dernal had taught him all those days ago.

Slowly and with some difficulty, he managed to stem the bleeding, if not heal his leg completely. It took his weight easily now and Knox unloaded his strongest spells on the alligator while he could. The fight didn't take nearly as long as with the bugbear, but not for a moment during the fight did Knox feel safe. In the end he was victorious, using a close-up Luminous Surge to nearly blow the head off the alligator as a last-ditch effort.

Collecting his second C Ranked Monster Core and getting that much closer to his next Level, Knox continued on his journey, this time making sure he kept the black orb activated as he sensed stronger monsters than the low C Ranked ones around now.

CHAPTER 42
GUILD CHARTERHOUSE

WHAT HE ENCOUNTERED next as he neared the edge of the swamp surprised him. It was a log cabin of sorts, but several times the size that a single person would need, more like a log mansion. It lay right on the border of the black-barked trees and wet ground of the swamp, as if someone drew a line and decided to build it half in and half out of the swamp.

He had gotten only within sight of it when a team of three humanoids appeared, approaching him at C Ranked speeds and giving off no sense of their aura. Meaning they were likely masking their auras, a common thing for C Ranked Adventurers to do as the power of auras above C Rank tended to stifle those with a sense for power.

"Halt and identify yourself," came a stern voice from the largest of the three, his face obscured by the heavy plate helmet he wore, matching the armor that covered his every inch. He had a hand on his sword, but he hadn't drawn it yet.

The other two were easy enough to identify, a leather wearing ranged attacker with a bow and pointy elf ears, while the third was an elderly gentleman with white hair, flowing grey robes, and a gnarled wooden staff that radiated power. Atop the staff was a gem, glowing a gentle white light. This team was a balanced attack party ready for any foe.

"I'm Knox, I take it this must be the Guild Charterhouse and my sign that I've finally escaped the Shadowfall Swamps," Knox said, infusing his voice with as much friendly of a tone as he could.

"You see his aura, its red. That can't be right," the elderly gentleman said, his head tilted to one side.

"I am Sir Garrick Stonehelm, Guild officiate over this Charterhouse. These are my companions, Faelar Swiftnook and Master Thaddeus Loreweaver," Garrick said, pointing first to the bow-wielding elf and next to the elderly man. "By the looks of your aura, you are well into the A Ranks or above. However, I know all fifteen A Rankers, and none match your young visage. Besides that, the intensity of your power gives off that of a high D or low C Ranker. Why do you choose to only slightly mask your aura?"

It was Knox's turn to tilt his head to the side as he tried to decide how best to handle this line of questioning. Should he be honest about what he'd gone through, would that bring about more suspicion than it was worth? There was also the Titan Complex to be considered. If more people were to find out, they'd likely want to study it and find out more for themselves. Something about that gave Knox pause so he decided that a small lie would be in his best interest.

"I can't speak to why my aura looks as it does, but I can assure you I am in the high D Ranks. Perhaps you could show me how to best mask my aura to avoid confusion in the future?" Knox asked, turning the inquiry into a possible learning experience for himself.

"How have you survived the Shadowfall Swamps if you are merely D Rank? I know there are several high C Ranked Monsters that roam within, you would stand no chance against them," Garrick asked, lifting the visor of his helmet, and giving Knox a glimpse of his blazing golden eyes.

"I've been extremely lucky to have only faced several low C Ranked Monsters; I believe I am on the cusp of C Rank myself," Knox lied. If he could still pull essence straight out of the air as he had before, he might very well be C Ranked, or the Level equivalent, but no longer would the system allow him to collect essence in such a way. Instead, it naturally flowed from the monsters he killed and filled his Core with perfectly Pure essence. This had the added benefit that meant he'd not have to deal with impurities in the future to slow his advancement, but it also slowed his current advancement, as killing monsters or completing quests was the only reliable way to collect essence.

"Indeed, you have," Garrick said. "Follow me inside and perhaps Master Thaddeus could examine your aura more thoroughly, even giving you some tips on how to mask it if he feels up to it."

"Thank you," Knox said, following the armored man back toward the building. He couldn't help but notice the archer and caster, Faelar and Thaddeus, slowed until they were flanking Knox on either side and were just a few steps behind.

The first thing that Knox noticed when he entered the Guild Charterhouse was the warmth that washed over him. The chill in the air was getting harder to ignore, despite the enchantments he'd added to his armor, it hadn't extended to his face or fingers, so he'd been a bit chilly still. But a massive fireplace roared with heat in the center of the building attached to a large chimney.

To the left of the first room was a bar, tended by a burly older gentleman; only two men sat at the bar and the tables surrounding it were empty. To the right were a series of doors, and straight ahead was a hallway and a counter with a young female sitting behind a desk.

"We don't get many out this way," Garrick said, obviously watching Knox take the place in. "But we can accommodate up to fifty Adventurers at a time. I've business to attend to but if you would follow Master Thaddeus to the training room down that hall, the second door on the left, he will speak with you there."

Knox eyed Garrick for a second, but nodded, feeling as if he'd agreed to a trap or something. But so far no one attacked him, however, he did pull curious looks from the two at the bar and another woman who appeared out of the very door they were headed for. They seemed in awe of Knox, and he didn't know why.

Once they'd entered the training room, a massive empty space with a sand floor and several dummies set into the wall, Thaddeus rounded on him.

"You can give up the act, no one has a red Aura that hasn't reached A Rank or above. Tell me the truth why you seem incapable of hiding your aura and spare me the trouble of forcing the information out of you. I may only be high C, but I've lived a long life, and you don't give off the intensity of an A Ranker yet, so I imagine it'll take time for you to unleash your full power."

Knox nearly facepalmed at the direct words from Thaddeus. He really needed to learn how to hide his aura if this was the trouble it was going to give him. He almost pulled free a ring to flare his power and try to put this elderly man in his place, but another idea came to him.

"You are right," Knox said, casting his eyes down. "I am A Ranked, however, I wish to remain anonymous, so I've veiled my power. But I am new to my power and have come from a distant land. Surely you can give me some tips on obscuring my aura for my own good and those around me?"

"Garrick is searching for your name against the records for all living members named 'Knox' right now, if you are lying, we will know shortly," Thaddeus said. "Besides that, there is something strange about you that I can't put my finger on, but it has my mind swirling with ideas. I will help you if Garrick comes back with nothing, and perhaps in exchange you can help an old timer pass his C Ranked blockage? I've yet to come across the proper insight that will allow me to advance, but seeing as you've passed through your C, B, and A Ranked insights, surely you might be able to help."

"That is a deeply personal request you've made and I'm afraid it varies so greatly from person to person that I'd likely not be much help," Knox said, hedging against his request. He'd be no help in such an endeavor as he'd only had to pass up to the C Ranks, the rest being taken care of by the system.

"I understand," Thaddeus said, though by the downcast look he gave Knox, he wondered if he did. Either way, Knox was going to be of no help to him, so he was getting off just fine by not getting his help.

They stood in awkward silence for another minute before Garrick arrived, helmet off showing his pearly whites, oddly glowing golden eyes, and a full head of curly blonde hair.

"Can't find anything on him," Garrick said. "There was a Knox at the Mires Gloom dungeon before it got wiped out, but he was presumed dead and only D Ranked at the time, so no way it could be the same kid. You find anything out?" Garrick asked the last bit in a hushed whisper to his companion, but Knox heard him just fine.

"Nothing, he claims to be from a distant land and only newly come into his power. I'd suggest we get him registered and show him the proper way of masking his aura," Thaddeus said, collecting himself and looking the same as he had when they'd first met, slightly curious and academic.

"I agree, let me handle the paperwork and you teach him what you can," Garrick said, disappearing from the room only seconds after arriving.

"This should be a simple matter if you've been able to mask much of your strength, I just need to teach you to encompass the full might of your power. Think of it like condensing your power, not veiling it. You will be bringing all the strands of the power that represents you and pulling them tighter around your Core."

He went on and on like this for another five minutes and Knox listened attentively. After a bit of practice, Knox began to get the hang of it. Though he wasn't technically even C Rank yet, he found that he had much more control over the stray threads of power that made up himself than he'd ever thought possible. By the time he got the hang of it, he likened it to sucking in your gut and holding it.

At first it was difficult and there seemed like there was no way he'd be able to keep it going for any amount of time. But after an hour of doing it, the action started to become second nature. It didn't affect his actual power or Level, instead, it masked the outer glow of it. Thaddeus for his part thought he was either the best teacher around, he said so many times, or that Knox was a prodigy of self-control.

What really happened, as far as Knox could tell, was he was dealing with far less power to hold in than a true A Ranker, so it wasn't hard to learn. In fact, after several hours of holding the power back he didn't even have to think about it, his aura was no longer visible to others.

In that time, they offered him a bath, cleaning services on his ruined clothes and even helped patch some holes in his leg armor. The head of the Guild Charterhouse, Garrick, or Sir Garrick since he apparently held some land titles from the king, was all too kind to help whom he thought was a new A Ranker to join the king-dom. When pressed on exactly where he was from, Knox shut-down and pretended to be tired, effectively avoiding any further questions.

He was given a room on the second floor, just at the head of the staircase. After being provided with a hot meal of stew containing some type of gamey wildlife, he found it delicious. The room was about ten paces by ten paces big, held a good-sized bed, a storage trunk, a dresser, a mirror, and a wash basin. Overall, it was slightly better than the apartment he'd rented back in Keenlen's Vale.

Though he required little sleep, he decided to try and rest. His dreams were pleasant and filled with dreams of adventure and action. Only toward the end did his mind get invaded by the dark figure of a little girl singing odd rhymes that didn't quite fit what he remembered them being. He woke up in a cold sweat, nearly jumping out of his bed when he saw the shadow at the end where his trunk was, looked similar to the creepy girl.

It was not her, however. He checked under the bed and in every little hiding space; he was alone. Just then, the building shook and he had to catch the water jug before it fell off the basin. Throwing on a pair of pants and heading down, he saw that he wasn't the only one awake from the sudden ground shakes.

"Don't worry, don't worry," Garrick was shouting from down the hall. "We've been getting them more and more, but the geomancer I spoke with says we are sturdy enough to outlast something twice, if not three times as aggressive as the ones they've recorded."

That mollified the majority of the half dozen people, but Knox wanted to take a look outside and see that the building was truly alright. Garrick caught up to him just as he reached the door. "I'll have a look myself, just to be sure," he said, giving Knox a toothy smile that he was sure was meant to be reassuring, but came off as a sign of his nerves.

The doors swung wide and immediately something felt off. Stretching his sense outward, Knox felt nothing, but the last time a quake had happened one of those little black blobs had come out and he hadn't been able to feel anything then either. Something else inside of him told him he was not safe. That is when the words began to echo through from the swamp side of the building, just around the corner.

Victory, Victory, to the deep ones went the victory. Gone for now, we come again, victory, victory.

"Did you hear that?" Knox asked, turning to Garrick, but Knox turned to look where he'd been just a moment ago and Garrick was gone.

A cold shiver ran up his spine at that and he began walking around the building, keeping his eyes open and ready. He'd had the good sense to bring his axe, but more than that, he was ready with a spell if it should become necessary.

"Garrick!" Knox called, worried the man might have been attacked by the black slimes.

The building, for what it was worth, was entirely intact. Knox went around the building twice and though he could still hear the rhyme, it sounded further and more distant as he circled the building.

The door leading to the inside swung open and Garrick stuck his head out. "What are you looking for?" Garrick asked, his voice more monotone than Knox recalled and the golden glow of his eyes seemed almost dangerous as he asked.

Knox cleared his throat and without thinking, began the workings of a spell to blast the man backward from a sudden urge of self-preservation. But he caught himself, just as Garrick smiled at him and beckoned that he should return inside.

It was time to get back on the road, Knox decided, but first he had to get his things and armor. Garrick let him pass, his eyes locked on him as he went by and his face a mask of emotionlessness.

Something wasn't right here, that much Knox knew, but it wasn't his place to figure out every mystery, at least not right now. He made it to his room, barred the door and waited for the sun to rise and filter in through his shutters. He wouldn't say he was scared, but he didn't feel pleased with the situation. However, when a knock came at his door, Knox involuntarily jumped in surprise, despite sensing someone approaching.

"It's Thaddeus, have you seen Garrick? He's usually the first one up and his room is empty. Someone said they saw you leave with him last night but only you returned."

"He came in with me," Knox managed to say with a mostly clear voice. "I need to be off, but I will keep an eye out for him on my travels."

"Alright, well come down and have breakfast before you go, the least we can do for you," Thaddeus said, his voice a touch more cheerful than Knox remembered. He didn't at all seem worried about his missing friend who had one hundred percent welcomed Knox back into the building last night.

CHAPTER 43
MIRES GLOOM DUNGEON TOWN

Knox got breakfast and hit the road, heading for what he hoped was the right direction. He hadn't even tried to ask about the town or what they might know, not after the weird stuff that had happened the night before. Despite the heavy overhang of trees and brush, the sun was out in full force and something about the light put a pep in Knox's step. *The light is where he*

thrived as a Titan Born and it felt as if he were stronger just being in it.

What had happened to Garrick the night before and what was with the creepy girl following him and chanting those creepy rhymes? It had to be connected to the ground shakes and black blobs that were coming out of the ground, but how? Knox wasn't exactly a detective or very good at this kind of investigation, but he did believe in knowledge and figuring things out, so he'd keep his eyes open and see what he could learn.

What did he know so far? Well, there were the words she'd spoken to him several times now.

Victory, Victory, to the deep ones went the victory. Gone for now, we come again, victory, victory.

Who were the deep ones, where had they gone and why were they coming again? Unfortunately for Knox he wasn't even familiar with the rhyme that Frederick had mentioned it being similar to, since he was raised by his father since birth, and he wasn't much for nursery rhymes. Maybe when he got back to the village, he could ask Frederick about it or maybe someone else knew a bit more.

Until then, he tabled the weird as what it was, weird, and moved on. As he walked, he encountered a few monsters, weaker ones unaffected by the repelling effects of the orb, but nothing that gave Knox any kind of decent essence.

Knox began to recognize where he was on the second day of traveling nonstop, but he wasn't close to his town yet, no, quite the opposite really. He was right by the dungeon town that had been destroyed by that higher Ranked monster. Deciding he couldn't pass up the chance to check out the dungeon town and see if anything worth collecting remained, he altered his course to check it out.

He approached slowly and carefully, not sure what to expect, but what he did feel when his sense came into range wasn't what he found. A dozen, maybe more, humanoids all moving around the dungeon town not too dissimilar to when he'd been there the last time, except much less people around.

Finally reaching the gate, he found it manned by a single armored figure that locked onto him the moment he came out of the brush on the side of the road.

"Who goes there?" he called out and Knox raised his hands up in a pacifying gesture. The guard had on a tabard with the Guild symbol he'd seen before, so he immediately relaxed a bit.

"Just a wandering Adventurer," Knox said, putting his hands down as the guard took his own hand off his sword belt.

"Mires Gloom is closed until after winter; had another bad monster attack and we are still recovering," the guard said, speaking freely despite Knox having just shown up out of nowhere.

"What if the monster returns?" Knox asked, the same question had been running through his mind from the moment he decided to check out the town and what might be left.

"The Adventurer's Guild sent out a team to hunt it down, they've likely dealt with it; besides that," the guard leaned in closer as he spoke and lowered his voice, "the new lass they put over this place is said to be a High B Ranker, almost A Rank. She'll handle anything monsters in this area can throw at us. When she arrives, that is. Right now, our strongest is a C Ranker the Guild sent over. Most of us are High Ds, though; speaking of which, I can't see your Aura, you must be a C Ranker?"

"I am," Knox lied immediately, smiling at the guard as he spoke. "Any chance I can resupply and look around before I get back on the road?"

"No vendors here yet, but you go in, and they'll give you a hot meal and some conversation for the night. You can set out tomorrow but remember, the dungeon won't be open till after winter, so don't go getting any ideas," the guard said, his voice almost playful as he spoke.

"Name's Knox," Knox said, holding out a hand. The guard took it and smiled.

"Mine's Frank, nice to meet you," Frank said, he even lifted his helmet off and showed a curly mop of brown hair atop his head, nodding at Knox, then putting the helmet back on.

"Well, Frank, it's been a pleasure, but I think I'll go see about that hot meal," Knox said, eager to see what other information he could learn before he left. Though he wasn't very hungry, he could always eat.

Inside were the usual tents and whatnot, but all the wooden pavilions had been torn down and wood was being burned in massive piles. To the east, a larger building was being constructed as well as several sections of the wall were half rebuilt out of massive logs. Knox found someone around a large kitchen fire but was told food was another hour or two out, so Knox did what he felt was right.

He found someone in charge and got to work helping out. They were glad to accept his help after inspecting his aura and finding nothing, a keen sign of someone either C Ranked or above.

"Take this axe here and help the team fell a few trees if you can," said a burly man with black hair and eyebrows so bushy that it nearly hid his dark brown eyes.

"I've got my own, just point me in the right direction," Knox said.

He followed a few others out the back gate, it had been smashed to bits and by the path that had formed, was being used as a back exit to access the woods around the place. Knox readied himself for a few hours of welcomed exertion, but it never came. Each swipe of his axe bit deep and took almost nothing out of him.

He was dropping a tree in less than a minute, and soon they had only him cutting the trees down while the others followed behind him stripping it and pulling it into town.

Thwack. Thwack.

He lost himself in his thoughts and the rhythm of it all, enjoying every moment. Why didn't Adventurers lend themselves to physical labor more, he wondered. With the increased strength and endurance, he could do the job of a dozen men in half the time. But the strong were more likely to just participate in dungeons or wars for kingdoms who couldn't get along.

War was something Knox didn't need or like to think about. So far distant from the capital city, it was rare that they even heard of the drafts that were put into place, much less be required to send men of their own. It wasn't impossible, but it was unlikely.

"That'll do," A voice called out and Knox turned to see his guard friend Frank approaching. "They've got enough to keep them busy for a few weeks now. Come get some stew and tell us why you are roaming these accursed woods by yourself."

"Alright," Knox said, wiping sweat from his forehead and sliding his axe back into place. "But tell me you have something to drink that has a bite to it. I'm ready to relax."

Frank laughed, nodding his head that they did indeed have some drinks to share.

The night was spent in a blur of laughter, fun, and drinks. They served the most wonderful beef stew, along with a chilled ale that sang to Knox's taste buds. It had a kick to it too, much stronger than a drink you'd serve to non-Adventurers, but that was the point, everyone here was D Ranked or above and if they were going to feel the effects of it, then it needed to have a bit of a kick to it.

CHAPTER 44
THE HUNTED

KNOX LEFT EARLY in the morning, just as the sun began to crest the horizon and spill onto the trees. He wasn't even the first one up, despite the early hour, these were working men that didn't mess around when it came to working hard. He'd miss the acquaintances he'd made, but he promised to return and run some dungeons in the future, each of the men here planning on staying on to do the same after the winter settled down.

It was around noon the same day when he felt a presence at the edge of his sense, following his every move. He tried to travel closer to it to get a better read on it, but each time he did it would pull away as if it knew what he was about. Then, at times it would completely disappear from his sense altogether. He worried what it might be but carried on, not knowing what else he could do.

The thing was strong, that much he could sense clearly, but how strong he couldn't say. If it were somehow resisting the effects of the orb, then it might be much stronger than he could handle. It certainly wasn't like the monsters he'd been encountering so far, weak and barely worth the effort of killing. Just when he was worried that he'd be lunch for the more powerful monster, a pack of Dire Wolves attacked him, his sense pressed too far looking for the greater threat.

Knox didn't need any special abilities to deal with the pack of Dire Wolves, each one barely a challenge by themselves and only a passable one as a single unit. Keeping his axe between him and the lead Dire Wolf, he pulled his sense in and closed his eyes. The Dire Wolf took that as an invitation, diving in for a quick kill.

However, Knox was anything but vulnerable with his sense going full power all around him. Without even opening his eyes, he pivoted his feet, putting himself just to the left of the wolf's attack, and slashing down, taking off its ear in the process.

Knox's eyes snapped open as he realized he'd missed the killing blow that was so easily open to him. Time to stop fooling around, he told himself as he readied for the three that dove in on him all at once. Bending and twisting, Knox avoided each attack, delivering bloody blows to each of the Dire Wolves in turn.

Instead of fleeing, Knox really thought they might after he delivered such devastating blows, the wolves rallied and came at him with coordination that was worthy of praise. Twisting and dodging, Knox was forced to pull into his abilities to escape getting his throat torn out by the crafty Alpha Wolf.

Using Ethereal Step, he passed through the ethereal plane and appeared behind an unfortunate wolf who had its spine smashed a moment later, bringing them down by one. Then two, then three, then four. The battle was quickly coming to a close now that Knox decided to use his abilities to end it. A quick activation of Solar Wings brought him up into the air to deliver his final attack, aimed at the Alpha and his remaining two companions.

Focusing his mind he cast Luminous Surge, the very light of the sun empowering him as he did so. But to his surprise, the Alpha dodged, running away as fast as its feet would take him. The other two weren't so quick and died a moment later. Knox turned, ready to track down the bleeding Alpha with its missing ear, but according to his sense the Alpha was moving crazy fast.

Sighing at having lost one of his prey, Knox pulled out the skinning knife he'd procured during his visit to the Mires Gloom Dungeon Town and began to do his best job of skinning and dressing down the wolves. He wasn't a hunter by any means, but he knew enough to get the skins and some meat. Of course, he'd have to smoke some of it and that took time, but he had an idea of how to adjust some runes on the black orb, or at least he hoped it would work.

If it did, he'd not have to worry about lower Leveled monsters or higher, but that was for after he'd smoked the meat and prepared the skins. Pulling up the next wolf, this one was mostly intact and had far less burns from his attacks. First, he cut from under the chin being careful not to go too deep, because the deeper you went, the more blood you'd encounter.

It was slow and careful work, several times he went too deep and released a fair bit of blood. Once he'd gotten most of the skin off, he cut it free and began looking for the Cores. Weak as they might be, it would be helpful to advance even a little. He found one at the base of the skull, this was attached right to the back side. Normally, they were harder to get to, sometimes attached to the spine or found within the skull.

He was lucky to have gotten this one intact, the sack of

organic flesh that held the Monster Cores ensured that they were almost always clean, so he pocketed it and went about his way to the next wolf. One after another he did the dirty work and prepared the meat for smoking.

For this, he was going to have to use his bedroll to ensure the smoke didn't escape, but first he needed to get a fire going and let it go down to embers.

While paying attention to the more powerful monster with his sense, it wasn't currently appearing at all, he pulled his sense back and went to work. First, he built a fire, then a tripod out of sticks to hold his meat. When the fire was burnt down to embers he wrapped the tripod up, leaving space for smoke to escape out the top. Then, he cut several small thin slices of wolf meat. The process was slow and laborious, but Knox was used to working hard, and soon he had a good portion of meat cooking.

There would be a good bit of waste, but scavengers would see that it was taken care of, already his sense picked up several smaller predators skirting the edge looking for a decent meal.

With all of that taken care of and nothing left to do but hurry up and wait, he turned his attention to the black orb and the runic formations that lay within. Rummaging through his pack he found the device he'd taken from the workshop that allowed for markings inside of objects. It was like a pen, but it had a gem on one end and took a bit of his essence as a way to power it.

Concentrating his sense just on the orb, the full spectrum of the runes within became apparent. There was one particular area that he was focusing on that he hoped would be useful. He found it easily and began to look over it. Sure enough, his theory was right, there were blocks that selected the strength, both high and low, the orb could focus on and someone had deliberately set it to the strength range it was currently operating on.

Using his notes and being as careful as he could, he began to add a few more filters to help the flow of power, hoping that would be enough to allow for a wider range of repelling. Of course, there had to be a reason why they'd only opened it up for a certain range of repelling, but Knox was willing to bet that his method would work just as well.

His first idea was to open it up to the low ends and high ends, but a sudden jolt of fear had him sending out his sense and feeling his stalker approaching. So, he did what he had to do, focusing on the higher end instead. Carefully and methodically, despite the anxious fear he felt growing inside of him, he worked to adjust the runes.

It took longer than he'd have liked, but he did it. He fed a small bit of essence back into the black orb and all at once a wave of something shot out from it. Pulling his sense from the orb, he shot it wide as a net as he could, feeling for the predator. It was right there, some half a mile away but it had stopped suddenly.

Knox monitored the mighty beast, but it came no closer, and eventually it disappeared from his sense altogether. There was still much work to be done, so Knox went about it, breaking camp where he could and collecting the skins together. Some eight hours later, the meat was ready, his cuts being thin enough that the smoke took to it nicely. He gathered his bedroll, using the tight roll to hold the skins, while he put the meat into a little leather bag he had attached to the outside of his pack.

He was well prepared and supplied now.

The orb worked wonderfully, Knox broke camp and was on his way and the entire time he didn't sense the greater threat that had been stalking him for the better part of a day. Instead, he ran into smaller threats, so many in fact, that he thought for sure it would take him over the edge and level him. He checked and hung his head as he walked, he was still several thousand away from the next Level. He'd kept all the Cores, deciding not to use them after all, so he had a bit more if he wanted to crack them open, but he wasn't there yet.

It was a day and a half later when he neared the village. He could sense nothing from within and immediately began to worry. Before he got close enough to see what lay ahead, his nose took in a whiff of acrid smoke, and he knew things weren't going to be good. The winds shifted, relieving him of the other smells that lay ahead, but he guessed at what he'd find far before he saw it.

The wooden palisade around the village lay in ruins with entire sections broken apart and burning. How could this have happened to his village? Sure, they knew there were great threats out there, but nothing so powerful ever left the Shadowfall Swamps, or at least that was what he had believed before his encounter with the draconic creature that attacked Dernal's party.

There was a scent of death in the air as Knox walked through a broken section of the palisades, but no bodies were visible for as far as the eye could see. The inside of the village was in ruins, even the mayor's mansion at the top of the hill inside the town was leveled to nothing. It was like something huge came through and just rolled around until most of the buildings had been laid flat.

Even Mr. Tome's complex had been flattened, which for some reason surprised Knox more than he could explain. It was by far the sturdiest place in all of the town, built by Mr. Tome himself to withstand almost any natural disaster or storm.

Emotions, raw and tumultuous, rolled through Knox as he took in the damage. His eyes fell on a building-wide bit of dirt that had been upturned and he didn't need to dig it up to guess at what he was seeing: a mass grave. But a grave meant survivors, so all wasn't lost yet. It was obvious by the size of the grave that many had fallen, but not all.

A sudden pulling in his stomach had him running through town toward his family home. What did he want to find there, he asked himself, but he had no answer, only emotions. By the time he reached the door, his eyes were wet with tears that were slow to form. He should feel sad that he'd likely lost his father, but the tears seemed more for the expected loss of his family home than the memories he had with his father.

So sour his last ten years with his father had been, that it blotted out what little good memories remained. The emotions were hard to pin down, but a wave of relief washed over him when he saw that his home was intact. Two around it were crushed, barely standing, but for some reason, his home was intact.

As he stepped into the house, the door left ajar, he wondered if he'd find his father inside, oblivious to all that had happened and waiting for Terrim to bring his next meal. But as he entered, that odd thought fled as he checked the rooms and found the place to be empty.

Sighing, Knox sat in his father's favorite chair and stared into the ashes of a fire that had long gone cold. How long had it been since the monster attack and why had they fled the village instead of rebuilding? The best Knox could figure was they must have lost too many people to rebuild, which meant over half of the village would be casualties.

So many dead, his friends, and neighbors, all gone. Deciding he wasn't in a hurry anymore; he went to his room and lay on his old bed. This house, for whatever reason, had been spared and now he was alone. Did his mother's runes have something to do with the protection, Knox wondered. But he pushed the thought away, as he knew better, or at least he knew better about the ones around the door. As he lay there, he fully opened his sense up and examined the house around him.

Since he'd last been here, his sense had grown substantially and what he could see with it now was leagues ahead of what little he could before. It was because of this that he was finally able to see the tiny hundreds of runes built into the very timbers of the house around them. Ones for protection, reinforcement, and more that Knox didn't understand. This place was a virtual fortress of magical protection and powerful wards.

"But why did you do all this, mother?" Knox asked the air around him.

Just another mystery that he'd failed to work out or understand. He had her journals, but what good did that do to help understand why she'd put so much work into a crappy house in the middle of the worst neighborhood in a far-flung town? So many questions pounded on his head, and he wished for nothing more than to understand what motivated her to do all of this before she passed.

A noise, distant yet closer than Knox would have liked, rang out and he pushed his sense out. The monster that had been following him had appeared once more, this time in the middle of town, knocking over more buildings by the sound of it. Knox's heart clenched and he wondered what he ought to do.

A realization formed in his mind as the tightness in his chest subsided. He was a Titan Born walking the Path of the Titans. No longer would he allow himself to be pushed around by the whims of a greater foe. This son of a bitch had killed his friends and likely the last member of his family.

It was time for this monster to die.

CHAPTER 45
ON THE WAY

SURE, it was foolish to face such a superior foe, but at that moment, Knox wasn't thinking about that. No, he had a deep rage bubbling up and for the first time in his memory, he wanted to really tear into something. It wasn't like he didn't have a plan. He looked down at his hands and the rings on each finger. Mic wouldn't like this plan, but it had merit.

Sure, as a low D Ranker, or Level 21, he didn't stand a chance against what was likely a B Ranked Dragon, but if he took one ring off, he'd be equal to a C Ranker and then two rings he'd be a B Ranker, but if he took three off, he'd be equal to an A Ranker. And if he knew anything from all he'd learned about Adventurers, the differences between just a single Rank was worlds away.

The only major drawback that he could anticipate would be the loss of essence and Levels that Mic had warned him about. So, he'd need to move fast and fight hard. He didn't know how fast the essence drain would be on his body with just one ring off, much less three, but he had to try.

Whatever happened, this fight wasn't likely to be a long and epic battle. No, he'd have moments to cut this beast down or be overwhelmed by the loss of his power. A trickle of better sense filled his mind as he walked to the edge of the door, and he wondered why he was doing this. Surely his plan would work, but at what cost and how much risk was he putting himself in? Maybe he was making a mistake.

"Damnit, I'm no coward," Knox whispered to himself, the rage beginning to bleed away. He would fight and die against the same monster that stole away his friends and family. Suddenly, his sense—still stretched out and monitoring the monster—took his focus as the monster bolted in a random direction, moving at impossible speed and out of the village within seconds.

"You truly meant to fight such a powerful monster?" a familiar voice said from just outside his house. Knox drew his axe, readied a spell, and took a step out all within moments. "Ah, very skillful response, but I fear you are still too weak to challenge that monster, much less me."

Aetex, the mysterious mountain of a man from before, stood with his arms crossed in front of him, a gentle smile on his face. He wore a simple tunic and pants, no armor, but his arms were bare, and they bulged with more muscles than Knox had ever seen on another person. He was beyond intimidating, despite the friendly demeanor on his face. What was worse, Knox's sense couldn't get a read on him at all, which was different from the aura he was letting off before, the yellow B Ranked aura.

"How'd you know my name before?" Knox asked, remembering the question he'd meant to ask the mysterious stranger before. Why had he followed him this entire way and what was his deal?

"I knew you by sight, young warrior," Aetex said, his face beaming with a proud smile. "I thought I was going to have to stop you from doing something stupid, but seeing as the monster has gone after other prey, you should be safe, and I ought to return to the shadows. Farewell, and remember, you matter!"

Before Knox could so much as speak another word, Aetex blurred and disappeared as if he'd not been there in the first place. Knox wondered if perhaps he'd been hallucinating, but no, he could see the prints in the dirt, so he'd been there.

Prints in the dirt, tracks, maybe Knox had a way to find any survivors after all.

Running free of his room, Knox went to the edge of the town and found what he was looking for. He'd guess that Mr. Tome had survived, before his large wagon with the massive wheels left deep and easily followable tracks in the ground. It must have been very muddy and wet when they left, because the tracks were solid and frozen now under the cool air of an approaching winter.

Knox followed the tracks, seeing where they led and made himself ready to follow. He would find his friends, perhaps even his father, it wasn't the end for them. Knox repeated this in his head like a mantra as he traveled into the wilderness, axe and magic ready to strike out at any that might oppose him.

Several times Knox lost the tracks and had to double back, all the while keeping his sense open to any possible dangers. It was on the fifth day of traveling like this when he finally picked up two humanoids in the very far reaches of his sense. Wasting no time and hoping that it was the town's inhabitants, as the tracks had all but disappeared at this point, Knox ran onward.

He got a better sense of the pair as he neared, and his heart skipped a beat. There was no doubt in his mind who he was about to sneak up on, his smile grew to a wide crescent on his face.

"Terrim you huge walking sack of shit!" Knox called out from behind a tree, the larger of the two hadn't noticed him yet and he jumped a full foot in the air from the sudden insult.

"Knox?" Terrim said, not returning the insult as he usually did, but instead turning toward him with tears nearly instantly filling his eyes. "You were dead? You've been dead, how?"

"It's a long story, my friend," Knox said, sensing as Beth circled around behind him. He turned just as she approached with a dagger posed to strike.

"What kind of monster are you?" She shouted the words with more venom than Knox had ever heard from her before. She stepped forward threateningly and yelled, "Tell me what you really are!"

"Relax," Terrim said, coming forward with his hands raised. "It is really you, isn't it?"

Knox looked at them, truly looked and took all the details in before speaking again.

Terrim looked rough, his hair longer than he usually let it grow, his clothes dirty and torn. He had new scars, red and angry, on his face and his exposed arms. He held far too tightly to the shaft of his axe and looked at Knox now with a suspicion of his own. Gone was the joking and lighthearted friend he'd left only weeks before, though in reality he knew it had been nearly a year. What challenges had his friends overcome to get to this point and why were they suspicious of him? Surely, they hadn't encountered monsters that took the shape of other people.

"Do you see any black in his eyes or ears?" Beth asked, her voice still hard and unyielding.

"I don't," Terrim said, leaning forward a bit to get a better look at Knox.

Knox turned his attention to Beth and realized she'd changed even more than Terrim. She had a jagged scar running up her neck all the way to the bottom of her left eye, though it thinned considerably, and he'd nearly missed it with how dirty her face was currently. She wore armor, but it had seen better days as well, and what was more, it had a few runic formations on it for protection and detection. Knox squinted to make out all the work, seeing as it was crudely carved into the surface, they would be suboptimal at best.

"Look," Knox said, holding up his hands to pacify the pair of them. "Ask me something no one else would know and I'll answer, easy way to tell if I'm a fraud."

"Beth it's gotta be him, and I see no signs of infection, so he isn't one of those either," Terrim said, his eyes pleading for Beth to agree with him.

Knox turned his attention fully on Terrim, ignoring the dagger to his back. "Ask me something, go on."

Suddenly, a flash of the old Terrim appeared as he smiled and an idea must have occurred to him. "If you truly are Knox, then there's one event you'll never have forgotten." A playful smirk touched his lips. "Tell me, when we were fourteen, what did we do that got us banned from the Harvest festival for two years and sworn to secrecy by the mayor?"

"Hah," Knox said, shaking his head. "Only three people know about that, you sure you want to let Beth in on it?"

"Go on," Beth said, the point of her dagger clicking against Knox's armor.

"Fine, it wasn't so bad. Remember that traveling merchant and his wife that used to visit all the time. Well, we snuck a little of my father's favorite drink into the community punch bowl. What we didn't expect was then walking in on the very drunk mayor and the merchant's wife when we were sneaking about afterward."

"Really?" Beth said flatly. "That's not even really funny, that's gross."

Knox shared a look with Terrim, and they both laughed out loud because there was more to the story, but it looked like Terrim wasn't going to force him to say it.

"No way anyone shared that story, I'd say it's him," Terrim said, his posture going back to a relaxed ease.

"Fine," Beth said, her face still hard. "Let's get him back to camp, you've got a few people that will be happy to see you."

"But not you?" Knox asked, eyeing Beth critically.

"Not me," she said, not meeting his eyes.

CHAPTER 46
WINTER IS COMING

"ARE you going to tell me what happened?" Knox asked after they walked for a solid, few minutes in silence.

Terrim shared a look with Beth, before Beth shrugged and Terrim sighed.

"So much has happened since you left," Terrim said, then taking another deep breath he launched into it.

He explained that weeks after Knox left, Dernal showed up in town with three of his companions. This surprised Knox, but he didn't interrupt as Terrim went through it all. The injured man turned out to be Caleb and somehow, against all odds he survived, but his injuries didn't heal as they should have. Though, as soon as he could walk, he left town by himself in the dead of night.

The other two, John and Leo, stayed with the village for a while longer before leaving as well. However, Dernal stayed, leaving for weeks at a time to search for Knox but never finding any trace of him. It wasn't until two months ago that he finally gave up and declared Knox dead. This had a mixed reaction for Knox, both making him grateful that he searched for so long but also sad that he'd declared him dead and given up. It wasn't like he could expect the man to look for him forever, but what came next was worse.

Apparently, Dernal took the declaration of Knox's death badly, turning to the drink and staying outside the village for weeks at a time just to be alone. For a time, he even began to drink with his father, which led Knox to immediately ask if he was alive —his father and Dernal really. Terrim assured him that both were, at the very least, still breathing and alive.

That alone loosened a hard knot from within his stomach, one that he almost hadn't noticed as it had been there for so long. When asked who had died, Terrim said he'd get the full list later, but he wanted to finish his tale. He went on to explain that merchants didn't show up this year, so supplies had begun to get low, since the crops were all dying due to some black rot. The same black rot that started to spread into the wildlife like it had the owlbear.

Then they began talking about people disappearing and showing up weeks later, strange and nonverbal. Those same people had blackened eyes and erratic behavior at the best of times. The first wave of their attacks started only a month or so ago. By that time, several dozen villagers were afflicted, with more getting infected or going missing each day. Then they started seeing a little girl with black hair in the woods, mostly the wood-cutters and like that spent time out there.

Terrim said he heard and saw one himself, though he just turned tail and ran, not wanting to get mixed up in whatever hellish curse had befallen the others. When they finally attacked, the villagers were overwhelmed. If Dernal hadn't appeared and killed so many with such efficiency, then most of the townsfolk would be dead.

Knox listened with rapt attention as the tale continued and they neared the encampment where the villagers awaited at the edge of his sense.

Apparently, most of the initial damage came from fires that overtook much of the town, even taking out the mayor's mansion. But then a wave of monsters came, literally hours after the people turned. Dernal fought hard, but it was too much and eventually they all ran into the woods, those of them that were left. They feared he wouldn't be a match for the monsters, so when he found them, all hiding out toward Frederick's farm, imagine their surprise.

The town was in ruins, crops failing, more dead than alive, and no merchants showing up before the winter meant some-thing drastic had to be done. They buried their dead, including those infected, and set off toward the nearest larger city, Thornhaven.

Knox recognized the name; it was several weeks' travel down the mountains, and the roads this time of the year were hard trav-eled due to the rock-hard nature of the frozen ground. They were well on their way, but still, it would be weeks more travel before they arrived, and on top of that, there was no guarantee that Thornhaven would take them in as refugees.

"You say Murdoch and several others have gone ahead to secure lodging or help in Thornhaven? When are you expecting them back and why didn't his father go?" Knox asked, trying to work out the best way forward. He had the means to grow food in the Titan Complex, Mic had gone over it in detail, but Knox hadn't paid much attention as he had plenty of food and hungered less than he'd ever had in his life since becoming Titan Born.

If he remembered the conversation right, he had the means to feed a few hundred at worst and twice that at best. There was even some kind of ancient plumbing system that fed water into the complex through several outlets on each floor. Not to mention that area, while cold, didn't have nearly the temperature drop that he was experiencing right now.

"Within a week or so, actually," Terrim said. Beth had gone ahead, and Knox walked side by side with Terrim, who towered over him. "They set out on horseback a while ago, they might even be back within a few days. Beth and I are a part of the Guard, so we will need to get back out there and scout for more monsters once we bring you in. Our watch just started, you see, so we won't be back in for another two days."

"That seems a bit extreme," Knox said, sweeping a two-mile area with his sense and feeling nothing but the humanoids ahead. "I can sense the area around us and not so much as a Dire Wolf is within a mile or two."

"Dernal says he can sense a bit around the camp as well, but nothing like a mile or two. It was his idea to have a few teams of scouts roaming the area for threats. He's even given us all a bit of enchanted armor; says he will teach us how to use techniques if we prove useful. Though, I say the idea makes him right angsty when I push him on his promise," Terrim said, shooting Knox his signature shit-eater grin.

Knox could understand that Dernal thought that once more he'd lost someone who he'd tried to set on the path of being an Adventurer. How surprised will he be when he sees that Knox is still around, Knox wondered.

Turns out he didn't need to wait long to find out. A humanoid giving off barely a hint of an aura, broke from the encampment a mile away and began to head in their direction fast. Knox didn't even have to guess who it might be, and before he could so much as verbalize his thoughts, Dernal ran into the clearing looking and smelling something fierce.

The smell wasn't pleasant, but Knox did his best to ignore it as the shorter man, black beard all out of place and rough looking, slammed into him and pulled him into a bone jarring, one armed hug. He smelled of piss, shit, and alcohol, but none of that mattered in that moment.

"You're alive and where is your aura?" Dernal asked, his usually calm and measured demeanor completely gone for the moment. Maybe sensing that, he cleared his throat, took a step back and spoke again. "Hmm. You've hit the C Ranks, good job." His normal stoic tone returning.

Knox cleared his own throat, his smile so wide it could hold open barn doors, before speaking. "I did, and so much more," Knox said, unable to keep the excitement from his voice.

"Tell me everything," Dernal said, then thinking better of himself he looked around. "Another time, I should get back. I fear I scared your father half to death by calling out your name and disappearing into the woods. It is good that you are alive, stay that way, will you?"

"I'll try," Knox said, still a bit in shock as Dernal turned, teetered a bit from what must be drunkenness, then bolted back toward the cluster of townsfolk.

Terrim leaned down, took Knox by the shoulders, and looked him in the eyes. "What exactly did happen to you and where have you been this entire time?" he asked.

Knox shrugged, unsure how much he ought to start telling everyone, but wanting to make sure he told Dernal first, trusting him to better guide his words, but this was Terrim, and he couldn't resist.

"I died, basically," Knox said, waiting a few moments for the words to set in before continuing. "I won't go into it all now, but I got stronger than ever before, was being hunted by a monster, and discovered something that is going to change the world forever. Oh, and I slept for nearly a year."

"You what?" Terrim asked just as the encampment came into view.

Beth turned to regard Knox, then looked to Terrim. "We should get back out there. Winter is coming and Dernal says monsters will migrate right through here, so we have to be ready."

Knox again tried his best to convince them that this wasn't necessary, but Beth was a hard ass and displayed none of her flirtier personality. So, Knox had to let them leave after they got him into the encampment.

Nearly three hundred people moved about doing one task or another. But it was Dernal once more that greeted him first, his father nowhere to be seen, despite Dernal's mention of him.

"We need to talk," Knox said the moment Dernal was within speaking range.

"Indeed," Dernal said, turning and motioning him over to a nearby tent he'd come out of. "Your father has gone to help gather wood, so we have some privacy."

That didn't sound anything like his father, but Knox just shrugged and followed him into the small tent. There were two bedrolls laid out and Dernal sat atop one, while Knox took the other. By the smell of it, this was where his father had been staying, as it stunk of alcohol.

Dernal, for his part, didn't smell as much and he was very wet.

"Did you take a dive into a water barrel?" Knox asked, eyeing the usually stern man with more than a touch of humor.

"Hmmm. I did," Dernal admitted. "But enough about me. Tell me everything. How are you still alive?"

Knox told him everything, sparing no detail as he went from his flight into the Shadowfall Swamps, to his discovery of the Titan System, his ascension to Titan Born, all the way to the pirates he'd enslaved by accident and how he'd remedied that by changing the runic formations. Then, ending with his last meeting with Aetex and finding Beth and Terrim in the woods. The entire time Dernal showed no emotion, just quietly listened.

"That's trouble," he finally said, shaking his head. "Oh boy, you've unlocked a heap of trouble."

"What part?" Knox asked, confused by his reaction.

"All parts," Dernal said. "First, you've somehow tapped into an ancient force that changes magic down to its core, then you've interacted with powerful forces, you're being hunted by that damned draconic beasty, you've uncovered a horde of pirates, and it sounds like the darkness is on to you as well. We've had our own dealings with it and if you are seeing that girl, then it's got its eyes on you as well."

"Okay, so it hasn't been a walk in the park, but I've managed," Knox said, shrugging off the stern words of his mentor.

"Uncover your aura for a moment, I want to have a proper look," Dernal said, scratching at his beard as he spoke. It was slightly more kempt than when he'd first seen it out in the woods, but not by much.

Knox did as he was asked and Dernal reared back as if struck. "Cover it, cover it back up," Dernal said, raising a hand over his face. "A red aura like that means A or above. But you say you are only equivalent to a D Ranker? How do you know without seeing the color, is it that Titan System you mentioned? You are seeing things that no one else can see?"

Seeing where this conversation might be going, Knox rushed to his own defense. "It isn't like that," he said, holding up his hands. "It's real and it can be for you too if you get close enough. In fact, I was going to suggest the entire town go into Shadowfall Swamp with me."

"Hhmm. Won't take kindly to that suggestion, I'll tell you that much. Returned hero or not, you'll see that these stubborn mules prefer to do what they want."

"Well, I'll be returning at the very least. I think I'm pretty much obligated at this point, but I'll see you all to Thornhaven first," Knox said, letting the future play out in his head. He didn't want to be alone, but if he had to be, at least he'd know his friends were safe.

"That isn't even worth considering," Dernal said, shaking his head. "The entire Adventurer's Guild is going to come down on you once they learn what is happening in the Shadowfall Swamp. You think these villagers don't like change, just wait until you meet the ancient heads that rule over the Adventurer's Guild. Not to mention what the royalty would think. This new Titan System might seem like a boon to you, but it'll be a curse to those who like things the way they are."

Knox hadn't thought about it like that, assuming that people would just accept the system for what it was and go with it. How foolish had he been? But he couldn't and wouldn't forsake the Path of the Titans, no matter what the cost might be. Sure, he'd wanted to be an Adventurer his entire life, but now he had a higher calling to attend. He could be a force for good and change, spreading the Titan System to all corners of the world. It was the surest way to get stronger and not be blocked by corruption buildup, and he had to convince Dernal of it.

"I can Level just as quick and easy in the D Ranks as I can in the A Ranks now," Knox said, successfully getting Dernal's attention. "The Titan System gets rid of the buildup of corruption and the necessary cleanup. It is as if all the essence it collects is pure, so you don't need to cycle it in the same way."

"And you think those that already made it to the B or A Ranks want others to be able to reach it? There is a reason so few make it to those heights, much of which falls on those already there, picking off anyone with high potential that can't be controlled. And it doesn't sound like you want anyone controlling this Titan System if such control could even be exerted on it."

"I'm going back, and I want you to come with me. I'll be inviting all those who want to grow stronger and care enough to come along as well," Knox said, firmly laying down his plan and hoping Dernal could get behind it.

"I might go," Dernal said, not looking Knox in the eyes. "But you better be prepared for the backlash when this gets out."

"I will be," Knox assured him, despite not being sure he would.

CHAPTER 47
BREAKING APART

KNOX GOT the pelts to the right people and passed off the majority of his meat as well. He saw several familiar faces but no one very close to him. However, everyone seemed surprised to see him. At one point, he thought he saw Frederick but whoever it was lost themselves in a crowd around a cooking fire and Knox didn't pursue the matter. Then he saw his father, and a mix of emotions played across his face, eventually landing in a knot in his stomach.

On the one hand, he looked well enough; he hadn't even noticed Knox yet, as he was actually helping out the camp— moving firewood from one place to another as best as he could with one arm. On the other hand, Knox still couldn't forgive the way he'd talked to Beth or how he'd treated him over the last ten, odd years. Figuring he ought to at least say hello, Knox walked over and reached down to help move some wood.

"I've got it well enough," Askar said, before looking up to see who was helping.

"I don't mind helping," Knox answered and Askar flashed a glance in his direction, a look of utter bewilderment on his face for several long moments.

He dropped the wood and stood up straight. Knox caught the barest scent of alcohol off the man, but not nearly as strong as even the smells that had come off of Dernal. For a solid few seconds, they just looked at each other, Knox trying to read the complex emotions playing off the older man's face, while Askar struggled to find words.

Knox took a deep breath and took the first word. "You look good, Dernal tells me you've been helping out a lot, that's good," Knox said, immediately cursing his words as inadequate for the emotions he was trying to get across.

"Work needs doing, after what we went through, no one is complaining about having a one-armed man around to help. Could have used your help, Adventurer, where the hell were you?" Askar asked, his voice going cold at the end and all the familiar feelings of disdain rushing to the forefront of Knox's mind.

"Not really any of your damn business. I'm happy to see you well, but I've got business to attend to," Knox said, cutting off the conversation before it became even more heated. He turned and walked away, but not before Askar had the last word.

"Just like your mother," he said, and Knox almost turned to question him about her. He knew so precious little that even the angry ravings of his father would be helpful in understanding who she was. But he didn't have it in him to challenge his father at that moment, so he continued walking onward to find someone else to speak with.

Several days passed and they'd traveled only a handful of miles, each day the entire group seemed able to only go half a dozen miles before it was too much for them with the rough terrain. It didn't help that they had to clear trees for nearly every mile because the road was covered with fallen logs. Nor did it help that Mr. Tome's wagon carried much of the town's supplies and broke down on the rough road twice in four days.

A change of things came about when Murdoch arrived back with two other horsemen. A small council was called together and once he learned Knox had returned, he insisted he be a part of it. Knox came early, hoping to catch a word with Murdoch beforehand, but found that Dernal, Terrim, Beth, and Frederick had already arrived as well.

"Good evening," Knox said, startling a surprisingly skinny and pale Frederick who had his back turned to the opening of the tent.

"By the gods' own luck, it's true!" Murdoch shouted over any others trying to say a word as Knox approached. Murdoch pulled Knox into a tight hug, before releasing him and giving him his signature wicked grin. "You must tell me every bit of your tale when we have the time."

Knox nodded and took a long look at the man to see what had changed. However, Murdoch, down to his loose fitting yet stylish tunic, seemed much the same as before. It was when he got to his eyes that he noticed the first difference. Where normally he had a light of excitement gleaming within them, now there was a heavy weight that seemed to add to the circles around his eyes. He'd been through some things; that much was apparent. But judging by the smile he wore, he wished to keep up spirits—classic Murdoch.

"I was hoping to get a word with you in private before the meeting," Knox finally said after finishing his close examination of his friend.

"And so you have, tell us your tales of wonder and adventure. Dernal tells me you single-handedly fought off a dragon and won?" Murdoch said. Dernal tried to protest his words, but Murdoch held up a hand, silencing him.

"Not so grand an adventure, let me assure you," Knox said, shaking his head.

"I'm sure you are just being modest," Murdoch said, winking. "Imagine the stories we could tell and the coin we could charge to those that wish to listen."

"Has Dernal told you about what I found?" Knox asked, ignoring his greedy friend's antics.

"He has not," Murdoch said, his chest deflating a bit as he sat back on the only chair in the medium-sized tent. There was enough room for another three or four people to stand comfortably, but not much more room than that.

Dernal confirmed the same by a simple, "Hhmm."

Knox bit his lip, he hadn't planned on telling so many people, but these were his friends, so he launched into the tale. He kept it a bit more clipped and left out key details, but he got the general gist of the story to them, most of all that they had a place that they could go and survive, a place with food and fresh water for the winter.

"Timely news indeed," Murdoch said, bouncing back to his feet. "It'll be a hard sell for sure, but once the general populace finds out that Thornhaven is not taking refugees and seems to be embroiled in a conflict that spans the entire kingdom, they might change their minds."

"What do you mean?" Knox asked. There hadn't been a war that involved the entire kingdom in his lifetime.

"I mean what I said," Murdoch said sarcastically. "Besides that, they were very interested to know how many able-bodied men and women we had in our group. I think they meant or still mean to recruit camp ladies and fresh soldiers from our numbers. It's why I snuck out in the middle of the night and paid my way out of their fair city."

"If the kingdom is at war, then isn't it our responsibility to-" Terrim began to say but was cut off by a grunt from Dernal.

"Hhmm. You owe those lords and ladies not a single drop of blood. What did they or are they doing for you out here in the wilds?" Dernal asked, the question weighing down on all of them.

He was right, of course. Out here, they were lucky to get merchants to visit, much less troops to help fight off bandits or monsters. Knox wasn't too worried, as he'd be immune to any summons as an Adventurer, but the others wouldn't be so lucky. If he was recalling correctly, the Adventurer's Guild could call their members to war, but it rarely happened, if ever.

"So, how do we best sell the Shadowfall Swamp to everyone?" Murdoch asked, biting his lower lip as he spoke, adding a measure of uncertainty to his tone.

They talked back and forth until the true council formed, several older gentlemen and a single elderly woman joining them. Murdoch told a lavish tale of treachery and deceit, saying he was nearly taken into custody and hanged for crimes he couldn't possibly have committed. He painted Thornhaven as a lawless place that wouldn't look kind to visitors, then ended his tale with an announcement that Thornhaven was taking young men and women for purposes he couldn't be clear on, that going there would mean the end of their town's population.

By the time he finished, he had all the elderly members

wringing their hands in distress. He could paint a story so well. By the time he got to mentioning an alternative route, they were eating out of his hands. Up until he slipped that it would be far east.

"The only thing east is the Shadowfall Swamp," the elderly woman Agnes said. Her voice sounded like an old creaky door hinge that was in desperate need of an oiling. "Surely, you don't think we can survive such a place."

This is where Knox could hold his tongue no longer and he injected himself, talking over whatever Murdoch had planned to say.

"I've got an artifact," Knox said, pulling out the black orb. "It repels monsters and will get us safely to an ancient complex that will provide fresh water and food for all."

"We are to believe the word of an Adventurer, a nasty untrusting lot you all are, down to the last of you," Agnes said, turning her nose up at Knox.

Knox tried once more to convince her, but this time it was Murdoch who drowned out his words.

"He speaks as one of us, not as an Adventurer. Surely, you know of Knox's deeds, always a hard worker, he even helped save poor Frederick last season in that unfortunate tragedy. I implore you to hear us out as we are limited in time, for winter is coming."

That last phrase was enough to put a chill through all of them. Winters were harsh and unforgiving. If they were lost out in the wilderness when the first full freeze hit, they were as good as dead.

"How many weeks?" Agnes asked, and the discussion evolved into plans for how to get there in time and how to keep the general populace calm during the trip.

In the end, they broke the news to the entire remaining group and one-third straight up refused to go that way, saying they'd take their chances at Thornhaven. A small part of Knox was surprised that his father wasn't among them, but he tried not to dwell on it.

It took them another day to work out how to split supplies, but they did it, and soon their group of nearly three hundred became a group of one hundred and ninety.

CHAPTER 48
SAFE TRAVELS

"So, how long have you and Richard been together?" Knox asked, doing his best to keep his true emotions hidden. He'd recently found out that one of the reasons Beth was so cold toward him, was she was sweet on someone else now—or at least that is what Knox told himself.

"Why would you care?" Beth asked.

They were standing in line for the cook pot to get their evening meal, and this was the first chance Knox had to speak with her alone, despite learning much of the gossip of the year from Terrim.

"I don't know," Knox said, shrugging even though Beth had her back to him and wasn't able to see the gesture. "Just thought, maybe we had something going."

"You left, then died. I think I was fine to move on," Beth said, her voice as cold as before and such a contrast to her usual jovial self.

"Did I suck the warmth out of you when I left, because you are being pretty damn cold to me and all I did was try to survive," Knox said, a bit of heat entering his voice as he struggled to control his emotions.

He liked Beth a lot, sure, he figured she'd move on but a part of him hoped that she'd stick around for him as he was only going to be gone a little while. That was, of course, before he'd been made into a Titan Born and slept for nearly a year. He didn't know what the right thing to say was, but he was damn sure what he'd just said wouldn't be it. Sure enough, Beth turned and stared daggers at him.

"I've lost more than just you, you stupid fool," Beth said, glaring at him. "Before I started seeing Richard, I was dating a fellow named Brian, you remember Brian, right? The super nice guy with big muscles? Well, he caught the stupid black sickness and tried to rip my throat out. Richard has been the only drop of sunshine in my life since and you want to make me feel like shit for not waiting for you? Think before you speak, Knox Trelling. Damn, you infuriate me."

She said the last bit while stepping closer, and for a moment, Knox thought she was going to hit him. But then she let out a breathy sigh and suddenly, he was less worried about being hit and more worried she meant to kiss him. Just then, Richard showed his ugly mug and Beth took a step back.

"Mind if I cut in," Richard said, doing a cutting motion with his fingers and raising his eyebrows.

"I do," Knox said, a flat smile on his face.

"Take my spot, I'm not hungry anymore," Beth said, stepping out of line and stomping her way across the encampment.

"What's with her?" Richard asked, oblivious to the entire situation and stepping into line in front of Knox.

Knox shrugged and stepped out of line to follow her. However, she lost herself in the crowd and instead, Knox ended up finding Terrim. They chatted for a while before Knox went off to his tent to rest for the night.

"Several monsters are closing in from the east," Knox whispered the words to Dernal, who nodded.

However, Murdoch must have overheard because he leaned and spoke next. "Thought you said monsters weren't going to be an issue," Murdoch hissed the words through clenched teeth, but Knox heard them well enough.

"These monsters are so weak that the orb doesn't affect them. I'll take care of them myself," Knox said, pulling his axe free and cracking his neck to the side.

"Nonsense," Murdoch said, sounding suddenly excited. "I'll be going as well."

"And me," Terrim said, he was the only one close enough to have overheard.

"Fine, but stay sharp, I don't want to spend the entire time saving you all," Knox said, grinning when he saw the looks on their faces.

So it was that Knox, Dernal, Murdoch, and Terrim headed out in front of the caravan to meet the forces arrayed against them head on. They'd gotten about a mile out when Knox's sense picked up what they were facing. Some type of four-legged monster, but not a Dire Wolf. No, it was something different, something he'd never encountered before.

Knox focused on it just as it came into view, but no information presented itself. Something that looked to be a cross between a Dire Bear and a boar, shambled into view. All around it, shadows seemed to cling and warp, and black goo dripped from its eyes.

It was massive, nearly eight-feet-tall from snout to end and half as thick. The head was disproportionately large and the fur under the moonlight breaking through the trees, seemed to shimmer and glint as if made of some sharp material.

"That's a Grimmaw," Dernal said. "And when there is one, there are more. Be careful, their fur is sharp and will infect you with a slowing poison."

Knox let his sense reach out, and sure enough, there were two others coming in fast, smaller than the first but still a threat to those they'd brought.

Knox stepped forward, confident in his ability to deal with something weak enough that the orb didn't repel it. The Grimmaw charged, showing surprising speed, but Knox was faster. Slashing down with his axe as it passed and stepped lithely out of the way, he drew first blood. The beast roared in rage, pivoting and coming for Knox once more.

This time, Knox raised his hand and cast Arcane Pulse. It slammed into the Grimmaw, throwing it off to the side just as the other two arrived. It was time to show off a bit, Knox thought as he cast Solar Wings. The light struck out at the closest two and they seemed more hurt than he expected from the small bit of light damage.

As the wings withdrew and he fell several feet toward the ground, Knox used Radiant Ground, slamming his fist into the ground and igniting it with light. All three of the Grimmaws were roaring in pain at this point, but Knox wasn't finished. He cast Lustrous Chains, lashing each of them to the ground. Moving forward with a slow and purposeful gait, he ended the monsters one after the other, black goo and all.

"Oh, the stories I'm going to tell of this fight," Murdoch said, shaking his head in disbelief.

"You really have found incredible power," Dernal said. "Those Grimmaws were at least D Ranked, you should have been outmatched by three of them."

"I walk the Path of the Titans," Knox said. "Just wait until you all get to pick a Path to walk. We will be unstoppable."

CHAPTER 49
INTO THE SWAMPS

THE DAYS CONTINUED on like this for a few weeks, winter growing ever closer and the border of the Shadowfall Swamp looming over them like a specter in the night. When they finally reached the edge of the Shadowfall Swamp, another group of about fifty men and women had left the party to go their own way, deciding it wasn't safe after all. Knox wasn't sure he could blame them, as the monster attacks had gotten worse, and he had been forced to activate the lower end of the runic scripts within the black orb.

For a week now, they'd had no attacks at all, but the damage had already been done to morale. However, Knox left Murdoch to deal with that, as he wasn't built to be a leader among his peers, as far as he was concerned.

It was because of the fine tuning he'd done with the black orb that he knew when it failed, about two miles into the swamp.

"Dernal, we have a problem," Knox said, rushing to the Adventurer's side. "Several C Ranked Monsters coming our way, maybe even some B Ranked. The stone has failed... we are doomed."

Dernal took it all surprisingly well, just giving Knox a 'Hhmm', before pulling free his daggers and calling for the caravan to march double-time. "How long?" he finally asked.

"Till the monsters get here? Minutes. Till we reach the complex? Days," Knox said, unable to hide the fear in his voice as he considered what was going to happen.

"Can you go ahead and get another Orb? We might be able to fight them off for a few hours," Dernal said. Knox nodded but suddenly several more marks appeared on his sense, and he realized a cold hard fact.

"We are out of time, make ready for battle," Knox said, pulling his axe free.

The first monster to appear was a Dire Alligator, similar to what he'd faced before, however, it was followed closely behind by a slew of other monsters. Being closer to the Titan Complex, Knox felt a bit of an influx of power, but it wasn't going to make a difference.

The townsfolk gathered together in a huddled mass, some with weapons, most without. Murdoch, Beth, Terrim, and Frederick all had weapons out and stood ready to face whatever came, but they weren't going to be remotely strong enough to face what was coming.

Knox shot forward, using Ethereal Step to get ahead of Dernal and struck out with all he had on the alligator before it could grab ahold of him. His axe sparked and barely broke the skin's surface. Using Solar Wings, Knox flew upward and into the dead branches of the swamp trees. Then, writing in the air, he inscribed a Glyph of utter destruction.

If it worked as he hoped, molten fire would pour out and consume his foe. The string of runes was long and complex, but he managed to get them finished before his wings gave out. Heat beyond anything he'd ever felt, slammed out of a hole in the air in front of him. With one final swish of his wings, he put distance between himself and the fire, gliding downward slowly as the wings failed.

The alligator didn't stand a chance, nor did the two monsters coming up beside it as Knox's fire came upon them. Even from the distance of ten paces or more, the heat was intense enough to redden Knox's face and cause him to sweat.

"Careful," Knox cried as Dernal changed course mid-sprint to avoid crashing into the fire. He corrected himself right into a harpy that lashed out with its wings. Dernal took the strike but thrust his palm up into the breasts of the ugly beast. Rays of light shot out of his hand and pierced through the harpy's midsection, killing it instantly.

Never before had Knox seen Dernal use his powers to such deadly intent, not even when facing the dragon in the dungeon they'd run before meeting the real thing out on the road.

Back and forth they fought an impossible battle with no end in sight. Knox had taken one or two bad hits, but Dernal had been there to heal him almost immediately. The biggest problem they were running into was their flagging Stamina. Eventually, it would be too much, and they would fail. But until then, they were pulling in the essence—or at least Knox was—from kill after kill of C Ranked Monsters.

Just when they felt like they were going to be overwhelmed and fall to the ground in exhaustion, the fighting ended. The waves of monsters suddenly cut off, but Knox could feel them at the edge of his sense, prowling in an all too familiar way.

"We need to prepare ourselves," Knox said, eyes going wide in sudden realization.

"What is it, boy?" Dernal said, looking even more exhausted than Knox felt.

"Last time C Ranked Monsters stayed back like this was because another, stronger monster, had decided I was prey. I can feel it coming now, two miles out and closing fast," Knox said, his sense catching the larger predator as it moved to close the distance on them.

"Here, take this," Dernal said, pulling free an orange pill and taking one himself. "It'll replenish your Stamina and give you a boost in essence. We need every edge we can get."

Knox took the pill and swallowed it without so much as a second look. A sudden surge of power filled him, and he felt ready to fight a dozen more monsters at once. Lucky for him, he thought, that he only had to fight the one.

CHAPTER 50
DRAGON'S IRE

THE GROUND QUAKED AND SHOOK, but not at the approach of the monster. It was one of the shakes again and as before, the ground cracked, and black ooze came out.

"Hit it fast and hard," Knox cried out, pointing at one of the half dozen oozes that had appeared.

Dernal moved like light itself, blurring as he did so, slashing down the goos one by one. Knox got to his first one by the time Dernal had taken care of three. His axe came down and the ooze fell apart to nothing. One by one they took care of the oozes, luckily not letting any escape or infect anymore. But Knox couldn't help but wonder how many were released outside of their view.

The ground stopped shaking just in time for the monster to approach and send it shaking once more. This beast, whatever it was, closed in on them fast.

"We need to go out and meet it, otherwise the townsfolk will be killed in the backlash," Dernal said, his voice stern and commanding.

"Right, stay here and keep them safe," Knox said, turning to Dernal. "I've got a plan to deal with the monster."

Dernal ignored Knox's request, running right on beside him toward the terrible fate that lay ahead. The dead swamp, with its many dead trees and stench, blurred around them as they closed the distance.

Knox found himself thinking about all he'd been through to get to this point. Starting off as a mere woodcutter that wished to share in the freedom of being an Adventurer, and then actually becoming one. From there, he had his life turned upside down— probably by the very monster that they were about to face—and now he thought himself able to face off against it? This monster was everything that he hated in life right now and it had to die.

Step by step, he grew closer to his inevitable death or victory. It was so uncertain to him that he honestly didn't know which would be the outcome.

"Never fear, for I am here!" Came a voice that filled Knox with a sense of relief. It was Aetex, the powerful B Ranked Adventurer. "But be wary, this A Ranked Dragon isn't going to go down easy."

Then, just like that, his stomach was pulled into knots again. The Dragon they were about to face was an A Ranked Monster. That was so far above him that he couldn't help but feel the impossible task ahead of him, even with a powerful C Ranker and B Ranker at his side.

Bursting through the woods they came upon the beast and for the first time, Knox got a good look at the reptilian creature. It was unlike the dragon they'd faced in the dungeon, all muscle, and red scales, no, this one was sleek, skinny, almost snakelike, with ruined wings of bone and rotting flesh. From its eyes and several wounds, black goo dripped out and suddenly, Knox knew that this monster had to be put down fast.

Then the most surprising thing happened, it spoke, halting its forward momentum and staring down at the three of them.

"Knox, Titan of Light, I am here for your head by command of my queen," the great serpent dragon said, its voice a low and spiteful hiss.

"Your darkness will no longer infect this land foul creature!" Aetex bellowed at the dragon. Then, without warning, he literally flew up to meet it, leading with his fist. A mighty smacking sound filled the air as he was wacked out of the sky by the serpent's tail.

"Your friend is foolish to attack straight on," Dernal said. "I'll flank to the right and distract it, you hit it with everything you got."

Knox nodded his head and reached for the first band around his finger. He'd be no good as an early Level 20s or D Ranker. The ring came off easily, but the power hit him like an avalanche. C Ranked power coursed through him and he knew he was stronger than even Dernal at that point, but it wouldn't be enough.

Before he could pull the next ring off, he dodged to the left and out of the way of a tail smash. Raising his hands instinctively he fired off a Luminous Surge and it lit up the evening sky. The dragon screamed in pain and Knox knew that they had a chance in that moment. The power of his light was enough to do some serious damage, but still, he needed more.

Reaching down, he pulled off the next ring and the flood of power was so great that he could feel his body begin to give under it, a flood of essence going from him to feed the overpowered state of his body. At this rate, he'd not be able to take another ring off, it was already so painful that he had trouble seeing straight. Pocketing the rings, Knox went to work against the serpent.

Aetex arrived back on the field a moment later, just as Knox activated his Solar Wings and took to the sky.

"Together we can slay this abomination. I'll go high and you go low," Aetex said, his booming voice a reassurance against the dread and pain Knox was feeling.

Knox dove for the serpent's lower section, staying just out of range of its tail, as he fired off Luminous Surge after Luminous Surge. Each one infused with the power of a B Ranker at the peak of B Rank, taking entire sections of flesh and blowing it away.

Aetex took the higher altitudes, summoning forth dozens of blue orbs of energy. With a battle cry worthy of legend, he threw them down at the serpent. They struck the dragon's wings, piercing through rotten flesh, destroying what little use the wings might have still had.

Dernal, meanwhile, circled around the dragon's side, using his superior agility to dart in and out of range. Every time the beast lunged or tried to strike with its massive jaws, he was always a step ahead, holding its attention and narrowly dodging its attacks. With each pass, his daggers left lines of red on the rotten flesh, but the damage was superficial at best.

In response to the combined onslaught, the dragon opened its gaping maw, inhaling deeply. The winds stirred and the tree branches began to bend inward toward the great dragon. Realizing the imminent danger, Knox shouted to his companions.

"Shield yourselves!"

Knox first activated Prism Ward, creating a shimmering barrier of light around himself. Then, because he had a moment to do so, he also activated Mystic Armor, giving him that much more protection from what was to come.

The dragon released a cataclysmic blast of dark energy, a torrent of shadow and black flames. The force of the blast was so intense that it created a crater in its wake, uprooting trees and sending them spiraling into the night.

The force of the attack sent him crashing into the forest, the ground cracking against him on impact. From his side he could see that Dernal was thrown against a nearby boulder, stunned momentarily, while Aetex weathered the blast full on—his body a torrent of blue flames, covering him from head to toe. The power around him was so great that, for a moment, Knox's sense ran over Aetex, and his aura appeared to be blue as the fire surrounded him.

Pushing the nonsense from his mind, Knox struggled to his feet. In the distance, the dragon roared in triumph, perhaps thinking its foes defeated. But as the dust settled and Knox began to rise, the light of his shielding making him glow in the dark night, the dragon's roar cut off abruptly.

"This fight isn't over," Knox said, spitting out a mouthful of blood. A sudden surge of pain within him made him realize he'd just lost another Level and soon his body would shut down. "We need to end this now!" Knox shouted up to the blazing blue Aetex.

"I will protect you, hero, even if it costs me my life," Aetex said, his words proud and mighty.

He dove forward, the flames around him seeming to lash out and burn the dragon. But whatever powers he held, they wouldn't be enough. The dragon, with its full focus on Aetex, easily beat him back. Aetex, unarmored and unarmed, began to bleed. It was odd, though Knox could tell even from a distance as he ran to aid his peculiar companion, that the man was bleeding blue. So, he wasn't human after all.

Dernal recovered enough to get back into the fight, but the dragon all but ignored him now, focusing on Aetex. Dernal wasn't a fan of being ignored, so he held up his hands and ran them straight into the side of the serpent, unleashing a torrent of Light and Life essence.

The dragon roared and suddenly, Dernal had its full attention. But that, of course, left it open to attack by Aetex, who grabbed the back of the dragon's neck and let his flames wash over it. Knox appeared suddenly, Solar Wings lifting him above the dragon and beside Aetex.

Casting Lustrous Chains, the biggest and most impressive chains of white light appeared and wrapped up the dragon. It roared in pain and began to shatter the links. But Knox was already working on his next attack, casting Luminous Surge. When the light hit the dragon with more power than Knox had ever mustered before, he knew it was close to dying. But in that moment, as Aetex and Dernal fought for their lives, something inside of Knox gave way and he began to fall toward the ground, half conscious.

Without thinking twice about it, he struggled to get the rings back on his finger before his entire body gave out. Foam, thick and wet, bubbled from his mouth and he couldn't control the shaking of his body any longer.

Getting ahold of one ring, he slipped it on and immediately felt relief. Then, as he was about to put the next one on, a mighty tail smashed into him and he went flying, his ring getting lost in the spray of dirt and roots. Pain, unlike anything he'd felt before, rocked through his body and he thought he could hear someone speaking to him or a long-lost memory trying to resurface.

Then, in the midst of all the pain and anguish, he saw a face. A beautiful brunette woman looking down at him with her arms folded. She had a proud smile on her face, and she held a hand outward for him to take. Knox took it, knowing exactly who it was he was seeing. His mother was appearing to him at the moment of his death, as a hallucination.

She pulled Knox into a hug, but it was short-lived.

"Put it on," she said, her words a magical tinkling of bells to Knox's ears. He'd imagined so many times what her voice must have sounded like from reading her journals. To get this small gift before dying was enough, he thought to himself as the pain reached a crescendo. "Put it on!" she said with urgent insistence, holding out an open hand to Knox.

In her hand was the ring.

Knox grabbed hold of it and slipped it on. Suddenly, the pain ceased and the world around him snapped into focus. Gone was the illusion of his mother or even him standing. He lay in the dirt, his hands wet with mud and blood. Aetex and Dernal struggled to finish the mighty dragon and Knox had to help.

He stood, ready for the final round against this impossible A Ranked foe. To his surprise, his chains were still working to keep the serpent slowed, giving Aetex and Dernal the space they needed to beat it senseless. Knox walked slow and steady toward the dragon, it moved slower and slower, even as the chains began to dissipate.

"One more blast ought to do it," Knox said, though his words came out a bit slurred, due to a fat lip and a mouth that kept filling with blood.

Holding his hand up in the air with his other hand, he cast Luminous Surge. The dragon, focusing on dealing with the other two combatants, had ignored him. Light poured out of Knox, weaker than ever before but still hitting with enough force that the dragon gave off one last roar before teetering to a stop.

"Darkness is coming," it hissed as the light in its eyes went out and the corpse of an A Ranked Monster fell dead at their feet.

They were able to recover a Core from within it, but then, Aetex used his blue flame to purge the rest of the corpse.

"Good thing that monster was only operating at half power, that goo really hampered its ability to fight. A true A Ranked Monster would have killed us by nature of its speed alone," Aetex said, as he rubbed at the back of his neck.

This caught Knox off guard, and he stopped peering into the A Ranked Core he'd collected. Surely, Aetex didn't mean that? But no, he had a very serious look on his face and Dernal nodded along with him.

"So, we just got lucky," Knox said, letting himself fall backward to sit on a fallen tree. "That didn't feel like luck to me."

"Because you fought valiantly and without regard to your safety, only the safety of others. Well done, hero," Aetex said, but by the look on Dernal's face he didn't agree.

"It was foolhardy, and luck was the only thing that saved us. We need to get back before the camp is overrun by C Ranked or B Ranked Monsters," Dernal said, his words as gruff as ever.

"We've the scent of the dragon on us," Aetex said, dusting his shirt off. "That alone will keep you safe till you make it back home. I, however, must be off. My quests are many and my responsibilities a legion."

And just like that, Aetex took off, literally flying up and off into the distance. Dernal looked at Knox then and just shook his head.

"I'm right behind you, go on ahead," Knox said, standing and brushing himself off. He wanted to look around the area really quick before returning, but he wanted to do it alone.

"Hhmm," Dernal said, but without any argument, he was soon jogging back to camp.

Going over to the corpse of the dragon, Knox began pulling teeth out of the burnt-up pile. Aetex had done a good job incinerating the remains, but teeth were sturdy, and Knox couldn't help but think they might be useful in crafting later.

However, he didn't think Dernal would approve of using tainted dragon's teeth. So, as carefully as he could, he collected them all and dug a little hole, placing them safely inside. He'd come back later and collect them when he had a functioning black orb.

It was while he finished burying the teeth and marking the tree that he felt the hairs on his neck stand on end.

Turning, he was face to face with a pale-skinned dark-haired girl. Knox stumbled backward in surprise, falling on his ass. She stepped forward, tilting her head to the side as she watched him.

"Titan of Light," the voice said in its same girlish singsong tone it had used when chanting the rhyme, "in darkness' sight, we Come to claim what's ours by right. From years ago, to this day's woe, the Shadows rise, their power to show."

Knox blinked and the girl was gone.

The entire swamp around him lay still and silent. Something was coming, and defeating this weakened dragon was just the tip of the iceberg.

Knox stood, brushing himself off and letting his mind wander back to simpler times. Sure, he could have lived his life out as a woodcutter, but all of these events would have probably still happened, and he'd have likely died along with so many others.

The canopy above filtered the rays of moonlight, casting dappled shadows on the swamp below. Knox closed his eyes and took a deep breath, feeling the weight of the world on his shoulders. The woodcutter's axe, the familiar weight of it, came to mind. The rhythmic thudding as it cleaved into wood, the scent of freshly chopped timber, and the simplicity of a life where every day's goal was clear-cut.

But as the memories warmed his heart, they also brought with them a sharp pang of realization. His destiny had always been more extensive than the confines of the forest. The universe had its plans, and Knox was intricately woven into its tapestry, whether he acknowledged it or not.

He thought of all the lives he touched and those who had touched his. The adventures faced, the dangers overcome, the bonds forged, and the lessons learned. The world was so much bigger than the woods he grew up in, filled with wonders and threats alike.

But if he had chosen the life of a mere woodcutter, would he have been content with knowing the looming darkness that threatened his world? Or would ignorance have been a blissful reprieve? Knox realized that the path he had embarked on was inevitable, driven by an internal compass that sought purpose and meaning.

A gentle breeze rustled the trees, and Knox felt a renewed sense of determination. The journey ahead was uncertain, fraught with challenges that would test his resolve. But with every challenge he had faced so far, he had discovered a part of himself previously unknown. And now, standing amidst the silent swamp, Knox was ready to embrace whatever lay ahead, armed with the wisdom of reflection and the strength of his past.

In the grand narrative of life, each of us has a role to play, a path to walk, he thought. And as Knox began his trek back to camp, he knew that his story was far from over. It was merely another chapter in the endless journey of self-discovery.

-Ending Knox Status-
-Personal Status-
-Name: Knox-
-Level: 19 (E Rank, Tier 9)-
-Essence To Next Level: 3,201/4,700-
-Health: Fair Tier 9-
-Mana: Fair Tier 9-
-Stamina: Fair Tier 9-
-Mind: 87-
-Body: 87-
-Spirit: 87-

The End of Book 1: System Activation.

LEAVE A REVIEW

Thank you for reading. Please leave a review!

If you really liked the book, please consider reaching out and telling me what you enjoyed about it at, Timothy.mcgowen1@gmail.com.

Join my Facebook group and discuss the books at: https://www.facebook.com/groups/234653175151521/

Join my Patreon at: https://www.patreon.com/TimothyMcGowen

ABOUT THE AUTHOR

Timothy McGowen, a Kansas-based author, cherishes the joys of family life with his wife and two daughters. His journey in the literary world began in grade school, and it's a passion that continues to flourish. Inspired by the imaginative realms of Terry Brooks and Brandon Sanderson, Timothy endeavors to follow in their footsteps, crafting stories that resonate with fantasy and adventure enthusiasts.

Prior to dedicating himself to the art of storytelling, Timothy honed his skills as a Software Developer, an experience that not only enriched his technical knowledge but also subtly influences his narrative style. This unique blend of technology and creativity is evident in his work, where he seamlessly integrates elements of Fantasy with splashes of Sci-Fi and the innovative concepts of LitRPG/Gamelit.

Timothy's passion for both reading and writing books is the lifeblood of his creative journey. For those who share this enthusiasm, he warmly invites you to join his newsletter. Stay updated with the latest news and embark on an exciting journey with each new book release.

His debut novel Haven Chronicles: Eldritch Knight has sold over a thousand copies of both ebook and audible so far. He writes Fantasy that contains a splash of scifi and Litrpg/Gamelit stories. Consider signing up for my newsletter for news on book releases as they become available.

LITRPG GROUP

Check out this group if you want to gather together and hear about new great LitRPG books.

(https://www.facebook.com/groups/LitRPGGroup/)

LEARN MORE ABOUT LITRPG/GAMELIT GENRE

To learn more about LitRPG & GameLit, talk to authors-myself included-, and just have an awesome time by joining some LitRPG/Gamelit groups.

Here is another LitRPG group you can join if you are looking for the next great read!

Facebook.com/groups/LitRPG.books

List of LitRPG/Gamelit Facebook Groups:

- https://www.facebook.com/groups/LitRPGReleases/
- https://www.facebook.com/groups/litrpgforum/
- https://www.facebook.com/groups/litrpglegends/
- https://www.facebook.com/groups/LitRPGsociety/
- https://www.facebook.com/groups/AleronKong/

www.ingramcontent.com/pod-product-compliance
Lightning Source LLC
Chambersburg PA
CBHW031023030726
47497CB00004B/971